Items should be returned on or before the last date shown below. Items not already requested by other borrowers may be renewed in person, in writing or by telephone. To renew, please quote the number on the barcode label. To renew online a PIN is required. This can be requested at your local library.
Renew online @ **www.dublincitypubliclibraries.ie**
Fines charged for overdue items will include postage incurred in recovery. Damage to or loss of items will be charged to the borrower.

Leabharlanna Poiblí Chathair Bhaile Átha Cliath
Dublin City Public Libraries

Baile Átha Cliath
Dublin City

Leabharlanna Taistil
Mobile Libraries
Tel: 8691415

Date Due	Date Due	Date Due
25. JUN 15		

PIPER

Helen McCabe

The Piper Trilogy
Book 1

First published in the UK by Myrmidon, 2008.

This edition published in 2014 by Telos Moonrise: Dark
Endeavours (An imprint of Telos Publishing Ltd)
5A Church Road, Shortlands, Bromley, Kent, BR2 0HP

www.telos.co.uk

Telos Publishing Ltd values feedback. Please e-mail us with
any comments you may have about this book to:
feedback@telos.co.uk

ISBN: 978-1-84583-885-0

CONTENTS

PROLOGUE   9
Burbor Psychiatric Hospital, Cluj-Napocka,
Romania: July 1990

BOOK ONE   21
Arva District, Carpathian Mountains,
Romania: July 1988

BOOK TWO   113
Sunny Mead, New Hampshire: July 1988
Burbor Psychiatric Hospital, Cluj-Napocka and
Cologne, Germany: July 1990

EPILOGUE   305
Arva District, Carpathian Mountains:
July 1990

APPENDIX   307
The Pied Piper of Hamelin, Robert Browning

ACKNOWLEDGEMENTS

I would like to thank the following for their help and support in the preparation of this book: Shahrukh A Husain for her advice on the historical background of Eastern Europe; my agent, Hazel Latus; Linda Mulas and Doreen Munn; Dr Keith Nash for his meticulous checking of my figures; Rafał Stanecki, Lilian Tasker; finally, Jacek Wasik for his very beautiful photographs of Romania.

PROLOGUE

Burbor Psychiatric Hospital, Cluj-Napocka, Romania,
July, 1990

Burbor Hospital was chilly and depressive; a site condemned to rust out its iron days until the new Government got its act together.

As Dr Sasha Marcu, accompanied by Robert, his charge nurse, crossed the footbridge linking the West site of the hospital with the East, he suddenly felt his depression lift at the thought of his project's recent success. And he had needed that boost.

Burbor Hospital was forced to welcome the whole of the human detritus spawned by an authoritarian regime. It was now the recipient of those affected by massive unemployment, social unrest and, not least, an inexplicable taste for superstition. To a psychiatrist, the individual's response was understandable; a grasping belief that God would help them if the Government would not.

But Marcu had to admit some things were slightly improving under the new Prime Minister. Bridges were being built but, unfortunately, not the one at Burbor.

They hurried across and on to the grim concrete floor of the East Wing corridor, which spat the hard sound of the men's footsteps up to the tired flaky-paint roof of the unit, forcing a flat, dismal echo.

Over the last five years, Marcu, white coat flying out behind him, had run and walked that miserable corridor thousands of times. He was as familiar with every metre of its concrete length as he was with the baggage of misery that traversed up and down it daily.

But that particular morning, as he and Robert finished their ordinary rounds and began the extraordinary, Marcu's ears shut down on the familiar echo and concentrated on a fragment of piping sound. He blinked, his conscious mind frozen with recognition. The high-note he was hearing was one that periodically issued from Irina's lips. 'Irina's song,' as Marcu called it, was hardly a tune. More of a whistle, recurrent and string-thin. *Grandsire's song.*

He knew that Irina was attracting him, letting him know that she was still around. She probably sensed he was on his way.

He walked on warily, glancing sharply at the charge nurse. Evidently he hadn't sensed anything amiss. Marcu had seen Robert in action. When disturbed, he shot to his destination! If the nurse had heard, he'd probably flagged the shrill note as insignificant. Hospital sounds were extremely diverse, but Robert knew instinctively which were trouble. Then the thought struck Marcu that, perhaps, the skinny-string reediness had been only in his head? The young psychiatrist suffered from tinnitus, which had once descended suddenly during a session with Irina and had been plaguing him ever since.

'Okay?' Robert's perception was uncanny. He must have picked up Marcu's uneasiness. Working in psychiatry developed a sixth sense. Marcu nodded in response. They turned out of the main corridor in the direction of the Acute Unit, where Irina had been ever since Anka's funeral. As he and Robert bounded up to the first floor, Marcu knew the tune was stuck in his head again, like an annoying insect swiped and crushed on the glass of a window or a helpless crane fly entangled in a spider's web. He found himself humming snatches of it at odd times, but always reassured himself the fact wasn't surprising, given how much importance was attached to the song.

It seemed louder now, yet Robert was still oblivious. It would not have been appropriate to mention it. Instinctively, the psychiatrist quickened his steps. It showed Irina was alert. She'd been sleeping for the last two days. And he needed her awake, knowing that a limit had been set on his time with her; that he was constrained by whether it was her will to go on living or to die. Her condition was slowly deteriorating and, soon, she would choose not to speak to him at all. She would be lost to him, as would the secret of Grandsire's identity, and all his patient efforts would have been for nothing.

The men hurried on down the upper corridor, which stretched the whole length of the monotonously ugly building with its smoky, black windows of unbreakable glass – essential for the acute wards of a psychiatric unit.

Marcu's daily sessions with Irina had been a fight against time, highlighted by apparent breakthroughs, only to be followed by dismal disappointment as his patient's mental and physical health deteriorated.

When they reached her room, they paused outside. 'I only need you for a while today, Robert. I know you're busy.' Marcu took no chances with Irina. Sometimes, he needed help when she turned violent. But her moods were less volatile under sedation. The trick was getting the right dose.

'Suits me,' said Robert, withdrawing his keys …

Irina, dressed simply in a hospital nightgown, lay motionless in the foetal position; her long, black hair flowing loose down her back, an incongruous touch of contrast, startling the room's pristine white.

She had heard them coming, but she did not move as the sound of footsteps echoed down the corridor, making their way towards her. She seldom knew herself if she was asleep or awake – what was real or was not.

The grating of the key in the lock had no effect, nor did the entrance of the two white-coated men into her cell. She watched them through half-closed eyelids and relaxed her pursed lips. She had not made up her mind if she would play the doctor's game today. They stood quietly for a minute or two, going over their notes. Then the one with dark, curly hair called Robert was looking down at her. She didn't like his expression. She was no-one's plaything.

'Not much response today, by the look of it. You won't need me.' He grinned and clapped Marcu on the shoulder.

Irina was sorry for the doctor. Things were bound not to go well for him in the future. He knew too much.

'Yes, you can go if you like. Irina and I will be okay. Won't we?'

She didn't move. Marcu was a handsome man, tall, blond, with deep, brown eyes. And so young. It was such a pity. Maybe if she kept still he'd go away. She was adept at pretending to be asleep. He thought he was clever but he didn't know that she was trying to save him pain. He couldn't see that. And he never went away.

'No, I'll stay for a while,' replied Robert. 'She's not awake yet.'

Marcu sat down. He was willing to wait. He was used to it. It had been the same ever since Irina Petrescu had been admitted to Burbor. In fact, it was the way with most of the Arvan women he'd seen. They shut off from normal life and shunned human contact, content to listen to their voices. Several had harmed themselves. But Irina was watched over very carefully. Well looked-after, but watched over. Even her husband's visits were monitored through the concealed two-way mirror.

He looked down at his patient and took out his small tape recorder. Nothing must happen to Irina. Other members of staff saw her as a guinea pig. But to Marcu, she was more than just a patient. Not only did she hold the key to what he'd been researching for several years, but he felt real pity for what she'd been through. He was a doctor, not a monster. Whatever she thought.

And he was determined to continue. To find out all he could about the strange happenings in Arva. He knew that he was on to something striking, which was based not purely on science, but which was rooted deep in the female psyche of Arvan women; something that had existed perhaps since the isolated settlement had been established. He believed wholeheartedly that the first part of his psychological research was compelling enough to gain academic interest internationally. He had been right. An American university had already contacted him. But, now, he had to finish, and the second part was going far too slowly. It was a matter of personal pride that he finished the project successfully. It had taken a long time to get his research published in Romania and taken notice of abroad.

Marcu was not a mediaeval historian and it had become clear to him he needed one. Now he had his contact, the bookseller, Nicholas Eisenmann in Cologne. In fact, he had great hopes that the German would be particularly interested, given the background to the ritual. But the man had told him that his response would be lengthy as it would take some time to digest the work; and, of course, to assess its eventual merit.

Nicholas was a figure of considerable influence, and well-known publishers often passed manuscripts to him for his opinion. He was something of an enigma – successful in business; a recluse in his private life; a specialist in Indian and Chinese mythology, as well as mediaeval European history. He rarely dealt with private inquiries and, as an obscure Romanian doctor of psychiatric medicine, Marcu had been lucky to attract the bookseller's interest in his research. Marcu could hardly wait to hear from Eisenmann. He believed the man had the power to provide him with leads that might shed some light on 'the secret of the marriage bed,' the key to which Irina Petrescu most certainly held, but as yet had not bestowed on him. And might not.

She was the first Arvan woman who had spoken about things forbidden by her culture. There were still so many things he needed to understand – to learn from his frail patient

– and he had so little time. So much depended on Irina.

'Well done, by the way!' Robert seemed determined to talk. Marcu grimaced. He didn't care to speak about the publication. He had gained the interest he wanted from outside Romania, but he didn't need to discuss it with his colleagues. Still, Robert was a good friend.

'Thanks,' he answered agreeably.

'You might make us all famous in the end!' The charge nurse grinned. Marcu knew Robert's attempted joke was a half-truth. The University to which the hospital was attached needed as much foreign notice as possible.

'We'll see.'

'Great! I'm going to read the whole thing when I have time.'

Marcu asked himself what Robert would have said if he'd also known about the file that had been passed to him by Inspector Valentin, who'd had recent contact with the New York Police Department. Valentin had been a good friend to him too.

Great was not the word Marcu would have used about the file. He knew Robert well enough to guess what he would have thought too. But Robert was not in his confidence and no-one, except Marcu himself and the police, had the faintest idea what the file contained.

The charge nurse had only heard, like the rest of Marcu's colleagues, that the Americans were 'interested' in his clinical knowledge and expertise. They assumed the knowledge was entirely academic, whereas the information the police file had contained was bizarre, sinister and, yes … *unscientific* to an astonishing degree.

It worried Marcu that the boundaries of his research seemed to be taking account of the role of the paranormal. But then he always told himself that a good scientist must display an open mind.

'Anyway, don't bet on me being famous, Robert,' replied Marcu, his fine-cut features relaxing into a smile. His eyes couldn't hide the exhaustion though. 'I've so much to do. So much still to find out. Then I need to go over it again and again. There's not enough time, Robert. She's weakening physically – and mentally!' He stared at his patient and frowned. Then, putting up a hand, he rubbed his forehead hard under his short blond hair.

'For a start, there's all this about her birth date. 22 July 1952.' He paused, while Robert waited expectantly. 'She seems to attach a lot of significance to it.' He pulled a face, tapping the thick file, which he set down on the small table by the bed.

'Some astrological thing maybe,' replied Robert shrugging.

'No, it's more complicated and specific than that.' Then he shook his head and sighed. 'She thinks she's to blame for what happened to Anka by being born on 22 July.' Marcu had almost forgotten he was telling someone. He spent a lot of time talking to himself. 'You know, I only have to take … one little step.' He made a fist with his fingers. 'I need to examine every possibility.' He frowned. 'I'm nearly there.'

Robert was watching him carefully. 'You've been working too hard,' said the charge nurse. Everyone said that psychiatrists were a bit mad. That it all got to them in the end. But Marcu didn't seem to hear. He kept staring down at the sleeping Irina.

'She insists she was forced into marriage at 19, but she'll give no reason. I've thought of trying to find out something from her husband again.'

'From what *I've* seen of Petrescu over the last couple of years, I'd say he'd be no help,' offered Robert. 'He only grunts when I speak to him.'

'Arva men seem to be as difficult as their wives.' Marcu shook his head. 'But perhaps Petre doesn't know anything about the secret, incredible as that might sound. The whole thing is astonishing. As for the dead child …'

'Anka?' asked Robert … Irina stiffened imperceptibly as she heard her daughter's name …

Marcu nodded, 'Poor woman! She's suffered all right. More than any mother should. Is it surprising she ended up like this?'

'But there were all the others.'

'Yes, I know. I don't need reminding.'

Robert flinched. Marcu could be touchy, but no-one took any notice when he was irritable. They were lucky to have him at Burbor. And no-one upset him, because they wanted to hold on to him for as long as possible. It was unusual to find a doctor with Marcu's excellent qualifications working in a provincial hospital. One of his academic standing would have been welcomed with open arms at any institution in Bucharest, but he had chosen them; although, privately, it was rumoured that he'd be off as soon as he'd completed his research.

'Sorry!' Marcu said. 'Sometimes this job gets to me.'

'You and me both.' Robert sighed. 'Bad enough losing a child anyway.' He looked down at Irina. He didn't know she was taking it all in.

If she could have snarled at him, she would have. It was not his business.

Marcu shook his head. 'But in those circumstances! If it hadn't been for Inspector Valentin's involvement, I mightn't ever have been able to get this thing together.'

When he had started to investigate the records of the female patients from Arva who had been admitted to Burbor, he had been surprised to find how their schizophrenic hallucinations had so many similar elements. That was when he had started to dig deeper, to realise that this was something striking, very different from patients' usual random delusions.

At first, he had relied only on clinical evidence, until he had realised that there was more to it than that. He had discovered that an assault on a young girl, culminating in death, had taken place in Arva in 1952 – the year of Irina's birth! Then, luckily – for him, but not for Irina Petrescu – the same thing had happened again in 1988. This time to her daughter, Anka.

The initial testimonial from Valentin regarding Anka's death had set out in the most brutal police language what had happened in Arva, but, off the record, although he had several witness statements to go on, the chief inspector had confided to Marcu, several incidents he was at a loss to explain.

'As a policeman he was just doing his job, I suppose. Without the finer feelings.' Robert wasn't keen on the State Police, having had some experience of what he saw as their forerunners, the brutal *Securitate*, but he was dying to know what that file from America contained.

'Don't be hard on him. Rape and murder are his business!' added Marcu.

'Same as ours then,' Robert said.

The psychiatrist sat down on the bed. 'I'm sure Irina knows a lot more about the crime, but will I ever get it out of her? Talking about it may be her only chance of partial recovery.' He stared at the notes. 'As for the rest of them ...' he shook his head, '... Arvan females just seem to have the bad luck of history repeating itself again and again. Especially in their tendency towards schizophrenia.' He looked up at the charge nurse with a wry grin. 'But you and I don't really believe that, do we, Robert?'

'The collective impulse perhaps?'

'You mean the psychopathology of the masses rooted in the psychology of the individual? The reasoning behind the behaviour of countless numbers of hitherto civilised people who become totally uncivilised and act in the most brutal way. We saw plenty of that in Europe with Hitler. But the archetype that drives such people together and makes them behave in that way, is the one I'm after, Robert. What has driven these poor women to the brink? I believe this particular model is rooted in some kind of myth. A deliberate agency at work.'

'That's clever,' said Robert.

'No, that's Jung. It's very useful and adaptable in this case. But it doesn't give me the answer. I need to find the source.'

'But you made the link in your research.'

'Yes, but with other people helping. For instance, Dr Baescu's helped a lot. He noticed a pattern in their behaviour and referred his patients. For a provincial practitioner, he certainly has an inquiring mind.' Marcu knew that without Baescu's referrals he'd have been sunk.

'I like the title, by the way. *The Feminine Folk Culture of North Transylvania: A Psychological Study.* Great stuff!' he reiterated. 'You've put Romanian medical research on the map again!'

'I have her to thank most of all. Then Valentin's connection with NYPD, which got me the American university's interest.' Marcu put out his hand and lifted Irina's limp wrist, counting the pulse. He frowned.

'If she continues to refuse food, we might have to set up a drip,' suggested Robert.

'I don't want that. We have to keep her alive. She's been through enough. Remember, Robert, she's the only Arvan female ever likely to open up to us. The rest are sane enough to keep quiet – or dead! I haven't got enough data on Grandsire yet … Okay, I can manage now.'

Robert nodded and left Marcu to continue the job, with which he'd persevered since August 1988, when Irina Petrescu, the farmer's wife from Ruare, had been admitted to their clinic after her only daughter Anka's funeral.

Marcu switched on his recorder and, with real concern in his face, leaned close to Irina's ear and whispered, 'Hi, can you hear me? It's Marcu. How do you feel about talking to me today?'

As he waited for her response, his mind sifted the information that he'd been given about the day of the ritual when Anka had been chosen by Grandsire. The story had been truly harrowing.

He closed his eyes, hoping that soon she'd start talking again; that once more he'd be able to piece together the mystery that had begun for him in late 1988, but that, as his subsequent research revealed, went back ages before that. Until Irina had been admitted, the trail had gone cold.

Her first revelations had been a mixture of hearsay from the old farmer, Claudiu Basa, and Irina's best friend, Simona Murgu. He was not likely to find out any more from the farmer, and, certainly, nothing from the village priest, who had heard his last confession. And Murgu remained silent, although there were some signs she was heading Marcu's way as well. Of course he couldn't rely on the fact that Simona might end up in Burbor, which, in any case, would have been ethically untenable. Who would wish that fate on anyone?

'Okay, Irina. Let's try,' he said, leaning towards her. She opened her eyes. It was his own fault. He wanted to know. What was she going to tell him today?

BOOK ONE

1

'Quoth one: "It's as my great-grandsire,
Starting up at the Trump of Doom's tone,
Had walked this way from his painted
tombstone".'

Arva, Romania
22 July 1988

'The girl is flying!' Claudiu Basa crossed himself, his skinny work-worn hands reaching hurriedly for his forehead under the black hat, the long, dirty nail of his forefinger scoring his skin and down to the left shoulder for the Son, to the right for the Spirit.

'Flying, flying,' he moaned as the raw tobacco juice dribbled between his open lips and spotted his scrawny chest like brown and sticky blood. And he had been chosen to see it. He wanted to curse the Father for letting it happen to them all again. They had suffered enough, hadn't they? But he was too old for blasphemy, too scared, knowing the date.

'Anka Petrescu flying to the Inn!' he whispered; and, in spite of his 90 years, he was feeling a fear as strong as when he was a boy, which made his legs weak. He was constantly afraid he might lose the only power he still harboured in the left calf. He had been walking on that useless leg from childhood, had always feared that he would have to crawl like a cripple. Even his name meant 'the lame one'. That was the cross Claudiu had to bear. He thought it was light indeed in comparison with the one that would soon burden Petrescu, as he watched Petrescu's daughter flying down the hill from the church.

Old Claudiu stood at the cottage door, his weak hand trembling on the lintel. The child must not see him; if she knew she had been chosen ... He stared up at the ridge. He had seen Anka 'go up' slowly, carrying the flowers; he would never have believed it could have been she – the stolid, small daughter of Petre and Irina Petrescu. Now she was moving faster ...

Claudiu squinted into the eastern sky, blood red and hard gold. There were streaks of silver in that dawn like flying ribbons from the tails of bolting horses. In the Carpathians, morning flamed into life suddenly and left the air breathless. The old man did not see the light whiten the tips of a thousand firs, only the small, black figure flying down from the grey stone church on the ridge.

He had no eyes for the conical blue of the tower piercing the fiery sky, only for little Anka's crazy progress. She had careered through the iron gate and was weaving in and out of the slim trunks of the forest trees like a mad spectre destined to dance forever like the night's fireflies.

The girl ran madly along – her arms flailing the air like windmills' sails. Claudiu could be forgiven for thinking of flight. So fast was her progress, her mad desire to get away, she used her arms to pump her body forward like some ugly fledgling falling from the nest. She dared not look behind, only in front. Her braids flew behind her – that hair, the prettiest thing about the Petrescus' daughter, was trying to free itself from the little doomed head.

The old man watched her small silhouette framed black against the eastern sky. Where would that One's evil spirit wander in the great space beyond? When would Grandsire return?

Claudiu spat the bitter tobacco taste from his lips; it was

the taste of gall, the bitterness soon to be felt by Petrescu and his wife. Claudiu was near to blaspheming now. It was happening again. He shivered in the presence of Death.

'*Moarte, moarte*, murder, murder!' The words forced themselves through the old man's broken teeth. He could stand no more ...

The Petrescus' smallholding stood, remote, in a field. The farm was situated in a small valley, one of many mountain farms in that part of the Carpathians. The Petrescus kept cows, two pigs, a few sheep and chickens.

The small, white farmhouse had a grey-tiled roof, half-covered by lichen, from which two red-brick chimneys protruded like listening ears.

On the evening of 21 July, the surrounding landscape was ominously quiet, as if waiting for something to happen. Inside, despite the sultry weather, there was a fire in the grate, but the chimney took little of it. Instead, the smoke rose to the ceiling rafters and blackened the bacon. It had always been the way in the farming communities of Transylvania.

Irina fed her family on raw onions, sheep-milk cheese and raw green peppers. Their diet was supplemented by yellow corn meal mush called *mamaliga*, which the family used in the place of bread. In the summer, Irina and Anka, her daughter, went out gathering wild raspberries. In the darkness of the evenings they made lace and embroidered tapestry.

It was a simple life. It had been so for many years. Irina and Petre, her husband, prayed such peace would never end. In Arva, cut-off by forest and mountain boundaries, they were almost self-sufficient and had managed to evade the dictator's land-grabbing programme.

The house had a natural boundary of wooden fencing, partly built by Petre and added to by nature. Here the Petrescus lived in a kind of stockade, undisturbed except by their neighbours and the seasons. As they ate the soft white cheese and steaming corn meal, their only concern was to get a living from their land and feed themselves and their family. And so it had always been.

But the evening of 21 July was a strange one. It did not linger into night as normal summer evenings. One moment it was light and then the lowering clouds bent down like dark blankets and covered the landscape. Petre had been in the barn using his torch. He recognised the signs of a coming storm with the experience of a man who had worked the land all his life. The sky was full of midges and a deep stillness had settled over the fields, where the cows were lying down.

He came in and switched on the lights in the rooms that had electric bulbs, which were always in short supply. Usually they would have lit only the living room in the summer, but that night they needed to light up the whole house in case a bear was wandering around. A few months earlier, a neighbouring farmer had been mauled by one that was attacking his sheep and had died defending them. Petre couldn't take that chance.

There was little they could do that night except go to bed. The next day was an important one for all of them. Anka, their daughter, went upstairs first. She was a placid young woman not given to imagination; not much upset her. She wasn't even afraid of a summer storm, which by the look of it, might be on its way. But she was young and didn't realise what that could mean on a day like the next.

It didn't take the farmer long to fall asleep. His hoarse breathing and heavy snoring soon filled the cottage. Irina slipped off her skirt and lifted her cotton blouse over her head, laying them down on a wooden chair. She had embroidered the blouse quite carefully with flower motifs depicting life in the forest. That pattern had been handed down from her forebears.

It was easy to sit on the night of 21 July without clothes. It was a relief in that heavy atmosphere.

Irina sat at the small table in the bedroom and stared into

her mirror. She knew she was a woman old before her time, strained with hard work and the struggle to scratch a living from the land. Too old, at any rate, to have any more children. Only Anka had come to them. Though their daughter had come to them and had always been a blessing, Petre hadn't been happy when she'd first told him about the pregnancy, because it had been the wrong time. Getting pregnant before you were married was a dangerous thing to do in Arva. But she had known Petre wouldn't abandon her.

Like the rest of her countrywomen, Irina had been exhorted by the government to have more children, but after two subsequent miscarriages, she had given up. It was only God's mercy that had saved her only child, Anka, in the womb.

Why was she thinking of things like that on a hot night in July? Perhaps it was because it had been a night like this when Anka was born – and conceived.

The pregnant Irina had been forced to go outside and help her husband during the storm. A great forest tree had blown down so near to her that she had been laid low to the ground. But the baby had survived. It had indeed been the mercy of God, whom Irina fervently believed would watch over and protect her little family.

She got up from the chair and, kneeling on the bare boards of the bedroom, gave thanks that Anka had survived until her sixteenth year. There was no way that she could be taken from them again. God would not have saved her for that. Whatever happened the next day – it would not be to Anka!

As Irina Petrescu went through the Litany of Saints, she was confident that when her Anka went up to the churchyard early the next morning she would come back the same girl she went.

Then the mother crossed herself, feeling guilty, thinking it might be another of her neighbours. Six girls in all, almost 16, and the first 'grandchildren' to take flowers to the grave. God willing, all would 'come down' unchanged – or perhaps only five would return. It was a terrible thought.

Irina's lips were set in a thin line. Wasn't it a very good year with six to choose from? Some years there was only one; some none – and then the harvest failed. No, Irina could pray confidently. Anka was sturdy – not like the last one – and why should it be this year that Grandsire came back, anyway? Whatever the old women predicted, Anka would be safe.

She rose from her knees, comforted not only by her unswerving faith in God, but by her knowledge that Anka must be unsuitable, that evening of 21 July. Perhaps the next day would be an end to it all.

She went over to the bed and sat down, wondering what five other women in the village were suffering that night.

When, long ago, she herself had gone up to Arva Church on 22 July, Irina had been very much like her little Anka. And she had known nothing of it then. It was a secret shared only in the marriage bed. A monstrous secret that lay heavy on any woman in Arva village, whose stomach was swelled with a first child.

She had prayed for a son – a male, who would not have to 'go up' in his sixteenth year and lay flowers on the grave. But, like five other women that year, she had not been lucky enough to have a boy. Irina had often asked the Lord why women should suffer like they did, and she knew that all those other mothers would be lying awake all night.

Anka Petrescu didn't want to take the flowers to the churchyard so early in the morning. She had begged her mother not to make her. It gave her the creeps walking up the ridge alone. It was different when she was with Mother and Petrushka.

'Why should I go so early in the morning?'

'Because it is the custom,' her mother had replied. 'You are the first 'grandchild' and you must take flowers to the grave.'

'But it's so early!' Anka liked her bed – she didn't see enough of it, having to work in the fields summer through. And Sunday, as well, the day of rest!

'The others will be going,' was all her mother had said. But, so far, Anka had seen none of them: no Tania, who was exactly her age, had enormous brown eyes, and was really beautiful, so different from Anka herself; no Marika, a month younger than she; no Ira, who was much thinner than all of them. Anka would have liked to be slim. Ira had a lovely figure. They all must have been too lazy to get up, thought Anka. Ira's mother never made her do anything!

Anka's heart was thumping and she felt cold and shivery as she looked up the hill she was going to have to climb. Why did she have to do this? She was scared, really scared. She could feel the sweat trickling down between her breasts even though the atmosphere was chilly. Why did she have to 'go up' at dawn? She clutched her flowers tightly. The red roses were looking limp already. She would have liked to have thrown them away; she couldn't hold the things without getting pricked – but she didn't dare; she knew what she had to do with them.

Anka wasn't scared of much and she didn't really believe in all those old tales, but she had to admit this wasn't a very pleasant experience. But there was no way she, nor any of them, could get out of it.

Arva girls had always done it, probably always would. It was just their luck. And her mother said they were keeping the old customs alive. She knew her parents were fiercely traditional and she had to be as well. There was no way that she could refuse to 'go up' to Grandsire. He stood for freedom. He had brought them here to Arva, to a better place – and they should honour him!

She wasn't going to think about what could happen. That was all superstitious nonsense. Nor about the 'secret of the marriage bed'. What rubbish!

But Anka had still shivered when her mother had turned her round three times and set her feet on the stony path.

They all said that when a girl was married she'd find out what it all meant. That was what made this experience so unnerving. She and her friends had talked about it for weeks. They'd giggled a lot – now she didn't feel like giggling. That kind of thrill had left her completely. She wasn't looking forward to passing the farm. The thought of the *Sowfucker* being around wasn't nice.

Anka paused for breath. She was getting in a state because she had things on her mind. Bad things – and you shouldn't 'go up' like that. She'd been lying to her mother for ages. But she'd had to, as her mother had a tendency to panic.

What had happened to her was embarrassing enough anyway. It made Anka feel different. She wasn't going to let anyone know. She'd managed to see a doctor about it in Cluj.

Anka remembered her embarrassment at 14 when her mother had taken her to Dr Baescu, their local practitioner, to find out why she hadn't menstruated. He'd pronounced Anka 'fine'. He'd told Irina that she wasn't little and pale, but sturdy – and just late.

In her sixteenth year, when still nothing had happened, Anka had decided to do something about it. She hadn't dared to visit Baescu and chose instead to find herself a doctor who practised in the city. She felt guilty about lying but even more so about what she was doing – deceiving her mother monthly. She couldn't discuss things like that with her mother, who just kept on and on, asking, 'Are you sure you're all right? Now don't forget to tell me every month.'

Irina was obsessed and it had given Anka a complex. It had made her feel different, and she couldn't stand her mother prying into what was, after all, her own business. If only her mother had tried to explain why she was behaving like that it wouldn't have got her back up. So, finally, Anka had told Irina what she wanted to hear – that the curse had started. It had been quite simple. When Petrushka – her pet name for her father – had killed one of their pigs, Anka had soaked some cloths in the blood.

She had known it was a dishonest thing to do – but it had

made her mother happy. Sometimes she wondered if her mother was going round the bend because, afterwards, she had gone about the farm singing for days. It wasn't normal.

And Anka hadn't been able to tell a soul. Well, at least her mother was satisfied. But she did wonder how long it would be before she was 'a proper woman'. That was the phrase her mother used to use when she kept questioning her, before Anka fooled her.

Seeing another doctor had taken some planning, but she'd confided in her friend, Ira, who could wind her parents round her little finger. She'd soon persuaded her mother to take them both shopping in Cluj. The money Anka had been saving for new clothes had been spent on the consultation. Ira had sat outside giggling.

Anka had been so relieved when she came out. The doctor had said she was quite healthy and she shouldn't worry about growing up just yet.

He'd added there was nothing wrong, but if her periods didn't come on in the next six months, it might be a good idea to investigate further. He had asked her if she had headaches and lots of other medical details. She had come away with a clean bill of health.

She really hoped the curse would get under way soon or she'd have to tell some more lies before she trekked off to Cluj again!

Anka was nearing the farm. The thought of that part of the ritual made her feel horribly nervous. Shiver-making! A light wind rose as she climbed higher on the ridge. She was very conscious of having nothing on under her skirt.

What the hell was she doing? Why did a girl have to go through something like this just for old time's sake? It wasn't very nice!

And where were all the rest? It was forbidden for them to 'go up' together, but they'd planned it between themselves. Anka would have been happy to have seen Ira, Marika or Tania.

She hurried past the farm, thinking about Claudiu. They

said he was just a dirty old man. He looked horrible, dragging his leg. When she had been small she had thought he was the Devil in his black suit. That was because he was crippled. She was sorry for that now. But Claudiu was a crackpot. He lived up here on his own, never saw anyone, and spied on girls.

As she passed the farm, Anka Petrescu was feeling very unhappy. Somewhere, at the back of her mind, her memory was listening to the old tales ... *Grandsire* only liked children.

The old women of the village had never elaborated; that was because of 'the secret'. But snatches of it had escaped and, now, these were drumming in her ears with the sound of her beating heart.

All the dry bones of those whispered conversations of her childhood were rattling in Anka's head when she finally reached the churchyard gate, its iron railings thrust against the red sky of dawn.

The hard little poopy she was carrying was her only companion. She stared at the ugly doll and hesitated. And there was no-one to be seen. She made a mental note that soon she would hear the bell. It must be near *Angelus* time.

She stared up to the conical tower of the church and prayed briefly and earnestly for help. Still clutching her flowers, she passed through the gates and the dark bushes that skirted Arva graveyard. Although the dawn was up, she couldn't hear the birds.

Would she see Claudiu? At school they said he lay in wait. But he never did anything, only looked. She wondered why the police didn't stop him. It must be an offence – but if he didn't do anything ...

The slight wind was stronger now. Anka held down her skirt with her free hand, conscious of her nakedness beneath. She was making her plans as she drew her breath in firmly and headed for Grandsire's grave.

She was just going to drop the flowers, bury the doll, perform the song and run. She almost considered running straight away, but years of practice and warning had been drummed into her. *Grandsire had to be satisfied …*

The wind was even stronger because of the churchyard's height. Anka thought she heard the first sound of the bell in the tower. She looked up and her mouth was dry. She really hated this. Why had she been born into a village where they had to pay thanks to someone like Grandsire? But he had brought them here and they had to.

Now she was reaching the rectangle that surrounded his vault. She was too frightened to look up at the stone obelisk with the missing cross. It must have been a shocking storm to tear the cross right off! She wasn't going to think about it.

She clutched the poopy closer as if it gave her courage, looking for the spot to place it. It was ugly, uglier than she was – she wished she was pretty like Tania and Ira. She had to build it a house in the stones. *A house of refuge …*

With a timid step, she bent and placed the wooden doll in the rectangle. Then, still bending, she placed her flowers against the arch of the tomb.

Slowly, she began to build the stones reverently over the doll's body.

She could hear the wind howling, and a flicker of light, as if it had flashed on some instrument, pierced her vision. There was a low rumble.

God! Lightning! thought Anka, scrabbling now to finish. The wind lifted her skirts and she was kneeling naked on Grandsire's grave. Struggling to control her clothes, she pursed her lips to begin 'Grandsire's Song', the final part of the ritual, then froze with cold and fear.

She was looking at the earth, watching the grave's shingle part like a river of stones. The scream forming in her throat blended into a piping whistle. Bright, little eyes were looking into hers, watching her in that dark river that was flowing from the stones, moving beneath her.

She gasped suddenly as the pains struck. The last thing she ever truly felt to be real were the most piercing and exquisitely painful sensations in her throbbing buttocks. Then Anka's knees buckled and she was thrown full force by the wind, face down and naked on to the moving earth of the grave ... That primeval piercing seemed as much in her head as in her body; like a cold thrusting, a scraping and scrabbling, breaking her insides into dumb submission. The coldness of it! As if the hardest of metal had struck her soft parts, kneading them into a glutinous mass of quivering jelly. That bent-inward pointing, that curved and vicious sniping, searching for her very self, silenced her.

She could not speak or even cry, only let it have its mastery. Struggling was useless. Suddenly, she seemed to hear millions of chattering voices in her head, telling her this was what she was born for. *Little and Chosen for Him*. Her self was cleft in two. Broken.

She felt the flap of his long garment; sensed the slivers of fur as he thrust again and again. And her head seemed severed from a bursting body that was not hers. She was a head full of sawdust; a male's plaything; a doll in his hands, which rent her in two ...

Time passed ...

Anka's eyes stared, the balls seemingly stuck in their sockets. Her body was stiff too, mechanical as she dragged it up. Her legs felt useless, but she found herself heaving them, one after the other.

Her mouth was closed tightly, stiff with dried blood. Her throat tasted full of blood too. Her lower parts were awash. Between her legs came surges of throbbing pain that cut her through, the like of which she had never experienced in her short and shortening life.

Finally, Anka jerked through the hard, bright dawn and stood on the ridge, an ungainly figure, braided hair sticking out stiff behind. All that was still in her brain was the squeaking laughter and the searing pain of the music he played. And what was human that was left in the little girl, now yearned for human warmth.

She caught sight of the farm as she began to fly down the ridge. The man who lived there was nearly 90. He would not carry her; he was deformed. He could not take her where she had to go. She could not look back; only look forward to a room at the Inn.

Claudiu's heart pounded with fear as the girl's feet went flying past. He stood there, hands over his ears to staunch the squeaking, pressed against his door in case she tried to come in.

He jammed his body hard against the old wood. That other year – what had the girl been like? He was groping for the clues in his memory. Ah, he had it now – yes, she had been a pale little girl, more of the type – corpse-like and pitiful.

A scrawny body, no figure at all, not much hair, eggshell blue eyes. What did they call her? Catina Albu! Her mother had been a Vaduva before she was married. How could he forget Catina? The girl's name was cut into his memory. And what had happened had broken her mother's heart – but then she'd died instead of going mad like the rest.

Claudiu looked at the crucifix above his mantelshelf. The small bunch of basil still hung about the dying Christ. The old man had been happy, felt forgiven when Father Pathan had brought in the crucifix and the basil to bless his home at Whitsuntide.

Now, just weeks later, Claudiu was ready to curse his Maker and his religion for letting him witness another happening; letting him be alive still to linger beside the stony path that led to the church and could not be meant for the feet of children!

An hour later, after he had cried and prayed, he found he was full of pity for himself as much as for the *Little and Chosen*. God's Mercy must be for him too. There would be as much relief for him as for her, who would soon be gone.

He begged then to be released from the terrible burden of watching another innocent victim, another little broken girl flying down the ridge. Prayed for time to run out for him. Both his manhood and his middle-age had been marked by the sound of little and chosen feet – this day he knew they had pattered out his death-knell.

Limping ungainly, the old farmer pulled out a brush made of hog's bristle, which lay in the drawer of his dresser. He brushed himself down meticulously. Lastly, his hat, which always sat like a squatting frog on the wardrobe. Finally, he dressed himself in his best he kept for funerals. Then he lay down on the bed and waited.

As Anka Petrescu made her stiff, doll-like progress towards the Inn at Sancipia, Claudiu lay thinking of Death and its peace.

He was also thinking of those other sights from which only Death could absolve him. His lips were mouthing his thoughts; those sights of those twenty-second days of hot July, past and present. Three times he had seen Him. How could a man ever forget their song, even on his deathbed? The delirious, confused words came fresh as the blood in his mouth; witnesses of an old man's guilt:

> *Buttocks, those curving crescents of moon*
> *Left in the pale, pink dawn.*
> *Bushes – from heaven – to be stared at.*
> *Juice in the mouth – the sad lot of the cripple.*

Claudiu's eyes opened suddenly, seeing it all again. The thoughts, which had always disgusted him, were still there. The thoughts he could not help. He had to be absolved from guilt. To speak about it before his death. He needed a priest! His head tossed on the pillow as he dreamed of past forbidden sights. His muttering was almost demented …

'That was some "going-up", that was! She wasn't like the fourth girl, who came after. All alone. She was late. Little, unformed, not like a woman. Catina Albu.

'Afterwards, I heard her pass. How she was, what she did, I never knew. I only heard her, lying there in the mess and heat of my guilt.

'Forgive me, Father. Forgive my guilt. Burn me for spying

on little girls and their "going-up".

'Forgive me, Lord, for the day she came down. She wanted it too.

'God have mercy on my soul. I've been a beast.

'Have mercy on my soul and on Anka Petrescu and her thrusting breasts …

'Have mercy, O Lord.

'*Absolve me, Domine, mea culpa, mea culpa, mea maxima culpa.* Father, forgive me!'

Claudiu's private *Confiteor* was nearly over – like his life, where the summer 'going-up' of little girls was the only pleasure left to a birth-made cripple, who had always been the subject of ridicule, who had borne every insult hurled at him and every accusation.

He had been hungry for women, but the recipient of much injustice. He was as ugly on his death-bed as he had been hysterical and fearful at 18. But he was determined to cleanse himself of guilt and make his last confession.

Back at the farm, Irina Petrescu waited until the morning sun crept over the patch where she had planted Grandsire's flowers. To add to her anxiety, she realised the rose bush was wilting like a dead thing. She couldn't bear to wait any longer!

Six o'clock had passed, seven had struck – she'd had enough – Anka had not 'come down'. Those words repeated in her head until she thought she would go mad. They were like shrieking voices, arguing within. It couldn't be Anka! Yes, it could!

Petre had finished the milking so, leaving him in charge of the house, she threw on her shawl and knotted her headscarf. She didn't speak to him, but the miserable look on his face was almost too much to bear. Like any man in Arva, who had a daughter in her sixteenth year, he was bound to be morose on 22 July.

She decided, first, she would go to Tania's, afterwards Ira's, then all the rest until she found Anka. She must have come down! If Anka had stopped to chat with her friends rather than come home straightaway she was going to get the brunt of her mother's tongue. Irina had never touched Anka, but sure as God she would, if the girl had been that thoughtless ...

Irina walked through the village, which seemed strangely asleep on that summer morning. She had visited all the girls' houses, and found them empty.

Finally, her feet carried her to the place she begged they could not be ... But they were there – five girls and their mothers drinking solemn toasts at the appointed place *as was fitting when someone had been chosen* ... They shook their heads, not trusting themselves to speak, knowing in their hearts that what they all feared had happened.

Irina's dry lips mouthed the questions ... No-one, girl nor waiting mother, had seen Anka 'go up' or come down the path to the church. There was no sign of the Petrescu daughter.

'I must be dreaming,' said Irina out loud. Cold panic was making her heart flutter as helplessly as the chicken she had killed the night before to celebrate the end of 22 July, which every Arvan mother prayed for.

'I must be dreaming!' she repeated to the chattering voices in her head, allowing her shrieking brain to shrink from the torture of reality. 'Anka will come down. She will come home to us. I know she will. She has to! It couldn't be her! It's impossible. I saw the blood on those cloths myself. Grandsire wouldn't take her. He only wants children. Lord,' she prayed wildly, 'if you exist, let her come back. Let me be dreaming!'

The five mothers and their daughters, who had 'come down' safely, stood silent with shock as Irina Petrescu ran around inside the circle they'd made to protect her, mouthing hysterical questions, hands over her ears, shutting out the voices in her head.

Finally, she collapsed, tears streaming down her work-worn peasant's face. Then they were bending over her, drawing her to them, trying to protect her from the ugly realisation that, once again, He had made His choice; that, now, Anka Petrescu would be on her way to the Inn at Sancipia, the only place she would find room.

It was then that Irina lifted her eyes, fixed as a sleepwalker's, and cursed the church and its stones, standing high and lonely on the ridge, for what it had seen and what it stood for.

2

'And what's dead can't come to life, I think,
So, friend, we're not the folks to shrink,
From the duty of giving you something for drink'.

Anka Petrescu just kept on running and running until she could run no more. Then the Arva girl stood on the ridge, fighting for breath. Sancipia – a resting place! Anka felt so different. Exhausted. Old. If only she could reach there, Dobos would fetch her parents. She needed them … She couldn't go home … She needed a refuge … Her mouth was loose with saliva, she was dribbling. Behind her the ridge had mountainous proportions.

Then, with one mad spurt, Anka lurched herself into the air and rushed down, her braids flying behind her in the slipstream her frantic body made. Sancipia. The Inn. There would be room! It was decreed!

Gheorghe Dobos fiddled about the hotel's reception desk. He wondered for the thousandth time what he was doing in the Arva district. The village, which bore the district's name, stood at the head of the lake's valley, close to the border. Its settlers had fled the Romanian plains and found shelter in the Carpathians. Where they had come from before that nobody was sure, but there were plenty of legends. The locals often talked about independence for Arva and were always spreading superstitious nonsense.

The hotel proprietor had just about had enough of it. He'd been getting it in the neck all the week from his wife, Ruxandra, and he didn't have time for fairytales. He was the one who had to keep the Inn going.

Sancipia was remote but picturesque – a haven for any tourist who could find it. It had been rundown for years, mainly because it had needed proper management. The building had been left to Ruxandra. She remembered as a child that it had been little more than an empty barn with hay lofts and a cellar. Her family had owned it since the Middle Ages and it was handed down daughter to daughter. Strange. He couldn't understand why everything in Arva centred on women. But she said *it was the custom*. How many times he had heard that phrase!

What had happened this week, for example? Ruxandra's nonsensical and nervous behaviour had got right up his nose. She was no good for anything – and certainly not for fucking!

And it had rubbed off on everything! For instance, Gheorghe could have kicked Ion, the porter-cum-handyman, right up the arse. The man hadn't even heard the night bell, so Gheorghe himself had had to check in the American tourist.

What a time to turn up. Four minutes after midnight! But Gheorghe had no power to refuse guests. He had masters now.

Sancipia was meant for hikers. Once, in Ruxandra's grandfather's time, it had been a hunting lodge; that was before Communism. Long before that, according to his wife, it had been a stopping place for pilgrims. It had religious connotations. Now it was run by the State, who called it a 'cabana' and equipped it well to accommodate dozens of hikers. The rooms were enormous; one had ten beds. Gheorghe swore under his breath at all masters. He was in a foul mood. Who wanted to live between the edge of a lake and Arva ridge? And he couldn't stand the locals who came to Sancipia to eat and drink because there wasn't any other accommodation. It was no good complaining to Ruxandra about them. She was an Arva peasant herself.

How many times had he thought he'd have done better to marry that girl back home in Brasov? But he knew she would never have buried herself in this godforsaken hole. Then, when he was looking for a business, he'd met Ruxandra. He sighed. The way she was behaving this week was driving him mad. She wanted children, but she said she was afraid. What could a man do with a woman like that?

Take last night. She had been down on her knees praying at nine in the evening. He'd been hoping for a good fuck. At least it would have been something to do to make him feel better, but Ruxandra would have none of it.

'What's up with you, woman?' She had looked at him from under the narrow black brows that made her pupils even blacker. Then she was crouching by the bed, hugging her knees to her breast. He could feel himself rising at the sight of her.

'I'm worried, Gheorghe.'

'What about?' He was still hoping as he unbuttoned his shirt and opened his trousers. Ruxandra had rolled over on her back but, before he could touch her, she had the goosedown fast about her and was lying on her side. He reckoned it was still worth a try, but she put out a slim leg and pushed him back.

'Worried for our people,' she answered.

'Oh, you and your people!' He was really irritated. He loved the woman, but not her endless philosophy of independence for Arva! What was the place but a backward piss-hole?

'Tomorrow's *the day*.' Her voice was muffled.

'What day?'

'Oh, what's the use?' she said. 'You'd never understand.'

'Don't give me that,' replied Gheorghe. 'I certainly don't understand *you*. Roll over, please.'

'No. It's 21 July,' she said stubbornly. *My God*, thought Gheorghe, *this woman is the last straw!*

And that was why Gheorghe was in such a bad mood, as well as being woken in the night. Ion had been sleeping like a churchyard corpse and Gheorghe himself had had to get up and let in the stranger. Ruxandra had been awake, he knew, but when she had heard the bell, she had pulled the quilt up and round her ears.

'I'm not going,' she had said.

'I didn't think you were,' Gheorghe had replied sarcastically.

When the man had handed in his passport, bearing the eagle of America, Gheorghe had given it only a brief look. The Americans were all mad – otherwise why would they come to Romania?

Curiosity, perhaps? Since they had got rid of the dictator, the mountains seemed to be crawling with foreigners. And as for being out in the mountains in that kind of clothing – what was it? Red shorts and a yellow T-shirt. And a case – no rucksack. What was the world coming to?

He had glanced briefly at the American's name. Walter Arvarescu. The ending showed the man was of Romanian origin. Another pilgrimage to find his roots? Trust the Americans!

'Call me Wally,' the man had said. His voice was not pleasant. More like a woman's. His skin was exceptionally smooth and tanned. He looked like a nancy boy. Blond hair tied back in a ponytail and an earring!

Gheorghe snorted as he ruminated over the man's arrival that night. Or should he have said that morning? After all, it had been past midnight. And now the man was sleeping in one of his ten beds.

'We shan't get very fat on him up there!' he growled to Ion. Gheorghe squinted out of the window at the early morning. It had been an exceptionally red dawn, presaging bad weather.

'Perhaps today we will get some more tourists,' said Ion.

Gheorghe doubted it, with the summer storms they were having. He blamed it on what the Russians were putting up into space. They weren't that backward in Romania not to have heard of the greenhouse effect.

Take the man upstairs. If he had been caught in a summer storm he would never have made it to Sancipia. The Carpathians were treacherous mountains even in summer. But what could one expect from an American anyway? If Gheorghe could have, he would have charged him double. But he wasn't allowed to. He had to be civil to everybody; otherwise *he'd* be the one to pay.

First Gheorghe had been dictated to by a Ceausescu and now, even with a new government, Sancipia was just the same. Gheorghe sighed. Nothing was going right for him. And his wife, full of superstition. She wouldn't even make love on 21 July! He snorted again.

Ruxandra Dobos heard the knocking. Faint at first, then increasing to an insistent, desperate drumbeat. She stood by the long curtains in the dining room, frightened to look out of the window, her heart thumping.

Down in the cellar, a frightened toad jumped, striking Ion's gaunt face, distracting him from his work.

Upstairs, Gheorghe was glad to stop what he was doing. He felt listless and unable to drag his steps to the door as the humid fingers of summer had pushed the *Little and Chosen* to demand rightful entry at the Inn Sancipia on the morning of 22 July.

'Gheorghe, the door!' called Ruxandra. She couldn't have moved if she had wanted to. And she didn't.

'I can hear. Why don't you go?' shouted her husband irritably.

'I can't. I'm doing something,' she shouted back.

'Ion! Where the devil is the man?' Her husband was really growling with anger now.

The knocking increased to a staccato two-fisted hammering. At seven in the morning! Who could want shelter so desperately early? It could only be her! A shivering Ruxandra made a reverent Sign of the Cross.

She felt safer now. The whole of her was terrified but thrilled at the same time. Could it be *the Chosen* come to the Inn? Come to Sancipia? She had never thought to see it in her lifetime.

The last happening had been 15 years before her birth, so her mother had said, but that might have been the ravings passed on from Simona Murgu and the rest. An Arva woman's importance was counted by her sightings.

But the Sala family was bound to the Inn. Whatever the State did or said. They had their part to play and she would carry on the tradition. There would always be room for Him or her as long as Ruxandra lived. She must bear a child to carry on the tradition. She'd married Gheorghe because he was a stranger from Brasov. Perhaps there was less chance then of anything going wrong. But she had to be careful about when it was conceived.

Ruxandra thought of her true emotional life as being only in the past, when as a shy teenager she had kept from her mother the sacrilegious secret about her relationship with Toma Matei. It would have been a disaster if she'd become pregnant. She'd been very lucky. But Toma hadn't.

She knew now that 'going-up' had made her the woman she was, still wary of men. The State Police had been very thorough in their examination of her. The thought made her shake as well as the remembrance. And she had been not quite 16. She had told the police all she could about that particular July morning in 1982 in a full statement.

Ruxandra remembered poor Toma so clearly. She had truly loved him. And he had died so cruelly. What was most painful was the knowledge that her attempt to cheat on Grandsire had cost him his life. As she waited for someone to open the door to that dull hammering, Ruxandra tried to conquer her over-breathing, stirred up by the coming visitation, tried to think of nothing but her undying love for Toma.

Toma, Toma, my first boy; brown arms, silky legs, curls at head and groin. Killed by nature, the light of the storm. Blackened beneath the forest tree, pinned to the ground, a cruciform shape. A victim of my 'coming-down'.

Ruxandra sobbed for him again, as she had done every day since her love had been wiped from the Earth, but not from her heart.

She had taken Gheorghe as her husband only because he was a man from the city, who knew nothing about 'coming-down', who had no knowledge of an Arva woman's burden and would hardly persist in trying to find out …

She caught her breath, dragging herself back to the present. With every knock, she knew for sure that one girl was destined to be unlucky this year. There had been six to choose from and Ruxandra herself was about to harbour the chosen. She shook her head in disbelief.

The ignorant man she had married, who had wanted her on her knees that very night, was now stumbling to the door to let in whatever was going to disturb Sancipia's peace for a long time. It was a shocking thought. At that very moment he was groping his way across the hall, ready to open the door to the devilish hammering that set every nerve in Ruxandra's body tingling with ominous excitement. She crossed herself quickly – and waited.

3

'With sharp blue eyes, each like a pin
And light loose hair yet swarthy skin,
No tuft on cheek nor beard on chin …
There was no guessing his kith and kin …'

The door would not open. Gheorghe realised that it was not sticking; rather something was stuck behind it. Once, a drunk had slipped down outside, his body jarring the door, his trunk half-propped, and his legs splayed wide.

But the one outside, out there, was not drunk, but hurt. A girl was crying, sobbing in great snuffling hiccoughs.

'Ion!' roared Gheorghe. 'Come here, I need you!'

It was quite dark in the cellar. There was only one electric light. Ion was busy rubbing away the dry feel of the toad when he heard Mr Dobos call from above. He was very glad he was getting free of the damp mustiness and up into the daylight.

'Coming, sir,' his voice echoed as he hurried along the flagged corridor. And he was shivering.

The two men managed to shove the door open. The girl had been seated against it, slumped forward, her feet and hands stretched out stiffly like some awkward doll. Gheorghe and Ion stared at the child, incomprehension on their faces, as she swivelled round and shuffled forward on her backside as if she had no power to walk – almost as if she were a baby.

She fixed them with a mechanical look from the brightest eyes either man had ever seen. She did not seem to be looking at them, only through them.

Her round cheeks were scarlet, her lips parted slightly showing pearly teeth. Her face was cut into the grimace of a smile, yet there were tears coursing down it.

'Who are you? What's happened?' asked Gheorghe. He went to help her, but the child would not be helped. She put up a little hand to ward him off.

'Christ, look at her hand,' said Ion. They stared. It was one mass of small open bites.

Gheorghe swallowed, his mouth suddenly dry. 'Can you speak? Tell us what happened?' He could see bites on her neck as well, like those on her hand. Her white dress was spattered with bright flecks of blood. Her black apron had red streaks of clay upon it. 'Ion! Get Ruxandra!' he ordered. Ion was glad to get away, unnerved by the sight.

Suddenly, the girl toppled over with a doll-like movement. She lay awkwardly on her side. Gheorghe drew in his breath. She was naked under the voluminous traditional skirt! He didn't want to look. All that was decent within him, was horror struck.

Her soft buttocks were a mass of bites too and blood was oozing between her thighs. With an awkward gesture, and almost afraid to touch her, he flipped back her skirts and covered her.

Inside the hostel, Ruxandra still stood by the curtain. She had heard it all, sensed what was going on outside. She felt as if she was standing there in a dream, where you can't move and, when you do, you get nowhere. She was conscious too that Ion was about to fetch her.

'Mrs Dobos, quick. There's a girl dying outside!'

'Dying?' Her voice was shaking.

'It looks like it!' The barman's face was white.

Ruxandra came to. 'Ring for Dr Baescu, Ion,' she said. 'Go

on!' The young man nodded, a terrified look on his face. Ruxandra started for the door …

They carried the victim in very carefully. The girl winced in agony when she was lifted, looking like an absurd, pathetic doll when they laid her on the bed in the special room downstairs that Ruxandra insisted be kept for any disabled visitors who might come to them during the season.

Ruxandra knew what she should do but had no notion of how to do it. *Comfort the Little and Chosen* was drumming in her head, a word-memory come from years of training. So she sat holding the child's fingers, chafing them gently, averting her eyes from the mass of bites, asking herself over and over, *Could the Great One have done this by His choosing?*

And the girl continued to cry wordlessly from her shining, staring eyes. What had she seen? She had been with *Him*.

Ruxandra still could hardly believe that it was her time to behold the phenomenon! All she knew was that she was in the presence of the *Little and Chosen*, but she had never thought it would be as horrible as this.

The women of Arva always spoke in whispers about 'the unlucky one' – never what happened to her. And Ruxandra had never asked. *'Blessed are those who have believed and not seen.'* Ruxandra had been one of those; now she had witnessed His coming with her own eyes. Through this little one.

And this morning, after all her own years of waiting for Grandsire's Resurrection, she wished she hadn't! But that was sacrilege! She prayed for forgiveness, but all the time she kept asking herself, *What really happened at Grandsire's grave?*

The girl was identified as Anka, Petrescu's daughter. Nothing could be hidden for long in a village like Arva. In any case, immediately after Ion had telephoned the doctor, a villager had turned up for a drink. It hadn't taken him long to let the news out. Soon the place had been full of silent people, shuffling about, trying to peer into the downstairs room. Dr Baescu had arrived, accompanied by the girl's mother, who was almost out of her mind.

Irina Petrescu had been distraught when she'd been brought in. She had been barely able to speak for crying. Her eyes had been staring out of her head. She had kept shaking and shouting, 'Not my Anka, it can't be! It can't be her.' And the old women had crossed themselves.

The dining hall of Sancipia was full now. Ion had his work cut out to serve them all. Bottle after bottle, glass after glass! And they drank it all in silence as a mark of respect to the *Little and Chosen*. Many times they raised their glasses to her. Gheorghe kept shaking his head in disbelief.

'Are you all mad?' he said to Ruxandra. 'What does it mean? Is this a village of nutcases?'

'I don't know what it means either,' lied Ruxandra, cleaning the glasses as quickly as she could. She had been glad to leave the child's side. But her task was over now the mother had come.

'You do!' hissed Gheorghe, clutching her arm. 'And you're going to tell me when these idiots have gone!'

It was a very small room off the one in which his daughter was lying. It had a sturdy washbasin and chair. Next door was the lavatory. Petrescu had been sitting in there for ages, his head in his hands, slumped forward just to get away from what was in the next room. Anything was better than standing, sitting or kneeling beside his only daughter, who couldn't speak, didn't appear to recognise him and only cried wordlessly from strange, glittering eyes.

He couldn't bear the thought that it was happening to him. He would never have believed it could! That he could be the father of the *Little and Chosen*. It was something that happened to other men, to other parents, once in a blue moon. It hadn't happened since 1952, they said, when Simona Murgu had 'gone up' and there'd been all that trouble about Claudiu, when the men had taken it out on him.

Why should it happen to them now? How could it be his

daughter? His little Anka! He ran clean water from the big brass taps and plunged his head into its iciness, wishing that he might drown and never show his face again. Then he felt a hand on his shoulder.

Dr Baescu looked a troubled man. His lined face, framed by a wild beard, was screwed into a frowning mask. He had been sickened by the sight next door and now was coming the hardest part. What father could face what he was about to be told? The man was a simple peasant, not bad-looking, an average human being who was now having to face a catastrophe. Baescu sighed.

'Petre,' said the doctor. 'Petre, I need to talk to you.'

Petrescu had never been ill in his life: that is, except one day when he was ploughing and he had dislocated his shoulder. He didn't like doctors one bit. And he certainly didn't want to hear what this one was going to tell him. He set his teeth together. Then he straightened himself, shook the water from his face and grabbed a towel, burying himself within it. He couldn't look at Baescu but he knew he was going to have to listen to what he had to say.

'Go on, doctor.' His voice was a muffled croak.

'Anka has been raped.' Baescu made it sound an everyday occurrence.

Petre groaned out loud, then thrust himself out of the towel and threw it on the floor. Suddenly he clenched his fists and strode away from the doctor towards the window. He couldn't trust himself to be near anyone. He just wanted to lash out at anything.

'Oh, Christ!' he cursed, then he crossed himself.

Once more, Baescu was beside him, taking his arm. 'I'd like to make it easier for you, Petre, but how can I? Your little girl has succumbed to an attack of the greatest force. We're doing what we can for her regarding her injuries -'

'How badly hurt is she?' cried Petre, turning back to the window. Outside, the landscape was still; not a breath of wind, as if the whole of nature was struck dumb with horror.

The doctor was following him again. He put a friendly arm

about his shoulders.

'Quite badly, I'm afraid.' Baescu knew he should tell the farmer that his daughter probably wouldn't recover, but the shock would be too much at present. The mother had lost her wits completely. And who could blame her? She needed counselling. They both did.

Baescu already had a plan forming in his mind. He would get that psychiatrist Marcu at Burbor Hospital in Cluj-Napocka to have a look at Irina Petrescu afterwards. He'd made it known to all local medical practitioners he was interested in any schizophrenic tendencies in the Arva region. He was writing a book on the subject, which interested Baescu a great deal, given how much he had speculated on the phenomenon himself.

Just now, the woman was needed to care for her daughter for however many days the child survived. How long Irina had been hearing voices he wasn't sure, but she was certainly hearing them now.

That might have been brought on by the shock too but, according to several of her neighbours, she'd had problems like this for some time. And in Baescu's experience, they knew about voices in Arva!

Petrescu's face was contorted, 'How could He have done it? I'd like to -' He held on to Baescu for support, his legs almost giving way. The doctor nodded in sympathy, trying to calm his pleading.

'I don't know how anyone could have done such a thing. It's beyond my comprehension! I understand how you feel, Petre, but that's a police job! It is - you *know* it is - and they *will* get him, I promise you. It's Anka that matters now —'

As the doctor talked, all Petrescu wanted to scream was, *You stupid old bastard. Call yourself a doctor? They'll never get Grandsire. Never. No policeman will ever catch him!*

'I want Anka to go to the hospital,' Baescu was adding, 'I've done all I can at the moment. Besides she is in shock. That's a dangerous condition in itself.'

'No!' cried Petre. 'She can't be taken from us! She can't!'

54

The two men stood together for a minute or two without speaking then Baescu tried again.

'Petre, I understand how you feel, but you have to leave it to the authorities. He *will* be found. But the best you can do for your wife and child -'

'Child?' said Petrescu bitterly, '*Child?*' He was thinking of Anka, her little round face, her happiness as she bobbed up and down on his shoulder all those years ago. 'Oh my God, what am I going to do, doctor?' The other man looked at him helplessly,

'You have to comfort them both, Petre. Stand by them, do everything you can for them. Anka is still a child, who has been through a terrible experience, and your wife is suffering terribly too. They both need you.'

'All that blood ...' Petre said it almost to himself, his own horrified voice drumming in his ears, 'all that blood, doctor? How?' he appealed, shuddering.

'There *seemed* to be a lot of blood, Petre, I know that,' said the doctor. 'But it was not quite what it appeared.'

'What do you mean?' The farmer's voice cracked with pain.

'It was *menstrual* blood, Petre,' replied the doctor. 'Your daughter is menstruating. Probably the shock.'

'The bastard!' swore Petre.

'And that made it all look worse. I think you should know something else, Petre. Your wife brought Anka to see me some time ago. She was worried that Anka had not started her periods. Why, I've no idea. Your girl was perfectly healthy then – but, later, I received a report from a doctor in Cluj.

'Anka, herself, had visited him for a consultation. She was not accompanied by her mother, and probably unaware he'd get in touch with me. Evidently, her condition was preying on her mind. Can you add anything of value? Was your wife obsessed with Anka's maturity?'

Petre lifted his eyes, red and swollen from crying. He was only a man; he knew nothing. The doctor was trying to comfort him; he knew that too. But it was no use.

Anka had been chosen as the victim. Who ordained it, he

didn't understand. What it was to do with birthdays and weddings, were old wives' tales. Anka had been only a child when she went up to Grandsire. Irina was going to pay for it! Petre would make her. How could she let her own daughter 'go-up' when she knew there was a risk? She should have stopped her!

Baescu waited while the farmer stood dumbly. How could he understand the man's feelings really? He had no children. Yet, in all his years as a doctor, he had never witnessed such savagery. Of course, in the war – but who counted that? No, he'd never seen anything like it. And the vermin? How did they fit in?

But there was no way he could tell this to a father, tormented by what had happened to his daughter; that her assailant must have been in a psychotic frenzy and had almost bitten her to death.

But how? The doctor had never seen human bites like that; they seemed more like animals' teeth! Probably rats! Perhaps they had swarmed over her as she lay on the ground after the crime. But how could that be true?

No, he wasn't going to surmise, just get her to the hospital, and let the police sort it out.

They had all forgotten the American. He was still fast asleep upstairs.

'What am I going to do if our guest comes down?' said Gheorghe to Ruxandra. 'He will think he has come into a mad house.'

'Well, he's managed to sleep through it all,' Ruxandra said.

'Nice welcome to Romania though, isn't it?' said Gheorghe nastily. 'This is going to ruin Sancipia's reputation.' His wife looked at him carefully:

'Just like you, Gheorghe! No thought for anyone but yourself.'

'That's not fair.'

'Yes it is, and I've had enough of it!' Suddenly, Ruxandra threw down her glass cloth and walked off into the press of visitors.

'That's right, Ruxandra,' called Gheorghe after her, 'go and hide with your own people. Let the devil take them for all I care!' When she was out of earshot, he sniffed and muttered, 'It looks as though he might have already.'

Police Chief Valentin stood in the foyer of the Inn Sancipia, looking round. He was a middle-aged man, who'd seen plenty of changes in his time. And plenty of crimes. Nor was he given to flights of fancy.

When he looked pleasant, his men knew that there was trouble on the way. Today, he looked less than pleasant. Rather sick. He'd had no food as he'd got out of bed in response to the call. Besides it was a hell of a journey to Arva from his office. Not that far, but the roads were bad.

And he'd drunk some wine, which had been a bad idea. His stomach, which didn't turn easily, was all churned up. He passed a hand over his brow and flicked back his fair thinning hair. It was too early in the morning for rape.

Gheorghe waited humbly behind the reception desk, the American passport in front of him. He didn't want to get on the wrong side of the police. They might close him down. And the inspector seemed in a very bad mood. But he was a man of intelligence. It wasn't Gheorghe's fault that the victim had ended up staying in his property. He couldn't be held responsible; he'd only helped to bring her in.

Valentin turned to the desk and taking the passport, stared at it, his brow creasing into a deep frown. He flipped over the pages. New York. He didn't relish this inquiry at all. Besides, he hated rape and especially when it had anything to do with children! There had been also too much suffering with regards to children in present-day Romania. He had to get his hands on this maniac very soon.

'What time did the foreigner come in?' he asked the landlord curtly.

'Just after midnight, sir,' Gheorghe replied. 'And he's still up there, fast asleep in bed. Ion says he is sleeping like the dead!'

Valentin sighed. One line of questioning over before it started. Not that he had anything against Americans. But he would have been the prime suspect, of course. If the man had been in Sancipia since just after midnight, he couldn't have done it to the girl. Not according to the police doctor anyway.

'I know what you're thinking, inspector,' said Gheorghe, 'but there is no way the man left here in the early hours. The whole place is locked and bolted.'

'And what about the fire risk?'

'Oh, we have a porter on duty all night.' Gheorghe could have bitten out his tongue. If they inspected the place and implemented new fire regulations he'd be ruined. 'Ion would have let anyone in or out,' he added to cover himself. All he hoped was the lazy bastard hadn't drunk himself to sleep.

'Well, I shall want to talk to this Ion afterwards. And possibly the American.'

'Very good, inspector.'

'Right.' Valentin looked across to the dining room, where a mass of silent, hostile villagers were staring him out. He knew the police weren't popular in these backward places, but he was having no insolence.

'What in Hell's name are they all doing here?' he asked.

'Search me,' replied Gheorghe, 'you'd better ask my wife. They're her people!'

'Come on, get rid of them!'

'You mean close up?' The landlord was horrified. He needed their custom. They'd spent a fortune toasting the victim's health.

'Get rid of them. Sensation seekers! If you won't, I will!' snarled Valentin, the wine making his stomach burn like fire. He strode towards the dining room followed by two of his men – both looking sinister with their weapons jolting against their hips. 'Come on, you lot. Out! There's nothing to see. The kid's gone.'

Gheorghe watched Valentin and his men moving from table to table. He could see the villagers didn't like it. For some bizarre reason, they were determined to stay. According to Ruxandra, it was the custom. She was as nuts as the rest!

They began to disperse, grumbling quietly.

'Bang goes my business!' said Gheorghe Dobos, but it wasn't meant to be a joke.

Because of the girl's inability to help herself, and her mother's obstructive behaviour, it was left to Baescu and the police doctor to administer emergency medical aid. After the latter had collected his evidence with swabs and tests, they repaired Anka's injuries in Baescu's surgery under local anaesthetic.

Afterwards, Petre carried his silent daughter out to the horse and cart without a look behind, while his wife stayed gibbering at his elbow. Petre had kept his word. Neither he nor his wife would allow Anka to be taken to the hospital. All Irina kept repeating in the surgery was, 'I will keep her with us as long as I can. She's not leaving me yet!'

When the doctors had finished, she'd burst into hysterical sobbing, holding the dumb, doll-like figure of her daughter to her fiercely. But the girl made no sign that she had even heard, just stared at them all with those unnerving eyes. Just what horrors had she seen?

Neither would she talk to the policeman who waited outside. It was as if she was dumb; probably hysterical shock. Baescu had warned them not question her further and Valentin had complied, also demanding in an authoritative voice why the hell hadn't he insisted Anka was sent to hospital. But Baescu knew the people of Arva region. They didn't give in easily.

However, the doctor was worried by the ceaseless menstrual flow from the girl. Great clots which tore from her body. Almost a haemorrhage. And there was good reason for it. The girl had been badly torn. Both he and the police surgeon agreed she needed expert attention – and probably a blood transfusion – a risk in itself these days. So he kept on trying,

'Can't you make Irina see sense, Petre?' begged Baescu.

'You don't want Anka to die, do you?' He was sorry after he'd said that, but he had to say something. But her father just stared at him impassively as if he'd already given up.

In a way, Baescu could understand his attitude. In that antiquated village, rape was death. Petrescu couldn't face the truth his daughter had suffered such iniquity. The whole thing was a paradox.

But, on the whole, Baescu didn't really understand the people he served. He knew something of their background; but it was clear they were a sect. Practically every one of his young women patients had been married at nineteen. It was the custom. He said 'practically' because the only exceptions were gypsies who were a law to themselves and were paying for it at present, given the recent racial attacks – and the village prostitute, old Eva Kirchma's daughter.

He wasn't surprised some researcher had got hold of their history at last. That it was Marcu, was good news. He had a reputation. He was also much indebted to Baescu given the amount of patients he put the psychiatrist's way. Arva was a breeding ground for hysteria, which invariably led up the road to a type of schizophrenia. Whether it was of the true variety, organic in origin, Baescu could not tell. He was no expert. He just sent every one of the women to the institution at Burbor in Cluj as quickly as he could.

And, now, Irina Petrescu. She'd be following. What had happened to her daughter was certainly pushing her over the edge.

Baescu looked at Valentin, who seemed to be suffering from a severe bout of indigestion. He'd been running round like a mad thing. Up and down to the station, examining old documents for any local suspects and waiting for the police computer to throw up the national records.

He'd insisted he had Baescu's medical report along with the police surgeon's. The latter knew Valentin better than Baescu and had hurried it through. Valentin was staring at the one by the region's doctor:

'You think she's in some kind of hysterical trance, brought

on from shock? And these bites?'

The doctor shook his head hopelessly.

'This is the first rape I've had in this area since I've been in charge. But we'll get the bastard. Whoever he is! Now, come on, doctor, what about these bites? I'm looking for a pervert anyway, but what sort of teeth has he got?'

'It couldn't have been him,' replied Baescu. 'Not unless he's a rat!'

The inspector's mouth twitched.

'I'm sure the bites are animal. Even your man is agreed. We discussed it when we had the girl on the table. We shoved in some tetanus, I can tell you. And I've seen a lot of rat bites round here on the farms.'

'But she was covered. It must have been a horde of the buggers!' Valentin hated rats; it made him shudder to think about it.

'We can have no idea what happened. Maybe the poor girl was savaged by them after?'

'She was lying there after what had been done to her and a horde of rats started on her?' The policeman's voice said it all.

'But what other explanation is there?' replied the doctor.

'I have no idea,' said Valentin, sitting down. His stomach felt worse as the thought of what had happened to that little unfortunate child made him shiver under his uniform.

The men were silent for a moment, then he added, 'I'll see the pest control officer gets in. We're examining the scene of crime now!' He coughed. 'Their damn superstitions! These damn people!'

'It's their culture,' replied the doctor. 'They feel and believe there was something supernatural about the rape of Anka Petrescu.'

'Supernatural about being covered with rat bites? About rape?' The doctor shrugged helplessly in answer to Valentin's questions. 'No, there's nothing supernatural about any of those, Baescu. They are facts of life. And death, in some cases. That child will never get over it. She'll always be haunted by it. We have to get him. And I intend to if I can!'

He and his team were going to check the records of every man, first of all in Arva, and then they were going to throw out the net over the whole region. It was summer and there were hikers about. But they would have to try locally first. Then they'd start making a search of all the hostels and hotels of the area. Whoever had done this to Anka Petrescu had to be caught. Anyway, one or two things had come up in the records already which seemed of interest. Valentin had a few visits to make urgently.

The American was still not awake at midday. Gheorghe himself went up to see if the man was still alive. He had reported to Valentin and already given a full description of the American's clothing and other details.

According to the doctors, the man was in the clear. The Petrescu girl had been raped somewhere between five and six. There was no question of it – nor any doubt that their foreign guest was asleep in his room at the time. He had witnesses. And they'd all verified the facts to the inspector, looking as haggard as any guests Gheorghe had ever seen. He was sure they'd never come back to Sancipia either!

It must have been Ion's lucky day. He'd been able to verify also that he hadn't been asleep and let the foreigner creep out. Because, at that time, he'd been called upstairs by several of the hikers, who couldn't rest for the noise.

They were complaining about the snoring coming from the American's room. It was worse than snoring, they said; more like a high-pitched squeaking, accompanied by snuffling as if the fellow had a shocking cold and a dirty, wheezy chest. They couldn't all be wrong, thought Gheorghe, although he and Ruxandra hadn't heard a thing.

Ion said the noise was so terrible it shot through his head like lightning pain. But Gheorghe knew the porter, who was an Arvan like the rest of them, had had too much wine earlier on.

Ion told Inspector Valentin that he had been at a loss as to what to do and had finally decided to hammer on the American's door, while the other guests stood cursing in their pyjamas. Anyway, it seemed to do the trick, because the noise stopped. Gheorghe suspected there would be no problem with the American's alibi. Especially with all that snoring. He must have been dead-beat after such a restless night. No wonder he hadn't got up early. Still, he had to wake up some time, especially if the police wanted to talk to him.

When Gheorghe used the key to get into his room, the man didn't stir, but his breathing was coming quietly and naturally and he seemed quite relaxed and wonderfully peaceful in sleep.

As the short and bald Gheorghe looked down at his guest, he was struck by the man's physical beauty. The American was sleeping naked with his sheet close to his loins, his legs thrust apart and his finely-formed foot protruding from under the sheet.

He looked a bit like a golden statue. His hair was long, giving him a feminine appearance. The sun was shining on his earring. Gheorghe didn't know what he was doing standing staring at his guest. It would have been different if he'd been a woman.

Gheorghe felt suddenly uncomfortable. The man was so boyish, and there was down on his cheeks. As Gheorghe turned to go noiselessly out of the room, the American's finely-cut mouth suddenly worked into a smile.

Gheorghe thought he was awake, was ready to speak, but then he realised he was having pleasant dreams. The man stretched his arms over his head and his armpits were as smooth as the rest of him.

As Gheorghe went out of the door, closing it behind him, he said to himself, 'Well, I reckon you're a nancy boy. Even if you had been out, I couldn't imagine Valentin pinning that sort of crime on you!'

Valentin had the police files looked through systematically by his team. The girl's was a strange case and, through a lot of careful and tedious detective work, because his own office was not completely automated, his departmental records finally threw up another such incident that had happened over thirty years ago and, strangely enough, in the village of Arva.

A girl had brought in the file and handed it over impassively. She was pretty and small, with highlights in her smooth brown hair and always dressed in a smart brown suit. But in spite of some of his young lads' efforts in that direction, she wasn't interested. She was from the big city and thought they were all peasants.

He had the file in front of him just now. It was heavy, blue and dusty. Flipping it open, he realised it held several documents. He sighed. Unfortunately, there were times when an inspector himself had to look up the old records. The documents had been filed under *Rape* in the *unsolved* section. Where else but there would he start?

1952 wasn't that long ago. What? Thirty-six years? The pervert *could* still be about, although it was very unlikely that he'd strike again after such a long period of time – a sex drive like that would need to be satisfied at much shorter intervals.

As he opened the file he was thinking of the bites all over the poor kid's body. He'd had the local rodent operator alerted but he'd refused to go to the churchyard. Valentin frowned. Damned superstitions! After that, he got in touch with the town council and they'd sent a couple of their men to look for the rats.

Then he settled down to read the files, beginning with Case History 005406.

Cluj-Napocka Police Files. Case History 005406:
Claudiu Basa.
Born 27.7.1900, farmer of Ruare,
Suspect, attempted rape – 22.7.1952.

Testimony of Simona Florea, spinster of Arva.
Statement taken: 25.7.1952.

… I was with Claudiu from four am. He was excited when he undressed me, especially when he found I was wearing no undergarments. We had intercourse several times. At no time did the farmer leave the bedroom.

At no time did he force me; I was willing. It was near to dawn in the morning when we heard footsteps hurrying past the farm buildings. I was afraid we would be discovered and begged Claudiu to go out and see who was passing. He was gone for approximately two minutes and returned to tell me it was Catina Albu, who had gone up after the rest of us …

Valentin read it all and made a note to interview Simona Murgu as well as Claudiu. Then he turned to the second document in the file:

Cluj-Napocka Police Files: Case-history 076338.
Claudiu Basa
Born: 27.7.1900, farmer of Ruare.
Convicted: 31.12.1982. Bestiality.

Testimony of Ruxandra Sala, spinster of Arva.
Statement taken: 23.7.1982.

Am I allowed to make this point first? My going-up was, in the eyes of the people of Arva, a sacrilege and a falsehood. I was not a virgin. I had known of Claudiu's sexual inclinations since Arva School. At that time, my comrades were not yet sworn to secrecy as we had no experience, but we were susceptible to rumour.

As I said, I was not a virgin, which, on the morning of the rite, caused me some mental anguish. I was unaware as to what was going to take place and I wondered if the fact of my seduction might come to light. I was an innocent in sexual matters, unwilling to commit sacrilege by visiting Grandsire's Grave when I was not in a state of grace.

I discussed this fact with Toma Matei. As I have told you, he was my young seducer. Although he, too, was unwilling to take any part in a rite exclusive to the female sex of Arva, he loved me and offered to accompany me. Together we concocted a plan. It was not difficult. I told you it was a bad year. I was the only one to 'go up' the twenty-second of July this year.

Our plan was that I should be able quickly to find a protector in Toma Matei should I be approached or appropriated by Farmer Basa. Toma was going to conceal himself in the graveyard some way behind the bushes where Basa was said to lurk.

I was dressed by my mother in the traditional way, completed the secret ritual, then my feet were set on the stone path. I was quite dizzy. I remember that. With my flowers in my hand and the poopy close to my breast, I set out, a little comforted by the thought of Toma hiding to save me if need be.

I remember one thing that worried me especially was the weather. There had been a storm late in the evening of the twenty-first and another was expected before dawn. No, I was not afraid of what I understood could happen. In fact, I had little belief in the superstitions attached to the visit to Grandsire. This was a direct result of my knowledge of a man. I could not be chosen. However, I was afraid of Basa.

When I was close to Grandsire, I followed the usual custom of laying the flowers on the grave then keeping him warm. At no time did I see Basa watching me. Later, coming down I met Toma, who caught my arm and dragged me quickly away from the lean-to sty at the side of the path, close by Basa's buildings. I can tell you Toma was very pale. Indeed, I remember he vomited. I understand I can repeat his speech now that he cannot himself. He had been witness first to the disquieting spectacle of Basa ogling my naked parts. In fact, he said it made him feel sick. Then, in case Basa should handle me on my coming down, he followed him into the farm buildings, but at a distance. There, he was treated to the disgusting sight of Basa relieving himself.

Valentin leaned back. The evidence compiled on Basa's sexual tendencies had been collected over thirty years. And there was more. The inspector picked up his coffee, looked at it and put it down. His stomach was really playing up. He felt in his breast pocket for an indigestion tablet, popped it in his mouth and, chewing, returned to the file.

After Valentin had read the whole document, he realised that the woman, Simona Florea's testimony was the only one in favour of Basa, whose record on police files was not one to be proud of. They'd got him in the end though. Bestiality. Common enough in backward farming communities. Voyeurism? Not much chance for that from what he'd seen of the villagers. But Arva was a queer place. Rituals? Valentin never failed to be surprised at what turned folk on.

He returned to the file, read parts of it again. The Florea woman's testimony was not what he was looking for. Others were more interesting.

He went on through the next lot of statements to find out what had happened to Catina Albu and in what way Basa had been implicated. He would definitely go up and see the farmer, but there was no way he could have been the attacker this time. He was far too old.

After reading everything about the strange case of the girl, Catina Albu, and her subsequent death, due to 'natural causes', Valentin closed the file, leaned back in the chair to ruminate on the evidence, hoping at the same time the acid in his stomach was abating.

He consigned the file once more into the hands of the girl with the patronising look on her face. He was tired. Whatever all this was about – he yawned – whatever kind of phenomenon – he yawned again – he might have been in the job twenty years, but it still surprised him to find how some people got their kicks.

After calling the supercilious secretary back in to take some notes, he then ordered a meeting of the detectives he had assigned to the equally baffling case of Anka Petrescu. Just what had gone on in Arva village in the past and evidently was still going on?

4

'… in Transylvania, there's a tribe,
Of alien people, who ascribe
The outlandish ways and dress,
On which their neighbours lay such stress,
To their fathers and mothers
Having risen out of some subterranean prison,
Into which they were trepanned
Long time ago in a mighty band …
But how or why they don't understand'.

The walls had been eggshell-blue, painted in Claudiu's mother's time. Now they were smoke-blackened by age. The small holy water stoup with the brass bowl for the fingers was as dark as pewter and the paper angel, which had been his guardian once, was half-peeled, wings downwards.

Although Claudiu had tried to keep his curtain nets clean, they were grimy and frayed. Above the bed was his mother's treasure, the hand-made tapestry of a rooster, squawking amidst rough flowers. There was no brightness left in the bird now.

The heavy furniture was as grim as the dour expression on the face of his parents, taken at their wedding. The old man's eyes fixed on their faded brown photograph as if it was the only familiar thing in the room.

He had been born in this bed and he would die in it. The

door of the heavy old wardrobe was hanging open, bulging with clothes, piled from its bottom. As the days, months and years went by, they had slipped to the floor of the cupboard in mouldering heaps. No one came into his bedroom but him, so why should he bother? Anyway, he would be leaving it soon. Today or tomorrow? But soon.

He had wanted Simona Florea once. Now she wasn't the woman he remembered. Anyway, she had married Murgu, the carter, to cover herself. He remembered how he'd struggled when she undressed him. He wanted to die in his funeral suit, but the woman insisted he get into his nightshirt.

Somewhere inside, he remembered she'd always been mad to get his clothes off. She'd twisted his useless leg unmercifully and clawed at his socks. He felt nothing when she pulled off his breeches. He just cursed her as she did it. At 87 years old, a man should have some privacy.

Simona had hauled the sheets off his bed, wrinkling her nose, which had been a pretty nose once. Now it was a beak! Poking into his private affairs.

'Can't a man even die in peace?' he'd growled. He didn't want to be bothered with this woman today; he was preparing to meet his Maker. Anyway, she'd called the priest, and the young one came.

When young Father Joseph went in to hear the old man's confession, his neighbours stood about the cottage whispering. That didn't last long, because Simona Murgu, who always had to be in the centre of everything, shooed them away. They sniggered as they whispered about the soft spot she had for Claudiu. Anyway, she didn't care. She knew he would want her to be around to keep the place going, when he couldn't.

Simona's brown, oval face was lined and her hair was pulled straight back from her forehead under the headscarf. She knew she looked older than she really was, worn out from hard work, not like the pretty girl Claudiu had known all those years ago. As she stood in the outside kitchen, she couldn't bear the stink of it. And Claudiu cooked his food here! Rough wood and planks formed into a shed – and beetles crawling everywhere! She wrinkled her nose, disgusted at the sight of the hob, large enough to feed a family, covered in age-old grease.

Simona put paper and wood shavings underneath it and started a fire with a taper. Swearing, she piled on more firewood until she got it going. Then she boiled water in a pan and scoured a pot so she could make the old man some *mamaliga*. He wasn't going to die of starvation anyway. She owed him *something*.

At just over 50, she was almost the same age now as he had been when she'd seduced him. He had been as helpless in her hands then as he was now. She felt pity for him more than anything else. Now her own husband, Murgu, had left her a widow, she knew she had to do something for this man. He had kept quiet about the child she'd borne.

She unbuttoned her brown cotton shirt and threw off the red, knitted cardigan. The sweat ran down between her breasts, which flabby and wrinkled, so different from when Claudiu had seen them last.

'Hell!' she cursed. But there was no malice in her thoughts as, continually wiping the sweat from her forehead, she tried to clean up, in between running over to stir the boiling cornmeal. 'What a life some poor woman would have had with you, Claudiu!'

But no woman would have looked at Claudiu. As a teenager, he hadn't had a girl. He hadn't been bad-looking; long in the nose, a trifle spotty, but lean and well-formed, except for his leg. He had been born with the deformity – the butt of his father's scorn, when he had wanted to take it out on someone.

Claudiu's mother had been hard too, but in a different

way. A woman full of secrets, who had seemed to resent her son from the day he was born. She'd known he would have to cope with the farm and with life itself after she'd gone, so she'd pushed him to do everything right, and beaten him with the yard broom if he hadn't. But he hadn't been strong enough to help her when *she*'d been beaten. The bastard had even used his son's crutch to do it.

That was the first time Claudiu had wanted his father to die and be out of their lives forever. Someone must have heard his prayers. The tyrant had been killed by a bear. Although the animals were rarely seen, they still roamed in the forests – and one had found Muger Basa and mauled him until his face was hardly recognisable.

Claudiu should have been sorry, but he could feel nothing. He just watched the box being nailed down, and the disgusting mass of flesh that had fathered him being closed away to putrefy.

After the funeral he went up to the graveyard a lot and kept on doing so. Sometimes, he cursed the old man, who would have been only bones by then. Other times, he used to sit by the grave and wonder what it would have been like if things had been different, if he hadn't been crippled.

He got a name for doing it. After all, if you lived by the church path and sat in the graveyard, you could expect it. He used to bring up the sheep, but the priest said it was sacrilege to have them feeding off the graves, so he would sit on a grave mound and keep the animals outside the palings.

It was only when he was a full-grown man he found out about 'going-up'. It hadn't been fair on him. He had never had a sister. Otherwise he might have known before.

In fact, he didn't know what feminine company was. All he did know was that women suffered. His mother used to lie there month after month complaining about stomach pains and, when he tried to help her, his father would order him out of the room.

There was blood too, things he didn't understand, pails of blood and stained cloths. Claudiu was a man alone in the world. He didn't have a friend. He felt set apart. Because he wasn't like the rest, none of the lads would speak to him. They said he was weird. Anyway, he wasn't sure if the lads knew any more than he did.

Some of them went to Eva Kirchma, the village prostitute, to learn about women. If he had done that, his father would have killed him. But he had seen her once at the gypsy camp by a stream. She was a small, dark-skinned girl, bending naked over the water. Claudiu had been transfixed by her beauty. A girl wasn't like a *man* after all. He had seen the back of her, slim and wonderful, but when she had turned and grinned at him, he had gone hot and cold.

That moment never went from his mind. After that, he wanted a woman of his own. But no woman would look at Claudiu. So he started looking at them. He had always been alone, his life measured by that day in high summer when the girls came up in their pretty white skirts and black-trimmed blouses to greet Grandsire at dawn.

There were three times in his life he remembered more than any other. He measured each year of his life by that day in the summer months when he saw what he wanted to see. In turn, the summer's heat was measured by the heat he felt on that special day in July when the village girls went up at dawn in all their glorious nakedness to meet Grandsire. But the three special times in his life were when Claudiu had seen Him.

The old man could see them now as he lay on his birth-bed, waiting for death. All the girls knew about him; he had never done them any harm – whatever anyone said. Whatever he had been accused of, he had only looked at their beauty. And tried to forget the ugliness. Claudiu closed his eyes. He wanted to tell Father Joseph about Grandsire – about everything he remembered so clearly:

A whirling mass of red and gold, those pale buttocks like lilies by the path. The flash of fire and ecstasy – legs astraddle like the heifer under the bull; a red shaft of light and her tears, always tears. There was blood from it – he knew that – he could scent it like a dog could – blood of the dawn and the girl. Afterwards, when the girl had flown down the ridge and He had disappeared through the cleft in the stone, which was called the Arch of Darkness, Claudiu had crept over there and traced his finger round the arch, when a big rat bit him.

Claudiu shuddered. The wound hadn't healed for weeks, leaking poisonously. The men in the village said Claudiu had done it to Catina Albu. She, the pale one, the pretty and thin one, who couldn't speak. They had put her away. Never saw her again. They pointed their fingers at him, muttered about him, shunned him. They hated what they couldn't understand. They even told the police. Claudiu hated those bitter Arva men, who didn't know his secret.

Luckily, he had Simona to vouch for him. She had been waiting for him when he came down from the graveyard, leaning against the lintel provocatively in her 'going-up' dress. He had been burning with excitement anyway, besides knowing she was naked underneath. So he had taken her to his bed. His first woman. He had kept most secrets well, until she cajoled him with her pretty pointing breasts and artful ways. So he'd told her about Grandsire and frightened her more than he thought he would.

But one secret he had kept on that 22 July. Those running footsteps they had heard coming down the church path past his house where they lay in bed had not been Catina Albu's, whoever had made them. The innocent lie Simona had told in her statement giving him his alibi had been his saviour.

A few days later, some of the village men had come up one night and caught him in the barn. They had beaten him with sticks, harder than his father ever had. He hadn't been able to pass water properly after that for a very long time.

Old Claudiu swallowed, working his Adam's apple, the mark of a man, a man he had never been, until Grandsire taught him how. He had been a recluse for 36 years, only looking at the women on a summer morning, fond of the only living creatures that loved him: his animals.

'Father, forgive me for I have sinned ...' he began. He would not have confessed to Pathan, even if his soul depended on it. The old priest had his own sins. When young Father Joseph left, looking pale and shaken, Claudiu felt easier, unburdened – but dirty, dirty – his dirty fingers plucking at the blanket. And he stared on at the faded face of that stern woman, his mother, who had died worn out with heavy farm work and that tyrant, who had made her life and that of his only son no better than the lot of serfs.

When Father Joseph came into the outhouse to tell Simona he was leaving, he was white to the ears. She knew he wasn't used to hearing confessions like that.

'Here, have some *tuica*, Father. The alcohol will put some colour back into your cheeks.'

Simona felt old and wise enough to boss this boy-cleric, who was evidently unused to such admissions. He had plenty to learn, and Arva was going to be the place to do so in the next few days. Simona had 'gone up' before the priest was even born. Yes, Father Joseph would be used to the stink of death again before the week was out.

She brought Claudiu the cornmeal mush. She would have to feed him. He was dribbling. She looked at the old man who had given her pleasure such a long time ago. She remembered what he had said to her about the stranger in the churchyard too. She had come to help Claudiu because she knew it had happened again. As she fed the *mamaliga* to him, she was thinking about the past and what she had learned in Claudiu's bed close to the church.

Simona's mother would have killed her if she had known. After the inquiry, Simona was afraid her parents would find out, but she felt much relieved when the police told her they kept those testimonies confidential. All that the people in the village knew was that Claudiu had got off again.

As she lifted the spoon to those trembling lips, she was disgusted by old age, which brought them all to quivering, ugly lumps of nothing.

His lips had been hard when they had crushed hers. She had never been loved again like she had been by Claudiu, the cripple. She had forgotten about his legs; his technique had been clumsy but madly passionate, and she had had a lot of knowledge too.

While she had undressed old Claudiu earlier that day and put him to bed, she had thought of that moment years before when she had unbuttoned his rough shirt, put her hand inside the garment and placed the flat of her palm against his hot and beating heart.

She and the farmer had loved each other in a frenzy: he because he had never loved a woman before; she fired up by the knowledge that what she was doing was both sinful and exciting. He had been in a mad mood then. After they had come together, he had put his lips to her breasts and consoled himself.

She fed this miserable old specimen of a man today because she remembered the past, especially the time when he had told her about Grandsire. She had been young and confident then and hadn't wanted to believe, yet the old superstition had terrified her. That morning she had coupled with Claudiu, she had discovered something about herself. As she had lain in bed beside him and he'd told her what he'd seen, she had recognised the burden all fertile women in Arva carried. Like the rest, she had hoped that they'd hear no more of Grandsire and what had happened to Catina Albu, that it might be over at last. Simona sighed – but it went on, and now there was another unfortunate girl lying half-dead at the Inn – the Petrescu child.

She looked down at his wasted body. Had Claudiu been the only living soul to see Grandsire and survive to speak of it? Perhaps he would be the only one ever. She hadn't understood about the *Little and Chosen* before Murgu took her as his wife. It filled her with dread to think about it now, as much as it had then, when she hadn't understood. The old primitive side of her as an Arva village woman still believed *the secret of the marriage bed.* She had been praying very hard, since her daughter, Emilia, fell pregnant, that she wouldn't deliver on the twenty-second, but there was nothing Simona could do about that now. Only go mad!

She should have been with her daughter really, but Claudiu had only a little time. She continued to spoon the food into his slack mouth, her mind fixed surely in the past. Claudiu must have seen Grandsire. What other man would be in Arva churchyard at dawn on 22 July? Except for the old priest perhaps. But that was another story! As Simona wiped his mouth periodically, she remembered Claudiu's words perfectly.

'The man was tall, slim and he sprang from nowhere. One moment he wasn't there, the next he was. The girl had just laid down the poopy doll when he just came out of ...' Claudiu had stopped abruptly, his face contorted with fear.

'What were you doing there, Claudiu, you naughty thing?' she had said playfully, trying to laugh it off.

'I was only looking.'

'Which one? Which one of us did you fancy? I went up early. Were you there then?'

'No.'

Both now and then, she'd wondered if the response was a lie. As Simona continued to stuff in the food, she began to feel sick.

Claudiu was also thinking about that morning when Simona had 'come down' from the church and into his bed. He had not slept after midnight. He had been sure that was how it was meant to be; so he could be one of the 'chosen' too; so that he could see Grandsire again. Why, he hadn't known. His instincts had told him that was how it was meant to be. A cripple allowed to see beauty, however cruel it was – but not to partake.

As Simona Murgu kept pushing in the cornmeal mush, he couldn't make sense of anything. He even began to believe that time it had been all in his imagination. Maybe he'd never seen Grandsire? Or perhaps the Great One had been with her when the *Little and Chosen* had passed the buildings and flown down the stony path? He'd heard her singing Grandsire's song. And those footsteps passing the house, had they been theirs? Then he dragged himself back from confusion. He must go to his Maker clear-headed.

He looked at Simona with dimming eyes. After her, he'd been lost. She'd never touched him again. She'd dared not – not after Murgu had taken her on. So Claudiu had turned into a beast and earned the name the women gave him in the village: the *Sowfucker*. After he had tasted what it was like to be a man and knew he would never have it anymore, he had descended to the level of an animal. *Sowfucker*.

The *mamaliga* dribbled its way out of Claudiu's mouth. He had no need of it now. He would never look at forbidden things again. Today, he would yearn for them no longer, be denied them no longer, sin no longer; today was his death-day. Soon he would know the *real* secret.

Simona put away the bowl; he'd had enough. She remembered how she had insisted on knowing what he'd seen …

'Tell me what you saw, Claudiu! And don't be giving me any fairy tales. What did the man do?'

Claudiu was silent for a moment. Then, he caught Simona by the shoulder urgently. She would have the bruise for a week. 'I've seen him before!' he said.

'Before?' questioned Simona eagerly. 'Does he come from Cluj?'

'A city, perhaps. But where I don't know.'

'When? Where did you see him?' Simona just had to know.

'It's no good me trying to explain. You won't understand it any more than I do – and you won't believe me.'

'Try me, Claudiu, try me!' cried Simona. 'You've tried everything else!' It was meant to be a joke, but it fell flat.

'The problem is,' said the farmer, his voice a harsh whisper, 'the first time I saw him was 36 years ago. And he looked just the same then. Just as young.'

There were goose bumps standing out all over Simona's flesh. She was terribly frightened when he said it. 'How could it be the same man?' Her voice sounded high and squeaky.

'I tell you it was!' said Claudiu, and his eyes were wilder than she had ever seen. She drew away from him a little. Perhaps he was mad – and dangerous.

'I tell you – he was the same both times. It wasn't right, Simona, he would have aged.'

'Stop it, Claudiu,' she said, drawing the old sheet about her, noticing his useless leg with a shudder.

'You said you wanted to know.' His face was close to hers. 'I know it was Grandsire! I think he lives in the churchyard and he ...' She was out of his bed, clutching the sheet, covering her soft and naked body.

'Don't tell me any more!' she screamed.

'Listen!' he shouted, swinging his good leg off the bed. 'Listen, I have to tell you now. Don't go.' She dropped the sheet and was scrambling into the white skirt and the black apron. They were as crumpled as his bedclothes.

'Don't go, Simona, please. I'm sorry I frightened you.' Simona was backing away, realising what she had done, that she had been truly in bed with a madman. All those tales the old women told to frighten young girls. They just weren't true. They couldn't be!

Claudiu was just saying it to cover what he'd been doing. She'd 'gone up' and never seen a thing. Then she had come straight back here and stopped off on the way. How could he have seen the man in the churchyard when he'd been with her? How could Claudiu have seen him that morning?

It was then they heard the running feet outside. She pushed Claudiu back on the bed, fighting to keep her head. 'Shhh,' she hissed. When the footsteps faded away, she was calmer. 'What you're saying is daft,' she said with the confidence of the young.

'I mean it, Simona,' he replied, pulling her back to him. 'I'm sure it was Grandsire.'

She was overwhelmed by fear then. She'd committed so many sins. First, she'd 'gone up' to Grandsire knowing she wasn't a virgin, then she'd cheated on her intended with Claudiu – and all on the morning of the twenty-second. Had she gone mad? Suddenly, she couldn't bear to think about the consequences. Either Murgu would kill her, or her parents would if they found out. She had to get out right away.

'I have to go, Claudiu,' she said. 'That person outside might have been watching us. I don't want to hear any more of your tales. No more. Do you understand?' She was in a terrible panic as she finished dressing.

He wanted her to stay so much that he caught her by the arm, saying, 'I'm sorry, I'm sorry. Please stay. Don't leave me. We can work something out. Don't be frightened! It wasn't Grandsire. It couldn't have been. It was just a man. A man who ...' But then she was gone.

Claudiu would take the knowledge he had to his deathbed. Why it had been his particular lot to watch the taking of the *Little and Chosen* he would never know. Perhaps it was something to do with the place Grandsire lay?

How many times had he traced his finger about the stone figure of the little cripple cut into Grandsire's tomb. All the other children had been laughing and looking to the west.

He had been alone, standing before the arch, when he used to do it. He would always be standing outside. And he was still alone. But what he had seen, he had seen. And today, it had all happened again. But this time of the *Little and Chosen*, he would have some peace.

At a quarter to midday, the convulsive spasm that shook Claudiu's body was, for the watching Simona, a hint of the farmer's end. He kicked out his useless leg and appeared to choke on his saliva. She knew she should send for Baescu, but what could she say, except that Mr Basa had decided his time was up. That much was written on his face.

It had been just the same with one of her great-aunts. Simona had seen her give up and just go. Claudiu knew his time had come. *And what a time it's been, you poor old devil*, she said to herself. She pitied him, living up here as an outcast. Life in Arva was bad enough anyway.

Claudiu had several small strokes before he died: the last leaving his lip hanging in a peculiar lop-sided manner, adding to his ugliness. He was working his mouth continually and she thought he was speaking to her – she wondered idly who was going to inherit the farm. Perhaps she … She dismissed the thought, but while craning her neck to listen and see if the old man had any last wishes, she was surprised to hear, in the last faint sounds of his breath, that he was singing, or trying to sing.

The recognition of that squeaky, thin piping made her flesh creep. All that was primitive in her nature screamed at him to stop, screamed at Claudiu that it was *their* song, not his; not a man's, but theirs! The song taught to the little girls of Arva before the occasion of their 'going-up' – Grandsire's song. Forbidden to any male.

Claudiu floated high on that song, out to the opaque edge of a world where reality is half-hidden and the unknown begins. He was moving so easily, better than he could ever have imagined, floating into the midday sun with no desire for the things of Earth, away above the ridge, flying as far as Anka Petrescu.

Simona knew when it was over. She closed his eyes, which had nothing of him in them anymore, and pulled the threadbare sheet over his head. Then, looking up at the crucifix and its sprig of basil, she crossed herself and began to pray for a sinner's soul.

Later, she brought the policeman into the bedroom. Valentin turned down the sheet and looked at the corpse.

'What time did he die?' The woman had done the necessary things and the old man looked pale and gaunt like any carcass with the spirit gone from it.

'Four minutes after midday,' she replied.

'Are you his wife?'

'Only a neighbour.'

'Was he married?'

'No! He has always lived on his own,' she replied. Valentin looked round the room.

'Would anybody know where he was early this morning?'

She hesitated before she replied, 'I know what you're here for – he couldn't have done it. I know.' She was twisting her simple wedding ring.

'Do you now?' asked the policeman, catching on to her nervousness. 'You seem to know a lot about him.'

'I've known the man for a long time. There was no harm in him, whatever they said.'

'Who are *they*?' asked Valentin, sensing he might be on the right track.

'I can't tell you that. But I can tell you who did do it. Grandsire.'

'Grandsire? Whom do you mean?'

Simona Murgu began to laugh. She shook her head in delight. The sound of her laughter seemed to offend in a room that harboured a dead body.

Valentin could see what was wrong with the woman. She was overcome by the situation. He caught her by the shoulders. The old man's death was certainly getting to her; and, besides, the atmosphere in the room was cloying.

'Come on now!' he said, not unkindly, but he was not disposed to take any nonsense. She was holding her hands to both her sides as if she was in pain. 'Let's get you a glass of water.' He thought it might bring her to her senses.

Standing outside by the pump, he tried again. 'Right, sit down,' he told her. 'And remember who you're talking to now. A girl's been almost killed, and you say you know who did it! Who is this *Grandsire*?'

It was impossible. Now the laughter had deserted her, she seemed to go into a kind of trance. He left her, head buried in her hands, seated on a block of wood by the path. She was even whistling when he went. As he got into his car, he decided that he'd send a woman officer to interview her later. Some people were still terrified when they saw a policeman. He turned to look at the seated woman, rocking herself to and fro.

'I'll see the doctor comes up,' he called. 'If I were you, I'd get some rest. You'll feel better then.' She didn't seem to hear.

He had been right, there was something weird about the whole business. He couldn't discount the similarities of this rape and the others that had happened over the years in this village. But the length of time between!

It was just his luck. He was a hard-bitten detective and he would go on looking for the answer. He'd get to the bottom of this Grandsire, go on looking for whoever or whatever the name represented; for the nutcase who thought he could go on perpetrating this kind of crime. Grandsire! He was already using the term himself.

As he switched on the ignition, Valentin had a sudden feeling that they would never catch this one. By the time he was driving away, he was pushing that negative thought as far from his mind as he could. Whatever happened, he was going to have a damned good try to nail the beast and whoever was protecting him.

Wally Arvarescu came down Sancipia's curved and broad staircase running with a light step. Everything he did was athletic. He moved with grace, and Ruxandra, who was working below at the reception desk, looked up and stared.

The American was grinning as he ran his supple fingers through his long, blond, wavy hair and glanced at himself in the large mirror at the bottom of the stairs. He was satisfied with what he saw. The hotelier's dark young wife was staring at his reflection from a distance and he smiled back.

'Hi!' he said. 'Great bed you got upstairs. I never heard a thing!'

'You have missed your breakfast,' she said. She was glad he spoke their language.

'No sweat. I never eat in the mornings. Nice place you got here.' He was looking round, still smiling. Ruxandra thought how perfect the man's teeth were – and his eyes – they were very light-blue, like the centre of a flame; the pupils reminded her of – she couldn't think …

'My name's Wally, by the way.' He put out his hand and Ruxandra took it. It was as cold as ice and she could feel his hard, sharp nails. She let it go again quickly.

He didn't look cold. Just the opposite. His expensive red shirt was open, knotted at the bottom, exposing the perfect circle of his navel. His shorts were of yellow, heavy cotton, fairly long in the legs; his thighs and calves were symmetrically formed and, if they had not been so well-muscled, would almost have been feminine.

Ruxandra was intrigued as she caught sight of the mouthpiece of a thin instrument protruding from his side pocket. His strange eyes followed hers and she reddened when she realised he had been watching her appraisal.

'Tin whistle,' he said, taking it out. 'Never travel without it. Keeps me sane. I'd like my passport.'

'You speak very good Romanian,' she remarked, unlocking the drawer. For a moment she was worried in case the passport had not been replaced after the police had inspected it. No. It was there! 'For an American,' she added, handing it over. Then she offered him a pen. 'You have to sign for it, I'm afraid.'

'Okay.'

She was surprised. She didn't think she'd handed him a red ballpoint? He had a lovely signature, flowing, almost antique. Like a blood-red river. 'My forefathers came from here,' he said. 'I'm just looking round. We always speak Romanian at home.'

So he was on a pilgrimage.

'Have you been here before?' she asked, just for something to say; he was looking at her in the most disconcerting manner.

Suddenly, the entrance hall of the Hotel Sancipia went quite black, as if a very dark cloud had covered the summer sun.

'What time is it?' he asked. She glanced at his watch. He looked too. 'It stopped when I came in this morning.'

'What time was that?' Her voice was faltering.

'I got your husband up, I'm afraid,' the American added, and now the smile had entered his voice. 'A few minutes past midnight. Bit late for a young fellow?' He grinned and she could have let him go on for ages. She was entranced by that charming, twinkling curve of his mouth.

Then, all at once, she knew what his eyes reminded her of – their china blue was wolf-like. And the hall still seemed unnaturally dark.

She tried to look out of the window, so she could break free from staring at those enticing lips. It was so embarrassing just to be opposite him and the mesmerising smile that made her heart thump.

'Well, I hope the weather holds for you,' she said weakly.

'Oh, yeah, but I'm finished here now. Back to the States. How much?' He paid by travellers' cheque. American Express. She felt disappointed, because she'd been hoping for some dollars.

'I'm glad you had a good night,' she added. She wondered about his snoring and asked if he had heard anything that had happened that morning.

'Didn't everyone?' replied the American jauntily. It was a peculiar thing to say. She had to follow it up. He was waiting for a reply. Anyway, she was curious about the noise in his room.

'Well, you did miss a little excitement.' Ruxandra knew that wasn't quite the right thing to say. 'A little excitement' was a snide and facile phrase to mask the horrors she had seen a few hours earlier, which she couldn't relate to him.

She felt a trifle faint – as though the strength was seeping away from her body like water trickling through a broken bucket, emptying itself into a drain.

'Go on,' he said.

'We had a bit of a crisis. A girl was attacked in Arva.'

'Arva? Where's that?'

'Oh, it's the village up at the head of the lake.'

'Was it a bear?'

She smiled at the question. She didn't like bears but, in this case, she wished it had been one. The American was so eager to know. Trust a tourist!

'Oh, no, it was an assault – a man.'

'You don't say!' he replied incredulously. 'I thought things like that only happened where I come from.'

'It's never happened here before,' lied Ruxandra. He was looking at her in the strangest way. Did he guess she wasn't telling the truth? 'Not that I know of, anyway,' she added hastily. 'I was just telling you because the police were here. They were asking about the guests.'

'And I was fast asleep through it all. When did it happen?'

'About five in the morning. Close to the church.'

'That's a pity. Poor kid. Let's hope they get the bastard.' He didn't look in the least bit sorry. In fact, he was smiling again and turning the handle of the tin whistle in his fingers. She had never seen such dexterity. 'Concert artist,' he added, picking up the passport. His nails were long. He slipped it into his pocket and lifted the tin whistle to his lips.

Ruxandra couldn't believe it. Surely the American wasn't going to give her a recital in the entrance hall? As if he was reading her thoughts, he lowered the whistle and picked up the case. He must have been travelling light. Where was his luggage?

Ruxandra stared at the case. There was something about it – she couldn't think what. How could it be familiar? His eyes probed her face.

'Do you like it? It's antique.'

She nodded. She had never seen one like it, the leather richly tooled with small figures holding hands. But, deep within her consciousness, back in her memory, something familiar stirred, although she couldn't think what. Her hands were sweating.

He squatted down in front of the counter, his back masking the case from her eyes. When he got up, the tin whistle had disappeared.

'I'll be going along now,' he said. 'I've had a wonderful time. I feel like a new man after that sleep. So long.' He put out his hand to shake hers.

Ruxandra was afraid to touch him. She didn't know why, but the feeling of danger was exceptionally strong.

'I'm glad you've enjoyed yourself,' she said. 'Where are you making for now?'

'I told you, I'm going back to the States. I'm hiking to the train station. That's where I left my luggage.'

'Oh, I see,' she said, relieved.

'But I'll be back, you can be sure of that,' he said, turning in the doorway. His thin, tall shadow was thrown crookedly across the wall. Then he was gone.

Instinctively, Ruxandra pulled her shawl about her and made the Sign of the Cross.

The man strolled up and away from the Hotel Sancipia, on through the forest trees and scrub. He didn't have to make an effort in that rough terrain. If any soul had been watching, they would have thought his feet scarcely touched the ground.

At the top of the ridge he paused, a strong figure. His summer clothes of red and gold fluttered in the breeze, like a flag, silhouetted against the skyline. He yawned deeply, as if he'd been asleep too long.

Setting down the music case, he flexed his muscles and punched the air in a gesture of joy. He put the tin whistle to his lips and, in the full sun, the instrument took on a golden and beautiful shape. For one second the mountains quivered with its music. Then the notes began to die.

He was free! Mechanically, he bent towards the case and looked across toward the iron railings, where the red and yellow station wagon was waiting for him, like an eager animal lurking in the bushes. He whistled:

'Okay, let's go!' There was a sudden rush of wind making the man's hair stand straight back and away from his handsome head.

Excited squeaking and chattering were in his ears as he began to load the wagon, its engine purring patiently. When he'd finished putting in the gear, which had been piled beside the churchyard railings, still dusty from its time below ground, he slammed the trunk shut and jumped into the driver's seat with a sudden burst of energy.

He was ready, and free to go wherever he wanted in the world. He touched the open passport that lay beside him on the seat, glancing cursorily over the details. A very good name – even if he said it himself. He was finished with 'Arvarescu' now. It had fitted perfectly. Had been conjured successfully. And the fool had been a musician too!

The man grinned and his strange blue eyes sparkled unnaturally. Suddenly, he was feeling very good to be alive once more! And he had that ancient, insatiable urge for children again!

5

'The music stopped and I stood still,
And found myself outside the hill,
Left alone against my will,
To go on limping as before.'

Inspector Valentin's inquiries had drawn blanks everywhere. He was almost ready to admit that the best police practices the country could offer had failed and he was left with another unsolved crime.

But he would wait. That was the nature of police work. And the charge might soon be changed to murder, because it was apparent the girl was not going to recover. The rational, clinical side of Valentin's nature reviewed the rape with nothing but the disgust it deserved, but of all the crimes he had investigated, this was the strangest and the most intriguing.

There was something else to it, something he couldn't explain away. He didn't even know how he felt about it or about the superstition he encountered everywhere in and around the village.

Anka Petrescu's family had been persuaded by Dr Baescu in the end. The physician had told her father the girl was dying and, in spite of the mother's pleas, she had finally been taken to the city hospital and treated. The clumsy repairs he and the police doctor had cobbled together were allowed to stand but, finally and as predicted, the girl had lost so much blood that the staff had insisted on a transfusion.

After that, the parents had brought her home, discharging her themselves against the hospital's wishes. It seemed that when she had got in there Petre had been swayed by Irina's opinion after all, and that neither the farmer nor his wife could bear to have their daughter treated anymore.

Really, there wasn't much that could be done for her after the surgery to repair her injuries – and the hospital was a grim place anyway, short of both drugs and comfort. She was probably better off at home, except for the transfusion. The bites were healing, but they were far less a threat in comparison with the treatment they had warranted. The risk of infection from transfusion was high and it was only the most urgent cases that merited it. Anka Petrescu had been one. There had been no option.

Valentin shrugged to himself at the thought of it. Whatever precautions were said to be taken, patients were still getting infected plasma; the parents must have felt the same horror at it all and decided to bring her back to the farm.

Since the mother had been unable to co-operate with police questioning – she was still half out of her mind – and the father had nothing to add, inquiries had proceeded at their own pace and extended through Moldavia and Wallachia and, of course, in Cluj-Napocka and its close environs.

Valentin's office had contacted Interpol, because the inspector now believed a foreigner must have been involved. But the only foreigner listed in the region at that time had been the American at the Hotel Sancipia, and he had a cast-iron alibi; he was in the hostel all night.

However, Valentin's frequent incursions into past police files had left a lot of unanswered questions. What was going on in Arva village? What had been going on for years? That was where the conflict arose in Valentin himself. The clinical logic on which the inspector prided himself came to an end there.

Five days after the rape, he went to see the girl at her home. He stopped off at the scene of the crime on the way. He closed the iron gates of Arva churchyard behind him and stepped into a province of deathly quiet. The impassive faces of Arva's dead stared forlornly from their photographs on the tombstones. If only they could talk!

The inspector thrust his hands deep into the pockets of his trousers. He could feel the sun boring through the shoulders of his shirt. There was not even a breath of kindly wind.

He wondered if the officials had managed to exterminate the rodents. That the girl's body had been a mass of animal bites had been disgusting – in fact, rats made Valentin feel sick – but infestation by them was even worse. That they lived in a graveyard was even more horrible, especially when he thought of the poor girl lying almost unconscious in her own blood with vermin trying to make a meal of her.

He walked slowly over to what Arvan folk in police files called 'Grandsire's Grave'. It stood in the corner of the churchyard. The scene of the crime had been cleared up efficiently.

The only thing that looked in disarray was the obelisk where the cross had been torn from the top. Valentin had read about the fierceness of the storm that had done it. It had featured in the police files as well. Reading the testimony of the girl Ruxandra Sala, whose fiancé had been killed by the falling tree, had given him some idea of the extremes of weather the village suffered.

Then he wondered if the rat catchers had set the poison, and decided he would get one of his men to make a telephone call and find out if the extermination of the vermin had been successful. He found himself wondering where the rats could have come from. There seemed no other answer but out of the vault.

Valentin inspected the rectangular structure. The top of the tomb was made from shiny mountain rock. He bent to inspect the fretted figures about the lid. He had never taken much notice of them before.

He was very surprised to see that they were the figures of children. Children, who linked hands in an everlasting 'ring-of-roses'. Whoever Grandsire was, he must have loved children. It was ironic that someone had chosen to rape one upon his very tomb.

Then, to his surprise, he noticed that at the western end there was a break in the children's circle. When he looked closely he saw that it had been broken by the image of another child, a child who was bent over – Valentin strained to look – a pair of crutches. A cripple! What did it mean? Suddenly he was thinking of Basa, the *Sowfucker* as the village women called him, the man who would have been his prime suspect if he had not been too old and now freshly laid in his grave.

Valentin stared on, committing the details of the tomb to his memory. He felt that tied up in this ring of dancing children was the answer to the rape of Anka Petrescu, an answer that could be found only in the ancient culture of a silent village. Below the disabled boy, and Valentin knew instinctively it *was* a boy, the tomb's panels were recessed, and he realised he was looking at an arch.

He walked round the other three sides of the tomb and did not find the same carving. He returned to the arch in the stone. He put out a hand and rubbed the mountain rock.

He could feel under the lichen and stale growth of years, the outline of a door. A door cut into the rock. When he brought his hand off the stone, it was vermilion. A red ochre of rust and dust. As though the mountain stone was iron. Valentin blinked at the discovery. He wiped his hand down his trousers.

It was then he realised with a sudden shock that the arched door cut into the stone of 'Grandsire's Grave' was facing not to the east like all other graves in the Christian world, but westwards. Into the setting sun! Each stone child's face was turned to the west towards that door.

A shiver ran through Valentin. The hard-bitten policeman took his foot off the grave and straightened up. He looked at his hand that had touched the door. It was quite clean. He looked down at his trousers. There was no sign of red ochre or iron, rust or anything.

As he retreated, stepping backwards, he noticed the loose chippings piled untidily about the rectangular shape that enclosed the tomb. His men had made a brief inspection already and reported the fact of the burials. He remembered the police files: the poopy dolls referred to by the girls. He looked at the stones, which were arranged haphazardly, like molehills. This superstitious nonsense ought to be stopped. But that wasn't his job. He was only a policeman. These people were backward in every way. Their ignorance had caused a girl of barely 16 to be subjected to a vile and horrible assault. He swore under his breath and kicked one of the clumsy piles. The stones fell away and Valentin caught his breath.

The hollow painted features and staring flat eyes of an ugly wooden doll confronted him blankly, with the expressionless gaze of a buried plaything, never to be returned to its owner. The clothes were mildewed, half eaten away.

Valentin looked at the damage his foot had done, feeling oddly ashamed of such self-righteous anger. Whatever the village women of Arva were up to, it still seemed like sacrilege to reveal to the world the bizarre, grotesque but harmless vagaries of a forgotten culture. It was only when he went around to the western side of the tomb and looked at the larger pile of stones beside the door, that he felt cold on that hot day.

Instead of his foot, he parted that pile with his hands to reveal an identical poopy, clad, not this time in half-eaten clothes, but in a dress stiff with the blood of its owner. Its head was writhing with the new maggots of blowflies.

The inspector winced and kicked the offending remnant of what once had belonged to a child, against the iron palings at the back of the grave. It was then that he heard a rumble of thunder.

Making a mental note of all the disgusting details, he made another snap decision. He would have workmen come and clear away the remnants of this degrading ritual dreamed up in the sick minds of a superstitious people.

He had been so carried away by the sight that he had almost forgotten to pick up the evidence. His men were going to be kicked up the backside for missing this one and not bringing it in. It could be an important lead. He went over to the railings where his foot had placed the doll and, taking out his large handkerchief, he covered the body, picked it up gingerly and carried it towards the car. Then he drove on to Ruare.

Valentin's visit to the Petrescus' farm was to leave an indelible mark on his memory.

'Come in, Inspector,' invited Petrescu. His rough features were haggard. A lifetime of hard work had not managed to do the damage that Petrescu suffered to his features that day. He looked haunted, morose, overwhelmed by what had happened to him and his family.

'Is there any news? Have you caught him?'

'No,' replied Valentin. He would have given anything to have been able to reply in the affirmative. The beast had to be caught and Valentin was going to do it. 'I've come to see your wife.'

'You'll get no sense out of her,' replied the farmer. Valentin could see by the look in his eyes that the man was desperate. 'What am I going to do, Inspector? Without either of them?'

'Your wife?' Valentin wasn't sure what had happened, or what Petre was referring to.

'She's gone off the deep end. Cracked. She's with the little one day and night, babbles on about nothing, while the child cannot speak at all.'

Valentin looked at him. Was it possible that he knew something about the mischief that went on up at the church? Yet the policeman's instinct told him that this man knew very little.

'I would like to see her anyway.'

'I would rather you didn't. She isn't making any sense.'

'Where is she?' asked the inspector.

'In the back.' He meant in the bedroom. The farm house had only two rooms, which served all functions. 'But I don't want you to. There's nothing either of them can tell you.'

Valentin looked at the closed door that interlinked the rooms, the brown paint scored by the claws of farm dogs. His eyes took in the poverty of the Petrescus' living quarters. He was feeling enormous pity for what had befallen the simple peasant.

'What was Anka doing up at the church, Petre, at that time in the morning?' His question was never answered. A thin scream cut through them from behind that poor, scratched door.

'In God's name, what's up?' Petrescu was running, followed by Valentin.

The farmer's wife was on her knees beside the low bed. She was rocking her body to and fro, crazy with fear and despair, crossing herself again and again. Her wild mane of black hair flowed down her back. Her hysteria was too much for either her husband or Valentin to comprehend. Then they looked at the bed where Anka lay.

It couldn't be – it wasn't her.

Her parents were clinging to each other in horror. Petre was trying to quieten Irina and the two of them were tangled together in an embrace that seemed to be giving them the strength to stand up.

Valentin stared at the small, doll-like figure, lying on its side, the knees drawn up in the foetal position. Anka's unbraided hair flowed over her shoulders, masking her face. The hair was white.

Valentin caught his breath. He'd heard of the hair turning white after some trauma, but he'd never believed it. Irina Petrescu moaned as the policeman caught the girl's shoulder gently and turned her.

The three stood horrified as the soft, wrinkled face stared up at them. There were spots of age on the brow, and the eyebrows were rough and beetling, tinged with grey. The once round, doll-like cheeks were sunken and the eyes open, but without lustre. Anka had aged 50 years in a week. She was an old woman.

Valentin had seen many terrible sights after being a policeman for 25 years, but nothing like this. How could a young girl have changed so much physically? What metamorphosis had taken place? This final visit of a very strange day found his logical self fighting for survival against the insidious workings of his imagination. He could only stare at the little crone with increasing horror.

A rigorous examination of the bloodstained poopy was carried out immediately when the inspector returned to the station. He got the report back the following afternoon. He shivered even more as he began reading it.

PATHOLOGY
Subject: Artefact
The object resembles a child's doll, made of wood, length 20cm. The carving is crude but displays human characteristics and apertures, oral and anal.

HISTOLOGY
A: Blood type: O Negative: (compatible with blood in report 100697 22.7.88.)
B: Traces of other haemoglobin, not in the human band, probably rodent.

C: No semen traces …

At this, Valentin stopped reading, and referred to the hospital report on Anka. It had been a puzzling fact before, that her examination had not revealed the presence of semen. This had precluded DNA testing. He had been careful not to let the parents know that the quality of her rape had been inhuman, insofar as a blunt instrument could be called inhuman.

The rest of the report was routine procedure except for the fact that minute traces of gold- and red-coloured fibres and hair, not belonging to the object, had been found in the poopy's clothes.

It was then that Valentin remembered the American. What had Dobos said the man was wearing? The landlord of the Hotel Sancipia had been most co-operative and had given a full description of the guest sleeping upstairs.

It was Inspector Valentin's first significant breakthrough. He would bring in Walter Arvarescu for questioning – if he hadn't left the country.

Valentin was in luck. All he had to do now was wait. The American had been traced relatively easily. He couldn't escape; he was safe on a flight from Otopeni Airport, Bucharest, to New York. The Boeing 707 had taken off on time at 13:00 hours and it would be met by Austrian police as well as some of their own at the stopover in Vienna. He wanted to keep the guy in Europe for as long as he could. Naturally, the New York Police Department had been contacted, and he was waiting for anything they might have on Arvarescu. In the meantime the man would be apprehended on suspicion until further inquiries could be made and laboratory work, including DNA testing, be carried out on the fibres on the poopy's clothes.

Valentin was as satisfied as he could be. He had done as much as was possible.

There was no way he could get the picture of Anka out of his mind. The Arvan victim had died the morning following his visit, and her unnaturally wizened corpse was now resting in the State Mortuary. Her mother had pleaded for her body for burial, but that would come after the autopsy and further developments regarding her murder. And it *was* murder now.

Whatever bizarre or supernatural happening had occurred – Valentin didn't want to use the latter term – the girl was dead as the result of a criminal act. It wasn't for a policeman to question the whys and hows. It was a fact, and every suspicion would be thoroughly investigated.

Valentin also knew that he had fouled up. The man should have been held for questioning at the hotel, rather than given a chance to escape – but his alibi had been sound. For this very reason, all Valentin wanted was to get his hands on Arvarescu and question him face to face. It was a matter of pride; Inspector Valentin was not a man who had ever been accused of any kind of professional error – and he didn't intend it to happen now.

That day when Arvarescu had left Romania the weather was unbearably sultry. Police Headquarters sweltered and buckled under the strain. The sweat ran freely off Valentin's face and forehead, making his skin red and uncomfortable. He looked at the wall clock. The only touchdown by the airliner would be in Vienna – about now. Although Arvarescu must have thought he'd got clean away, Valentin had him thoroughly covered.

The inspector went to the window and looked across the street. He was feeling some relief already, but not from the weather. If ever there was going to be a summer storm it would be this afternoon. The clouds lowered over pointed, old, red-tiled roofs and the flat, expressionless tops of the blocks of ugly flats.

It was then that the staccato tap of the Telex brought in a message that made Valentin's red face go white. *A Tarrom Airlines Boeing 707 has been struck by lightning while touching down at Vienna. The emergency services are at the scene …*

When the survivors were identified and the corpses taken to hospital mortuaries, Valentin's suspect was not amongst the living. As usual, the seating had been checked meticulously against the names of the passengers and the American's charred body was numbered among the unfortunates. They would have to wait for dental records – and even those could be inconclusive, given the force of the fire. Valentin had to admit the line of his investigation as to the Petrescu murder was most probably at an end. There was no doubt about one thing: whatever the American had done to that girl in Arva village – if he had – he had paid for it, and there was no chance of him committing such a terrible crime again.

Valentin consigned the Petrescu file to criminal records and decided to forget the case until either he was proved right about Arvarescu or another suspect presented himself. He'd be hearing from the States soon.

After the Viennese crash, a lot of travellers were scared to fly. Crash talk was on everyone's lips. However, those who had to get out of the Austrian capital for one reason or another had no choice but to stay at the airport and wait for the next plane.

The tall, slim American handed in his passport at the check-in. He was a natty dresser, creamy-yellow suit, red tie and gloves on that hot night – an eccentric certainly by the look of him. As he waited for the official to scrutinise his passport, he was smiling.

'Musician, eh?' remarked the officer.

'Yep. Flute-player.' He grinned, that strange smile flicking around the corners of his mouth. Arvarescu was done with forever.

'Thank you, Mr Koppelberg. Have a good journey.' The man handed over the document, its golden American eagle staring fiercely. The smile on Diep Koppelberg's face didn't reach those pin-pricks of eyes. He was leaving Europe, the land of his birth such a long time ago, without a regret. He was glad to be free and wandering again.

He was travelling very light. His music case, which alerted the security scanner through which it passed, revealed a handsome antique golden flute. His most precious and prized possession!

Once the plane was airborne, the lights went off to indicate that seatbelts could be unbuckled. Diep Koppelberg got up from his seat and went into the cramped toilet. It was in there that he began to peel off his gloves.

With curved talons extended, the fair man flexed his ugly hands, ready to do their work. Lifting his wrist to his mouth, he sucked his burns dry with blood-red lips, while the awful chattering in his head drowned the sound of the jet's mighty engines.

6

Arva,
August 1988.

They buried Anka Petrescu quietly. In attendance were Young Father Joseph, white to the ears; Irina, half-crazy; a silent Petre; and Inspector Valentin. Only the four of them knew of the wrinkled old body under the coffin lid.

Everyone else stayed away. It was their custom. It was considered bad luck to attend the burial of the *Little and Chosen*. Anka's place of burial was chosen too. It had been ordained. Facing the west like the others who had been chosen before her – *Grandsire's Girls.*

Arva had designated the place, which was marked off for the purpose and had been so for almost seven hundred years. A place of horror and of pilgrimage where the *secret of the marriage bed*, once tasted, was revealed to some.

Arvan women knew that only red and gold roses would grow on Anka's grave, tended once a year in July by Petrescu. It was decreed there should be no photograph of her set in the stone. She could remain in the memories only of her parents and of the initiated of Arva. That was the custom too.

As they lowered that unfortunate little girl into the earth, Inspector Valentin caught a flash of black in the corner of his eye. He looked across the churchyard, but there was not a soul to be seen.

After Father Joseph had led the weeping parents away, Valentin decided to investigate. They had buried Basa on the fringe of consecrated ground. The *Sowfucker* was given his satisfaction too. He was to watch in death, as he had in life. What he had seen, he thought he had carried to his grave.

The day of Anka's funeral, Simona Murgu, dressed all in black, knelt in the mud beside his resting place. When he had died, she'd laughed; now she was crying.

'Claudiu, are you listening?' she whispered to the red earth. 'Why did you tell me? I didn't want to know. And now, I must pay! I must pay!' she repeated, rocking herself back and forth.

The inspector touched her shoulder. She jumped; then stared up at him. The watery sun made her peasant's face, wrinkled from hard work in the fields, a thing to pity.

'Come along,' said Valentin, not unkindly, recognising the woman from the farm, who appeared even more deranged than at their first meeting. 'You must stop crying for the old man now!' He was thinking of the Petrescus. They had a lifetime of pain to come.

The woman got up from her knees. She turned her back on the grave. 'Do you think I was weeping for Basa?' she asked, and her voice was fierce. 'For that old cripple? Not for him! But for myself! Myself and my children!' She looked quite crazy. Valentin remembered how she'd laughed after the farmer's death.

'Okay, have it your way,' snapped the policeman, walking away. He wanted no part in this madness. He was glad that his interest in Arva was a purely professional one. He'd leave the psychology to those who thought they understood. Like Baescu and that shrink in Cluj. Marcu was a pleasant young man, but Valentin couldn't understand why he wanted to probe into things like this when he didn't have to. Valentin had no option. Anyway, he'd give them anything he could on these mad women of Arva.

Simona Murgu was still watching Valentin as he got into his car. As he turned the key in the ignition, the police inspector wondered if he'd ever get to the bottom of what had really happened in that sinister little village. He was hoping that the American police might come up with something he'd missed.

Valentin had got on surprisingly well with the FBI agent who had been his contact in New York. The detective's Romanian was excellent. In fact, he had told Valentin over the phone that he'd been recruited originally for his proficiency in the language.

Valentin had liked the American's warm and friendly approach and had been especially gratified to communicate how happy he was that the Cold War had come to an end and that he was now able to talk freely with a colleague in the West.

Now, as the supercilious secretary handed him a package that had come express from the States, Valentin thought back over his conversation with his American counterpart. They had chatted for a while about the suspect, Arvarescu, and his suitable death by fire. Valentin remembered the American's words quite clearly:

'I'll tell you a bit about Arvarescu if you like. I made a few inquiries. He was picked up on our precinct. I wasn't there then, of course, but I heard about it from one of our old-timers.' Valentin was about to ask where he'd served before, then changed his mind. The American was paying for the call, not his office. The cop continued, 'The nut definitely was out of his head. Hearing voices, you know.'

Valentin knew about voices all right.

'He had these – what you call them – hallucinations. Thought he was some fairy or something. Thought that was an excuse.' Valentin laughed politely at the joke.

'He said he'd been after kids forever and that *they loved him*. Imagine that! The creep. He spent a lot of time in the prison hospital. Then they transferred him to the nut house in Weser. The guy finally got what he deserved I reckon, although it's a pity we didn't nail him a long time ago, before he did all that damage.

'If there's anything I hate – I guess I speak for all cops – it's child abuse. And, if it's in a guy's blood, it doesn't matter how old he is. It just goes on and on.' Valentin heard him give a heavy sigh at the end of the phone. 'I'm not religious but, somewhere along the line, I'd like to think these guys' crimes will catch up with them.'

A few days earlier, before Arvarescu had been burnt to a crisp, talk of catching him would have been music to Valentin's ears. The Yank added, 'Yep, I guess strange things happen in our business.'

'You're right there,' replied Valentin, his voice full of gloom.

'Anyhow, I'll send you out the info! Have a nice day!'

Valentin felt even more morose. He'd quite enjoyed their conversation. He'd probably never hear from him again.

And here it was, in a neat little package, straight from the New York Police Department. How the American psycho had got out of the States and had ended up in Romania was anyone's guess. Anyway, thought Valentin, at least Arvarescu can't molest any other innocents now. He settled down to read the material.

His American correspondent had enclosed photocopies of all the written documents relating to the escapee, including a passport-sized police photograph. Valentin stared at the haggard features, the straggling yellow hair and the light-blue eyes. He was going to show the mug shot to Gheorghe Dobos to get a positive identification, even though the man was dead. He'd already had a good description of the American from the innkeeper and the criminal in front of him certainly resembled their suspect. But he was going to make sure anyway.

He'd had plenty of shocks during the investigation of the rape and murder of Anka Petrescu, but the last was still unexpected. When he turned over the photograph and stared at the date stamped on its reverse, his mouth went dry. *July 1952!* How could it be? Arvarescu would have been an old man by now! So the young American couldn't have been their suspect! What kind of coincidence was that?

Valentin sat still in the chair, his eyes focused anywhere but on the photograph. He saw that the girl was still working in the office, bent over her word processor. She'd stuck it for a long time and was becoming less uppity now. He'd realised a long time ago that she thought provincial policemen were all peasants. Maybe she was right. He had certainly got this one wrong. But it was an inexplicable coincidence. Same name, same crime. He studied the photograph again.

Arvarescu's staring eyes seemed fixed on his own. It was all too much for an ordinary policeman, caught up in something extraordinary. And how was he going to tell his American colleague – the phrase still sounded so good – that the Romanian police department had made a cock-up of it – that the Walter Arvarescu who had perished on the plane at Vienna couldn't be the same one, and that the US files on the sex predator couldn't be closed?

Feeling as if he had been cheated, Inspector Valentin laid down the photograph and began to look through the enclosed photocopies. Attached to them was a friendly little note:

'Hope this gives you some idea what kind of nut we're dealing with. I've sent you part of one of the transcripts provided by the man's psychiatrist. Dialog 17 will sure give you an insight into how a pervert like Arvarescu ticks – or ticked!'

Valentin flipped through, looking for the transcript. He couldn't shake off the feeling of being cheated, nor the sense of incredulity at the coincidence of two similar crimes and two matching names – and he could still hardly believe how much time had passed between. Thirty-six years. That number stuck in his mind.

When he saw the title of Dialog 17, he swallowed hard. This was getting worse:

The Rat and the Piper: A case study of poly-personality traits derived from a series of interviews with WA; in-patient, Weser Psychiatric Institute for Sexual Offenders, New Jersey. June 2nd, 1950 – June 3rd, 1952.

Suddenly, Valentin was thinking about the little Arvan girl, her body a mass of rat bites. He pulled himself together and began to concentrate on the copy that his foreign colleague had made. It was a conversation between Arvarescu and his psychiatrist, Dr Dietmann. Valentin thought of Marcu. This was probably the kind of thing he did at Burbor. Dietmann had written a short introduction:

Walter Arvarescu, a male Caucasian of Eastern European origin, probably Romanian, a sufferer from schizophrenia since his early teenage years, has always maintained that his series of attacks on young children (mainly pre-pubescent girls) were prompted by his principal alter ego, the mythical Pied Piper of Hamelin (ref. the poem of the same name by the English poet, Robert Browning) and his accompanying bête-noire, a rat named Snipe – believed to be an anagram of the male sex organ and used by Arvarescu as the scapegoat for his savage and insatiable sex-drive. In the following interview, the offender blames 'the rat' for his 'failures', another metaphor for his guilt complex after committing the crimes. Walter Arvarescu's intelligence quotient tested on the 99 percentile and his musical and literary abilities are believed to have contributed to his schizophrenic fantasies.

The following extract is taken from 'The Rat and the Piper', a case-study made while Arvarescu was an in-patient in our institution. Dialog 17 is particularly interesting as it was the last recorded before

Arvarescu absconded – never to be recaptured in spite of an extensive nationwide search.

DIETMANN: Why do you always go back to Hamelin, Wally?

ARVARESCU: Because it was the best, doctor, the best day of my life.

DIETMANN: Tell me about it.

ARVARESCU: Why should I do it? Let him.

DIETMANN: Who, Wally?

ARVARESCU: The rat.

DIETMANN: Can you see him now?

ARVARESCU: He's right there. Sitting next to you.

DIETMANN: He's not real.

ARVARESCU: Go on, Snipe, tell him.

DIETMANN: He's in your head, Wally.

ARVARESCU: He's always in my fucking head. I can't get him out. He's always telling me what to do.

DIETMANN: Why do you take any notice?

ARVARESCU: Because I'm the Piper. (Here Arvarescu began to whistle)

DIETMANN: Is that the music you played for the children?

ARVARESCU: No. It was better than that.

DIETMANN: Tell me about Hamelin. The rat can't. He isn't real.

ARVARESCU: I told you, ask him.

DIETMANN: I can't, Wally. He isn't real.

ARVARESCU: The kids liked my music. They followed me. They loved me.

DIETMANN: It wasn't love, Wally. You have to face facts. They weren't old enough to love you. They didn't understand.

ARVARESCU: I don't like grown-ups. The rat made me do it.

DIETMANN: Do what?

ARVARESCU: He's the Devil in me. He escaped.

DIETMANN: When you were in Hamelin?

ARVARESCU: He got away. There were so many children. All the little boys and girls, with rosy cheeks and flaxen curls.

DIETMANN: Where did you hear the poem, Wally?

ARVARESCU: I made it up!

DIETMANN: No, you read it. You're not the Pied Piper. He only exists in here. In your head. It's a legend. Where did you read all about it?

ARVARESCU: Somewhere – and I'm him, but there aren't any children. Where are the children?

DIETMANN: You took them away, Wally. Do you remember?

ARVARESCU: I have to find them. Go out and find them. (Here Arvarescu begins a conversation with his mythical rat, Snipe)

SNIPE: You mean like I found you, when I escaped. You tried to kill me, but I escaped. The only rat to survive from Hamelin. But you were after children before that, weren't you? You had plenty of children on your Crusade.[1] And what happened to them? That pretty boy, Nicholas, who you told what to do. He had hair just like yours.

ARVARESCU: I don't want to talk about that any more. I was a good guy once.

SNIPE: Before you got a taste for children. I like the taste of them too.

ARVARESCU: Stop it, you filthy beast.

SNIPE: You can't face it, can you? But I keep you going. There will be plenty more times. Hamelin was the best though!

---

1 A reference to the Children's Crusade in 1212, reputed to be a likely source of the Pied Piper legend, when 30,000 German peasant children flocked to follow the mysterious boy, Nicholas, in the hope that they, as innocents, would triumph in taking Jerusalem where adults had failed. Many died on the way, or were sold into prostitution or slavery.

ARVARESCU: It's all your fault! If it hadn't been for you, no-one would have known about me. But I let you go. The only survivor. All the other rats died, but you got away. If you'd drowned like the rest, I'd have been free. But I'm stuck with you. You're bad news!

SNIPE: You have to face facts. You're stuck with me, so make the best of it. And I mean the best! It wasn't about money, was it?

ARVARESCU: Mind your own business. I did it for love.

SNIPE: Very funny. (Here Arvarescu breaks down)

DIETMANN: Can you go on, Wally?

ARVARESCU: I don't want to discuss it anymore. I don't want to talk to you anymore! (Here Dialog 17 breaks off)

Valentin stared at the pages, trying to make sense of the thing as a whole. At first, the coincidence theory seemed the only explanation: that the brute who had perpetrated such horrific suffering on a young girl was still roaming free somewhere. Whoever the Arvarescu was who had died on the burning plane, it couldn't have been this one. He would be 70 by now.

Where could they go from there with their investigation? Maybe the American had been using an alias and he'd slipped off somewhere else. But that couldn't be right. He'd checked in at the airport under the name Walter Arvarescu. The whole thing was making Valentin's head ache and his stomach play up.

There would be no positive identification ever – even from dental records. The crash victims were too badly burned. Perhaps they would never know who had perished? It was as inexplicable as the sight of the little girl turned old woman. He shook his head at the thought, not allowing himself to contemplate what would happen if Dobos made a positive identification when he was shown the photograph. That *would* defy belief.

The inspector couldn't concentrate on a thing afterwards, and at about two in the afternoon he ordered the secretary to find him a copy of *The Pied Piper of Hamelin* by the English poet Robert Browning.

She had a puzzled smile on her fine lips, and her eyes said plainly: *Inspector, why are you asking me to bring you poetry when you should be out catching villains?* But she brought the book – in a German translation. It wasn't a nice story. What fairy tales are? In fact, it made Valentin shiver. He shivered even more when he read the Foreword. Legend had it that, after the children disappeared into the bowels of Koppelberg Hill, the *Rattenfanger* led them eastwards into Romania. Where had they settled? He read the historical background again more carefully. Right until the end of the Second World War, Germans – mainly from Saxony and the surrounding districts – had been one of Transylvania's biggest ethnic groups.

Ideas kept leaping around in Valentin's brain. He was a rational man, not given to belief in children's stories, but he was still telling himself imagination was sometimes necessary for the detection of crime. There was certainly a ring of truth about the legend of the Pied Piper. The Foreword also explained how German settlers had moved East in mediaeval times for a variety of reasons, one of them being the plague. That made him think of the rats again and the tomb in Arva churchyard with its everlasting dancing children, clutching their poopy dolls.

Was it possible that the *Rattenfanger* had come this way and that there was some kind of link between the Grandsire the villagers spoke of and the legendary figure of the Piper?

Valentin shut the poetry book with a snap and pulled himself together. He would think about it all when he had time. At that moment, he felt too old for fairy tales, and a searing headache had suddenly struck him. He took a couple of strong painkillers and, shading his eyes from the harsh electric lights in his office by cupping his forehead in his palms, shook all those fanciful ideas out of his brain and got back to his work.

Some weeks later, after thinking about it very carefully, Valentin sent all the material to Marcu, who then rang him up and thanked him profusely. He didn't know why the bloke was so happy, seeing as how the rapist was probably still free. But he was a psychiatrist, wasn't he? Probably as nutty as his patients.

Valentin felt slightly sick when Marcu added that Irina Petrescu had had a complete breakdown and was now in his care. Valentin decided that, although he'd witnessed some horrific sights in his time, nothing could compare to seeing that little girl turn into an old woman. He would never forget it, and he hoped fervently that he would never have to see such a thing again. He didn't understand it then and he couldn't now. Maybe Marcu would be luckier and find out from the mother what had really happened.

Leave the medicine to the medics, Valentin, he said to himself, putting his feet up on his desk and popping another indigestion tablet. He still craved to get on with solving this mystery. But these were turbulent times and the department was dealing with a sharp increase in crime; none as strange but some just as brutal.

Valentin couldn't see into the future, but he had a theory that it would get worse before it got better. He realised that Anka's rape would probably be consigned to the 'Unsolved' section, like those rapes in the past. After all, he was only a policeman with one pair of hands and a very bad stomach.

Later that week, he felt even worse after the trek over to the Inn at Sancipia to see Gheorghe Dobos. The man looked nervous. Valentin understood what that was about. It was bad for business to have the police around.

'What's up now, Inspector?' he asked.

'I've a mug-shot here I want you to look at,' replied Valentin. Dobos looked scared as Valentin withdrew the photo from his file. 'Nothing to worry about,' he added. 'Now – is this the American who was staying with you?' He'd had the image blown up.

Dobos stared at it for quite a time. Then he made a face.

'The one who was here –' he considered, '– was not as scruffy,' he said, 'but, yes, I'd say it was him.'

Valentin looked down at the floor. Somehow, a nasty little instinct had told him the man was going to identify him positively. 'Are you sure?' he asked.

'Yes, I think so,' replied Dobos. Valentin grimaced. 'But Ruxandra was the one who talked to him.'

Ruxandra stared at the photograph. It gave her a queasy feeling just to look at the man's face again. He'd certainly gone down in the world since she'd seen him last, and it was only a few weeks.

'Is this the same man?' said the inspector.

'Definitely. But –' she hesitated. 'He was a lot better-looking when I saw him last. But I'm sure it's him.'

Valentin would have laughed at the couple's illogical answers if he hadn't been feeling so baffled – and ill-tempered because of his indigestion. Besides, you could hardly ever rely on a witness to give you a straight answer.

'Thank you very much,' he said, trying to hide the sarcasm in his voice. He slipped the photograph back into the file and consigned it to the depths of his briefcase.

'Have you got him?' asked Ruxandra. Her dark eyes were wide and scared.

'I can't tell you that, Mrs Dobos, but our inquiries are progressing,' he replied. When he was outside, he opened his car door, but didn't get in. Instead, he stood, blankly staring up at the mountains. *Now what the bloody hell am I going to do about this?* he asked himself, and popped another indigestion tablet.

BOOK TWO

7

'And nobody could enough admire
The tall man and his quaint attire'.

Sunny Mead, Lakes Region, New Hampshire, USA,
July 1988

The station wagon crawled. Then it pulled into the parking area off the highway at the peak of the incline. The driver sat without moving while the smoked glass windows slid down noiselessly.

Putting out an arm, he drew a long, sensitive finger through the dust caked on the outside of the door. He had come a very long way.

He brought in his arm and stared at the red deposit. The corners of his lips flicked a smile. With a quick, animal movement, he lifted his finger and smelled it as if scenting the spoor.

A red dust stain lingered on the dashboard control as he made the window close. The air conditioning unit left the vehicle as cool as a tomb, compared with the 91 degrees Fahrenheit outside.

Then, its engine growling, the station wagon snaked its way down the long incline of Scenic Route 113 into the valley – passing the old bridle path that led to West Rattlesnake –

on towards the small resort of Sunny Mead, that lay peacefully vulnerable, wrapping its scrawny legs around the lakeside.

Diane Durrant jumped. For a moment, she didn't know what the quick movement was. The door was open and she'd thought some animal had come in from outside. Then she saw Pip's pet toad on the drainer.

'Get off!' she shouted. The toad's vocal sac ballooned like a silver bubble of washing-up liquid. Its guttural croak had the same effect – to spook Diane, as always. 'Get off!'

Its golden eyes looked lazy, like it had been watching too much television. It squatted on the draining board. 'Dave!' she yelled, 'Dave, come in here, will you? Bufo's escaped!' But there was no reply; her husband must have gone to the station. 'Rose? Teddy?' Where were the twins?

Diane stood, wiping her hands down the side of her skirt, while the toad ballooned in full. She felt a movement at her elbow. Teddy was looking up at her contemptuously.

'Mom, it's only a toad!' His shiny fair head barely came to the top of the drawer. 'Come here, Bufo!' He stretched out his hand. She watched her six-year-old catch hold of Pip's toad and grab it.

Di breathed with relief. She didn't want to deprive her older son of his pets, but Bufo's webbed toes and warty back gave her the creeps.

'I'll take him back up,' said her son, turning his back on her. The contempt in his eyes had annoyed her.

'Do that!' But Teddy didn't notice the acid in her voice. Why should he at six?

It was proving to be a difficult summer. There was a time when Diane Durrant wouldn't have been scared of catching a toad. She hadn't even been scared by Grade 11 Senior High, who blew down their brass and woodwind like they blew up the rubbers that the Vice Principal was always finding in the playground. Kids!

116

She walked over to the kitchen table, sitting down heavily, leaning her head in her hands, rubbing her tense facial muscles with her fingers. She had good skin, was a little wrinkled about the eyes, but who wasn't at 42?

It was this School Board business. Sam Drury, the Mayor, was turning out to be a real bastard. Dave had always said he was awkward. She would have called it small-minded. What else in a place like Sunny Mead?

Unable to settle, she walked over to the window to look out at where the goldenrod in the back meadow was making the landscape pure yellow. Branksome Lake was a great place to be in summer. A resort that could hold its own with the best. And full of tourists. A popular place for boating, swimming, everything. But when you lived there all year round …

She could hear Pip upstairs – the hip-hop of his crutch. Diane flexed her neck and facial muscles, trying again to relieve the tension. Drury didn't know what it was like to have a child who was different. His son, Sam Junior, was the Romeo of John Branksome High. Her eldest didn't have that kind of future to look forward to. Not unless things changed.

Diane breathed in deeply. It was no use. She couldn't see things working out yet – but she was still hoping. Maybe this new teacher would do them all some good?

'Hi, Mom!' It was Melanie. Her almost-17-year-old daughter had done her three hours as a cashier in the local store and was home for lunch. She would be looking in the ice-box in a minute for food.

And Diane had only just finished doing the breakfast dishes. The reason she hadn't put them in the dishwasher was that it was still full from the night before, and she'd forgotten to switch on right now. She'd never been fond of household chores.

And, presently, her whole preoccupation was with her pet scheme. Damn the Mayor! Why wouldn't he go along with it? *Drury, you've got a lot to answer for!* she said to herself as Melanie came through the door.

'How did it go?' She looked at her daughter, hands fast in the pockets of her jeans.

'Boring as usual.' Melanie said it with conviction. Diane was always amused by the pout she could put on, which changed her blonde daughter's fragile beauty into a thoroughly unpleasant stubbornness.

'But it pays!' said Di. Her tone was just as irritable.

'Sure. What's for lunch?'

'You know what!' Di gestured at the ice-box.

'Oh, Mom!' was the impatient reply.

'You could have eaten out.'

'I could have,' said Melanie, 'but I prefer to come home.'

Diane was sorry. She didn't want to get into an argument with Melanie. When she had taken the part-time job, she had told her parents that it was good practice for getting ready for college. And Diane desperately wanted her to do well. She was a talented girl – a wonderful musician.

'Are you practising today?'

'Sure. As usual.' That was the end of their conversation.

Melanie's lunch consisted of a large pizza and Coke. She hardly seemed to notice how Di could do with some help, either, because her head was hidden inside a teen mag.

Teddy and Rose were easier to please. Di wondered how she'd ever had the six-year-old twins. After Pip, it had been some five years before she had even considered getting pregnant. It had all been too much of a shock. But it had been Dave who'd persuaded her.

As Di poured milk for the twins and handed it to them, she recalled once again the conversation she had thought about so many times since:

'Look, Di, Pip was okay when he was born, you know that. What happened wasn't any of our faults.'

Dave hardly ever played the detective at home but, on that occasion, he had treated her to a reasoned explanation as to why it was worth them extending their family. He loved kids anyway and Di knew he was hoping for a son who would grow up strong and whole. But the risk! If one accident could happen, so could another.

But he had managed to persuade her.

'Look, Di, you know what they say. Lightning never strikes twice! What happened to Pip and me doesn't bear thinking about, but it did happen. Is it going to spoil all our lives? Is it?'

He had won.

She had caught just as easily as she'd ever done and, before she'd known it, the twins had been on the way. And she wouldn't be without them now. She looked fondly at their silver heads; they looked like angels, but she knew better. And yet they were quite different.

Rose stared at her mother across the kitchen table. Diane recognised the challenge in her eyes. She was looking into the opaque and milky emptiness of her glass. The little girl felt angry the milk had gone, because it gave her a nice cold feeling down to her tummy as it slurped and gushed its way over her tongue, rolling round with the spit.

'More,' she said.

'More,' the twins repeated in unison.

'*Please*,' Diane added mechanically.

Rose felt angrier. Why should she beg for it? Why should she say *please*? What did please *mean*?

'*Please*, Rose,' her mother repeated.

The little girl wasn't going to say it, so she sucked on her straw insolently, trying to make the end feel like the lost milk.

'Please,' sneered Teddy, his sandal sole scraping Rose's ankle. 'Go on,' he muttered, 'say it, say it, you cow, say it.'

'Shut up,' said Rose.

'What did you say, Teddy?' asked Diane.

The boy was hanging his head. Rose was smiling.

'He said I was a cow. I like cows.'

Melanie put down the teen mag and made a face at both of them. 'Shut up! Both of you!'

Rose looked round at the lot of them. Teddy was being nasty; her foot was hurting. He hadn't said it in a nice way.

She wasn't a cow! She didn't like him this lunchtime, not one bit!

'Teddy, what did you say? I'm asking you! How dare you say that to Rose?'

While her mom shouted at Teddy, Rose was getting angrier. She didn't like her brother, she repeated to herself. Not a bit! She wouldn't say 'please', she wouldn't say it after that.

She caught at Teddy's foot and ground at it under the tablecloth. Her brother gasped.

'Why do you let them do it, Mom, why?' Melanie protested. 'Why can't we have a minute's peace?'

'Shut up,' said Rose.

Melanie was on her feet. 'What did you say?'

'Leave them alone, Melanie, I'll deal with it!' Diane had had enough already. Teddy was sniffing. Melanie was blazing angry and Rose was looking as if she liked it.

Rose liked it especially when Teddy's face went red. It was like when he made a wee wee. Why did he have that thing anyway. Why did he have a pee pee and she didn't? She chewed her straw until it was flat. All the time, Rose knew her mom was looking at her. She didn't want to see Mom's eyes. She could get awful angry. Suddenly Teddy pinched her, just as Mom was opening her mouth.

'Aaaah!' screamed Rose, diverting Diane's attention.

'Stop it, stop it!' shouted Melanie. 'Make them, Mom, make them!'

Rose looked at Melanie. Why did those things poke out at her front? She looked down at her own flat little chest.

'You're very naughty!' said Diane accusingly.

'We're not!' said Teddy defiantly.

'We are,' said Rose, and waited for the outburst.

It ended with tears all round. Diane sighed. Twins were supposed to be friends. They were sometimes, but there was sibling rivalry. She'd learned all about that in college when she'd been doing her teaching degree.

'Mom, how can they be so awful at six?' asked Melanie.

Diane sighed. How could they? 'I'll take Pip's tray up,' she said, avoiding her elder daughter's question. 'And I hope you're going to do some practice!'

Melanie nodded. Teddy and Rose were staring. Diane wasn't going to say the same to them. They had both taken to the violin, but this wasn't the time. 'Now, behave yourselves, while I go up to your brother!'

She shouldn't feel pity for him, really she shouldn't. It was the worst thing she could do. Yet the sight of her 13-year-old filled her with dread. She would never get over it, never. What she would have given for him to be behaving like the others below.

His back was turned to her when she came in. He was seated by the window, his crutches propped beside him against the chair, their grey handles curved as if patiently waiting for his sensitive fingers to curl about them again.

Diane had asked herself a thousand times what it must be like to be deaf and mute; never to hear Mozart, never to hear anything, never to speak!

A wave of protectiveness towards him surged through her. She had to stop wanting to cosset him, but how could she? She just went on and on, deep, deep down within her. Yet, one day, Pip would have to fend for himself. That was why feelings like this were wrong.

'Hi,' she said, although she knew he couldn't hear. She walked round to face him, in case she startled him. 'Hi,' she said again. The dark, cropped head, so like Dave's, lifted. The green eyes flecked with hazel, again all his father's, stared up at her. His sensitive lips were closed in a thin line. He looked sad. Alone! Reproachful? Then she relaxed. 'Hi, I've brought your lunch.'

Pip smiled. Today he could have thrown the French fries and the Coke right into his mother's face. He couldn't help it. The strength of his feelings towards her was something he couldn't handle at the moment, so he was putting all his energy into his arms like he did with his sticks and the wheels of his chair, or with the murderous flicking of elastic bands at the flies that hung round his bed.

He took the tray, continuing to smile, making the thin skin of his face wrinkle right up under his eyes, feeling it taut round his mouth, clenching his teeth together. He muttered. He didn't know what sound he was making – he couldn't hear himself making it – but he was forcing that fucking useless tongue to do something instead of just lolling out of his mouth, drooling with spit.

It was his age that was getting to him – he knew that. His age. That made him angry even to think of it, not being able to help what he was doing – and he was doing it to himself – not his body, but *the rest of him.*

His head was still full of the explosion that had made him like he was, made him do it …

Dad, Dad, Dad, Dad – look! The tree! It's on fire! Dad, Dad, help, help! The pain, oh, the pain! And the smell of burning. Is it light now, Dad? Is it dark? I can't hear! It's all gone. My strength's all gone. All sharp metal and falling – falling into the dark …

Pip thrust his nose into the glass of Coke, and its effervescence wet his chin with sweetness instead of spit. He looked up over the rim of the glass, reading her lips,

'Drink it up; don't mess with it.'

He nodded, taking a gulp, setting it down. Then he got rid of the French fries very quickly, except for two that he placed carefully aside for his white rat.

Mom didn't like him giving Cass his food, but Cass liked it. And Pip realised in a satisfied way she wouldn't stop him feeding the rat. That was the only good thing about being like him; you got away with lots of things.

He watched his mother moving about the room. She looked good in jeans. Not as good as Mel, but good. She smelled good too from here. Not of perfume but of downstairs, where everything was real; where they did things and heard things and laughed and had a good time.

Downstairs was the place!

But he liked it up here. Pip watched Diane fussing about. She belonged up here with him, not down with them. They had her all the time. This was his time. It was precious. Not that he didn't like them downstairs. He did. What about the twins then? They were great guys, but little bastards as well. The toad didn't mind being picked up and carried upstairs by Teddy, but the newt dived every time Rose stuck her fat hand into its water.

And they could never remember to feed the garter snake. It would have died if it hadn't been for Dad. Mom wouldn't touch it. And Melanie hated it. What about Mel then? Everything where it should be, except she couldn't get her head together. And that was his family. And this was his place.

It was an attic room. It had been converted especially for him. He had an elevator to go downstairs. He could roll his chair right into it, then press the button, and down it would go. It made him independent. He didn't really need much help, except to get heaved into the car and be pushed about when he was tired. Sometimes he got them to push him when he wasn't.

Pip's room was rectangular; he had the whole length of the house. From the back windows he could see the street, with its white houses all laid out like a checker board.

He liked the buildings in Sunny Mead. They were friendly. They meant everything to him. They had grey sloping roofs with attic windows in the top. One of them had what was like a little belfry, but it was a fake chimney for show.

Lakeside, the houses were different. They called them 'chalets' for the visitors. They had cable television and private porches where you could sit out naked. They had a deck too with a lake view, and you could rent out a boat. Pip sat at his own attic window for hours, watching everyone.

There was nothing Pip Durrant didn't know. Who was fucking whom, who slept where, which kids were out. From the other side he could see the lake. Branksome. He called it Golden Pond. It was better than Squam Lake, the real one, where you could get a boat or go on a tour of the film set.

It was great having had a movie shot round your place. He liked Jane Fonda – she looked good for her age – and he liked the boy in it too. It was a boring story, but good. But not as great as *The Terminator*. He fancied himself as Arnie, blasting away at everything.

Pip watched Diane smoothing the bed. He pushed away his plate of French fries, set the tray down on the table and reversed his chair in his mother's direction.

It was a great room to be in, nothing to get in your way, no furniture that stuck out like downstairs. It was a hell of a job to get about below. That's why they'd done this conversion. So he'd be free. But what did free mean?

Get me out! He'd been trying to shout it. He had! He had heard himself saying it – when he stopped hearing – stopped saying anything. But when they had got him out, all he'd been able to do was stare up into the light and into Dad's face. He'd thought he was dead. Then he'd known he was. But he wasn't; he just couldn't be free anymore.

Pip propelled his chair across the attic, past his mother, towards his aquaria. He had the glass cases stacked against the wall. His pets.

He felt a wave of warmth through his body. He wanted to hold one right now, feel its fur, see its face. Animals were kind. He liked animals. He liked them all. Every sort. Golden Pond was where he had found them, except Cass, and the white rat was the one he was itching to hold.

Cass was climbing, climbing frantically, twisting in and out of the little run that he had made for her. He kept seeing her nose and tail, whisking in and out continuously. She was very intelligent and there was something up.

She came out like a shot and, while he was handling her, the rat's face seemed strained. It was an intelligent beast and Pip knew all his animals very well. Cass had something on her mind. When he started to stroke her she tried to run up his sleeve.

Diane was mouthing something. He read her lips quite easily. 'Don't let it up your shirt like that!'

Why shouldn't he? Just because she didn't like rats. He sighed an impatient refusal. Cass needed him; if she was upset for some reason, she needed his warmth, like he needed hers.

Diane disappeared back downstairs, and now he was alone he could concentrate on all the animals. There was no sign of Strangler. Mom said it was a horrible name, but it was only a joke. Strangler wouldn't hurt a thing. He was a garter snake and completely harmless.

Pip peered into his cage – wherever he was, he'd gone to earth. And he hadn't touched his dinner, just like Cass hadn't even sniffed at the French fries he'd saved.

It was the same with the salamander. It was splayed in the back quarter of its watery prison, one bulging eye inert, death-like. He tapped the glass, but it didn't respond.

'Get up, you lazy son-of-a-bitch,' he mouthed jokingly. But it didn't make any difference. The salamander lay there, uncaring.

There was no sign of the mole. He had given it a big case, and he liked to watch the animal digging and groping its blind way through crazy tunnels in the mounds of earth that Dad had shovelled in. Mom had said it was cruel – but she would have yelled if it had been out on the lawn instead. Pip liked its pink feet and its snout best. And its blind eyes gave him comfort. It was like him in a way. Its other senses were as keen as his. Things that made up for what was lacking in both of them.

For a moment, Pip panicked. What if they were all dead? Where was the toad? He didn't keep Bufo in a case. That's why it was always getting out.

Pip wheeled about, looking anxiously at the glass-fibre structure his father had rigged up in the corner of his room. It was a series of green humps really, like the monkey mountain at the zoo. It stretched up to the rafters, and Dad had positioned a couple of bright spotlights to warm it up and make it look pretty. It stood where once there was an old wash stand, which his father had ripped out, connecting the cold water pipe to a little fountain like the ones in the garden centre. The whole effect was meant to be like a waterfall. Pip couldn't hear it, but he could imagine the noise. That's where Bufo lived most of the time, except when he got bored like he had when Mom had found him on the drainer.

Pip envied Bufo's ability to find a change of scenery at will; just leaving the attic door open while he was in the vicinity gave Bufo the chance to hop downstairs and make a nuisance of himself.

But now there was no sign of him either. Pip would have called him if he could, but instead he ran his strong, sensitive hands up and down the green glass-fibre and drummed. His animals knew the sound. It meant their master was frustrated.

Then, quite unexpectedly, in one terrifying moment, Pip felt a lightning-swift blow between his nose and his chin. He threw himself back in the chair and spluttered. Bufo had taken a flying leap into his face and hit him full in the mouth.

Pip swore in his head. What was the crazy toad doing? He'd never done that before. Then Bufo hopped and skittered across the room towards the window, where he leaped for the sill and squatted, his glutinous eyes fixed on the street below.

'I'll get you!' mouthed Pip, though he was shaking after the sudden encounter. The toad cowered as he came closer, sensing his capture.

Downstairs, Diane had managed to get them all practising. At least, whatever else her children were, they were musicians through and through. It was in their blood like it had been in hers.

Rose was the image of what Diane herself had been: listening to the piano at two, face alive, head on one side;

starting to learn an instrument at the age of four. And Teddy, thankfully, had the same bent as his twin. At least the two agreed on something.

Diane swallowed in satisfaction as Melanie made the oboe speak. Its mellow throatiness was a joy; she caught her breath.

Mel was really talented, and if anything got her into college it wouldn't be her SATs but her musical aptitude. She had been voted Musician of the Year in her junior year at John Branksome. Now she was set for graduation and, hopefully, a place.

Diane was hoping that Mel would get a grant on account of her music, which would be something at least towards the fees. People said being married to a policeman had its advantages, but there were times when she couldn't exactly see what they were. She sat down to accompany her kids on the piano, her alert, intelligent, but tired, face bent over the keys.

Upstairs, Pip was still trying to catch Bufo. Every time he nearly succeeded, the toad hopped away and returned to the window sill, as if an invisible line was reeling him in, or like a fly drawn to a fly-paper.

Finally Pip let him sit there while the two of them stared down into the street below. Downstairs, the cacophony of noise reached high decibel level; upstairs, there was only silence.

Somewhere away on the fringes of Sunny Mead, an engine's growl was turning into a purr, as a station wagon swung its stealthy way from street to street and down the lakeside. It crawled to a halt outside 107 Camellia Grove. Pip had a great vantage point of the Grove. It was called that because of the trees clustered near the end, so near in fact that some of their branches tickled the chalet's windows. He knew when every occupant moved in or out. Mel said he was *real nosy.*

The vehicle was long, almost like a funeral wagon, but a deep chestnut brown, almost red. When Pip looked closer, he saw that sections of the paintwork were actually yellow, but obscured by a coating of red dust. Strange-looking, thought Pip. He couldn't see the driver, because he hadn't made the window slide down. It was like the wagon had arrived all by itself.

Look at that, he said in his head, addressing the toad. *The guy must be fried.* Pip couldn't actually feel the heat outside, because the air conditioning kept the long attic cool, but he knew what it must be like in the street, and the driver clearly had his engine switched off. He was just sitting there inside.

Pip didn't recognise the licence plate. The guy wasn't from around hereabouts. Maybe he was a salesman travelling through? The boy and the toad kept looking; human, alert and hunched; animal, squat and nervous.

But he was just an ordinary guy after all. Pip watched him as he got out. The man was casual in red shorts and a yellow vest. He was tall, slim and tanned. He looked like a tourist. Judging from where he was parked, he'd be taking one of the lakeside chalets.

Branksome had lots of strangers in the summer, but they were usually families – not a guy alone. This man was certainly counting on staying. He had gone round to the back of the wagon and was pulling out his stuff. He couldn't be a tourist. He had too much gear.

What interested Pip most were the five long cases stacked on top of one another. At least, the boy thought they were cases, something like his own aquaria. But the man's were taller. What was the guy going to do with them? They were covered with a kind of black sheeting except for the ends and Pip couldn't see them properly.

While the man was bending inside the back of the van, Pip suddenly saw something sticking out of his pocket. He couldn't make it out so he reached for the pair of binoculars he kept close by him. They were his town eyes. Simultaneously he glanced at Bufo. The toad's sac was ballooning madly, thin and rubbery, as Pip brought the glasses up to his eyes.

Gee, it was a tin whistle! Pip grinned suddenly. Cool! So the guy had heard of Branksome Music Academy. He was surely down for some concerts at the Bowl. He probably didn't care having to drive some to get there.

He looked cool in other ways. He believed in matching up. A thin yellow scarf was floating out of his pocket. Pip blinked. It seemed to be getting longer and longer, like a conjuring trick. Pip blinked again and took the glasses from his eyes, which hurt a bit, rubbed the lenses, then put them back. The guy was stuffing the scarf back in.

Then he was reaching deep into the back of the wagon when, suddenly, he jumped back as if he'd been shot. Pip almost laughed, but something stopped him.

The guy was sucking his thumb like a kid, but Pip knew instinctively that he was very angry. He was staring into the trunk, the afternoon sunlight glinting on his earring. No, he hadn't been shot; he'd been bitten!

Pip's curiosity increased as the man reached back in. Whatever was there was vicious. Then Pip looked at Bufo again.

The toad was going crazy, suddenly arching its warty back, hopping to and fro. Then it leaped for his face once more. Pip jerked back his head and it crashed into the v-neck of his shirt, going up and down on his chest with the beating of his heart.

The boy laid down the glasses very carefully and put up a wily hand. Got it!

'Got you,' the satisfaction of those wordless words echoed in his head. 'Got you, you crazy toad. What's the matter? What's the matter?' He soothed the amphibian with a shivery finger. Then, putting it inside his shirt, he trundled back to its favourite place and dropped it in the little pool. Bufo shot off, running crazily for a hiding place.

Pip was mad to get back to the window to see what the guy had got in the back of the wagon. He wanted to know what had bitten his thumb. But then he saw the rest of his pets. A cold feeling ran up and down his back. All the little guys were going crazy!

Cass, the quietest, gentlest white rat he'd ever had, was scraping up and down the glass with savage teeth. Pip felt sudden tears start in his eyes. He loved them all. They were going to die – they must be. They were going crazy. It must be the heat. Maybe the air conditioning was driving them crazy? Maybe something had gone wrong?

He took his walking sticks and drummed on the floor. He rang the small bell Diane had given him over and over again to tell them to get up here from down there. But no-one came.

The mole was spade-digging, blundering its molish way through tunnel after tunnel, always coming to a blind end. And the salamander was dipping like a mad, quick fish cutting the water, turning its yellow belly up like a fried egg. Pip could hear nothing, but he could imagine the confused squealing and guttural croaking. He couldn't sit here and watch his animals suffer.

Dad, Dad, Dad! He was shouting, he knew he was. Not only in his head. The golden belly of the salamander was like the lightning in his brain. The mole was throwing up the earth frantically like Pip had done when he'd been blinded by dirt, half buried under the wrecked car, after it had hit the tree.

Pip thumped the floor in unison with the thrashing of his manic pets, but still nobody came. He knew they must be practising their instruments. Diane had once said that when they were, they couldn't hear anything. Desperate, he decided to go down in the lift. He was going to fetch them.

Downstairs, the family had reached the crescendo. Diane thought they had never played so well. They'd really got it together. She wished Dave could hear them.

The sound was getting to them all, holding them with its

spell. All those years she'd tried to give her children music, had paid off. She was excited, and her excitement seemed to be spreading through her fingers, right up her arms, towards the twins, who weren't looking at their music anymore, their small fingers rat-tatting on the bridges of their instruments, their right hands fretting – it was marvellous. And Melanie … well, the oboe was perfect – just glorious.

Diane forgot she hadn't gotten any further with this piece. It was fresh to the children. It was only a long time after that she realised that.

She didn't hear Pip thumping on the floor in his misery but, suddenly, Melanie dropped her oboe and was looking up at the ceiling. The whole piece was ruined.

The twins looked like when Diane told them they couldn't have their favourite candy. Diane jumped up from the stool.

'You spoiled it, Mel, it was wonderful and you spoiled it!' she almost shouted.

'I thought I heard something,' said her daughter, still staring. 'Pip.'

'Well, you could have waited until the end of the piece.'

'I'm going up to him,' said Melanie – and Diane could have slapped her. Kids didn't care about anything, did they? However talented, Mel didn't care!

Diane was so disappointed. She'd been carried away and out of herself by the music. She looked at the twins, who'd put down their violins simultaneously. She didn't like the look on Rose's face. There was going to be trouble.

Suddenly she realised how selfish she was being. If Mel had heard Pip, she should go too.

'No, Mom!' Diane stopped dead, because Melanie had put up her hand as if in warning and stood at the foot of the stairs. She went and sat down.

Mel was feeling the strangest impulse as she looked upstairs – that she shouldn't go up to Pip, but should have carried on with that piece of music so it could stream out into the street and fill all those smug little lakeside chalets, full of nosy interlopers – and drive them out!

Mel swallowed, blinked and began to worry what stupid things she was thinking. She could hear Pip's rat squeaking and squealing. There was something wrong.

That's what she had heard before in the music – that damn rat. She didn't know how, but she had a feeling he was out somewhere, running about, and she couldn't take it. And the snake! Looking up the stairs again, she decided that now she'd go and find out what tune Pip was playing himself.

As the frightened boy propelled his chair into the lift, his eye caught the garter snake, twisting its way up its aquarium, seeking his help; then it fell back, quiet, coiled, normal. Cass stopped crashing about her cage, and the salamander floated on the surface of his tank. Suddenly Bufo appeared, crouched on the side of the pool. They were all right!

Pip was sweating. He remembered the guy outside. He turned back to his window, his hands manoeuvring the chair skilfully in his hurry. As he reached the glass and looked down, the station wagon was empty. Someone must have helped the guy – he couldn't have got all the boxes out on his own. All that was left in the back was a big, covered animal cage and an attaché case.

Pip raised the glasses. A bird, that was it. It was a birdcage – the guy had been bitten by a parrot or something. Pip's mechanical eyes didn't take a close look at the case.

It was then his vision was suddenly impeded, as the lenses were filled by a body shadow. The guy was back. Pip put down the glasses as the man leaned in and lifted the cage. He was making heavy weather of it – it must be made of iron or something. Pip shrugged, picked up the glasses and fixed his attention on the man.

He swallowed. The guy was looking straight at him. Pip's face felt hot. He couldn't think how the guy could see him up there in the attic. But Pip knew he didn't like the man's face. He had really strange eyes. They spooked you. Pip sensed that, even though the man was quite a distance away from him. And he knew somehow that the man could see his face too. It was garbage, but that was the feeling.

The guy had a long, thin nose, but not too long. Bony. Old. Why had Pip thought he was young? The ugly nose had a flaming red spot on its side – was it bleeding? Yes, it was blood. There was another red spot on his cheek. But it was his thumb that had been bitten.

He must have had his face down to the cage when he dragged it out. And he was smiling in a funny sort of way, still looking straight in Pip's direction. He had a sharp chin a bit like Cass. Pip put down the glasses.

He couldn't stare at that guy anymore. He watched him with normal eyes, watched him carry the covered case down the path through the garden of one of the chalets. Which one though?

Suddenly, he remembered! His heart thudded. It couldn't be! He hoped it wasn't – what day was it? Where was his diary?

It was a neat little book, but Pip's black loose-spring scrawl filled it with graffiti and doodles. Whenever Mom told him anything he had to remember, he was supposed to put it down in here; he promised himself he would, when he was feeling guilty for not doing what she said; when he wanted just to keep in touch with life downstairs; but he forgot just as soon, and, instead, dashed in those things he could imagine himself doing one day when he was well again.

He flicked through the pages: June, July – here. He'd drawn a couple of large breasts right across the day. Feeling an idiot, he scored the nipples out with the soft black pencil while he squinted at the almost illegible scrawl beneath.

NEW MUSIC TEACHER

Pip swallowed – then jumped! He was sweating when he looked up into Melanie's face. He covered the breasts with his hand. But she wasn't looking; she was gazing at the window.

'What are you doing up here, Pip?' she asked. It was easy to read Melanie's lips. He liked looking at them even if she was his sister. She had a great mouth. 'What's the matter with Cass?'

He took that other little book, which was his life, his only means of communication, and wrote with the black soft pencil:

'I'm not doing anything. All the little guys have been going crazy!'

Melanie walked over to the window. He followed in the chair. He was going to have to ask her if the new music teacher was due. She might know. Maybe that *was* him. His hands were wet with sweat. He caught at her T-shirt and let her drag him along. She turned.

'Get off, Pip! You're spoiling my top.'

'What are you doing up here?' he signed.

'I heard it. The rat was making a hell of a noise. We were practising and I just came up. I thought something was the matter.'

How could he say there was something the matter? He didn't know what it was; he only knew it was something to do with that guy over the road.

They were both at the window now. Melanie stood beside her brother and stared at the unfamiliar vehicle, its trunk open and empty. She could still hear the music playing in her head. She felt like that sometimes after she had been wrapped up in it.

With one brief moment of insight, she thought about the Pip she'd known once. There were four years between them; she could remember him as he used to be. It had been a hell of a crash and it had spoiled all their lives. She and he had had some great times together.

How did he cope? Maybe this guy who was coming would help him – all of them. Things were surely getting on top of Mom; maybe this was the answer. Although she and Mom weren't getting on so well, she appreciated her problem. She had her hands full.

Mel couldn't have done it. She couldn't have sacrificed her

life like that for someone else. It seemed hard, but that was it. She loved Pip, but she couldn't have done what Mom had done.

Mom's was a great plan – whatever Sam Drury and the School Board said. Drury was a creep and Sam Junior could be just as much a creep as his dad sometimes. Once she'd called Mr Drury 'Uncle Sam'. That was when they were all friendly. He wouldn't even listen to what her mom was saying. Didn't even want to know! There were people on the Board who did see her point, but he was the chairman and had the casting vote.

There was no way he was going to let children like Pip into Branksome Music Academy. He believed that they should be somewhere *special*, somewhere where their *special needs* would be catered for. What he really meant, considered Mel, was he wanted them out of the way: where no-one could see them; where no-one could be upset by them. Granted, Pip was funny sometimes; who wouldn't be, with his problems? But there was nothing wrong with his head. He just couldn't speak nor hear nor walk very well. Did that mean he could never have a normal life?

She was thinking of how Pip would cope with sex and stuff like that when she saw the guy walk out of the house. A tingle of interest made her look harder. She'd bet he had a really nice ass under those shorts.

To cover that thought she turned quickly to her brother, who was seated, motionless, beside her. Sometimes, it almost seemed Pip had the ability to read her thoughts. Maybe it was because they'd been so close? He probably knew she was wondering what it would be like making it with that guy. But he was just staring mechanically into the street.

She looked at the young man again. His physique was perfect; her eyes travelled down slowly from the sleek head with its long blond wavy hair tied back, his earring, the smooth tan all over.

'Wow, look at those legs,' said Melanie; it didn't matter, no-one could hear her, she wasn't looking Pip straight in the face.

Who was the guy anyway? She watched him close the trunk, go round the front and check something under the bonnet. She turned to Pip again.

'Where's he staying? Do you know who he is?' Pip shook his head and Melanie was surprised to see how white his face was. He looked sick.

'What's up?'

He shook his head again. Melanie picked up the glasses and, pretending to sweep the lens about the street, she brought the stranger into sharp focus.

At that moment, the young man placed two hands flat on the closed bonnet of the wagon and looked her full in the eyes.

Melanie choked. What was she doing, staring at the guy like that? She wanted to take her eyes off him, but she just couldn't. She couldn't understand how he could see her, how he could be looking up at the window like that.

She withdrew a little, with the glasses still trained on him. But she couldn't get away from his stare. He had the lightest of light blue eyes; perhaps the lightest she'd ever seen.

He was grinning too. He must be able to see her. She withdrew even further, not wanting to put the glasses down, but still mad to watch him. God, his body was so smooth. Perfect!

She jumped as Pip's eager hand plucked at her sleeve. He was pulling her down towards him, mouthing something, but there were no words. She could feel his urgency. She squatted beside him.

'Go on, Pip, you can tell me what's the matter. If you can't sign it, write it down. Do you know who that guy is?'

Her brother shook his head with such violence that the pad and the pencil fell right off his knee. She picked it up, wondering what had upset him.

She gave it back to him, following it with the pencil. 'Go on,' she said, 'tell me.'

With shaking fingers, Pip wrote in his black scrawl: *107 Camellia Grove. He's staying there. I reckon it's the new music teacher.*

Melanie's heart gave a great lurch. *Must be her lucky day.* He was the greatest-looking guy she'd ever seen. A bit old for her. Thirtyish? But that had never worried Mel. She got on well with older men.

Her feminine mind was already concocting their first meeting. It would probably give him a shock when he found out the girl he'd been looking at in the window was his prospective employer's daughter.

She smiled, but her look changed immediately to seriousness. She couldn't believe it. There were tears in her brother's eyes. She had never seen him cry; she was sure he did, but she'd never seen him.

'Tell me what's the matter,' she said, 'please?'

He couldn't, he couldn't write it down. He couldn't understand it. They must all be against him. He loved Mel, but he couldn't see why she didn't say anything. The guy was a creep. He knew it. He'd never understand women. Instead, he wrote:

Do you think it is the new teacher?

'I hope so,' she signed.

He stared at her. Was she mad? How could she hope so? He didn't want anyone in his house who looked like that. Someone with a face covered in bites! No, thank you. The new music teacher had better keep away from him. He was horrible.

8

'I'm sure my poor head aches again,
I've scratched it so and all in vain'.

'Well, you see, kids like that …' he swallowed. The Mayor was sweating. 'Hot!' he said, wiping his forehead. Dave looked at him. Drury never had any difficulty saying anything. He let him go on. 'You see, Dave, Diane's a great girl, but the town–'

'The town? You mean the Board?'

'Yeah, the Board.' There were flicks of spit at the corner of Drury's mouth. He was chewing his words as usual.

'Give,' said Dave. He leaned his elbow on the table and went on filing the report. Anyway, what gave the Mayor the right to turn up in his office whenever he wanted?

'I can see I'm taking up your time,' said Drury uneasily. He was never sure what Dave Durrant would do. He had to pick his words carefully. Dave was lifting his head, looking at him again. The detective put down the pen and Drury didn't like the look in his eyes.

'If you've something to say, Sam, spit it out. 'Kids like that,' you said.'

'Not Pip, I don't mean Pip.' Dave was sick at the thought they'd elected Drury. He was so full of wind he could have farted himself right away. He was gabbling on, 'He's different, your Pip …'

'I know that. I'm also sure Diane's right. Someone has to do something about kids like Pip.'

'Right, right, but …' Drury was wishing he hadn't spoken to Dave after all; he should have gone straight to Diane.

'But not at John Branksome High?' The detective's eyes were scaring the hell out of him. Dave could be a bastard when he wanted to. That's what he was paid for. You just had to get on the right side of him. Drury was willing to try again.

'Let's put it another way.' Being Mayor of Sunny Mead was a bit like being a diplomat. And he had to be careful to be politically correct. 'Now how are two or three kids going to feel, pushed in with a lot of kids who can do everything they can't? How the hell would *you* feel, Dave?' This time he knew he'd said the wrong thing.

Dave was on his feet. Through the glass he could see the sergeant, Patsy Doran, watching. Patsy was a big, stolid Irishman. His real name was Patrick, but he'd gained his nickname because on occasions he took a long time to catch on. He was easy-going like a lot of the Irish and could take a joke in good part.

Drury was hard-going. Dave would have liked to have got on with him like he used to, but just now, it was proving impossible. Turning to the Mayor, he said, 'You asking me how I feel, Sam? I've got a son who's a normal, talking, hearing individual inside!' Dave stabbed a finger at his own chest. 'Inside, here where it matters. My son isn't nuts. He understands everything. This is the 20th Century, Sam! If a kid's a deaf mute, it doesn't mean he doesn't know anything. Got it?'

'Right, Dave, right. I understand completely. But the Board …'

'To hell with the Board!' Dave couldn't stand it any longer. This man's fat, smug face was getting on his nerves. 'Think of the kids! She only wants to try three.'

'But how can they appreciate JBH if they can't hear?'

Dave was really angry then. Why had Drury come to him? It was Diane who ran the Music Academy. She knew what she was doing. The sergeant was still watching. 'Sam, haven't you ever seen or heard deaf kids singing?'

'I know they do,' began the Mayor, 'but …'

'Not at JBH?'

'It's not my fault. It's the Board.'

'So you keep saying. But you're the chairman. Why can't you give Diane a chance? She knows what she's doing. You appointed her principal, then let her be principal. She's even engaged this guy for the rest of the vacation. He's used to working with the disabled. Why don't you give him a chance? See what he's like?'

Dave looked at Drury. The Mayor's eyes were just cracks in his flabby, porcine face. He was an unhealthy colour, blubbery, probably from too much red meat and booze. When you were a butcher, steak was even cheaper. And he was a rye drinker. It showed. But he was the boss.

'Who is this guy, anyway?' asked Drury. '*We* didn't appoint him.'

'I'm paying his wages,' said Dave. 'He's coming for a few hours a week to work with Pip to see how they get on until fall. Then the rest is up to you and the Board. He's only on trial.'

'Is he any good? Can he do the job? Where's he from?'

'Look here, Sam, I've a lot to do. I'm sorry. I suggest you give Diane a ring. She'll tell you everything you want to know.' The Mayor nodded.

Dave was assessing his success. Maybe it was working with Drury? Who knew what worked with him? He was a devious bastard. That was how he got to be Mayor.

'Right,' said Drury. 'I'll do that. Give my regards to Diane.'

Outside, Patsy was looking relieved. He'd seen the sparks fly rather too many times in that office between Drury and Durrant. He was glad they'd made it up, whatever it was.

'Have a nice day, sir,' he said as a red-faced Drury pushed hard at the swing doors and walked out of the building.

The twins had gone outside after Mel had spoiled the practice. Her elder daughter had been upstairs a long time but Diane didn't worry. Mel and Pip had always been close, and Diane wanted it to stay that way.

There was something else she wanted too. More than anything in the world. That something good would come out of all her endeavours. She was beginning to believe it. She felt hopeful, like when they'd bicycled through Hadley the year before Pip was hurt.

It had been fall then and the leaves had been thick on the lawns. Not all the trees had been turning, only some, but their leaves had been red and gold, matching the little red wooden houses. It had reminded her of the past. It had been so peaceful. There were times in Diane's life she wanted to forget, but like everyone else, she cherished the good memories. Like playing the pump-organ by the light of a kerosene lamp in that little church in the village where she was born. And music, music. That's what she wanted to remember. And that was what Pip remembered. She was sure.

That morning there had been a heat mist over Branksome Lake, as if it had been drawing itself up for something. She knew what the water would be like in the afternoon. The surface would be the face of a diamond, sparkling, faceted, molten silver. All the kids would be out in their swimsuits, and the water would be cool.

In spite of her sudden optimism, the time she didn't want to remember thrust itself into her mind: the faces of Lieutenant Steel and Patsy Doran when they had come to tell her about Dave's accident. She had really thought he was dead. But it had been Pip who had died – metaphorically, at any rate. Her talented musician, her lovely son, struck deaf and dumb and crippled. And it had been the lightning. Why had the tree had to fall on Dave's car? She'd asked herself why so many times she had sickened herself. At least now she was looking for a compromise.

The doctor had said there was no reason for Pip's deaf mutism – it was classed as hysteria. One day – and suddenly, perhaps – his hearing and his voice might return. And Diane was praying for that day. And she would bring it about by whatever means she could.

In the beginning she'd done everything she could think of to stimulate him, to try to make him remember, to unlock his ears and his tongue. But nothing had worked. So she'd started looking for other kids like him. And there had been two she had found almost directly in the next state.

They could walk pretty well, but in everything else they were like her 13-year-old. And she was going to help them as well. It was a crusade. But now, Sam Drury, who'd been their friend once, was trying to stop her.

It had been the biggest thrill of Diane's life when she had got to be principal of the Music Academy. That was what she had been working for. Now all she wanted was to integrate three disabled children, including Pip, into the next semester: three special children who'd been through so much.

And she wasn't going to be beaten. That's why she'd engaged Mr Koppelberg. He looked like the kind of man she was searching for – on paper, at least.

Of course his appointment couldn't be confirmed without the sanction of the Board, but she would worry about that later on. She had just invited him for a couple of weeks to see how he got on with Pip.

She had made that quite clear in the advertisement. A temporary appointment. And she'd been *so* lucky; he had the most wonderful qualifications. His reply had said he was looking for a new environment and that he considered children to be the most important thing in the world.

Although, to her surprise, Koppelberg's had been the only application, Diane had liked that part best. It was very unusual for a teacher to admit he loved children. He sounded like a musician after her own heart.

Another thing that was special about him: he hadn't typed his letter; it had been written in a lovely, flowing hand. *Artistic* had been Diane's first thought when she had seen his writing. And she was intrigued – he had used bright red ink. All this added up to an original guy.

So far they hadn't received his references. She herself had

rung up one of the referees he'd given and got only an answer phone. Later, though, one of his former principals had spoken to her. They'd chatted and he'd provided one of the most brilliant verbal references Diane had ever heard.

When she'd told Dave, he'd been naturally suspicious. He said the man sounded too good to be true. He'd rather have seen it in writing, he added; but that was what it was like being married to a policeman. In this case, it had had its advantages. There was no Koppelberg listed in national criminal records. So she had decided she was going to hire the music teacher on a temporary contract and wait for his references to show up. That way he would be on probation and, if unsuitable, they could part company without any problems.

Diane had been so lost in her thoughts that she jumped at Mel's voice. Her daughter had come downstairs without a sound.

'He's here, Mom.' Diane noted a certain excitement in her daughter's tone. She was quite laid back as a rule.

'Who is?'

'Diep Koppelberg! The music teacher.'

'You must be psychic. I was just thinking about him. How do you know?' She didn't wait for an answer. She had too many things on her mind. 'Oh, dear, and the chalet isn't ready. I always clean up properly at changeover.' She looked at her watch. 'I should go over there now.'

'Mom, you don't need to straightaway. He looks like he can manage fine.' retorted Melanie, thinking he looked exceptionally capable. 'Besides, I've got a feeling he'll be over here pretty soon.'

'I suppose he will,' said Diane doubtfully. 'Why is he so early? When he telephoned yesterday, he said he would be arriving late. So I told him where the key was.' Letting the chalet was an extra burden on an already busy Diane, but it brought in the cash and she'd made enough earlier on in the season to pay Koppelberg's wages.

'The place looked fine, Mom, last time I was in,' said

Melanie. 'I'm sure he won't mind.'

'Anyway, how do *you* know he's here?' Diane was puzzled.

'Pip told me when I went upstairs to him.'

'Pip?' Diane stared.

'Yes, he had it written in his diary. He's been watching him unload.'

'But Mr Koppelberg should have come here first. We'd have been able to help.'

'That would have been good,' said Melanie. Diane did a double-take at this. Eagerness to help was not one of Mel's strengths. She felt all on edge now, completely different from a few moments ago. What had all that been about the past and the 'feeling hopeful' bit? At that very moment, she saw the twins' fair heads dash past the kitchen window.

'Goodness, what are they up to?' she said. 'I suppose you couldn't go and look?'

Melanie looked less than enthusiastic at the request and wiped her forehead with a tissue.

'What's the matter?' asked Di. 'Are you okay?' Suddenly Di didn't like the look of her daughter. Her cheeks were flushed and her eyes very bright. She hoped she wasn't sickening for something.

'It's hot,' replied Mel.

'But it's quite cool in here,' said Diane, looking round. She hoped the air conditioning wasn't going to break down again.

'It must have been the stairs then. I'll have to get fit.'

'Good. Now, will you go and check on the twins for me?'

It was only after a grumbling Melanie had gone out to look for her brother and sister that Diane realised she had forgotten all about Diep Koppelberg again. What would he think of the place? It needed clearing up and fresh sheets putting on the bed. She shook her head in disgust. She'd really messed up. What was the matter with her today?

Rose stood very, very still in case it got her as well. She rubbed one leg up and down the other.

Putting her head on one side, she looked for a second, then closed her eyes and drew her lips tightly shut.

Then, making the biggest effort she could, she squeezed her mouth up until it hurt. *She mustn't scream, she mustn't! She mustn't cry, she mustn't!*

She was listening for Teddy. He wasn't going to see her cry. He never liked Annie Laurie anyway. He'd laugh!

Rose opened one eye again very carefully, then shut it, then tried both together. At the same time, she bit the soft inside of her bottom lip. 'Do you hurt, Annie, do you hurt?' She was sobbing inside.

Annie was lying on her back, her hands stretched up to Rose, her legs wrenched apart. Her little mouth was open, its pouting upper lip still frozen into a smile.

Rose sobbed, then shut up. Annie's snub nose with the dusting of five freckles was scenting the summer around her. Her little fingers were stretched out stiff and wide, begging for help. A tear rolled down Rose's cheek.

Annie Laurie, Bonny Blue Eyes – one hanging on a wire – flopping down her red, sawdust cheek. It had been pulled right out. And her head!

Rose scrunched up her face and, through a haze of her own making, stared at Annie's battered, red skull. Gee, that was what was inside someone's head. That was Annie's brains.

Her baby-soft head had been gobbled and pulled away as though someone had been digging deep into her mind. It had made a dark, empty tunnel into her body.

Rose squatted beside the storm drain, her plump legs straddling the gutter, her blonde hair falling over her face.

She could smell something really horrible. She wrinkled her nose. It was coming from Annie. Annie had done a pooh-pooh in the street! Yes, there it was between her legs. A nasty, black pooh-pooh, and there were more.

'Oooh,' she said. 'Oooh, Annie!' Rose bent over and, almost tottering, stared between Annie's flabby legs. There was a hole going right up to the hole in her brain.

Suddenly Rose couldn't stand it. Her lips split open wide

like Annie's and she screamed:

'Mommmmy, Annie's dead! She's dead! She's all ate up! Mommmmy, come here, Mommmmy …' The sound of her own voice had got to Rose; she was hiccoughing, letting the sounds of agony mix with those coming from Annie, who was lying on the ground, staring at her, without a brain. Rose coughed and snuffled.

'Rose, what's the matter? Rose, come here! What's the matter?' It was Mel.

Like a stone straight from a catapult, Rose launched herself at her sister's legs. She sniffed. Mel smelt nice, not like Annie. Rose hung on to her sister's slim brown legs, rubbing her cheek against their skin.

Mel put an arm down and hugged her close. Then she saw the rag doll.

'Ughh,' she said, holding her little sister even closer. It was obscene. She swallowed, looking down at the twin's fair head, wondering how to comfort her.

Suddenly Rose looked up. Her tears had stained her cheeks, but her eyes were now brightly inquisitive.

'Her brain's all out, Mel,' said Rose. 'Do my legs go through to my brain?'

The red-orange ball wouldn't stay in Teddy's hands. It was like a crazy thing, dazzling him. He was practicing catching it as it came off the wall with a rhythmical thump – thump. Then it struck him in the face, bringing tears to his eyes.

'Ball players don't cry; not in front of girls anyway!' The ball was speaking over Rose's yelling.

'Cry-baby, cry-baby, cry-baby,' said the ball's mouth, the chalk teeth taunting Teddy. He had painted them and now they were grinning meanly like the scary pumpkin at Halloween.

With a metallic, spring-like action, the ball suddenly jumped off the floor and hit Teddy right in the teeth again. He felt dizzy.

There was a hot, sweet wetness in his mouth. It was burning. He put up his finger and brought it down red. Making a face as ugly as the ball, he licked off the blood and swallowed it. He liked the taste.

He made another face at the ball. Then he caught it in temper and shied it at the wall, like he was trying to crush it. Its chalk teeth flashed by him and Teddy scampered after it in the direction of the lakeside apartments.

Ducking and weaving like one of his special footballing heroes, the small boy went after the ball. He could almost hear the roar of the crowd as he tried the pass.

Next moment he was sprawling. The ball was lying mischievously still where it had struck a water barrel. He'd tripped over it.

Teddy, rubbing his smarting knees, stained green from the grass and flecked with blood, put out his foot angrily. The ball was still by the barrel, still grinning.

He kicked it savagely and, with a terrific rebound, it flew back from the barrel's iron rings and struck Teddy right in the middle of his throat.

The blow to the small, fragile Adam's apple filled his neck with warm, strong shockwaves, rendering him speechless. Gurgling, he watched the orange ball arch high in the air and swing away over the lake at the same time as something ran over his foot, lunging at him with a pincer mouth.

Unable to scream, Teddy, rigid with horror, watched the huge, black rat scampering off in the direction of the disappearing ball.

Teddy gasped, stepped backwards in fear and tripped into the storm drain.

Precisely when he saw it, Pip couldn't say, but it was at the same time his mind heard Rose's thin shriek stabbing the air like a bodkin.

He could see her face and she was screaming. He knew that. What he was seeing, had seen, in front of his eyes was even worse. Teddy was playing with something that tricked Pip's eyes like the sun but, at the same time, could have been the product of Pip's imagination.

His brother was playing with a ball of fire. At least, that was what it looked like from the attic. It was bouncing to and fro between the boy and the wall. It was a circle of red-gold light, then a transparent arch, glowing like the image behind Pip's eyes when he stared at the light bulb too long. And Teddy was playing with it on the lawn.

Pip watched it stream towards his little brother's head, enveloping him, then roll on across the grass, between the houses, towards the lake. And Teddy was following it, trailing it on its dancing way. Pip was cold with fear. The ball of lightning dashed on, its beautiful spherical music ringing in Pip's head.

It came to rest at the foot of the barrel belonging to Adams's chalet. And Teddy was circling it warily. He seemed to be urging it out of its hiding place – until it sprang at him, knocking him backwards and then careered its crazy way up into the air to disappear into nothingness over the lake.

As its red-orange shape streaked into the evening sky over Golden Pond, Pip turned his head involuntarily away from his terrified little brother towards the glass cases at the end of the attic.

He didn't have to approach them; he knew what was going on. The little guys were at it again, scrabbling and screaming, begging him to let them out. Pip's quick eyes caught and held that rodent stare. Cass, the gentle white rat, was leering at him, snarling and showing her needle-point teeth.

Gripping the arms of his wheelchair, the boy sat, powerless to move or bring comfort, wrapped in the anguish of those he loved best of all. What was happening to his family?

Teddy lay face down over the storm drain, his body tingling like when Daddy had carried him into the house that winter when it was snowing and put him by the fire. But there was no snow today.

The water was gurgling deep down in the storm drain like the noise in his throat, and it smelled dark. It was a very wide hole. Teddy wondered what it would be like down there and if that was where the rat had gone. He knew there were turtles down drains, but were there rats?

'Get up, Teddy! What are you doing messing in the drain? It's filthy!' It was Mel's voice. Teddy felt angry again, so angry that his head was bursting.

Why couldn't Mel leave him when he was only looking down the hole? But she didn't go away.

'Get up,' she repeated.

He arched his back until he was bent double like an old man. Then the arch-spring of his body snapped erect and he faced both his sisters. They were staring. Suddenly the hot, angry feeling shot through his legs and feet away down into the earth and he felt cold and shivery, little and hurt, especially his foot. He sniffed and then he pointed in self-pity.

'Look.'

'It's bleeding, Teddy. What have you done?'

'It was the ball!' He wasn't going to tell them about the big rat in case it got him again.

Rose was staring at him – and he was suddenly on the defensive. 'Liar!' she shouted. Then he could see she'd been howling. Hadn't he heard her?

'Cry-baby!' he taunted, repeating the ball's little evil voice in his head.

'Stop it, you two! Twins are supposed to be friends. Why can't you be nice to each other? Come on!' said Mel impatiently.

Teddy followed the two of them at a distance. Nothing was going to stop him looking down that storm-drain again. He lingered behind, and when he was about 50 metres from Adams's rain barrel, he was sure he could hear triumphant squeaking.

'Just wait,' he said in his head, 'just wait, you son-of-a-bitch. Cass will get you and beat you up. I'm going to bring our rat down here to do it!' He could still hear the squeaking, which was like the horrible noise his violin made when it was flat.

Teddy pursed his lips and simulated it. The shrill, thin note pierced the air, shattering it like glass. It reverberated inside Teddy's skull.

Mel was shaking him, 'Stop it, Teddy, stop that horrible noise! Please!' She and Rose put their hands over their ears.

Then, suddenly, Teddy had a very bad pain in his head. He stopped the whistle and began to cry.

Mel came through the kitchen door with the twins hanging on to her arms. Teddy was hopping crazily like Bufo.

'Look what I've found!' she said to her mother, grimacing.

'Mom, Mom,' and the children were jumping round Diane, gabbling unintelligibly. When Diane could make some sense of what they were saying, she gave them both an arnica tablet from the medicine cabinet. It wouldn't do them any harm! She bent and examined Teddy's foot. The puncture was deep.

'How did you *really* do this, Teddy? Now, tell me the truth!'

'The ball did it!' persisted Teddy stubbornly. Mel and Diane looked at each other.

'I think it's a bite,' Diane said. Mel nodded, shuddering. 'I told Sam Drury that we were getting infested down here. It's all the rubbish the campers are leaving. He'll have to do something about it.'

'They were saying in Biology that rats are on the increase everywhere,' added Mel gloomily.

'Were they? That's horrible,' replied Diane, looking at Teddy's foot again. 'Where did it happen?'

'Adams's storm drain!' said Mel.

'Oh, dear.'

'It was the ball!' appealed Teddy. 'Its teeth are nasty! Yellow and horrible!'

'You painted them!' accused Mel. 'And you know it wasn't

the ball!'

'It's his imagination, Mel,' reproved Diane. 'What's the matter, Rose? Teddy'll be all right!' Rose's face was screwed up like a little, wizened, old woman's. 'Don't make that face!'

'You'll stick like it if the wind changes,' said Mel.

'My dolly, my dolly!' sobbed Rose.

'What does she mean?' asked Diane, preparing herself for more bad news.

'I forget to tell you,' replied Mel. She hadn't, but she didn't want to think about it. 'Annie came to a nasty end!' Rose began to wail, burying her head against Diane's breasts, nuzzling at her. 'I think you might be right about rats, Mom!' Mel said.

'She was all gobbled up!' snuffled Rose. 'Her brains were all gobbled up!'

'Cry-baby,' spat Teddy, pushing against his mother too. As Diane held them apart, she was suddenly praying for the vacation to be over.

'That's enough, you two,' she said firmly, parting them. She looked at Melanie again. 'Well, he's had his tetanus, so he should be all right. But I think I should check with the doctor.'

'So do I,' said Mel. 'And, personally, I wouldn't go anywhere near Adams's drain. No way!'

9

'So munch on, crunch on, take your nuncheon,
Breakfast, supper, dinner, luncheon!'

The Durrants had their first real taste of Koppelberg the evening after he arrived; the night he came to dinner.

'What's cooking?' Dave's lean stomach tightened at the smell. He'd grabbed only a burger at the canteen all day. The moustache hairs right under his nose prickled and his saliva came quickly into his mouth.

Diane was taking a lot of care over this meal. She had to impress the music teacher – *and* Sam Drury. Dave grinned, putting his arms right round her waist. She leaned her neck back and thrust it in the hollow of his shoulder.

'Get off, Dave, you'll tip the sauce!'

He liked her smell too, familiar, warm, enticing, lovely. But he wouldn't tell her now. Only afterwards when they were in bed. Still crazy after all these years. He liked that Paul Simon song. Twenty-two years, in fact, and still with one wife. Quite a record – especially for a cop. They were well known for their marriages breaking up; too many unsociable hours. He let Diane go, stood watching her move while she made dinner, thinking that when she pushed back her hair she looked like some impatient girl; her body was just as good.

She turned. 'I hope you don't get called out,' she said,

picking up the glass of red wine he had poured for her while they were cooking. 'It's so important that we're all together as a family tonight. I want Diep to impress Drury as much as he impressed me.'

'Diep?' For a moment he couldn't think who she meant.

'Oh, you're so silly,' she said. '*Diep.* Diep Koppelberg!' She felt exasperated.

'You've only just met the guy, Diane.' Dave was still wary. He just seemed too perfect. And he was a damned good-looking guy.

'I know, but I took to him straight away. I feel like I've known him for years. He's really easy to get on with. Dave, I know Pip's going to like him, and that's all that matters. Did you know that he gave up his vacation in Europe to come to Sunny Mead?'

Dave stopped chopping the garlic. There was an edge to Diane's voice he hadn't heard for a long time. Suppressed excitement. She was humming a little tune under her breath.

'Handsome, isn't he?' He had meant to say it under his breath, but it had slipped out unawares.

She laughed. 'Don't be silly,' she said affectionately, 'but, yes, he is in a strange way. Kind of boyish. Sensitive, I'd say. Takes things to heart. But he's a lot of fun too!'

'What did you do with this guy?' Dave joked.

'You two, come in or go out!' called Diane, suddenly noticing the twins. They were being a nuisance; they kept coming and peering round the door, in and out of the kitchen.

'Why can't you kids sit and watch television? Just keep out of here and let Mom and me get on,' said Dave in good humour. Then he noticed the bandage. 'What's Teddy done to his foot?'

'The ball did it,' said Teddy.

'What? What does he mean, Diane?'

'He was playing with his ball lakeside and something bit him,' smiled Diane.

'The ball!' Teddy's face was earnest, his eyes were squinting at Dave. His father regarded him, then shook his head. There were ways to get through to Teddy, who had a lot of imagination, but he shouldn't be allowed to make everything up.

'Now how could the ball do it?' questioned Dave, squatting to look.

'It just went boom, boom, boom,' shouted Teddy, jumping up and down, nearly knocking Dave off balance. Dave grabbed him.

'Calm down! What's up with you? Keep still! Let me look.' Teddy stood, balancing on one foot. Dave lifted the edge of the lint Diane had put under the plaster. His eyes narrowed, 'Di, what's this?'

The small puncture holes were blue-black and oozing pus. 'What bit him? It looks like a rat! Listen, son, didn't you see it?'

'Dad, that ball was horrible,' said Teddy deliberately. 'It kept going boom, boom, boom away from me. I'll never make the team now. It jumped right over the lake after it had bitten me.' Dave stared into Teddy's eyes. Having imagination was something, but not listening to anything was something else!

'Now, Teddy, this thing that hurt you …' Dave said. 'It couldn't have been the ball. Where did it happen?'

'By the storm drain,' Rose was standing close to him. She put her little hand over her father's.

'It didn't!' said Teddy.

'It did, Dad, it did!' Rose was jumping up and down.

'That's enough, both of you. Did you see it, Rose? Did you see what bit Teddy?'

'Annie's dead,' Rose's eyes were filled with tears.

'What?' Dave looked at the twins. They were pushing each other. 'Now, you two, level with me. What's it about, Diane?' he appealed. He looked up into his wife's face. The enthusiasm had left. She was biting her lip.

'I didn't bother to tell you but – Rose found Annie. She must have dropped her and Mel said the dolly was dead. All messed up!' Diane put a quick finger to her lips to warn Dave not to say too much in case it upset Rose even more! 'A dog must have got her!' Rose was beginning to cry already.

'Honey, come on, honey. Daddy will get you another Annie. Did you see a naughty dog, Teddy?'

'No, I was playing ball.'

'Listen, son. Did a dog bite you?'

'No, it was the ball!' Dave got up off his haunches.

'I think you ought to take him to the doctor in the morning. It looks nasty. When did he last have a tetanus shot?'

'I'm not sure. But I'll see to it.'

'Will you take Annie to the doctor, Daddy?' Diane sought Rose's hand.

'Annie can't be mended, honey. Daddy will get you another, I guess,' she comforted.

'I want Annie!' the little girl insisted.

'I want a tortoise,' said Teddy, 'like you got for Pip! Then it can go down the drain!'

'Okay, Teddy, point taken.' His son had been on about Ninja Turtles ever since he'd seen them on TV.

Briefly, Dave looked up at the ceiling. He should have known there would be trouble. Promising to buy a tortoise for Pip and bringing nothing for them. But Pip didn't have much pleasure out of life! Only his pets! Dave wanted to make up for what had happened to him. Probably too much! Then Diane started:

'It wasn't a very good idea to buy it this week, Dave. Pip will be so wrapped up in it he won't make a good impression on Diep.'

'Is that right?' This Diep was beginning to be a drag. 'I would have thought it was more for Diep to make an impression on Pip.' Dave felt exasperated.

He'd stopped off on purpose to get the reptile – perhaps he shouldn't have after all? He realised Diane could read what he was thinking. He was probably as unsubtle as any man who was examined in women's magazines. He could also see that she understood he wanted to make up.

'You are good, Dave,' she said, putting her hand up to his cheek and stroking it. He shivered. 'But when Pip gets a new pet it takes up all his time!'

'Well, it'll be hibernating soon,' was the only defence he could muster.

It had been a very funny day all round. Summer storms always made him nervous. He supposed it had been the accident. Naturally the weather reminded him of the crash in some deep-seated psychological way. Anyway, that's what a shrink would say.

The twins were quiet for a moment. He picked up the newspaper that was lying beside the bread bin. He looked at it. Fires in airplanes, disasters everywhere. He put it down again as Diane opened the oven. The twins were jigging up and down.

'Dead cow,' said Teddy.

'Shut up!' said Rose.

Diane straightened and sighed. 'I want both of you to go in the den and watch television. Do you hear what I say?' They were gone in a moment. 'I'm sorry,' she said to Dave, 'I always feel guilty when I send them to watch TV. But sometimes they're too much!'

'You don't have to tell me,' said Dave, 'but we wouldn't be without them.' They both laughed then and picked up their glasses of wine. 'But – I think you should take Teddy to the doctor. Or I could?' He kissed her on the cheek.

'Thanks, Dave. For everything,' she said. 'Now I have to get on or nothing will be ready when our guests come!'

Diane brushed away a gnat that was tickling her cheek. They were such a nuisance. How it had got through the screen she didn't know. Perhaps there was a hole somewhere? She'd have to get Dave check it out.

'Diep? Soup?' Diane was ladling it and trying to concentrate.

'Great.' He had a soft, warm voice, almost like a purr, with the trace of a foreign accent. As she handed the soup to him, the hot liquid slopped and scalded her fingers. She jumped, but didn't let go. He saved her embarrassment before all the guests, catching the plate deftly, just brushing her fingers with his cool ones.

'Sorry.' She felt extremely clumsy. Already a blister was rising on her thumb. Then, by the time they were all eating, Diane found herself the victim of completely unexpected memories.

Diane was holding the bowl daintily, nibbling carefully not to spoil her white Commencement frock. She was looking into his light-blue eyes. Maby had been her first love, that mean little shit of a basketball player, who had been making it secretly with her best friend.

And she'd trusted him totally! It had taken her ages to get over him. In fact, it had hit her so hard she had thought she would never get over it. She had just wanted to die when she had found out. She had known that everyone was laughing at her and she had wanted to kill him, even kill herself.

All the worst feelings she had ever had, rose up and rolled themselves into a ball of fury centred on Maby, whom she had done everything with and got nothing in return. All that petting, all those delicious dangers, those throbs inside, those things that meant everything to her, had disappeared in a moment, like magic. They had stayed out so late; she could almost hear him laughing, saying, 'I love you, honey, do it again, please!'

Diane blinked, glanced at the blister on her finger and realised that, for a moment, she had been far away from the table and her guests. That she had been thinking of things she hadn't thought of for ages; events that were as fresh in her subconscious as they had ever been.

Diep Koppelberg was smiling. It was him. It must have been his light blue eyes. They had reminded her of Maby's. She had forgotten the boy who had destroyed her for years; now he was fresh in her mind.

She glanced at Dave guiltily, but he was in deep conversation with Sam Drury. The mayor was looking at the twins. And Pip – Diane felt so sorry for him; his face was white – he'd hardly touched his soup. It was probably too much for him being downstairs with everyone like this. And

Diep was smiling still, his eyes turning from her to Pip.

'Can't you manage the meat?' Diep's voice was bell-like, high and clear. He knew how to make Pip lip-read. Then he was putting down his spoon and signing the words perfectly, his long fingers stretching like a juggler's, but with the skill of a musician. Diane was amazed. He'd never let on he knew sign language. What a stroke of luck!

Pip didn't respond and Diane felt acutely embarrassed again. Diep grinned, turned sideways, looking once more at Di. One side of his lip was twisted, like that of a little boy caught out in mischief.

'Never mind! Let the little guy get to know me. He'll change.'

'He's ...' Diane began, but Dave stopped speaking to Sam and turned to Diep. Di was hoping he wasn't going to say something awkward; intuition was telling her he hadn't taken to the music teacher. It was only because he was jealous.

Jealous? Why was she using that word even in her mind? Dave wasn't jealous, only perceptive.

'Pip, eat up your food.' Dave was leaning back in the chair, staring at Diep. 'He takes some getting to know, Mr Koppelberg,' he said.

'Diep, please.'

'Right, Diep,' replied Dave, but Di didn't like his tone. She was immediately angry. What was the matter with him? Didn't he know how important it was that this man stayed to help Pip? She cut in before her husband could say another word:

'Pip takes quite a long time to get to know people, Diep, because he's on his own a lot. By his own choice, of course. He could come downstairs any time he wanted, but he likes it upstairs with his pets.'

'Pets?' The music teacher's eyes seemed lighter, wider. What an attractive guy he was! He put back his head, stared up at the ceiling and nodded. 'I thought he had pets. He looks just like that kind of guy. That's another thing we have in common.'

'Did you hear that, Pip?' said Di. 'Mr Koppelberg has some pets as well.' She turned to Diep with a questioning look, urging him to go on, break the ice and tell Pip about his animals.

When she looked at Pip, she couldn't believe it. His face was blank, expressionless, his eyes as wide as Diep Koppelberg's, but unnaturally bright.

'Don't you want to hear about Diep's pets?' she signed. He shook his head so violently that everyone stopped talking and stared at him. Then Diane was angry with him, angrier than she had ever been.

Why did he have to behave so badly when things were so important? Couldn't he understand that she needed him to be pleasant, docile even? It must have shown on her face, because Dave was saying, 'Where's the second course, honey?' He made it sound like a joke, but the edge of the tone scissored through her.

'Okay,' Di said, 'now who's for beef?'

'Dead cow.' Teddy's voice was deliberate.

'Shut up!' Rose's even more so.

'Shut up, both of you!' said Mel. She looked right at Diep Koppelberg, 'I'd like to hear about your pets, Diep,' the tone was quite direct, 'as long as they're not snakes!'

'Sure!' Diep's laugh fascinated Melanie. 'But I guess this isn't the time, nor the place. You must come over to the chalet one day. And Pip must!' He looked into Pip's white face. 'When he feels better!'

'I'd like to hear about them now,' said Melanie.

'Melanie, Diep evidently doesn't want to talk about them!' snapped Di.

What was the matter with her mother? Mel didn't usually resent the fact Diane looked young for her age. Tonight her neck looked flabby. Diep must have noticed. He'd been looking at her enough.

Mel's finger strayed to settle the thin strap of her top, which was slipping a little. She knew she looked great in it. Perfect shoulders, Sam Junior had said. She wanted Diep

Koppelberg to look at her, not at her mother. They were grinning at each other again.

'Diep …' said Mel, laying down her spoon deliberately. She was conscious of the way her breasts were small, neat and firm beneath the cotton top.

Her eyes were holding the music teacher's. How come his eyes were as blue as that? They suddenly reminded her of the flame they'd made in chemistry, almost phosphorescent. She wondered if anyone else had noticed. And they were shining at her! Under the table, she closed her thighs together voluptuously, as if he was touching her.

'Do you play?' he said. She shivered. It was as if he was reading her thoughts.

'Yes,' she replied and her voice seemed to crack.

Di glanced sharply at her. It was not like Melanie to be so reticent.

'Mel plays the oboe very well!' she said.

'Plenty of wind then?' joked Diep. Suddenly Mel was very cold. She looked round and shivered. Didn't anyone else feel the draught? It was like she'd been drinking, gone out in the air and felt its shock.

Diep was smiling. The others had to notice how he was looking at her, but they didn't seem to. They were all talking to each other. Her mind was doing really wild things with the guy. They were taking each other's clothes off. And his body was so smooth. Mel had never really liked men with hair all over them. The guy was a dream. She swallowed. He grinned.

'Getting warmer now?' Her heart was thudding. She nodded.

'I think we're all getting warmer!' Dad's voice made Melanie jump. She picked up her spoon again, then put it down, remembering she had finished her soup and Mom was putting out the main course. She felt shaken.

Teddy knew his ball would come back, even though it had flown over the lake. He didn't want it to. He squirmed in his chair. His dad was making warning faces at him. He looked round for support. His foot hurt. He stared at the music teacher.

'My ball bit me.' Nobody laughed because nobody was taking any notice. They were all eating dead cow, except the new guy. Again, Teddy was conscious of Dad's eyes. Dad didn't like it when Teddy lied. 'It did!'

Mr Koppelberg was grinning. He looked a bit like Danny Adams. Mom didn't like Danny coming round to play with him, because he was naughty, but Teddy liked him.

Mr Koppelberg didn't look too much like a grownup. There was something in his eyes that made Teddy know he was going along with the whole thing; that he knew Teddy's secret.

It was a good feeling – having a grown-up on your side. A funny one, but it gave Teddy a buzz, just like lemonade fizzing up your nose, or pulling your pee-pee at night, or Danny's birthday party when they'd flobbed candy at each other.

'You're a good ball player?' asked Diep Koppelberg. It sounded like he knew that Teddy was a great one. If Teddy squeezed his eyes shut he could see himself screaming down the pitch. He did, fixing the image in his mind, grimacing, charging in and scattering the team for the hell of it.

'Teddy, stop making that face and eat up your dinner. He's being silly, Diep!' said Diane. Teddy opened his eyes to see them all staring at him – but Mr Koppelberg was laughing now.

'No, it's his imagination. It's good!'

Teddy could have kissed him! Suddenly the little boy grew red at the idea. It was sissy! He glanced at Rose to see if she'd noticed, but his twin was staring at Mr Koppelberg, rolling the meat round and round in her mouth.

'Rose, do you think you could swallow that?' Teddy heard Mel's disapproving whisper, but Rose didn't … The meat didn't taste like dead cow. It didn't taste like anything now, except wet cotton wool. Annie was dead.

Rose shut her eyes. She forced herself not to think about Annie's brain; she would think about cows. She liked cows. They gave you milk when you pulled those funny things.

They were rude! She chewed the meat harder and harder. Mr Koppelberg was looking at her. Did he know about cows? Did he know about babies drinking like cows?

Rose had a very funny feeling; she knew he did. A warm, runny feeling inside her that made her want to climb on Mr Koppelberg's lap and snuggle up to him like she did to Daddy – when he was not down at the police station, when he was there.

She looked resentfully across at her father. He wasn't there when it killed Annie. He had hair on his face – under his nose. Why did he? Why didn't Mr Koppelberg? His hair was really long – it was nice – it reminded her of Tara.

Tara was Rose's best friend – most of the time. She'd have to be all the time now Annie was gone. She had big blue eyes too. But not the same as Mr Koppelberg. He had eyes like Annie's, they stared at you, but they knew what you were doing, what you were feeling.

Rose's eyes filled with tears. The meat wouldn't go down. It was like chewing Annie's brain. Suddenly she spat it out on to the plate.

'Rose! Rose! Rose!' The sounds were all around her. 'What do you think you're doing? Rose!'

More tears dripped. She appealed for help and found it. Mr Koppelberg had a mouth like you could pop a sweetie in. He wasn't shouting at her. She looked straight at him.

'Annie's dead,' she announced.

'Jesus!' snarled Teddy. Dad was on him in a moment:

'What did you say? There was no need for that!'

Rose hoped he meant Teddy's nasty word. She hated him! 'She's a pig!' said Teddy.

'That's enough!' Dad was real mad. Rose didn't care. Mr Koppelberg was on her side!

'Annie's dead,' she repeated, appealing to him.

'She's just upset,' said Diane, defending her to Dad and everyone. Rose was staring right into Mr Koppelberg's eyes. No, he wasn't like Tara after all. He was like the prince who kissed the Sleeping Beauty.

'Annie was only a doll!' Mel said scornfully. Rose turned on her savagely.

'She wasn't!' said Rose. 'She wasn't. She was real. She was my friend.'

'A dolly?' smiled Diep. Rose was triumphant. Mr Koppelberg understood. 'You'll have to come over and see mine. I collect them.' Rose's heart jumped. She wanted to. She wanted to go to his chalet to see the dollies. 'From all over the world.' He was grinning. The other men were staring at him.

Now Rose was grinning as well. It felt like her face was cracking where the tears had rolled down. But it was also like waking up in the morning when she found she hadn't died.

She looked at Teddy in triumph – until she saw Dad's face. Dad didn't like Mr Koppelberg. All of a sudden, Rose felt very, very angry.

'You collect dolls.' It wasn't a question from Dave, more of a statement. Sam Drury had put down his fork and was listening too.

'Sure. Antiques, china-faced, wooden ones, the lot.' Diep smiled, and Mel knew it was for her.

'Wow,' said Mel, 'they must be worth something.' He was turning to her; he knew she was on his side – even if they were all against him. *They're all ruining it*, thought Mel. *The best-looking guy I've ever seen, and they're ruining it. All of them!*

What would Diep think of them? She could kill the twins, mouthing and spitting like that. Mom was middle-aged – she couldn't have the hots for him – and Dad … just because he thought himself macho. Sometimes he was really insensitive.

It was the work he did! A policeman wouldn't be able to understand someone like Diep. Someone with soul. Because Diep liked dolls, Dad thought he was gay. And that creep Drury staring at him like that, popping eyes and bald head. It was written all over their faces. Trust *them*!

She could have held Diep close to her breast, cuddled him and … she could feel her face going hot. Diep was smiling, but his eyes weren't. He was hurt. She knew it.

Rose was staring at Mel now. It was Rose's fault too. The

kid might be cut up about her doll, but she had no need to behave like that. Mel glared at her, then looked at Diep. In a very clear voice she said:

'Diep, I think it's so interesting. You should go over to Annalee. There's a factory in the wood. The Doll Museum. I'd love to come over and see your dolls. Oh!' A sudden pain made her catch her breath, draining it away. She stiffened. Her tension increased the dart that seemed to be skewering her upper arm. It felt like a big pin being poked in and out of the muscle.

Sam Drury kept on eating and no-one else noticed. Then the sharpness suddenly receded. She'd never had a pain like that before. *Gee, what's the matter with me?* The breathless words echoed in her brain, making Mel feel queasy. And no-one had noticed. Not one of them. They didn't care. Then she saw his eyes, swivelling towards her.

Bonny Blue Eyes, sang in her brain. *Bonny Blue Eyes*, called Rose's voice, but her mouth wasn't speaking.

'Sure, you must come,' Diep said to Mel, and she forgot her pain. 'And Rose as well.'

The softness in his voice made Mel feel better right away, as though he was giving her a spoon full of medicine like Mom did when she was a little girl and had tummy ache. This guy had to be him. She knew Diep Koppelberg was the guy she'd been waiting for all her life.

Dave didn't know what was up with all of them. He'd never seen them behave so badly, nor so strangely come to that. And he didn't like Koppelberg. But, if he could do something for Pip …

The boy wasn't his usual self either. Although he couldn't speak, nor hear, nor do what the others did, when he ate downstairs you knew he was there, scribbling on his pad, fun on his face, up to mischief. It was like he wanted to make up to them for what he was, to compensate for what Dave had done to him.

Dave looked at Di, who was chatting to Koppelberg as if she hadn't even noticed the rest of her family. Dave was angry inside. Why the hell did looking at her and Pip make him feel so guilty?

Dave stared at his plate. How could he sit here eating as if nothing was happening, when he was full of the strongest sense of disgust he'd ever had. Disgust with himself! It was like a sudden pain shooting through him and spreading through everyone.

If he hadn't been out in the storm in the first place, the accident would have never happened. He'd lied to Diane, said it was safe, that there weren't any storms about. He knew she was terrified of them, terrified of being alone, but he'd still gone with Pip.

Because he liked football. It had been his only afternoon off for ages. He'd wanted to take the boy to the game. So he'd taken no notice of Di. And he'd done that to Pip.

The meat felt bitter in his mouth, as callous as those thoughts in his brain. He could have spat out the food, like Rose. He pushed back his plate. He ought to be talking to Stella Drury. Sam's wife was obese, and about as objectionable as the Mayor himself. He was sick of the whole project. It stank.

This man was going to be no good to Pip. They had had to invite Stella and Sam Drury to dinner, just so they could suck up to them. 'Dolls, eh?' he murmured, almost to himself. But Stella must have heard, because she wiped her mouth with her napkin and looked up.

'Umm, delicious! I never could stand dolls. I used to pull their heads off and their legs. I liked boys' things to play with!'

She was an extremely ugly woman with a Teutonic accent that had never left her after 20 years in Sunny Mead. Her parents were immigrant German and had been exceptionally severe with their only daughter.

Stella had been deprived in her girlhood. She had determinedly pushed those sour old Europeans out of her life. She'd been glad when they'd both died, but she still felt guilty. It had been the dolls that had done it. All her father had ever given her when she was a child were wooden ones. No wonder she'd hacked their heads off. She'd never had a proper doll. She'd begged for a china baby, not a stiff wooden one with a painted face; the kind those old Germans had made.

Brunswick? Where the hell was that anyway? Stella wiped her mouth again. There was sweat running between her breasts.

'Umm, just lovely,' she said, picking up a large amount of food on her fork. It was poised before her mouth, 'See, Mr Koppelberg, Di's a wonderful cook. Done to a turn.' Stella filled her mouth. She chewed. The new music teacher was a strange-looking young man, blond like her father. He had the same alert look. That made Stella less than keen on him. And his name?

She pursed her mouth as she chewed, trying to think. Koppelberg … She sucked in her cheeks, making her look like a very old woman rather than one of 55. Diep Koppelberg. It was a strange name. It must have originated from Germany.

'Yes, I do,' he said.

Was he answering her question? Stella glanced up quickly, but their hostess was saying, 'Thank you, Diep. I'm glad you like the meat!' Diane looked extremely satisfied.

Suddenly, Stella was too! She blinked. Things were getting clearer. Surely Koppelberg was the place where … Immediately, she began to cough wildly and violently.

She clutched at her throat and gagged. Her tongue felt like it was bursting from her head. Her eyes, glutinous and terrified, stared right out of their sockets. There was a rasping and a rattling in her lungs. Her face turned blue. The veins in her head and neck distended and swelled.

'She's choking!' screamed Diane.

Dave's chair went backwards with a crash. He caught hold of Stella, who was slumping forward onto the table like an ugly rag doll. But she was still conscious.

He dragged her out of her chair, bent her over so that her head was lower than her chest and slapped her hard between the shoulder blades with the heel of his hand.

After no response, his police training went into full

practice. Gripping her in the prescribed position, he hugged her, forcing out the piece of meat blocking her throat. It shot straight from her gullet onto the table. Suddenly, she was coughing again.

'Thank God,' cried Di. Mel put a hand to her mouth in horror. She looked towards Diep for support but his face was impassive. He seemed to be concentrating on Dad's emergency action. He didn't know what to do either, just like her. She was proud of her dad, but he was a policeman.

Dave had managed to dislodge the meat, but it had been touch and go. Stella had been lucky not to have had a heart attack, given her size and everything. None of them had any appetite for dessert, but Rose and Teddy didn't seem to have been affected.

Teddy was glowing inside. He had that buzz again when Mrs Fat Drury choked. It had been so exciting. Like when the ball had flown over the lake and that sizzling had gone all down his body right into the earth.

He was proud of his dad, but Mr Koppelberg would have been able to do it too. Teddy knew that. But Dad hadn't given him a chance and Diep had been ever so nice to old Mrs Fat. After she'd thrown up, he'd held her hand. Teddy stirred his dessert into a globular mass and sucked the spoon.

Rose licked the red cherry. She wouldn't have been nice to that silly old cat. She wouldn't call Mrs Drury a cow because she liked cows. Rose had been very interested when Mrs Drury choked. She wouldn't have cared if she had died, because she was a doll killer, a torturer. She deserved it.

I bet Mr Koppelberg felt like that as well. He was only trying to be nice to her, thought Rose, smashing the cherry, mangling it with her tongue, sucking its juice. She had seen him holding Stella's hand. Rose was angry when Mrs Drury had pulled it away. She wouldn't have.

The Drurys left soon after. The incident had unnerved them all. In fact, the whole dinner party had been a disaster. Diep and Dave needed to help Stella to the car. She still looked a bad colour.

Diane passed a hand over her forehead as she watched them get her in. Stella Drury had nearly choked to death in her house! And there had been no opportunity to discuss anything about the project with Sam.

The men were returning up the path again. Diep's blond hair was like a halo under the security light.

'Don't worry, Diane,' he said, 'she'll be over it soon.'

'She's lucky,' said Dave as he ushered his wife and Diep Koppelberg back into the hall. Suddenly he was glad that the music teacher had seen what a policeman could do. But he was sorry for Di, very, very sorry.

All of a sudden, Diep Koppelberg had his arm around Di's shoulders. 'Don't worry,' he repeated again, 'there'll be another time,' he said.

What the hell was the music teacher talking about? What did he know and Dave didn't? What had Diane and he been arranging?

10

'In Tartary I freed the Cham,
Last June, from his huge swarm of gnats;
I eased in Asia the Nizam
Of a monstrous brood of vampire bats'.

The nightmare was hideous. Pip could hear his inside voice screaming. But he couldn't scream! He was dumb! Although awake, he was still half in it ... The rat had been on his chest, then it had scampered off. He thought he could hear its shining claws scampering around and around, twisting over the slippery floor. He couldn't get it out of his mind. It was real.

He tried to shake it out of his head. Perhaps it was because he'd had Cass in bed with him a couple of nights before. She had run like a little, white, bumpy ghost from the top to the bottom of his duvet. But this wasn't Cass ... It had a mouth like a human. It could talk. A small mouth with thin, real lips.

Pip banged his head on the pillow, trying to shake the dream out. He had to get up. And look. He stretched a small, cold hand towards his light and switched it on. The action shattered the glass bulb into pieces. Oh, Jesus, he was in the dark! And the rat was out.

He tried to calm down. He wasn't still in the nightmare,

he couldn't be. He'd just tried his light. It had just been a dream, one of those nasty things that happened to people; which reminded them there was something behind everything, that there was something beneath the surface of the world.

He took some big deep breaths like Mom had told him to when he got into a panic. But he could still hear it scampering. How could he hear it? He couldn't hear.

He stretched up his arms into the dark air of his room, as if pleading for help. He'd have to go down. In the lift! He was too scared. Too scared to move. He'd just lie there a minute, then maybe it would go away. The 13-year-old tried to rationalise things. It had just been a dream. A dream about him and a rat. His new music teacher and a rat!

Pip felt sick. He forced himself to think about something else. But then that whole disgusting dinner came flooding back. He could have puked over the table! He had to keep his eyes on his own food, anything to stop himself being friendly with the music teacher. But the way he looked at you – it was like being pulled into a shining whirlpool with great long scissors.

Pip made a face, pushing the dream out of his head. It must have been because of the bites. That had been the beginning. Koppelberg had one on his thumb. That figured. But why didn't the guy cover it up?

And no-one had looked at it. Pip couldn't understand why! It was so bad it could have dripped in the sauce. It was a big bite, red and festering. Like the one on Teddy's foot! The thought sizzled through his consciousness like lightning.

Maybe the rat was his? Perhaps he'd let it out? The horror of it made Pip shake. Maybe it had got up to the attic? Come across from the chalet? Up Adams's storm drain? Maybe, maybe, maybe … Pip stared blankly into the darkness; deaf, dumb, and blind.

Cut it out. You're not blind. Was it speaking? Had it spoken? No, he'd said it. In his mind. Pip was sweating. He wanted to call Mom. But he couldn't, could he?

He'd have to go down in the lift. He couldn't see anything! He'd have to stay where he was. When he was ill he slept in their room. He wanted them.

He'd have to get up and go down in the lift. He was too scared. Too scared to go down in his own lift. He'd never been like this before.

Pip started to cry. His tears were the only warm thing about him. They ran down his cheeks as he stared up into the darkness of the rafters. He let himself keep sobbing. It was a kind of relief. Crying in the dark, while he could hear it scampering. It was still there. It had been a terrible dream …

Pip had started to go down the hole after Teddy and the ball lightning. It was only when he was inside the black storm drain he knew he'd never catch them up. They'd gone on ahead. He could hear them laughing, chattering, he could see them hand in hand in a collusion of terrible togetherness. He knew he would never catch them up, because he was a cripple.

They moved along so easily, but he couldn't. He was behind the mole, which was digging its blind way on through the earth in front of him, frantically pushing on through the tunnel.

There was earth in Pip's mouth. He couldn't speak. There was earth in his ears. He was dead. He was dead and buried!

He kept pushing up above him with his strong hands, pushing away the earth that was pressing on top of him, pushing back the black hat he was wearing. It was very tall, like a chimney pot, and went up, up to where the sky should have been; where he should have been, up in the sunlight somewhere, outside. But he had to follow Teddy.

He thought he would never do it when the tunnel suddenly opened out. His crutches had gone. His legs wouldn't carry him. He was limping, crawling. He'd never catch up.

The arch was very, very high. It was bright beyond, bright as day. He could hear the little guy laughing, chattering to someone. There was lots of chattering.

They'd never let him in. They wouldn't hear him, because he couldn't speak. He couldn't even crawl into the brightness, because he was a cripple.

You dickhead, he said to himself, full of loathing. *What are you doing? You can't go in there.*

Then a tall shape was filling the doorway arch. Pip couldn't see its face for the brightness behind, a red hellfire of brightness. He couldn't see its face, because the shape had its back turned, facing the flames.

'Dickhead,' it said in a high, squeaky voice. 'You dumb dickhead. Don't you know me?' It was Diep Koppelberg.

He was very, very tall. Pip was crawling towards him, his crippled legs uselessly dragging him unwillingly towards the music teacher's back, compelling him to follow. Now Pip could see him properly.

Koppelberg was huge. He was kneeling. His long shorts were in rags, hanging down his legs, fluttering in tatters, mildewed, red, wet, gold, mouldy, raggy. It was very, very hot.

Pip was sweating as he got nearer to the fire that was blazing behind Koppelberg. He was burning with heat, with shame. Koppelberg's buttocks were very near. Pip could see the bites and the red, raw skin.

As Pip came nearer, trembling, Koppelberg swivelled, turned, like a raging beast. He was only a horrible shadow. There was nothing to him.

Pip could see right through him like a lightning flash on the surface of Golden Pond. He wasn't real. But Pip was staring down at his dick, screaming and screaming inside his head.

Koppelberg had a rat for a dick! It was level with Pip's face. The great rat's head waved from side to side. It was sick. It was grinning. It was mocking him!

'Dickhead,' it said in Koppelberg's voice, opening its thin lips. The rat's scissored teeth made a bar for the end of its tongue, moist, soft, red, dripping.

'Now you know who I am. I'm Snipe. I'll snipe you, sniff

you out, nip you, bite you, dickhead, dickhead, dickhead!'
Obscenities were dripping from its wet-bud tongue,
imprisoned behind the sharp bars of its teeth. 'Speak, you
dickhead! Speak!' it commanded.

Pip screamed and screamed, and he could hear Teddy
laughing. Then Snipe was jumping down, down on top of
him, wriggling – and Koppelberg's image collapsed on top of
him, all over him.

He screamed and screamed inside until all that was left of
him – and Koppelberg – was a heap of bones, a cairn of
stones, mounting under the arch of darkness. Then the fire's
light was out.

On the top of the mound of ashes sat a head, Diep
Koppelberg's head. A doll's head with Koppelberg's face –
but eyeless sockets. The light blue fire of his eyes was gone, a
broken skull, a sawdust brain – Bonny Blue Eyes – and
Teddy was singing that funny, funny song as Snipe, the rat-
penis scampered along the tunnel …

Pip banged his head against the pillow, trying to force the
dream out, but he couldn't, because it was still scampering
around his bed. Was it Snipe? Was it him? Shocking fear
made Pip stiffen. If it was – he swallowed down the sick in
his throat – he'd *have* to get out of bed and switch on the
other light.

He tried to rationalise those dark dream-fears. It was only
a dream. Maybe Cass had got out. God, if she had, she'd
have Bufo! He'd have to get up and switch on the light. But
he was too scared. Too slow.

Pip was sweating heavily, shaking. He couldn't
understand why he could hear scampering! He was deaf,
locked in a prison of his own making. He knew he could hear
once, could speak once! Pip felt stinking, hellish fear as the
scampering continued. What if Snipe bit him?

Like a flash of lightning across his consciousness, he
thought of Teddy. Snipe! Snipe had bitten Teddy! The big
rat-penis had come up the storm drain, wriggled its evil, red,
bursting way up from the hole and bitten his brother. Now it

was in Pip's room. He was screaming inside his head. He had to get to Mom and Dad. He had tried to tell himself it had been a dream when he had seen the ball lightning playing its ugly game. He must be dreaming again!

He put out one naked, defenceless foot, searching gingerly for the floor, then felt around for his crutches. The darkness had become merely dim now, a ghostly twilight as his eyes grew accustomed to it; where every light is a crack in the wall; every mirror, a dazzling slit; every block of furniture, a looming ghost. His blind little hand waved helplessly, looking for his crutches.

There! He had them! The feel of their handles gave him courage. Where were his slippers now? It couldn't bite him if he had his slippers. If only the light hadn't gone. He had to get to Bufo, light up the toad waterfall so he'd be safe.

But there were no slippers in the usual place. His feet would have to go unprotected. Hair wet with sweat, flipping across his eyes, Pip hopped forward, fixing his dark-blind eyes forward onto where he knew the looming mountain was – and the light switch.

It was quiet now except for his own thundering heartbeat filling his head and ears; pulsating in his neck, driving his freezing blood rhythmically in tune with his faltering steps. Hop, click, hop, click, went Pip and his crutches towards Bufo's mountain.

Then his foot got it first. Cold, wet. He screamed a wordless scream as his sensitive, vulnerable toe struck the mass on the floor. Its jelly coldness ran up through his body, making his teeth chatter.

Pip balanced on one leg, disabled by the reaction from his quivering foot, which had been shocked into disobedience. He *couldn't* move. He felt on the edge of fainting, but if he fell he would fall into it, whatever it was. Someone had crapped on his floor! He had to go round it. Still balancing, he used his crutch like he'd seen the guys do in war movies, when they were looking for mines.

His moving foot touched the mass again. Pip felt sick at

what was hanging onto his toes. Somehow, he had to make the light. *Sweet Jesus*, he prayed, *let me get to the switch!*

The toad mountain was looming. Pip was gasping with fear. One more lurching step and he launched himself forward and clawed for the light, his fingers painfully scraping down the wall, taking one of his nails.

Gentle Jesus, meek and mild ... He kept saying it over and over again in his head – the little prayer he'd learned at school – *Look on me a little child!* But it was still between his toes. In the sudden, blinding brightness of that attic room, he dared not look down.

He did. Finally. His stomach turned in a whirling, retching mass. There was slime on his foot. It wasn't crap. It was something else.

Scissors of fear ran along his scalp, zings of electric nerves ran their shrieking little way down the back of his neck, down his backbone and through to that obscene gloop in which he'd trodden.

He swallowed, gagged back the bile – and looked. What was left of Bufo was half of him, split and globular. Pip's foot had separated one of his legs. One glutinous eye stared balefully up at his shaking master, the other was gone and the socket and head were ripped right open.

Pip closed his eyes and swayed. One of Bufo's legs was stuck between his big toe and his first toe. He had trodden on Bufo! He couldn't have done all that, but he'd helped. What he couldn't bear were the half-eaten raw mass and the scraps of skin about. Bufo's skin had been torn off and the flesh nibbled beneath.

Snipe had done it. In his mind was that terrifying picture, that terrible little red penis-bud, sniffing and licking over Bufo's remains, the barbed teeth tearing out his flesh.

Pip swallowed the bile in his throat, heaving with sobs, shaking his foot to get rid of what was left of his pet. All that remained in his mind was that terrible image and the knowledge that only a scavenging bird or a rat will eat the flesh of a toad. Snipe had been there. The rat was loose. He prayed then for all of them, for Bufo and for all of them.

There was worse to come. Cass had gone. His pretty white rat had disappeared. Her cage was open. He knew he hadn't left it like that. He was so careful. He couldn't call her because of that bloody prickling sensation in his throat that stopped him speaking. His bleeding nail prevented his fingers from drumming.

He had shaken Bufo's leg off his foot, and as he stood there, defenceless, he felt a traitor. Maybe Cass had been the murderer? She had got out and she had killed Bufo. He might have left the door of the cage open. He was guilty and sick all at once, thinking of that horrible possibility.

All of a sudden, Pip seized his crutches hard and beat on the floor in a desperate paroxysm of fear, anger and despair.

Diane and Dave sat bolt upright in bed, looking up at the attic ceiling. Then, both of them were falling out of bed and running through the door.

Back in her neat little bedroom on Maple Street, Stella Drury wasn't so lucky. She woke with a pain in the chest, left arm and leg. She couldn't even move to tell Sam. The Mayor was snoring like a beast while his wife tried to fight that crushing steamroller of pain that clamped her arm and chest. Sam's uvula swung to and fro like a flap in his throat, letting the hoarse whistling of his strangled voice escape in rasping proportions. Behind his back, with the arm that was free of pain, Stella was clutching for the telephone, her useless leg trying to kick at Sam's, trying to wake him up.

But her heart had had it. Inside, a massive clot stopped dead in its tracks, blocking the artery. The machine of her heart couldn't break through that red light. It would never be 'Go' any more for Stella Drury.

All those fatty deposits had blocked the way. The frantic driver that had kept her body going for 55 years, was faltering. Stella's jaw felt thick and strange; as though it was pressing down on her neck. She was dizzy and cold, so cold. The engine of her pulse was winding down. A steamroller was crushing the life out of her.

With a convulsive jerk and a gagging sound, a massive heart attack arrested the life of a woman whose only crime was that the name Koppelberg had reminded her of a mountain in Germany where, on 22 July 1376, a tall blond boy had led a procession of dancing children; chattering, laughing children clutching their dollies; down into the depths of his unknown heaven. Yes, it had been a pity that Stella Drury's folks had come from Brunswick.

Diane sat on the edge of the bath, watching Dave. What a week it had been! 'Do you think that choking on the meat might have started it?'

Dave could see Diane's white-faced reflection in the bathroom cabinet mirror. It had probably contributed; but he was going to lie for her sake. 'No. A heart attack can get you anytime. It might have been coming on for weeks.' That worked. Di was smiling just a little.

Then the smile disappeared, leaving her face sombre, peaky, almost showing her age. Dave had never noticed before that Di's neck was a wee bit saggy.

A close but quick glance confirmed his neck wasn't like that – but he thought he could see a new crop of white hair, sprinkling the dark behind his ears. Now Di was regarding him critically.

The rest of her looked great, a good figure, broader round the hip now – she'd been skinny when they'd married. In that nightshirt she was desirable. Her eyes were provocative.

She looked at him from under narrowed lashes, 'Yes, you are going grey!'

Why couldn't she have said something else?

She got up and bent over the basin, picked up her toothbrush and squeezed half an inch of candy-striped toothpaste on to it. She was looking at herself in the mirror now. 'I got a feeling this is the end of the project,' she said, holding his reflection.

'Don't look on the black side,' he said, putting his arms round her from behind. She didn't respond. In fact, she stiffened.

'Drury will never get round to anything now. Not after this. He was bad enough before. I can't see him in the mood to discuss something as low-priority as this.' Her voice was bitter.

She didn't seem to notice that Dave's hands had moved up to her breasts and were playing with her nipples. She didn't want to notice. Then Di sighed, looked up at the ceiling, but the sigh had irritability in it.

'What are you thinking?' Dave asked.

'Pip behaved like a little moron at the dinner-party!'

That was the harshest thing he'd ever heard her say about their son. Normally, she made allowances for everything. It was probably because she was upset about Stella Drury. Maybe she blamed herself. But that was ridiculous. 'That's not a very nice thing to say,' he said slowly, bringing his hands down about her waist. 'You don't fancy it tonight, do you?' He did. He needed her warmth.

Then she was swivelling in his arms, away from him. He let her bend down and scrub her teeth viciously, spitting out the white foam. She clenched her teeth together, grimaced into the mirror, examining them, put out her hand for the floss. He passed it to her.

She drew the string up and down and through her teeth, pulling out every minute particle. Now Dave sat on the side of the bath and watched her. It was hard being married. But they were still together.

Suddenly, he was wondering if she'd ever been unfaithful to him. It just came like one of those thoughts that strike you dumb. He was thinking of Koppelberg with his arm about her shoulders in that easy, companionable way.

She finished, satisfied. 'I'm tired,' she said. 'Are you

coming to bed?'

'In a moment,' he answered. The desire had drained right out of him.

They lay in bed stiffly, not touching each other. Di didn't want his warmth. He knew that. Stella's death had upset her a lot. It had upset him as well. And it had nearly happened in their house. He wouldn't have wanted the twins to have seen. They were little and tough, but death shouldn't touch them yet. Not if he had anything to do with it.

Mel? He hadn't liked the look on her face either when she had been staring at Koppelberg. She hadn't been able to take her eyes off him all night. Dave had to admit that it took a father a long, long time to adjust to his own daughter's sexuality – if ever. Somehow the idea of Mel doing it with Koppelberg crept into his brain and made him want to retch.

And Pip? He hadn't taken his eyes off the man either. What was with this guy anyway? Pip's manners had been bad, granted, but you had to make allowances for the boy.

Usually Dave wasn't soft on his son. He had to teach him it was a hard world out there. But, in spite of that, there was a close bond between them. Pip had had a bad time in the last couple of days. The death of Bufo had been such a shock to him. Dave hated rats. He'd like to have caught hold of that miserable pet rodent of Pip's and broken its neck. But the boy shouldn't have left the cage open. Still it was a shit that it had all happened.

Treading on your pet's oozing remains in the dark! It made Dave's stomach turn, and he was used to everything. They hadn't found Cass although they had hunted everywhere for her. Dave hoped they wouldn't. The deviousness of rats was really something.

Dave, himself, didn't like thinking about it. He knew rats were intelligent, but the idea of it stripping the flesh off a pet toad and eating its guts revolted him just the same.

He snuggled himself into Di's back and thought again about Stella Drury's fight for life. She had evidently struggled against the heart attack, because she had been found lying half in, half out of bed with the telephone knocked off the receiver. She must have been trying to get help. Sam had been distraught when he'd called him in.

Dave's mind went over the events. Stella had been a heavy woman, difficult to move. And she wasn't a pretty sight. Dave thought of Diane and how he'd noticed her neck. How long would it be before they both got old? Stella had been only in her mid fifties. Dave swallowed. Drury hadn't even closed her eyes. What would it be like to wake up and find your wife dead beside you? It was funny how people just went. He'd always wanted to die naturally, rather than violently.

Every time he buckled on his gun he thought about that. But Sunny Mead wasn't like some big city. They'd got a different kind of hood. But to fall asleep and wake up dying – well, that idea really was enough to spook you.

He wondered how Koppelberg was settling in. Maybe he'd go over to the chalet and have a look. Probably lives like a pig! It was such a strong thought that Dave opened his eyes wide in the darkness.

Di's breathing was rhythmical. She was already asleep. He wished too that she'd never thought of her project. Look what it had done to them already. For the second time in the last hour Dave had sensed that Koppelberg was bad news. He didn't know why, but there was a distinctive hostility between them. Dave wasn't a jealous man, but the guy seemed to be getting to his family. How, he didn't know, because he'd only just met them.

But there was one thing Dave was sure of: he was going to keep his eye on the music teacher for as long as he stayed in Sunny Mead.

What remained of Stella Drury was not insubstantial.

'Shit, feels like a ton,' said one of the bearers under his breath. The four men carried the heavy coffin for about two hundred yards to the graveside. There were a lot of people at the funeral. Even though most of them didn't care for Sam, Stella had been well-liked.

The day was hellishly hot with the threat of a storm. In fact, as Stella's casket was manoeuvred over the grave, the thunder growled over Branksome. Sam Junior was crying when the rope slipped and they dropped his mother in the ground. Tears didn't fit with the macho image he'd been cultivating for the last two years at JBH. But the athletic form of the sportsman looked well in a black suit. And more than a few of the girls noticed.

Sam had had the church bell rung in respect for his wife. Its tinny tone reminded them all of their mortality as Stella was laid to rest in a grave that lay only a mile away from Adams's storm drain.

The storm was crouching over the lake now, enveloping the chalets in an eerie darkness. Inside 107 Camellia Grove, Diep Koppelberg bent over the heavy wooden table, writing in the dust with the pointed tip of his iron-hard nail.

GOODBYE, DOLL KILLER

The clear, red flourish of farewell oozed a thin trail of blood, dripping from his perfect flesh, which had been raised over the age-old skeleton of his bones.

His ancient trophies, his own particular brand of hell, stared glassily from the long coffin cases propped up against the wall, willing their master to effect once more a hasty resurrection.

'I want to go and see his pets!' Teddy's stubborn tone battered Diane's skull.

'He didn't ask you! He asked Pip,' said Diane sharply. She was still wearing the black cocktail dress that had been about the only thing she could find suitable for Stella's funeral. She wasn't in the mood for the twins' tantrums.

'He asked *me* to go and see his dollies,' said Rose.

'Yes, Rose, but not now! Do you think you two could go out and play for a bit until Mel comes back?' She was busy at the store.

'Nothing to play with!'

'Please?' said Di, filling the kettle. She hoped the twins were not going to be impossible. She was tired, and funerals always made her feel miserable. She had a lot on her mind. Too much. Dave had had to go to the station again and Pip hadn't been well since losing Bufo and the rat.

The whole thing spooked her. She half expected to see the toad pop out on the drainer or whatever. Deep down in her heart, she was really glad it was gone, but she was sorry for her son. Perhaps Diep had a pet that could make up for its loss? It was a new thought that cheered her a little bit. He seemed to have taken to Pip anyway, despite him being very awkward.

The kettle boiled and Diane made herself an instant coffee. She sat down and started thinking about the funeral again. Poor Stella! What a shock it had been, her dying so suddenly. Who'd have thought it? Diane put down her mug. That worry still nagged her. That awful dinner party! She shook her head. Everything had seemed wrong. She'd invited the Drurys to try and make up for the falling out she'd had with Sam over the school scheme. If she hadn't, Stella might be still alive. She'd never forget how she'd choked on that meat.

As for the scheme – she felt guilty even thinking about it now. She hoped she wasn't that selfish to put her own concerns before those of the Drurys. Poor Stella. And poor Sam! All one could do was to be sorry for him right now. This was *not* the time to be thinking about her ongoing feud, she told herself. But the scheme had been in the forefront of her thinking for so long, that she couldn't help herself wondering if Stella's death might make any difference to the Mayor's outlook. Of course, she wouldn't have admitted that to anyone but herself.

Who knows how the death of someone close really affects a person? She tried to imagine how she'd feel if she lost Dave. It didn't bear thinking about. She guessed she'd just go into her shell and not bother with anything. But, of course, she'd have the kids to think about. Then she thought about Sam Junior. How was he going to cope, losing his mother? It was all so depressing.

She sighed again and tried to focus on something else. Maybe Diep would play some music for them today. That might cheer them all up. Suddenly things seemed much, much brighter, especially when she saw the twins' fair heads bent close together beneath the kitchen window. They were friends again! More like partners in crime, smiled Diane, thinking of their inexhaustible enthusiasm for mischief. No wonder they got on so well with Diep. The music teacher was like a big kid himself.

11

*'And folks who put me in a passion
May find me pipe to another fashion.'*

Sam Junior loped head down, looking from side to side. The tongues of his high-tech trainers flopped limply like those of thirsty dogs. He was just bursting with anger – about Mom – about everything.

He kicked a dead Coke can, sending its battered body wanging against the wall of S J Hairdressing Co. He'd have liked to have kicked it right through the window instead. That was where he used to go and have his hair cut when he was a little kid. He knew the old guy who worked in there and all those sitting waiting to have theirs done. But no-one waved to him or nothing.

He could *feel* them gawping. He was used to that, because he was a great ball-player. Even the old guys used to come up and say so, then tell him how good they'd been themselves. And girls! Well, they couldn't keep their eyes off him. Now they weren't looking at his pecs, only feeling sorry for him. *He didn't want them to feel sorry for him.* Sam Junior breathed in and flexed his six pack. He hadn't changed. He was the same. He hadn't got the plague. He stared into the barber's. One guy nodded, but the rest looked the other way, or down at their dirty mags.

'Fuck you,' he muttered. 'Fuck you all! My mom's died. So what? She wasn't *your* mom. She was mine.' He was sorry for himself – and it was his own business. No-one else's. He put his hand under his windcheater and felt the Smith and Wesson .38 calibre, comfortable against his chest. He'd been feeling crazy when he'd taken the pistol out of Dad's cupboard. And it had made him feel better at first, like he was protecting himself. *'Why did you have to die, Mom,'* he said to himself. *'Everything's changed!'* Then a guy he knew, who was coming along, just stepped off the pavement and crossed the road.

'Hey, man, I'm here!' he shouted, and the guy pretended not to hear. He'd have liked to have blown him away. No-one cared that his mom was dead and buried. Why had it happened to her? For Chrissake, why? Why not some dumb kid from school? He needed her.

Mel Durrant was jogging towards him. She worked out every morning. Was she going to cross over too? She'd been at the funeral, wearing a black skirt and a black top. Her shoulders were brown toasted. He'd wanted her then to hold on to, but she'd been standing with her dad and her mom – who was alive. He'd wanted her like when they'd necked at the drive-in three Saturdays ago.

Mel was cool. She looked great. He was sure she wouldn't cross over. Her shorts hardly covered her ass. She wasn't wearing a bra! The football player watched her neat breasts as she approached him. But she had the same look on her face as all the others! Sam Junior, who had never wanted for anything, because his mom gave him everything, waited to see if Mel was going to cross over out of his way.

Mel was sweating freely, blowing the air out of her lungs in tune with her running action. Her first impulse was to pretend she hadn't seen him – the green visor of her peaked cap was dense enough. You just couldn't walk up to someone and say, calmly, 'Hi, Sam. Sorry your mom's dead!' Not like that, anyway.

Mel knew she should have been comforting him – but she'd gone off him. Things just changed from day to day now. Three weeks ago she could have eaten him alive. He'd given her a massive love bite on her shoulder, which had taken some hiding from her mother. Funnily enough, when she'd seen him at the graveside – a big, raw-boned kid – she'd known she didn't want him anymore. When had she begun to feel that? Probably when Diep Koppelberg had come. Diep was *so* beautiful.

Slowing down, she swallowed, put her hand up to her visor and brushed the sweat from her forehead. She stood, and a thin sliver of wind cut coldly along her hairline. Big Sam – that's what they called him at school – was right up against her now. Mel still stood her ground.

'Hi, how are you?' It came out easily enough, but the words seemed to stick in her throat as surely as the meat had in his mom's. She shivered momentarily as he slipped his long arm round her shoulders. 'What are you going to do now?' she added, looking up at him. The boy shrugged.

They strayed on together towards Branksome. They could hear a kid shouting. Mel was sure it was Teddy's voice. Early though – for him. Her brother was a lazy little devil. Rose was the one who got up.

They came round the corner below Adams's. The lake lay in the grey cool of morning, its corrugated surface lapping and licking the grassy shore. The front lawn of Diep Koppelberg's lakeside chalet was long, ending in a wooden landing stage with a springboard where the kids jumped off all summer. In an hour or so lots of them would be there. Mel might go herself – but not with Sam. She was thinking about being beside Diep in her bikini.

The two teenagers stared. The man and the boy were playing ball with unbelievable energy. Teddy was like a ball himself, bobbing and weaving, while the tall slim frame of his new music teacher pirouetted close about him.

Once, when Teddy got the ball from between Diep's legs, they collapsed laughing on the lawn, squeezing down the daisies and the goldenrod in a childish, puppy dog roll.

Mel felt like an interloper watching her brother and Koppelberg. He was more of a kid than Teddy himself – but such a hunk of a guy too! She could feel the same sharp pain in her side that she'd felt when the Drurys had come to dinner. It made her heart jump. 'Phew,' she said under her breath, thinking maybe it was her appendix.

Sam was silent, his arm making a lazy half-bracelet about her neck. If his mother hadn't died so recently, she would have shaken him off.

'What an asshole,' Sam said. Mel was so angry. She knew what he was thinking. A moment of innocence spoilt by such a shit remark, just because Teddy was splayed on Diep's back like a funny, ungainly little tortoise.

'Why don't you shut up?' she said.

'Who does he think he is?' said Sam Junior viciously. 'First team material?'

There was no need for any of it.

Diep was getting to his feet and Teddy rolled off him quickly, this time like a small, abandoned dog. The six-year-old righted himself with his hands, and then he too was standing erect, facing his sister and Sam Junior. Diep and Teddy walked slowly towards them. Diep was bouncing the orange ball, making its chalk teeth chatter like a cartoon flinging by.

Mel could feel the cold wind again. Then Teddy was on her, pulling at the bottom of her shorts. 'Let go, Teddy.' He was hanging on to them.

'Mel, my ball's back! Diep found it in the storm drain! It's back!'

'Great,' she said, happy for him.

'By the way you two were using it, it could have stayed there,' drawled Sam. Mel had never seen him so nasty before, but she also knew it was a challenge to this newcomer, who didn't know Sam Junior was the ace player in John Branksome High football team.

Men, she thought, shaking her head imperceptibly,

wondering how Diep would react.

As the music teacher continued to bounce the ball, he suddenly seemed very much taller. The rubber sphere obeyed his sharp, dexterous palm as if bewitched. He turned and began to run across the grass, together with the ball, which seemed to have a life of its own.

Mel looked down at her little brother; his eyes were shining with hero-worship. Then, in the middle of the lawn, Diep stopped, his light body taut like a string, fine-muscled and controlled. While the ball bounced on rhythmically under his commanding palm, he put up the other hand and motioned scornfully to Sam Junior.

'Come on, then. Come and get it.'

In one moment, Sam was throwing off his windcheater. Mel gasped as she saw the shoulder holster. The crazy kid was wearing a gun. Diep was laughing. It didn't worry him.

Teddy was pointing. 'Look, Mel, it's a .38 calibre!'

'Come on, then! Come on! Come and get me!' Diep's voice was high and taunting, but he had a grin on his face. Mel and Teddy began to laugh – though, afterwards, Mel would see there was nothing funny about what was to happen. Next moment the guys were facing each other.

Sam Junior looked across the lawn. It would be great, he thought, to make this new guy look an asshole in front of Mel. He seemed to think he owned the place. Maybe he could do with a taste of what a big guy from JBH could give him?

Mel looked at Sam, at Diep, then down at her little brother, who had sensed an impending battle.

'Diep will win! He will!' Teddy's voice was high and piping, while he wriggled beside her like a small electric eel. Mel shook her head. Why did guys always behave like this? A hostile Sam was staring at Diep.

'You wanna work out then?' he challenged. Mel shivered at the tone.

Diep was nodding slowly, a lithe, bright figure in his red and yellow. He was holding the ball tightly. It sat, quietly tucked under his arm, held there by his elbow, while his other hand stood on his hip like he was waiting for someone to tackle him.

'Wowwwweee! It's gonna be football!' Teddy's voice was even higher, more excited. 'They're going for a down!'

'Don't be silly. There's only two of them!' Mel couldn't take her eyes off Sam's gun, which hugged against his T-shirt. Had he gone crazy or something? What would Diep think?

Then Sam Junior's big body wasn't beside her anymore. He was making for Koppelberg.

'Come on, let's see how good you really are, asshole!' muttered Sam to himself as he ran onto the lawn. The new guy's arrogant face made Sam want to punch him right in the mouth.

'Okay, let's see how great *you* are!'

Sam blinked as the thin hiss of the words cut through the morning air. Surely the prick couldn't have heard him! Sam glanced quickly at Mel, but she was staring at Koppelberg. The Mayor's son felt jealousy flow right through him. Mel had the hots for the guy!

Sam turned and stared at his opponent. Yeah, a workout wouldn't do him any harm. Sam assessed the match, deciding on his approach.

Diep was a tall, slim guy, a wimp, whereas he himself was heavy and powerful. Sam had the advantage: maybe not at basketball, but at football for sure.

'Go for it!' screamed Teddy suddenly.

'Shut up!' said Mel, assessing the situation for herself. She didn't want to see Diep hurt. There was an ugly brutality about Sam Junior when he was angry – and he'd been angry ever since she'd met him that morning. Why were guys so stupid? Always having to prove themselves.

'Why don't the two of you knock it off?' she shouted. There was no need for any of it.

They crouched, facing each other – Koppelberg in possession of the ball – menacing each other across an imaginary scrimmage line.

Then, like a striking rattlesnake, Diep made a rush at Sam,

who was ready to block him – but wasn't quick enough. The shock of the impact had Sam on his back, winded. He shook his head and tried to get up. Diep was grinning as he struggled.

'Wow,' shouted Teddy, jumping up and down. 'Wowwweee!' His scream was a piercing whistle. 'Go for it, Diep!' Diep was just standing over Sam Junior.

Melanie winced. She knew Sam. He'd be up in a minute. Next moment he was on his hands and knees and Diep was moving away quickly.

'Hey, you guys, pack it in, will you?' she pleaded.

'Shut up, Mel!' Teddy's voice was sharp. Mel caught her little brother by the scruff of his neck.

'No, *you* shut up! Someone's going to get hurt. Hey, guys! Please … Guys!'

Then Diep kicked the ball with full force. It hit the struggling Sam full in the chest. Gasping, he started to topple and then righted himself, fumbling at its slippery surface. Controlling the ball, Sam stayed with it tucked under his arm, holding it with his elbow. He had possession.

His face was streaming with sweat and was very red. It was then that he saw Koppelberg coming. He tried to take evasive action but his opponent hit Sam with his shoulder just above the knees.

Sam toppled backwards towards the wet lawn. He could feel the music teacher's arms snake-tight round his legs, lifting him right off balance. With no protective gear, it was sheer murder.

'Stop it, *stop it!*' shouted Mel.

'Fumble, it's a fumble!' screamed the excited little boy beside her.

Mel ran onto the lawn and stood between the beaten Sam and triumphant Diep.

'Stop it, both of you!' Diep was grinning in the most relaxed way. He looked magnificent. 'You've made your point!' She was angry with him, but all the time she stared him in the eyes, she was thinking he was as good as any Redskins record-breaker.

Sam Junior was trying to get up. There was nothing in him but rage and hatred for the prick who'd outclassed him in front of his girl. His body ached; there was the salt taste of blood in his mouth. There were tears in his eyes. All he could feel was the hard imprint of the .38 calibre gun where it had added more bruises to his body when he fell.

Suddenly the rage in him turned to thoughts of murder. He just wanted to blow the guy away! With the whole of his bruised and humiliated self, he wanted to blow Diep Koppelberg's head off. And the guy kept on staring at him with mocking, arrogant eyes. Then, his lips twisted in a smile, Diep Koppelberg threw down Teddy's ugly, grinning ball.

'Okay, Mel, if this is what you want. Come on, Teddy, your mom says you need some practice. Music!' The taunt was obvious.

Mel stared at Diep. He was only a guy after all. And games were what guys took seriously.

'What else are you good at?' she asked in a teasing, challenging way, standing close to him.

'Most things.'

Mel felt hot. There was no mistaking his meaning. The smile about his mouth made him infinitely kissable. She shivered.

'Including swimming,' he added.

'Swimming?' They were both looking at the lake. She was thinking about her bikini – the black lace one – standing in it, beside him.

'Yeah, remind me to show you sometime,' he said. 'And the kids. You and I are gonna have a great time!' It was like Diep was reading her thoughts.

'You like kids, don't you?'

'I love them. I always have.' He said it simply, without a hint of embarrassment. 'But they grow up too quick.' She felt shaky with emotion. Diep Koppelberg had everything she wanted – tough and tender. But he was a strange guy. There wasn't one man in Sunny Mead who would have said what he did. None that she knew anyway.

She looked across at Diep's opponent. Sam Junior was seated on the ground, looking dazed. She felt she should have been sorry for him. But she wasn't – no JBH star could compete with Diep Koppelberg. In spite of his mom and everything, she found to her surprise that she didn't feel sorry for him at all. Still, she went over.

'Can you get up?'

'Yeah!' he growled, and Mel was afraid of the look in his eyes.

'Just leave him, Mel. He'll get over it,' said Teddy. For a moment Mel thought it was Diep who'd spoken, but the music teacher was walking away in the direction of his chalet.

'Where you going, Diep?' shouted Teddy, turning. 'I'm coming!'

Diep Koppelberg turned as well. 'No. You go home, Teddy,' he commanded. 'I'm just getting my flute. And getting changed!'

Teddy stood stock still, then he turned obediently and ran off in the direction of the house. Mel shook her head. Diep certainly knew how to handle her little brother.

Rose wondered if she dare go in. Diep was out with Teddy. They were playing football. Why did Diep want to play ball? With him? Teddy didn't want her now he'd got Diep. But Diep liked her a lot. She knew that – almost as much as Daddy!

Were there real dolls inside there? Diep had said she could see his dolls. She missed Annie. But it would be rude to go in without being asked. And Mommy had said never to go in a strange place, like she'd said never to talk to strange men. But Diep wasn't strange.

Rose squatted in front of the last of the three steps that led to Diep's apartment and squinted at the grass. There were ants everywhere. She didn't want them in her bottom. She wasn't going to sit down on the step after all.

So Rose bent right over and looked at them, just like rag-doll Annie did sometimes. But Annie was dead! She could see the steps through her legs. She had funny legs – all mottled at the top.

Suddenly Rose noticed the door to the chalet was open just a crack. She straightened up. Turned. Diep would have robbers go in if he left the door open. She'd just go up the steps and pull it to. Then she might see one of the dollies.

Rose went up slowly and carefully so she wouldn't put her foot through the wooden steps and fall. She didn't like open steps. The wood creaked and squeaked under her shoes. She'd only just peek and then she would … she wasn't sure yet just what she would do.

On the verandah, Rose held her breath. It was naughty. Mommy would be mad. Then she blew out, her cheeks scarlet with the effort. Diep had invited her! He had said so before Mrs Drury had choked on the meat.

She could see something just inside the door, and there was a real funny noise like in the zoo. Was it Diep's pets chattering and squeaking?

Rose gasped as she was grabbed from behind and held up in the air, her arms straight out like a squirming doll. Then with a little jump, he turned her. Diep held out the little girl twin at arms' length and he was grinning. He wasn't angry at all. He had a very nice face. He put it close to hers.

'Visiting?'

'I came to see the dollies. Can I, Diep, can I? You were playing with Teddy!' There was accusation in her voice. He laughed out loud and, bringing his face very close to hers, he kissed her. The kiss was like a burning, searing little pain in her cheek. It made her go zing, zing inside. She liked it.

'Not yet, honey. I gotta change.' He put her down and she grasped his leg. It was a funny cold leg, not like his kiss.

'Please, Diep?' She tugged at the red-gold cloth. He was looking down at her. Rose thought how big he was, much bigger than the prince in the story – but just as pretty though. She thought he was going to change his mind, because his tongue was creeping very nicely round his white teeth. His tongue was pointed. Wet!

Then he was stooping. He put his arms about her. She snuggled into them.

'Rose,' he said. His purring was a low growl. She liked it.

'Yes,' she replied. But it wasn't a question.

'Rose,' he repeated. 'That's a very nice name. I like roses …'

She was extra happy.

'… red and gold. When I was at home, a little girl brought me some roses.'

'Was she nice?' Rose felt jealous. 'Was she your little girl?'

'Yes, but she's grown up now. She's old.'

'But I'm not. Don't be sad, Diep!'

'Who's sad?' The force of his quick laughter made her jump. 'You crazy little doll! I'm not sad. I'm very happy! I just had my birthday.'

'Did you get a present?'

'No, but I'm getting one soon.'

'What, Diep, what?' She was jumping about in the circling protection of his arms.

'It's a secret.'

'Is it a dolly?' They both laughed and, quietening her, he put a pointed finger to his lips, then to hers.

'I won't tell anyone in the whole world.' She felt she loved him more than anyone. And he didn't smell a bit like her daddy when they were close. More like the woods, like when you picked up fir cones and they fell on the ground; a new smell. She closed her eyes and breathed it in. She kept them closed.

'Can I see your present, Diep?' She could feel his hot breath on her cheek. Would he kiss her again?

'You will, Rose. I promise. And I always keep my promises. Now, you get off back home and I'll be over in a minute. Go!' He put her down. She opened her eyes and he was straightening up, his long legs making an arch above her head. She looked up.

'Soon? You promised.'

'Go,' he said.

She ran off headlong at his command and, in a second, she was looking back, but Diep had already disappeared.

Pip was as scared as hell in case the dream came back. He didn't want to go to sleep at night anymore in case it did. His eyes ached from trying to keep awake. When he closed them he could still hear Snipe scampering about. And Cass had never come back.

He stared across at the tortoise Dad had bought for him. The reptile couldn't take Bufo's place nor Cass's. It was old and ugly. Like Koppelberg.

Nothing had been right since he came. And Mom was stuck on him, and Mel and the kids. They all were. All stuck on him – and they didn't know him.

Pip couldn't tell them how he was feeling. They'd think he was mad. Anyway, that dream had been disgusting – maybe it was just part of growing-up. He was sure that's what Mom would say. He was afraid he could see her lips saying it. If that was growing-up, he didn't want to. He wished he was very old like the tortoise.

There was only one thing. Now Mrs Drury was gone, Mom's plan couldn't work. She would have to send Koppelberg away. Sam Drury wouldn't want to be bothered with the idea of disabled kids when he'd just lost his wife.

Pip squeezed his eyes tight shut and prayed that Koppelberg would go away. He was as tired as that dog he had seen through his glasses, the one sleeping in the doorway of the hairdresser's, but he'd been afraid that if he put the binoculars down he'd miss something vital. He felt like he was the only one who could save them all.

There was Dad though. He didn't like the music teacher. Pip could sense it. But he'd do anything Mom said. And he was always so busy down at the station.

Pip kept his eyes closed, but the scariest thoughts were filling his head. He recognised their message. He wanted something to happen so Koppelberg would have to go.

Beating up Sam Junior didn't count. Pip had watched it all. There was no way Pip could fight Diep. The man was too strong. There had to be another way. What if something really bad happened again, like with Stella Drury?

He jumped and opened his eyes. Diane was shaking him gently. He read her worried mouth.

'Sorry. Were you asleep? You aren't ill, are you, Pip? You look pale.' She was feeling his forehead with a cool hand. She stopped, looked at him with pleading eyes, adding, 'Pip, I want you to come down. We're just going to practice with Diep. I know you can't hear any of it but it might just ... help – to see us?'

Pip was sorry for Mom, for himself, because she would think he was behaving badly. But there was no way he was going down there with him. He stood his ground. Diane squatted beside his chair.

'For *me*, Pip, please?'

He shook his head again, his hand trembling on the little pen. How could he write out all the horrible thoughts that were crowding towards him? She'd never understand. How could he tell her about the dream?

'Oh, well,' she said. 'We'll have to do without you then.' And there were tears in her eyes. She turned away from him, and he knew she was hurt. But there was nothing he could do. He could never, never let Diep Koppelberg get round him the way he'd got round them. Why couldn't they see what he was like?

He must have been trained at a conservatoire. Diane was truly astonished at Diep's consummate skill. They all were. Even the twins sat enraptured while Diep was playing. But she couldn't recognise the melody. Her head was swimming. It wasn't Mozart. At first she'd thought it was – Mozart was one of her favourites – but then it had become a *melange of* every other great master she loved. Not a parody, but a joy. Maybe it was some new piece? Whatever it was, the composer had pulled it off superbly. She told herself she would have to ask Diep, but then she lost track of any coherent thought, as the music seemed to captivate her, opening up her nature to Diep like a warm stream of consciousness. Mingling with him was the strangest feeling, mesmerising. Every tiny, meaningful moment of Diane's life was laid open and reflected in the rippling flute. She was drowning in the sound. Every sexy, salacious moment – every throb of life, wave of excitement, exultation of triumph, every damn wonderful, ugly thing she'd ever done – was back with her. Her excitement mounted. It was like having sex with him. No longer with Dave, but with Diep, Diep … Every note he played filled her senses like foreplay.

Her face was burning. Diane swallowed and darted a secret glance at her children. But they were ignorant of her thoughts, lost in their own, staring at him open-mouthed.

And, all the time, his eyes were as wide as theirs as he mouthed, drawing and pulling the life from his glorious flute as if it was a living thing.

And she couldn't get the melody out of her head. It was filling her brain; it wanted all of her. It was the most perfect experience of Diane's life. And Diep had brought it. The tears came then. She was crying for herself and for Pip, who was sitting dumbly upstairs, and had refused to listen to Diep's music.

All of a sudden, the staccato notes leading up to the climax of the piece transformed themselves into daggers of disappointment and resentment. As the experience withered and died, she was dragged back into the real world, which centred on the selfish son who had spoiled her pleasure.

As Mel listened to Diep play, her imagination drove her body to swing rhythmically from the waist, to dance to the tune as surely as the tortured girl in the fairytale was carried away on her heartless red shoes.

Mel hadn't thought of that story since she had cried over it at nine years old. She didn't know if the others could see her moving. She didn't care, but her fingers yearned for the oboe to take its own life from him and his flute. To join in his playing!

Her hands twisted about in her lap, wanting skirts to hide in. To play with him, to be played on with those slender fingers that explored the tortured rhythm! With a shudder she waited for the climax, so thin and painful, climbing to the very dizzy top of a mountain with Diep into the heat of his heaven. Physical ecstasy! She was pulling her jean-clad legs tight together in time to the music's tension, squeezing her pelvic muscles in and out in time with his playing.

There would be nobody but him. She would follow him out of Sunny Mead to the end of wherever.

Rose watched Diep. She loved him. Better than her daddy. Her fat little hands stroked the glossy, warm curve of her violin; slipped over its surface round its body as if it was a shiny, fresh-painted wooden doll.

Her palms explored the fretwork, making an imaginary face in her mind. Diep was smiling while he played. She wanted to play with him. His nice pointed nose, all wrinkled, sprinkled with gold. She loved him: loved him and his dollies. *I want to see your present, Diepee darling, sweetie …* Rose thought all those little things to him that her daddy said to her at night.

The flute's pretty crying made a tear trickle down her cheek for the prince who was changed into a toad. Bufo had been a prince and Bufo was dead. Two tears rolled down Rose's face, then three – poor Diep, poor Bufo, poor Annie. She loved them all.

Teddy was marching behind Diep along the scissored notes, up through the scales behind his golden-red hero, sword in his hand.

And the burnished ball bounced on before them, its

pumpkin head glowing with pride. Together they could take on the world – together they could do anything, anything together. They were invincible! He and Diep! Man and boy! Heroes! Teddy would march with Diep forever, and the cheerleaders would swing their batons and twirl their sticks and no-one could touch them; no-one could break that golden line as long as they stayed together always.

Upstairs in the attic, Pip spun round and round in his wheelchair, confused by what was happening, full of terror. His ears might be dead but his brain was spinning madly. It was as if unknown events downstairs were wafting up there, through and into his consciousness.

The animals could hear the whirl of Diep Koppelberg's flute; even the deaf young garter snake could sense danger and death. An exhausted Pip, head hanging in despair, watched the little guys going crazy again and knew that the music teacher was playing, waiting below, waiting for the only one who wouldn't follow him.

With a terrible, wordless scream, Pip put his hands over his ears, while his precious pets, crazed by the music, tormented out of their minds, lurched and battered themselves suicidally against their prison walls.

There was silence. Dazed, the twins looked at each other. The music had gone. Diep was laying the golden flute to rest in its special case, engraved with children who never stopped dancing, listening and following forever ...

Mel opened her eyes, stared emptily at Diane, whose response was dull and lifeless.

Diane looked round. Their house was drab and empty. He had finished. It was over. Diane flopped back in the chair and passed a hand over her forehead. She was very cold, yet her cheeks were bright red.

The corner of Diep's mouth worked in his clay mask of a

face, worked to bring the life to himself again, lulled by the strength of his flute. He could smell decay, the scent of new earth waiting. All that was superhuman in him cracked the clay mask of his face and brought its beauty back to life. 'Okay?'

Spontaneously, they began to clap, and Teddy brought his bow across the strings of his little violin, breaking two and not noticing. Rose was still sniffing. Diep came over to her. He reached down his hand and took hers.

'You're cold,' he said. 'I'm warm.' And she slid her trusting child's palm into his, bringing him young life and energy.

Rose was smiling at him through her tears, loving his moist pink tongue and his bright quick eyes. He reminded her of a lovely, sweet little animal, and she really cared about him.

His hand felt hotter now, instead of cold, hotter than a fire. It gave her the courage.

'Mommy, it's Diep's birthday, isn't it Diep? Can we have a party for him?'

Diep smiled at Diane and she came to, her bewitched mind discarding any earlier thoughts that might distract from his purpose. She yawned, stretched lazily as though she'd been sleeping, reaching back behind her head easily as though she had the whole of her life to live over again.

'Sure, honey. Diep can have a party any day he likes!'

'How about soon?' Diep said and, suddenly, the drowsy room was full of light. 'Remember, I don't have much time left!'

Sam Junior hung about the store. When the ice-cold coke hit the open nerve in his tooth, he thought his head was coming off. And people still weren't talking to him. They were frightened he'd mention his mother. He thought about Koppelberg.

'You bastard,' he swore. 'I should have done it!' Sam could feel the Smith and Wesson safe under his windcheater; snug against the ribs it had bruised. His head was muzzy. He needed a blow of fresh air. Suddenly, he wanted to get out of Sunny Mead, get away from them all. Forever.

As he drove his second-hand Japanese car very slowly past the Durrants' house, he could hear music. That was nothing unusual, but this was the most god-awful noise he had ever heard: a squeaking violin, a tinny piano and an off-key flute.

It set his bad tooth on edge, but the tune kept on irritating him like a buzzing gnat or a stinger. It was still in his head as he drove up the mountain road to catch the summer-league game over in Sun Falls. At least watching the Redskins would give him some real ball play.

Hours later, in the quiet of that dead July evening, clouds of gnats drifted across the twilight-red surface of the lake. In the sky a crescent moon hung low, a white wraith lost in the glory of the dying sun.

Diane had tiptoed out of Pip's attic when she had seen he was asleep. The mute boy, exhausted by the anguish of his pets and lack of sleep, had drifted into his uneasy dreams, while, beside the lake, the Sunny Mead houses, like little white wooden boxes, clustered together fearfully, waiting for night …

Sam Junior was losing the manic excitement of the Sun Falls game little by little. It was draining out of him, drop by drop, on the long drive home. He wished he'd taken Lou Bates with him – or Hank or any of them. Then the Redskins' failure might not have hurt so much.

He was having morbid thoughts of Mom again, of dying, now the anger had gone, leaving only the misery. He was eight kilometres from home and at the forest's very edge when he switched on the stereo. Its raucous blaring only jarred his nerves more, while the blackness of his depression began to merge with the coming of darkness.

He drove on mechanically through the infrared light of a truly bloody sunset. The sun was dropping reluctantly into the gaping hole of clouds; facing its daily ritual of death.

Back in the attic at Sunny Mead, Pip Durrant tossed in his dreams and screamed out a warning. From a great distance he sensed the small Japanese car, like a child's toy lost in the awesome landscape, skittering in and out of the forest trees, travelling west to overtake the sun's disappearance. Its windows flashed fire, reflecting the rays, as the helpless, insignificant box on wheels buzzed on to its final destination ...

There was a road tunnel to go through before Sam Junior could say he was safely in the valley. It was a short stretch carved out of the rock, a feat of engineering that withstood the tons of forest earth above. The half-circle of its cavernous mouth was clearly visible as the car sped on, ready to be swallowed in its gullet.

Sam Junior was humming the melody that had fixed into his head that morning. It was one of those catchy tunes that struck like a plaguing gnat, that kept biting at your brain, however much you hated it. Funny he wanted to remember the god-awful noise after hearing the Durrant kids practicing. He had the radio full on, but that tune wouldn't die.

Suddenly a flicker of light pierced his consciousness like when lightning strikes the landscape and only your senses notice. He thought it was the sun's reflection dappling the stones at the top of the tunnel.

Pip cried out in his sleep. Above the gaping mouth of the arch of darkness, Snipe and his master were one again, crouching above the entrance, waiting for another intruder, peering into the bright red landscape. The boy could see the rat wriggling, sniffing and slavering, its moist red tip of a nose scenting murder. The precious antique case lay beside Diep Koppelberg on the ground. His long red nails, hard as iron, prised it open, taking the blinding-bright weapon lovingly from its box. He raised it towards his face, near to the black 'O' shape of his mouth and the tight, thin bloody line of his lips. The sound of death was the music he played that night, and was to be the last melody Sam Junior would ever steal from him.

The reflected light blinded Sam Junior's eyes when he was at least 300 metres from the tunnel's mouth. 'Son-of-a-bitch!' he swore, braking violently but, at the same time, dazzled. What was it? A security light? His hand went up automatically to the visor to protect his eyes.

The man in the photo-chromatic red suit stood fully erect, terrifying, menacing, rigid. His strong legs were apart, feet squarely placed on the cold stone like an antique colossus straddling its insignificant victim. His wet and mildewed coat was spotted with red mould.

His iron-nailed hands, skin puckered and burnt, were clasped one on top of the other, protecting the murderous steel trigger-finger. At 20 metres, the red flames of his eyes glared, homing in, adhering to the head of his horrified target.

Sam Junior never had the chance to see the last of the sun's rays shine flat red off the .44 Magnum. The weapon, at 14 inches, was not quite as long as a flute, but the weight and the sentence it carried were fatal.

The 240-grain lead bullet, chosen so coldly, jacketed carefully so that it would not deform on impacting the windscreen, punched a perfect little hole, as neat as a rat bite, in the centre of the young football-player's forehead. Its high velocity explored his vulnerable brain, sending it spattering backwards out and around the toy box of a car as easily as a child daubs red paint.

The vehicle careered crazily to the left, striking the rock by the mouth of the tunnel. Then it toppled and rolled down to end its death dance, jammed between the fork where two giant forest trees grappled for supremacy. The car lay upside down, its tail screaming out to the sky – a cruciform shape. Then, in one thunderous ball of fire, Sam Junior's half-headless body was cremated.

His murderer replaced the weapon in its antique case and crawled away across the top of the tunnel. His mouth was red from too much piping, his fingers from too much death. The rat was grinning as well as it scampered away.

His poor dad'll go crazy, thought officer Amos, the traffic cop who had been detailed to redirect any vehicles that approached the tunnel. The crash investigators and the engineers had to make sure the outer wall was safe before they let any Big Falls traffic through. Amos was stockily built and had been attending accidents for the last 20 years. He was hard-bitten, and very little shocked him. But this crash was something different. He'd seen the kid grow up.

He was staring across the road at the rescue crew setting up the hydraulic platform to lift the Subaru from its bizarre resting place, when Detective Durrant drew up next to his Harley.

'How's it going?' asked Dave, leaning out of the window. He'd been called out as soon as the licence plate had been identified.

'Just brought in the hydraulics,' replied Amos. indicating the grim scene. 'They'll have him out soon. Poor young bastard.' The cop was a man of a few words. 'Lordy, here's another,' he said, with a grim expression on his face, as they heard a car's engine roaring towards them.

'Looks like it,' said Dave. Amos strode off to flag the driver down. Then Dave got out and stared down the slope. At that particular moment, he knew his presence would be more of a hindrance than a help. The corpse would be unrecognisable. *Toasted*. That's what they'd said.

The team knew what they were doing – and did it well. He guessed what was on their minds as they sweated under the arc lights below to prise the body from the wreckage. Some of them had known the boy as well as he and Amos had. Sam

Junior had been the number one star at JBH, whose high school team was the best in the county this year.

Besides, Dave had a particular dislike of accidents, given the one in which he and Pip had been involved. He swallowed. The burnt-out wreck that had been Sam Junior's car was rammed between two massive forest trees, and he knew personally what that kind of impact felt like. Thank God the car he'd been travelling in with Pip hadn't caught fire before he'd managed to get them both out. But it had been close. *Sam Junior must have fried.* He pushed away the memories.

He had a job to do too. The crash investigators were the ones who would find out later what had happened, but he needed to be around just now. The kid had probably been going too fast – he'd been pulled over for speeding a couple of times in the past – but there was always the possibility that it hadn't been his fault – that something else had caused the crash.

When Dave had first heard who the victim was, he'd almost puked. *Sam Junior.* As he'd driven up to Big Falls, a thought he didn't want to entertain had kept popping into his mind. Had the kid crashed his car on purpose? He'd been pretty upset after losing his mom. And why shouldn't he have been? But Dave dispelled the thought as Amos walked back towards him along the road. Sam had been a tough young guy
…

'Ain't much traffic this time of night, thank the Lord,' said Amos, 'but *that* guy …' he gestured and shook his head as the tail lights disappeared, '… tried to give me some shit. And he found out I ain't in the mood.' The glint of anger in Amos's eyes changed to something as near to tears as Dave had ever seen, as the two of them stared down at the burnt-out wreck. 'The kid was a great ball player!'

'Sure was,' said Dave.

'Are you going to have to tell his dad?' Amos asked. Dave nodded. 'Jeez, how do you do something like that?'

'I dunno, but …' Dave sighed. 'I know Drury well and,

somehow, I guess it would be better coming from me.'

Amos nodded. 'Well, I ain't religious, but I guess any guy having to do that needs a prayer.'

Dave was touched by his sympathy. 'Thanks, Amos.'

'Got something here, Chief. I found this by the tunnel.' Amos reached down into one of the saddlebags and drew the object out. It was one of Sam Junior's distinctive hubcaps, painted with a cartoon image of a bright yellow sun with a face, bordered by the JBH sports slogan. 'It was in the bushes. Must have been ripped right off in the impact. This might be a bad idea, but maybe the boy's dad ...' he shrugged, '... maybe he'd like to have it. My old man kept a couple of things that meant a lot to him from back when he was in the war.' Amos handed it over.

Dave stared at the hubcap, the reality hitting him. He was going to be the one to have to break the news to Drury. It was one hell of a detail.

'Could be evidence, Amos.' Dave could hardly look at the sun's sick grin.

'Mebbe. But you take it.' He turned. 'Hey, look, they got him.' He pointed.

'I think I'll just go over there,' Dave said.

'Sure,' replied Amos. They watched in silence as what remained of Sam Junior was zipped up in a body bag.

'Okay, let's get this over with.'

Amos offered him his gloved hand. 'Good luck, Chief.'

'Okay,' said Dave, surprised at the brief show of emotion. He left Amos straddled over his Harley and walked towards the slope where the corpse was being hauled up on its last journey towards the van that would take it to the town morgue.

I'll need that prayer, thought Dave. Amos had been right. How *was* he going to break the news to Sam Drury? For Sam to lose both his wife and his son within the space of a fortnight went beyond tragedy somehow. It was more than any man could bear. He'd never liked Drury, but he wouldn't wish this crap on anybody.

He thought of Mel then. How would she take Sam Junior's death? The kid had been sweet on his daughter, sweeter than she was on him – but this? He waited as the body bag was put into the waiting van. It wasn't hard to imagine what it contained. A charred stick of a body, that a couple of hours earlier had been a vital young man with a future.

Later, as Dave drove back to Sunny Mead, he glanced at the hubcap lying on the seat beside him. The bright yellow sun, Sam Junior's cheerful logo, had sustained a deep dent, obliterating one red eye. The other seemed to be winking at Dave while, below, its sharp teeth grinned as if it knew something he didn't.

12

'Unable to move a step, or cry
To the children merrily skipping by.'

Dave looked around at all the preparations. What was it all in aid of? Some guy his wife and kids had only just met and who'd wriggled his way into their affections!

It had been hell going to Drury the night before and telling him his son was dead. That morning, Sam had actually broken down crying when he'd come to Dave's office to pick up the hub cap. After that episode, no way did Dave want to discuss kids' parties. He felt miserable and irritable. And he was hungry too. He picked up a cold hot dog and put it in his mouth.

Noticing Dave's expression, Diane sensed trouble. It was a pity he didn't approve of the kids wanting a party for Diep. He wasn't usually so small-minded.

'It'll take the kids mind off it, Dave,' she said.

'Why the hell does Koppelberg want a party anyway?' said Dave.

'Oh, it wasn't him. It was the twins' idea. You know what they're like. As soon as he mentioned it was his birthday, they were crazy to do it!' She was glad to give the answer. She didn't want him shouting at them, making them naughtier.

'Where are they now?'

'They're at the store. Mel's taken them with Pip in the chair. And you have to agree, it will take their minds off all the horrible things that have been happening.' She swallowed and pressed her lips tightly together.

What had happened was too terrible to think of. The two deaths that the Drury family had suffered had hit the town hard. And Sam – how was he going to get over this, so soon after Stella? Dave had told her that right after he'd broken the news, the guy had nearly gone crazy. But now he was keeping himself to himself. He didn't even want to go out. Diane expected he was totally broken. She would have been if it had happened to her.

Like Dave, she didn't really feel like celebrating anything, but she had the children to think of. And Diep was so marvellous with them. He'd gone on just as normal. It was as if they'd known him for years, as if he fitted into the family perfectly.

She was glad though that she'd explained to him about Drury. She hadn't told Dave, but the first night Diep had arrived, she had taken it on herself to talk to him about their problems with the Mayor. How he couldn't be trusted.

She was sorry she'd intimated Sam Drury mightn't keep his word. Now she felt guilty. She shouldn't, because it was a natural mistake, born of her dreams for disabled kids. How many times had she told her pupils, 'All experience is an arch to build on'? Diane had studied Henry Brooks Adams in college.

She didn't know why she'd told Diep, except she'd hoped he'd make a wonderful impression and win the Mayor over. He was that kind of man. And it had been so comforting when he'd persuaded her not to worry, to have confidence in him. He'd said he'd had a lot of success with awkward authorities before and that one mayor was very much like another.

But external forces had now intervened. Drury had let the council members know he wouldn't be standing for Mayor anymore, and he'd resigned from the School Board – at least, temporarily. There was no way he could focus on town matters, she supposed.

Sam's deputy had taken over, and he had quite a different attitude from him. Now there was a real possibility that her scheme might finally bear fruit.

It was an ill wind – but she marvelled at the music teacher's intuition. Diep had promised her it would come out all right. And she hadn't known him two minutes. She remembered his excited expression when he'd said, when he first came, 'Drury will be so impressed with what I can do for the kids that he'll *have* to agree!' But no-one, including Diep, could have imagined it would happen as it had.

'What are you thinking about?' asked Dave.

'Everything,' she said.

'Come here.' He slipped his arms around her. She let him, knowing she'd been neglecting him lately. But she'd had her hands full with Pip. The night Sam Junior had died, he'd been like a crazy thing, crying and shaking when she'd told him. She'd never thought it would upset him so much. It was so strange. When Dave had been called out to the accident it had been as if Pip already knew what had happened. She was sure it was all the nightmares that were upsetting him. She wished he'd tell her about them.

'I'm sorry, Dave,' she said. 'I've had so much to do!'

'I know, I know,' said Dave, soothing her and himself as well. 'When things like this happen, folks realise just how lucky they are.'

'I don't know. I just feel … full up. Sick. I want things to go right. I don't want to see our kids hurt, I suppose.'

'That's life, honey,' said Dave, holding her tightly, stroking her hair.

'And death,' she added, closing her eyes, then opening them to look over his shoulder blankly. He turned her.

'Come on now!' He looked into her expressionless eyes. 'You get on thinking about that party. Maybe it'll do us all good!'

That seemed to cheer her up. She looked happier as she put his dinner in front of him. As he picked up his knife and fork, he knew he wasn't doing it for Koppelberg. He'd never taken to that guy. It was just for her and the kids. Ever since the man had come to the valley, there had been nothing but trouble for all of them.

But Di wouldn't have it: she liked him a lot – too much. Pip didn't. He seemed to be the only one on Dave's side. His father still wasn't sure why. Perhaps he ought to ask him?

Riding a wheelchair was okay except when they left you. And they had. Mel had shoved the ice cream into his hand and run off with the twins each side. To be fair to Sis, it was a big ice.

Pip stared down at the melting cone. It was dripping from his chin as he looked up and across the lawn towards the lake. He didn't resent the way the other kids had disappeared. Just who they'd gone to see.

Pip's probing eyes bored into Koppelberg's back. The music teacher was arching high, his body springing open like an elastic band as he hit the water with only a minor unsettling of spray. He was the best diver Pip had ever seen. No wonder Mel and the twins were looking. *Too good*, said Pip to himself morosely.

Pip thought about the giant turtle he'd seen on television, a cousin to his tortoise. Its flippers had flapped clumsily – and it was a water creature. This was a man, an athlete. Suddenly, the soft ice cream seemed sick and limp. Pip stared at his own useless legs.

Fuck you, Koppelberg! he snarled in his head, paying Diep out for those monstrous nightmares. His brother and sisters, mouths open, were standing lakeside where Koppelberg, music in every buoyant movement, played to his audience. Pip's deafness cut off the sound of their applause, prompted by the sight of that perfect body seemingly suspended in mid-air, but he could still see them all clapping.

Christ, cried Pip inside his head, *Christ, I want to hear, I want to speak, I want to tell them – not just to write it down!* Couldn't they see the man like he did? Pip couldn't be imagining it.

Koppelberg was too far away for Pip to see his skin, but the boy knew every puckered and spotted blemish, uglier than the salamander, which could just about equal the stranger's prowess in the water; warty like the toad, festering with rat bites. Pip felt sick. Bufo's entrails were still fresh in his mind.

The melting ice cream had left a sticky patch on his jeans. He pulled out his handkerchief and wiped up the mess.

Turning away from the scene, Pip began to wheel himself down the sidewalk. He couldn't get to the lakeside over the lawn to see Koppelberg's antics, but he could make it to the chalet. The idea came so suddenly it hurt! Now was the time to see what Koppelberg kept in that cage, what had bitten him and what was still doing it. He was going to find out if Snipe existed, the rat-penis that filled his sleep with disgusting dreams. And when he found out? He wasn't sure what he'd do. Who could he tell? Who would believe him? Every day his life was getting more like his nightmares.

Mel grabbed hold of Teddy's shoulder as he fought to pull off his shorts. He wriggled frantically. 'No,' she said, 'you're not. You're not going in!'

'Why?' Teddy snarled defiantly.

'Because I said so. I know you have your trunks on, but no way are you going in there!'

The twins' eyes begged.

'No, I can't let you. You'll have to ask Mom. And you know what she'll say. You're too little.'

'Come in too, Mel. Come on, please!'

'No, I can't, Teddy!'

'Why? Why? Why?' Both Rose and Teddy were shouting at her now.

'Never mind why I can't come in, just shut up, you little brats!'

Diep was shaking the water off himself like an animal and walking towards them. Drops, like sunny tears of fire, fell from his supple, sleek body and skin. The curved corners of his mouth were crooked in a smile.

'Hi, kids, are you coming in?' he asked. Mel swallowed. She was very hot, and her short top was clinging to her breasts. Besides, she was hot and sticky between her legs. What wouldn't she have given to go swimming with Diep? It was bad enough having her period now. The shock of Sam Junior's death had brought it on and she was afraid it might show through her white shorts.

'We can't come in, Diep, we're shopping. For the party.'

He grinned in reply, his bright blue eyes wide with excitement.

Teddy let go of Mel's hand and ran up to Diep, clasping his leg. 'I want to. I've got my trunks on but *she* won't let me!' He stared at his sister in a hostile way.

Diep's eyes were flicking over Mel, but then he laughed, showing the tip of his tongue. He caught Teddy firmly by the shoulders and the little boy stood squarely and defiantly in front of him, his small body blocking the man's pelvic arch and the swelling below.

Rose was angry. She let go of Mel's hand too, determined not to be left out, and ran to the music teacher.

'Rose!' he said in a soothing voice. The twins stood side by side, like they were ganging up against her. Mel hesitated. She swallowed, took a step forward.

'Come on, kids, we have to go. We've left Pip outside the store.'

Diep laughed. 'So? He'll be okay.' He squatted down between the children. 'One day, Teddy, when you're bigger, you'll be able to do whatever you want. And you, Rose. Just now, you have to do what everyone else says. Tell you what – watch this! I'm practising – for the party.'

'Watch what?' cried Rose. She was enchanted. They stared as Diep ran away, picking his way through the pebbles at the edge of the lake, lifting one leg in a clown-like gesture and shouting boyishly.

Then he dived into the water and came up, shaking his head, grimacing, acting the fool. They all laughed. Their chattering happiness was as keen and thin as the music Diep Koppelberg played on his pipe. He shook the water out of his eyes and floated lazily on the surface like a golden salamander. The prattling of children in his ears was all he craved in life. Now savagery had taken over, as ancient as the private hell he'd created once more in that tiny lakeside chalet.

Diep lay staring up into the sky. He had space and freedom now. And he closed those light blue eyes, drew the red veil of his eyelids to shut out the scorching sun, which burned as hot as any fire. There were other noises in his ears, besides the sound of children, blotting out the moment of peace. The raucous laughter of Snipe inside his head, urging him on to play the Piper again. He drifted lazily far out in the lake, ignoring the children's shouts from the side. His lips were busy humming his own shrill tune as he sent his thoughts to where the coffin-shaped glass cases loomed through the shadows, resembling a line of uneven teeth grinning through the gloom. Then he dived.

The day was too warm, too lovely to be trapped in a wheelchair. The thought made Pip more determined to see what pets Diep was keeping in the apartment. He was going to make it even if it killed him.

Two small, square windows squinted relentlessly over the lake; blank, unseeing spaces each side of the flat lip-line of the chalet's wooden veranda.

From below its two steps of teeth, a frantic twisting string of a path hurried away past the black menace of Adams's storm drain.

Pip manoeuvred his chair skilfully in the direction of the chalet. He knew he couldn't negotiate the steps, so he made for the back entrance, a simple door, located on the side of the wall like a listening ear.

He couldn't believe his luck. Not only was it out of sight of his brother and sisters but it was swinging back and forth in the strong summer breeze that was flying off the lake. Diep must have left it open.

Pip didn't feel quite right about being there, about intruding. But the string path had reeled him in. He simply couldn't stay away. He had to look inside to see what beasts the guy was keeping.

As he approached, he was sure he could hear something. It wasn't a noise in his head – he was used to those. This was different; a thin, shrill sound like the high drone of a wasp buzzing, or the noise he saw on the television screen, when he imagined what spacemen heard when they dropped to their knees in agony after being zapped by a laser gun. It never occurred to him that he might be hearing properly again, as he brought the wheelchair to a stop outside the hanging door. It was very dark inside.

Pip suddenly smelled the freshness of new earth, like when Dad was digging the garden and the wriggling worms were sliced by his spade.

Fuck, thought Pip. *Why did you have to pull the drapes? I want to see!* Craning to look, he leaned right forward, holding the door with one hand and warding off the insects buzzing around inside his head with the other. Straining eagerly to see, he fixed his eyes into the darkness of the hollow little chalet.

There was no way Pip could see what was in those menacing cases. He needed to go in. He clenched his fists. It was right that he should see what animals Koppelberg was keeping. There were laws about it. Inching the side door of the chalet wide open, he let the unsuspecting sun dart into the room. The buzzing noise in his head grew louder as if some insect was very near. He put up his hand to stave it off and held it there, trying to block the sound.

He could see nothing for a moment, except the bright motes of dust dancing in the beam of light, but the smell was overpowering. Pip let go of his ear and pinched his nostrils together to fight off a feeling of nausea. There must be something dead inside those cases! He'd have to tell Dad. The bastard would have to pack up and go. What was the guy doing? Was he crazy? He could see wisps of dirty straw rolling over the floor, escaping madly along with the breeze, leaving only wet and shit on it like in a pigsty.

Where were the boards Dad had put down? Now the floor was made of stone, with uneven cracks in it like crazy paving … It couldn't be. Was he dreaming? Was he in the wrong chalet? Pip was terrified, and swift fear of the guy rose like bile in his throat.

The sun was hiding behind him now, throwing Pip's own shadow and the chair's before him. He swallowed, his tongue sticking to his throat in fear, and threw himself back in his wheelchair, trying to reverse. The door was holding him. He bent, trying to push it open, but as he came up, the buzzing turned into a squeaking. *The guy must have some rats*, he thought. But the sound was coming from the ceiling.

He gasped as he squinted up. The rats were hanging upside down from the smoke-blackened ceiling, their wings folded around their listless bodies. At first he thought they were dead, then they began to stir.

Bats, he thought, relieved. Then he realised their noses were far too blunt and squashed and their nostrils too wide and red. They seemed to be growing bigger in front of his eyes as they opened their crocodilian mouths to reveal needle-sharp incisors. Pip's chin began to tremble in spite of him trying to block out his fear. *Vampire bats. What were they doing there?*

'That's their business, dickhead.' His stomach nearly jumped into his throat when he saw it. A monster rat with twinkling, slanting eyes was squatting on the table, its thin lips taunting him with a grin. It was the talking rat he'd seen in his dreams, and its clawing, pink, thin hands were holding the limp and twisted body of another grey-white rat. Cass!

Making mute little noises with his lips, Pip dribbled in fear, screwing his eyes up so he couldn't see. But he had to – otherwise it would get him. Then another voice burst into his head, above the rat's triumphant squeaking: *Diep's.*

'So you made it at last,' he mocked. 'You wanted to see. Now you can.'

How could it be Koppelberg? He was outside swimming in the lake. He couldn't have come in without Pip seeing.

With a scream of terror, Pip pushed himself backwards, and the chair toppled sideways, throwing its occupant full-length on the ground under the steady, merciless stares of the rodent and its master. Their eyes mesmerised Pip, drawing him closer and closer. He felt like a fish being reeled in on a hook. All he could do was gasp for life as he wriggled on, until he came to a breathless stop before the first case that stood like a sentry guarding some precious treasure, obscured in front by a thick black curtain.

Diep's face was very close to him now and his one lip seemed peculiarly lop-sided. His pale-flame eyes were sharp pins of light. He thrust out a pointed finger and rubbed away the bright red dust at the bottom of the case, revealing a glint of bright gold. His voice was savage. 'You're dumb and deaf, so I'll let you see.' He smiled cruelly.

'The doll-killer almost blew my cover. And the football player was just … irritating! I have no time for mistakes. I never used to make them.' Pip could hear the rat laughing behind. 'You came here because you couldn't stay away. I've never shown my trophies to a cripple before.' Pip's terrified eyes followed Diep's finger as the legend beneath the red film revealed itself at last. The bright numbers turned and marched into line in front of his eyes:

1212

The curtain slithered its dark way down, choking him with blinding dust. He started to rub the sting away, and when he could see again, Koppelberg and the rat had disappeared. Pip waited, trembling, in case they came back. But the dusty air was thick and silent.

Pulling himself together, he forced his eyes to look up. He had to see whatever was in the case so he could tell Dad. But he had to be careful.

He levered himself by his arms, bit by bit, until he was

level with the fly-spotted glass. The tall case was like a fairground attraction, with red button eyes at the bottom that glared at him, willing him to press them. *No way I'm touching you,* he thought. Once again, he twisted his head round, jarring his neck to check if Diep and the rat were behind him, but he was all alone. Doing his best to be brave, he peered through the dirty glass – and let out a relieved breath, his shoulders relaxing. *Only dolls.*

They weren't that frightening, just creepy. A strange male doll with a wrinkled face sat in the corner of the case on a plinth. It was big and took up a lot of space. It looked as if it was made of white marble and wore a three-tiered crown, a cape and a long skirt. A big cross was hung round its neck. In a way Pip thought he knew who it resembled, but somehow his brain wouldn't function. A kind of priest? And it looked new. He frowned. Diep had probably stolen it from some museum.

Then he noticed that the three sides of the rectangular cabinet were painted with garish pictures, one of which showed a black cathedral with massive towers and another church as well behind the marble doll. Pip squinted – he'd seen that one somewhere too. It had a massive dome. Suddenly, his brain was working again. *He knew* – but then the connecting thought disappeared.

In the squares in front of the churches were children riding in carts, happy children shouting and waving, but not like any children he'd ever seen, except in fairy story books.

All the kids were dressed like the big doll, lying face down in front of it. The old marble man had on silly tights and a grubby white shirt without any sleeves. Its hair looked like Mel's old Barbie doll, long and golden. Beside it lay a crucified doll, broken in half.

Pip screwed up his eyes and made a face when he saw it. Then he noticed the others lying around it. Why hadn't he seen them before? Hundreds of tiny dolls scattered around the bottom of the case – like the ones Rose kept in her pocket. *Midgets,* he called them, and she hated that. They were dressed exactly the same as the big one, but the girls had white skirts. Pip felt braver now and leaned right against the glass to have a good look. They weren't happy. They were disgusting. They had pins sticking through – he squinted to see – *No, not pins! Swords and horrible things*.

'Ugh,' he said. Some had no heads. Some no legs, nor arms. Pip pulled a face. He was getting a bad feeling about this, like in a nightmare when you want to wake up. He felt hot all over his head, as if the glass was melting it! He tried to draw back, but he couldn't, because a claw-like hand was gripping his shoulder. Then a lightning shiver passed through him. Koppelberg.

'Wake up, Nicholas!' He'd never heard Koppelberg purr before. 'Pretty little Nicholas.'

Pip screamed out as the big doll sprang up like a scary jack-in-a-box and fixed him with its blue glass eyes. It picked up the crucified doll and came towards Pip, then pressed its nose to the glass. It had a face like Diep's but it was too young. Then its shirt began slowly bleeding into a big red cross. Pip had seen crosses like that in his history book, but he didn't know they were made of blood. Over his head he could hear the vampire bats flying: they had picked up the scent. He knew what they fed on. He thought he could feel them brushing his hair with their wings.

He began to cry as the boy crusader turned from the glass and strutted around. Koppelberg's iron-nailed fingers still kept Pip a prisoner as a thousand chattering voices filled his ears. The walls of the cases had come to life and the children set off on their merry way round the painted walls, singing and shouting and waving their red-cross banners like at the end of a Disney movie.

Diep's voice was whispering in his ear now and Pip could smell his foul breath. 'That little crusader ran all across Europe with his broken doll in his hand, hanging from its cross. And what do you think happened to him? To all of them? Wake up, my pretty little ones.'

The little dolls must have heard his voice and began to stir beneath Pip's nose, filling it with the smell of death. They were like crawling heaps of maggots on carrion. The ones with the swords stuck in them stood up, bleeding, staggering, screaming and trampling down the others beneath who were trying to move. The ones without limbs were climbing on the ones without heads.

Then the host of tiny dolls began to grow in front of Pip's terrified eyes, to sprout into real children, who pressed their mutilated noses against the bending glass and cried out, 'Help us, help us!' They stretched out their arms to him in supplication, while behind them the little crusader was growing bigger too.

Pip tried to shuffle backwards, but the cruel grip prevented him. He was forced against the glass by his neck like a helpless rabbit to face those myriad tortured dolls. Then the white marble statue came alive, rose slowly from its throne and beckoned the young crusader, placing its skinny, ringed hand on his shoulder. Then, in one terrifying movement, it tore the cross from round its neck and held it high, where the Jesus figure wriggled his crucified arms into an open blessing.

'He blessed me,' Koppelberg snarled into Pip's ears. 'And I took my cue from him. 'Suffer the little children' he said, and that's just what I did.'

'Don't show me any more,' screamed Pip. He had to get out of his nightmare. But Diep's hard, cruel fingers dragged him along to the next tall case, which towered over him, hidden by its shrouding veil. Pip wanted to be sick. He didn't want to see. He wanted to go home.

But he remained – glued to the floor as he stared at the glittering bottom of the second case, this time only lightly covered in red dust that had almost obliterated the antique plate showing the date. The writing was in flourishes of red like ketchup, or blood.

1376

Nobody tweaked the curtain but, when it fell, the opaque

glass revealed the statue of a man, who stood life-size on his pedestal, his flute to his lips, straining for the high notes. When Pip's frightened eyes could make him out properly, he saw he was made of a mouldy green metal, which glistened dully. The statue's body was flecked by moving golden specks. They were all around his head and his feet; golden specks mixed with red.

Pip squinted up at it, tears running down his cheeks. He couldn't understand what he was seeing, and then he realised the case had no glass, but the guy was imprisoned in an opaque cage like a fly in amber. Then the buzzing in Pip's head reached a terrifying crescendo. It was driving him mad. He was being attacked by the specks. They grew larger than gnats and he could feel them start to nibble at his face and neck.

Pip waved both arms in the air to ward them off. But he couldn't run away. He flailed the air with his arms like windmill sails, jerking his body to and fro to rid himself of the specks. Suddenly, they stopped their buzzing and, their eyes bulging, crawled quietly up and down the outside of the case. The statue man didn't come alive. He stood still in his prison, his flute seemingly frozen to his lips. Pip let out a sigh of relief.

He hadn't noticed the painted walls until then. The ancient little town had crazy red roofs and a ring of high walls washed by a twisting river. Another fairytale? He'd seen that picture before too. Then he remembered. He'd loved it as a little kid. The rats running through every street, doing wicked things until the Piper charmed them away. *The Pied Piper of Hamelin.* He glanced up at the statue, but it didn't move.

He caught his breath, trying not look at what was painted in a seated pose on the back wall of the case. It had a panel all to itself. A black monster rat, like the one that had torn Cass to pieces! He'd seen enough. He didn't want anything to come to life. But as Pip tried to move away, he felt himself being drawn forward towards the feet of the statue.

A moment later he slipped through into the toy world of the Piper and it wasn't a fairytale anymore. He was seated on a small wooden chair, with a nibbled crust in his hand. Rats were swarming around his feet, running over his naked toes, squeaking and chattering: a frantic host, scrambling on top of themselves, smothering each other. Heaps of rats, falling down from the thatch, coming out of the cracks of the smoke-blackened walls.

Pip wanted to wheel himself away, but his chair wouldn't move. He gripped the crutches lying across his lap, but they had no handles. He looked down. They were made of rough sticks from the forest. Then the swarming rodents were pushing at his chair, rocking it with their force. And it moved. He thought he might fall out face down. Would they eat him like they had eaten his bread? *Like they had eaten Cass and Annie?* Cover his face with bites like Diep's?

Noises of a million rats were in Pip's ears as he and they tumbled together toward the door, where they joined more and more of their brothers and sisters, slimy wet and smelling of the sewers. Soon they were in the streets that led to the riverside. A riot of squeaking, mixed with chattering teeth assaulted his brain as Pip was carried along. He felt slivers of fur on their feet, caught the glint of hundreds of slanting bright eyes as they rushed on frantically.

Then, all of a sudden, the chair stopped rolling and the rats were tumbling away. He struggled to his feet, trying to make it back to his house. But he was paralysed. He watched the rodents slipping and sliding down the riverbank, screeching and fighting on the way to their deaths.

The crutches hurt his hands as he tried to run in case he was washed away too. Each step was a pain as it had always been. He wanted his mother. 'Where are you?' he shouted, and his weak voice dashed itself against the town stones. But there was only an echo for an answer. He was all alone in the town with the rats' death throes still fresh in his ears.

Then he looked up to the walls and his heart expanded with joy. Down the steps, children were trooping, boys in tunics and girls in quaint white dresses, with black handkerchiefs knotted round their heads, laughing and skipping down to the path by the river. They were waving and shouting to their parents, who were crying and hanging over the walls, begging them to come back. The children didn't even notice Pip as they rushed past, like the river below; they looked so happy as their small legs clattered over the stones. He wanted to go with them.

'Wait for me,' Pip cried. 'Wait for me! Don't leave me behind!' He could feel their warm bodies as they passed by in a seemingly never-ending line, brushing him, bumping him, ignoring him as they always had. He stood, a small pillar of misery, as the children parted each side of him, like turbulent water around a rock. He looked across the river over the bridge and up to the hill, where the statue man stood, silhouetted against the sky, piping them on. Soon there were doll-like midgets in the distance. *They were leaving him behind.*

He couldn't catch them up and he was all alone in that miserable little town with its weeping, bereft people. Then he felt a movement close beside him. Maybe one of them had stayed, who was lame like he was? He turned – and screamed. His companion was the monster rat, its shiny fur sleek and wet.

'Dickhead,' it said and grinned at him wickedly, then bounded away after the children. There was nothing he could do. Pip fell to the ground, crying, trying to open his eyes and climb out of the vision, but it was no use. He looked up and the green statue man was moving, shaking itself free of its casing, its claw-like fingers around its flute, its lips pursed and its chest heaving as its high, thin notes pierced the air.

The statue had eyes like daggered pinpoints of salty blue flame, which transformed themselves into orbs of fire. Beside it, the black rat crouched, skulking in its shadow. Pip knew they had come back to take him, like they had taken the children. He staggered and fell on his back onto the stones.

Then the statue man jumped out of the case and the monster rat bounded behind him, something hanging out of its mouth. Pip watched the rat carry away the sawdust-draggled remains of Annie, the poor little rag doll, and the mangled fragments of Teddy's orange ball, which hadn't sailed away over the lake at all.

The statue, whose face melted into Diep Koppelberg's, leered over Pip and hissed at him through his saw-like teeth. 'You won't betray me,' he said. 'You can only be on the outside looking in. You're a cripple. My music isn't for you. *Suffer the little children*? What crap! My kids don't suffer. He was supposed to be a good guy. The kids followed Him all right. All the way. And His price was high, higher than mine. A crazy dance to the ends of the world, and what did they get? Slavery! Death on a cross!' Diep laughed, showing his pointed teeth, and the rat's awful chattering whistle was filling Pip's deaf ears. 'Would you like to see some more?'

Sweat streamed down Pip's face and the room whirled round. He didn't know what was happening to him, and then the whole world dissolved into darkness.

'Where is he? Where's Pip? Pip, Pip, where are you?' Mel shouted.

'Pip, Pip?' echoed the twins in unison. Then a woman heard and came out of the store to help. She knew the disabled Durrant kid and had seen him wheel off from the lakeside. She pointed out the direction in which he'd gone in.

Hurrying, with the twins in tow, Mel returned to the lake. Her little brother and sister bored easily and they'd finally left Diep to scull about. He was in a very funny mood and wouldn't talk to them. Perhaps he'd seen Pip?

The pace was giving Mel sharp stomach cramps, and she was soaked with blood. Again she hoped it wouldn't come through her shorts. Where the hell had her brother gone? She worried about him being on the street, because he couldn't hear the traffic. But she also felt guilty she'd left him alone.

She couldn't see Diep in the water anymore. He'd probably gone to get changed. Suddenly she knew what she'd do. She'd just go to the chalet and enlist his help. It would be a chance to get in there.

'You stay here,' she ordered the twins. They halted abruptly. They were staring at her enquiringly.

'Why? Where are you going?' challenged Teddy.

'We want to come,' said Rose deliberately. It was always the same: if you told them to do something, however much they disliked each other at the time, they both disagreed with you.

'You can't. I'm going to ask Diep if he's seen Pip.'

'I want to see his dollies,' said Rose.

'Nuts to the dolls! I want to see his pets!' said Teddy. They were crafty little kids. They'd guessed where she was going. Mel hesitated and they stared at her.

Then Teddy sprang forward as if he'd been released on a piece of elastic.

'Diep!' She turned and gasped with relief. Diep was coming between the chalets – and he was carrying Pip. The three of them sprinted to meet him. Diep looked at their anxious faces. Pip's eyes were closed. He lolled in Diep's arms like a doll. His face was very white.

'What happened?' asked Mel, horrified. 'Where was he?'

'He fell off his chair and the wheel was buckled. I found him over there,' said Diep. 'I think we should get this little guy back home.'

'Is he unconscious?' cried Mel, hurrying beside Diep, trying to keep up with his long strides. 'Do you think we should take him to the hospital?'

'No, he's all right. He's just had a shock,' said Diep calmly, striding on. It was all the three of them could do to keep up with the music teacher.

Pip opened his eyes. The family were round his bed, all of them, just staring. But not *him*. Where was he? Pip trembled.

'Are you sure you're all right? What happened, Pip, what happened?' cried Diane.

The doctor had confirmed it was shock. He'd given Pip a thorough examination. But none of them would ever know why. None of them – only Pip. And he could never, never tell them. He was going mad. He needed a shrink. Perhaps his legs had affected his head? Maybe he was a nutcase?

He could never tell anyone. Not even Dad. They were private, private things that he couldn't even write down. They were horrible things that would come back every night to torment him. And he didn't know if they were real or not.

He didn't know if he'd really seen them inside 107 Camellia Grove, which used to be a neat little chalet, the day before, the week before, the month before he'd fallen out of his wheelchair.

It was just a wooden building with a landing stage in front of it, where the kids jumped off into Branksome Lake. It would never be Golden Pond to Pip any more.

Where had all the things come from that tormented him? He must have bashed his head when he fell. Maybe that counsellor could help? The one who had seen him after the accident?

He'd said there was nothing wrong with Pip's throat – just hysteria; that he could speak if he wanted to. Christ, how he wanted to! Fuck the counsellor! Fuck all of them! Nobody knew what he was suffering. He needed to tell them desperately; wanted them all to know what Koppelberg had shown him in there, in that wooden hell. But he had only been dreaming, hadn't he? And there had still been three cases to go. Would he see them in his dreams …?

'Take me home,' faltered Pip, but his voice was hollow. 'Please, don't show me!' he begged, but his lips wouldn't work.

As he crawled along the dusty floor where the chaff blew like rain, he could see the sharp, shining teeth showing up in Diep's pale and spotted face. The hysterical boy tried to drag himself away, but he felt the hand on his head like a weight beating him down. In his nose was the smell of death, as he was dragged unwillingly towards the third case.

'Such is my work,' crowed Koppelberg. 'Look!' The next legend was written in bright fresh blood.

1952

Pip's ears were filled with his heart, echoing eerily through the black emptiness that was him, the black hole he could see through the glass, where the twin wooden dolls moved slowly on towards the dark nothingness that looked for all the world like the entrance to Adams's storm drain.

'One of my best years!' whispered Koppelberg, holding the black rat in his lap, caressing the rodent's sides, which moved slowly and rhythmically with his breathing.

The case before last was only as tall as the dolls inside, which like automata had wooden faces and gestures. They stared through at Pip, their expressions hard and threatening.

Then their stiffness became cavorting and their blood began to run warm in their artificial veins. The man who looked like Diep Koppelberg stroked the children's hair and caressed them behind their glass prison. Their faces changed and changed from captive to carefree to wrinkled and old as they listened to the ageless music that was only in Pip's head. *Changed back until their painted wooden faces suddenly looked like Teddy and Rose.* All his worst fears. He couldn't bear to look.

'Who *are* you?' asked Pip again, but his silent voice was hollow.

'I am the Way, the Truth and the Life,' said Diep Koppelberg. 'And the children follow me.'

'No, no, no, no!' screamed Pip in his dreams, sobbing just as he'd done when Koppelberg had carried him home from the pretty little lakeside chalet ...

Pip woke up suddenly and looked wildly around. His mother was sleeping in a put-you-up bed so she could keep him company in case he had any more nightmares. He was happy she was there, but she could never understand. He could never tell her. In his feverish brain, he could hear Koppelberg laughing. 'Who *are* you?' he whispered, but no one could hear his words. 'What are you doing here? Who have you come for?'

Some hours later, early in the morning, when the brain rallies the dying and the dreams come walking, he had what he called, years later, 'the last vision', which was different from all of the others. That was when he changed from feeling helpless to knowing he could do something about Koppelberg …

He was in the chalet again, facing Koppelberg, who had a challenging look in his eyes.

'Only two cases left,' said Pip. 'What's in the next?' He couldn't believe how brave he felt.

'Find out for yourself,' Diep replied, sweeping his arm towards the last. 'But whatever you see, you'll never get me.' He grinned.

I will, said Pip, in his head. He had to find out what horrors were inside. The last case in the row was lying on its side. It was empty. The nearest to him had nothing in it either. It was clean and bright. As if it had never been used. It had no date written at the bottom; in fact the base and the sides were absent; it was just a frame. He ran his hands up and down the thin, shiny stuff. He'd never seen or felt anything like it before. The frame looked like a rectangle drawn in his school maths book; *unreal*, an empty frame standing on its end.

Then he saw a speck moving in one corner. But there was no corner, because he was standing in the space where the frame had been. *I must be inside it*, thought Pip. But the speck was still there in front of him and growing bigger.

At first, Pip was frightened. Was it an insect? Another rat? All those things he'd been afraid of? But he couldn't take his eyes off it as it grew. He realised it was taking on two human shapes. Soon they were full size. They looked like they were coming up in a lift. The man was carrying a small girl. They had their backs to him and the little girl had her arm round his neck. Pip knew her head was on his shoulder, because the man was holding her like Dad held Rose. He must have been her dad too.

He wanted to see who they were, more than anything. He wasn't scared anymore. He felt he knew them; that they would never hurt him.

'Who are you?' he asked. They were silent, as if they couldn't hear him. He said it louder and louder, until he thought his head would burst with the question. He had to know.

Then they turned and he gasped with relief. The man had a face like Dad's, but it wasn't him, because he didn't wear spectacles. But he looked like him. The girl resembled Rose, but she wasn't Rose. She had a little bit of Mel's face in her too. Pip remembered Mel when she was little. She'd looked just like that when they'd played together, before the accident when he'd got ill. All of a sudden his head was full of memories. Good memories. Good dreams. And he knew they had brought the memories for him.

'I like you,' he said simply.

'I like *you*,' replied the man, and the girl clapped her hands. But her smile wasn't Mel's. Or Rose's. Perhaps he didn't know her after all? Pip was puzzled.

'Who are you?' he repeated. But they didn't answer. He drank in their faces, committing them to his memory. Then they began to fade in front of his eyes. He was losing them.

'Don't go, don't leave me,' Pip cried. 'Where are you going? Shall I see you again?'

'Not for a long time, Pip,' they called, as their voices became fainter. He stood and watched as they slowly disappeared. He felt more alone than he'd ever done in his life, but strangely it was a good kind of loneliness. Theirs had been the kind of space he wanted to fill.

Pip sat by the window. He didn't feel like looking through his glasses at anyone anymore. He wanted to think what it all meant. The dream stayed close to him. In a way, it was keeping him going, thinking he would see them again. He couldn't get the two of them out of his mind. It was like an ache inside. He didn't know why *they* had been in Diep's horrible chalet. It didn't seem right somehow. It didn't fit. He thought about the man with the spectacles: how he came out of nowhere; how he disappeared; how he looked like Dad, who never wore glasses, because he had 20-20 vision.

But Mom had spectacles for reading. A sudden thought came to him. She had an old pair and he knew where they were. She'd left them up there when she'd been sitting by his bed, reading the newspaper. She did that a lot since he'd been brought out of the chalet. He remembered how she'd jumped up and said, only yesterday, 'These are no good. I'll have to get a new pair.' She'd shoved them into the drawer by his bed.

All of a sudden, he needed them. He rolled his chair back over to the bed and pulled open the drawer with trembling hands. There they were. Taking them out, he manoeuvred his way to the bathroom and sat in front of the mirror. Then he put on Mom's glasses, just to try. He couldn't see anything for a minute, because they made his eyes funny. Then he looked into the mirror. His face stared back at him. He didn't move, only kept on staring at it as if he was suspended in air. He felt as if nothing was moving anywhere in the world.

Who did he look like? It was so strange and spooky. *He looked like the man.* He took off the specs and shoved them in the bin under the washbasin. He didn't want to see any more visions. He was better now.

He knew he was braver too. They had to get rid of Koppelberg. *And he believed they would.* He wheeled himself back to the window and, taking his binoculars, he stared with determined eyes at 107 Camellia Grove.

Somewhere deep inside, Pip knew he would never forget the people he'd seen in the fourth of Koppelberg's cases. One day, when he was grown-up, he would find them again.

13

'All the little boys and girls,
With rosy cheeks and flaxen curls,
And sparkling eyes and teeth like pearls.'

Dave Durrant sat in his office. Spread open in front of him was the letter Diep Koppelberg had sent Diane. It was too perfect in every way. Dave didn't know why, but it just was.

He sucked in his lower lip and scraped it with his teeth. He leaned his chin in the fork of his hand and grimaced, moving his face from side to side. His head felt like a lead weight.

Whatever had happened to Pip hadn't been normal. He doodled on his office pad with his right hand, unconsciously drawing the lines of a wheelchair. Then he scrubbed out the drawing viciously.

'I got you into that chair, son,' he said under his breath, 'how the hell am I going to get you out?'

What had Pip been trying to do, going to Koppelberg's chalet? Probably to see his pets, that was it. But what had he seen inside? He would write nothing about it.

Dave didn't like it. Koppelberg was a nut. You could see it in his eyes. But he and Pip were stuck with him. Neither Diane, nor Mel, nor the twins would have a word said against him.

Take this party, for instance. They were dead set on it. It

wasn't natural to get so excited about a birthday party. The guy behaved like a kid, but there wasn't anything kid-like about him. He gave Dave the jitters, and Dave didn't mind admitting it. He'd seen a lot of creeps in his time, and Diep Koppelberg was one of the worst. Take his first letter, for instance. Dave had kept it after Diane had asked him to check the man out. Why wasn't it word-processed? Flowing handwriting was definitely out.

He put down his pen and walked over to the Dell and stared at the monitor. Koppelberg had no police record. Dave had checked him out before. Where did he go from there?

He looked at the letter again and at the telephone number Koppelberg had given Diane in case his references didn't arrive. Dave was deciding already. He'd ring up the music college and check on the man. He got the answer phone:

'I'm sorry, caller, but our office is closed on Mondays, Wednesdays and Fridays during vacation.

If you're enquiring about enrolment for the next semester, please ring ...'

He didn't want that number, so he listened to the rest, which gave him the general information number. Dave was going to have to wait until the next day. If the office had been in the same state he'd have sent a man round, but this was different; it was personal. Besides, he wanted to keep it to himself. In any case, he left a message with his own number:

'Hi, this is Dave Durrant, Sunny Mead Police Department, New Hampshire. I'm making a routine enquiry about a Diep Koppelberg' – he spelled it out – 'who is holding references from you. I'd appreciate it if you'd look out his details. I'll be calling back Tuesday. Thanks.'

That'll set them buzzing, he thought, replacing the receiver.

Dave went over to his office window and looked in the direction of the lake. Sunny Mead could do without that kind of creep. 'Right, Koppelberg!' he said out loud, 'I can play games too. Let's see who you are and where you come from after all.'

He turned very quickly, thinking he heard laughter behind

him, but when he looked there was no-one outside the office except Patsy Doran, who had his head down over his paperwork.

The morning of Diep's birthday was hot and sultry, with grey clouds gathered and lowering.

Diane shook the dainty cupcakes out of their patty tins. She felt touchy. She could have done without this party, because she was so worried about Pip.

'Ow,' she said, burning her fingers. At the same time there was a sharp tap on the glass of the kitchen door. Diane put down the tins and, sucking her fingers, went over and let him in.

Diep was grinning. He seemed to fill her stuffy kitchen with bright maleness. He eyed the cakes intensely.

'Take one. But, watch out, they're hot!' she said, smiling back.

He popped a whole one into his mouth. He didn't seem to have burned his tongue. She was surprised.

'Diep, the cakes are meant to be a surprise. The twins will be angry. You're not supposed to know. They were going to decorate them.'

'I can keep a secret,' he replied, putting a finger to his lips.

He was quite the best-looking guy who had ever stepped into her kitchen. He was wearing a red windcheater with a hood and yellow shorts. His legs seemed to go on forever. They were covered in the finest golden hair – like a girl's – but they were strongly muscled. He caught her looking. She turned, embarrassed, and found herself thinking of Pip. He would never look like Diep.

'Don't worry,' he said. It was as if he was reading her thoughts. He was so close to her; she could feel his breath on her neck. 'I think I'm getting under Pip's skin, Diane. And that's good, very good. He's responding. Once he starts doing that, who knows?'

'I hope you're right,' she answered. 'I've never seen him as upset as he was when you carried him home.'

'I reckon he came over to talk to me, Diane. There are other ways of communicating. You know that.' He was looking straight at her. Suddenly, the kitchen seemed cool. To Diane's relief, a breeze had come in the window. 'Pip and I have made contact,' Diep added. 'I guess he can hear my music.'

'I don't know what you mean.' She was puzzled.

'Inside his head. I know he understands. And there's a lot more to come. So, don't worry.' He touched her cheek with his long finger, and her nerves were tingling. 'What time do we start?'

She jumped at the pointed question.

'How about half-three?'

'Great!'

'Diep …' she paused, '… will you play for us?'

He shrugged childishly.

'Just for me?'

'For you? Yes!' He was grinning a charming, lop-sided smile. 'But only on one condition. You persuade that son of yours to come downstairs to my party.'

'I'll try,' said Diane, doubtfully.

'You do that. Or say I'll come and get him.'

She could hear the twins. He turned. 'See you.' He was gone so quickly that she only caught the yellow flash of his shorts in the corner of her eye. Then the kitchen was full of excited, young voices.

'Are those for Diep?'

'Yes, honey. Leave them alone, Teddy!'

'Have you seen him today?' her son demanded.

'Oh, no,' she lied, wondering how on earth he'd got out without them seeing him. Rose was already climbing onto the stool.

'I want to frost them.'

'Let me show you then, Rose,' said Di.

'I know how!'

'You don't!' argued Teddy.

'I do!' Rose protested.

Diane sighed. 'What are you doing, Rose? What's that?' Her small daughter was drawing a shape in the frosting sugar.

'It's a cow. I wanna put it on the cakes.'

'You can't put a cow on the cakes, honey,' replied Diane patiently.

'Stupid,' said Teddy. 'Why would he want any lousy cow you made?' The small boy squinted at the shape. 'It's a pig anyway – like you!'

'Teddy, don't let me hear you say that again,' warned Diane. 'Get down, Rose. You can do it when it's cool. Yes, Teddy, it looks a bit like a pig. But no cows, nor pigs on the cakes!'

Rose was making a face when, all of a sudden, Teddy began to whistle. The melody was thin and tuneless, setting Diane's teeth on edge.

'Teddy, stop whistling. Stop it, I say. What are you whistling, anyway?'

Immediately, the twins were standing together, grinning. Their moods were mercurial. Like a double-act, they defied her, pursing their mouths into puckered circles from which the horrible tune continued.

'Go on. Out of my kitchen!'

How they knew that tune she had no idea, but Diane didn't recognise it until they had disappeared through the door. It was the theme Diep had played before; but, whereas his had been wonderfully melodic, theirs resembled the shrill squeaking of a strangled animal. It must have stuck in their minds.

'No way,' signed Pip. 'I don't want to go to his party!'

'Why, honey? It'll do you good. Anyway, it'll be better than brooding. It's stuffy up here in the roof, in spite of the air conditioning. It'll be cool by the lake. You'll love it!' cajoled Diane. If Diep wanted Pip to come, then she had to do her best to persuade him.

But he kept on shaking his head stubbornly, and Diane was

angry he was being so awkward.

'Dad's coming. You can talk to each other,' she wheedled. If only Pip could …

Diane and Dave had discussed Pip over breakfast.

'I thought Koppelberg was here to work,' Dave said.

'He is – but he's here to help Pip most of all. You know that. And, at least …' she hesitated, '… he's getting some response.'

'What do you mean?'

'I mean Diep has already had an effect on him!'

Dave put down his fork and looked at his wife. 'And don't we know it!'

'I didn't mean it that way; only that since Diep came, Pip's more alive. Responsive. Things are happening. Before, he didn't want to know. He was content to leave things the way they were.'

'I don't agree.' Dave went straight to the point. 'I think the guy's upset him.'

'That's what I mean, Dave. Diep has made him think again, *live* again!'

She hadn't meant to be so vehement, so emotional, to praise Diep like that. Diane knew she had gone far enough, as she saw Dave's expression. After so long with one man, she could sense his every mood.

'You're really hooked on this character, aren't you?' Dave said. 'I suppose you haven't noticed the look on our son's face when we mention the guy. For Chrissake, Di, the kid hates him. I wouldn't call that living. He can't stand Koppelberg!'

'I don't know what's the matter with you both!' Dave was just about to remonstrate when she added, 'And you're jealous – you must be! Why? I only want to help Pip. I don't want to see him give up. I want him to feel again. Can't you understand that?'

'And so do I. But I don't want him half frightened to death! For some reason, Koppelberg has scared the shit out of him!'

240

Di slapped the lid on to the marmalade jar and began clearing away, swooping the twins' uneaten crusts into a brittle, misshapen heap. 'I can't see why you're like this!' Her face was flushed.

'You said it was jealousy. Remember.' Dave stood up from the table. 'I tell you one thing, honey, the guy has managed to get us two going. When did we last fight? And I am not jealous. But there's been nothing but trouble since that guy came. He's a jinx. And is it right, having a party with two of our neighbours dead? It doesn't seem so to me.'

'Point taken. But it's nothing to do with Diep. I thought you weren't superstitious.'

'I'm not. I just don't like kids' parties!' Dave looked so much like a kid as he said it that Di smiled. She came over and put her arms round him.

'I know, honey, but kids do. I'm doing it for Rose and Teddy. To cheer them up. They don't understand what's going on. They just want to have a nice time. Don't spoil it for them. Please?'

The emotional blackmail worked. 'Well, okay, but ...'

'Thanks, Dave. And Pip will come down if you're there. He needs something to cheer him up as well. Can I tell him you want him to go?'

'Okay.' He nodded. Di was satisfied. She could read her husband like a book ...

Di looked at her son, his stubborn chin thrust out. So like his dad – a carbon copy.

'Please, Pip. For me?'

Dad's really coming? he wrote.

She nodded. 'Everything's going to be fine. Just fine. We'll have a great time. It's ages since we had a party. And who knows? You might enjoy it.'

I won't, replied Pip in his scrawled, black writing. The defiant letters made her eyes sting. *But I'll come. Just for you.*

Di was so pleased. At that moment she could have gone

back to the kitchen and made a mountain of cupcakes and let Rose draw cows and pigs all over them.

'Great. You've made me really happy.' She squatted beside his chair and put her arm round him. 'I want you to like Diep. He can help you – if you'll let him.'

She had her face turned away as she said it half to herself. Suddenly she felt Pip stiffen and draw himself back from her. She didn't think anything about it at the time, but when she was back downstairs she realised it was like he'd heard what she'd said. Diane dismissed the idea as pure imagination.

Mel drew out the black lace bikini, thinking how Mom had told her to take it back to the store. She could almost hear her mother's disapproving voice. *Mel, where on earth could you wear that? What will Dad say?* It was brief all right – indecent – but today Mel felt reckless, uncaring. And why shouldn't she? The way her whole family was behaving lately was enough to scare any guy off, and she wasn't going to lose Diep. When he saw her in this, he would flip!

Mel turned to make sure her bedroom door was shut tight. She didn't want Rose coming in. Her little sister was nosy. Then she went over to the window and looked out. No sign of anyone. The smell of Mom's cupcakes was still wafting through her room. When she had closed the door, she had trapped their homely tang. She looked again. There was nothing homely about her black bikini.

Mel stepped out of her shorts and pants, lifted her arms and pulled her vest right over her head. She was just about satisfied by the sight. As she turned, her naked body looked okay in the mirror.

Wait – Mel screwed her head round – was she putting weight on her tush? The pale brush of her pubic hair blazed in the dim room. Suddenly she was thinking of Diep. At that moment he was as real to her as if he was watching.

Mel swallowed nervously and, bending forward, let her small rounded breasts fall into the lace cups of the bikini. Then she pulled on the bottom half, which settled gracefully, provocatively showing off her hips. She was humming his tune in her head.

Mel stood appraising her figure, cupping her breasts protectively. She really had the hots for Diep. She was going to wear the bikini that afternoon – nobody was going to stop her – and he wouldn't be able to take his eyes off her.

After she'd tried on the bikini, she took it off and laid it on the bed, then got dressed again. It was only when she was going out of the door that she felt a brief stab of guilt. How many times had she promised Sam Junior she'd wear it to the lake? Now he'd never see her in it.

'Still,' said Mel, under her breath, 'that's life!' It was only when she shut the door behind her that she thought how much she'd changed since the music teacher had filled her life and her dreams. There was no room to think about Sam. It was awful that he'd died that way, but she'd never really cared for him like *that*, had she?

'Rain, rain, go away!' shouted Teddy, feeling a big drop sting his warm forehead. 'Everything'll be spoiled!' His ball was grinning. It didn't care. 'What are you laughing at?' he growled. 'I'll kick you down the drain again!'

The yellow ball stirred in the hot wind, which was blowing in from the lake, as if it was going to take up the little boy's challenge. Then, suddenly, the wind lulled back and instead began to play with the tablecloth, lifting it off the trestle.

Rose caught the end of it and smoothed it down with her fat little hand. Where was Diep? What was he doing over there? Maybe he was feeding his pets? Rose wanted to go and help him.

Several big drops were falling now. The twins could see Mom looking out of the window and up at the sky. Suddenly, Rose and Teddy were standing side by side, squinting into space. They screwed up their faces, clenching their teeth together to frighten the storm away.

'Rain, rain, go away!

'Come again another day

'And not on Diepee's birthday!'

They chanted in unison, staring hard at each other in concentration, then fell quiet.

At that very moment the low, dark clouds let through slivers of light, which penetrated the surface of the lake, making it glitter near to the landing stage. Immediately, the twins lifted their palms and slapped them together in triumph!

'Look, Dave, the twins are going crazy,' Diane called to her husband. 'And not at each other for once! I can't believe it. They're playing nicely!'

Dave nodded, then turned, 'I guess you're right about this party, Di.' He was looking at the sandwiches, cakes, hot dogs on sticks. Di had really gone to town.

He regarded his wife carefully. 'But all this extra work? Is he really worth it? A birthday party? How old is the guy, anyway?'

'Thirty-six, I think,' she said. Diane wasn't sure how she knew Diep's age, but she did. At that moment she felt Mel standing right behind her, facing her father.

'Yeah, Mom, he's thirty-six. Why, Dad?' Dave shook his head. He realised Mel was challenging him to say something bad about the guy. He also knew his daughter was stuck on the music teacher. It was better he said nothing. Then she'd get it out of her system.

And yet, for one startling moment, Dave was disgusted that she'd forgotten Sam Junior already, when he was hardly cold in his grave. What made women so fickle?

Dave shook off the thought. What was the matter with him? His daughter was probably hiding her feelings for the Mayor's son. It had been a shock for all of them, never mind Mel. He was being insensitive.

A low rumble of warning thunder rippled above the house. Dave picked up one of the cakes.

'Can I?'

'I suppose so,' said Di, impatiently, 'but you're worse than the twins!'

As he was eating the heart out of the pink icing, Dave was praying the rain would come and wash away that son-of-a-bitch as well as his party.

It was the nearest thing to praying Pip had tried for years. The Durrant family weren't religious and, as for Pip, he had never forgiven God for letting the tree fall on Dad's car. He nearly believed there wasn't any God, because who would leave a kid like him, mute and crippled?

That afternoon Pip wanted to feel different. When the rat, Snipe, had been running round his room, he'd prayed then – in his mind. And in that nightmare of Koppelberg's chalet, after he'd fallen out of the chair and knocked his head, he'd prayed none of it would ever come back, that he'd forget it all. So far, it hadn't worked.

But, now, he needed God to take away the horrible feeling that was pressing on his chest, choking his throat like when Bufo had hit him. Bufo? Cass? They'd never found Cass. But Pip knew where she was. Snipe had got her. His eyes filled with tears.

He stared at his pets. They took no notice, were quiet and listless. The weather was affecting them; they were always like that before a storm. *Please, God, make it rain. Please?* he prayed.

But the feeling that nothing was right anymore, with himself or with anyone, just wouldn't go away. And Koppelberg had done it – made him think horrible thoughts, made him see horrible things that he'd never wanted to see.

Worst of all, Pip still didn't know if they'd been real. All he knew was his music teacher was bad, *very* bad, and that the man *knew* that Pip knew. What was going to happen to them all?

Nobody would listen to him, nobody! Except for Dad. He might. But what would he say, what would he do, if Pip told him about the things in the chalet? They couldn't be real. Maybe Pip was going mad?

God, he prayed, his eyes closed, *let it all come right! Don't let them take me away!*

When he opened his eyes, he was shocked to see all the little guys were staring at him. The mole's head bulged out of the top of a grey mound of its own making; its bright, hard, black, stony eyes were fixing him. On top of his case, Strangler's limp coils were heaped against the glass, but the snake's head was waving slightly, its dull, unblinking eyes focused on Pip. The old and ugly tortoise, which had no name, was spread-eagled against its glass, its thin V of a mouth cracked in a sinister grin.

Pip swallowed. Not even his pets liked him anymore. He was alone, stuck in the silent prison of his useless body. The boy threw himself back in his wheelchair, shaking his head to get rid of all those terrible thoughts. After two minutes of frustrated silence, he began to bang on the floor for his mother to come up.

14

'And when all were in to the very last,
The door in the mountainside shut fast.
Did I say all? No, one was lame,
And could not dance the whole of the way.'

The sun was still sending shafts of light onto the lake surface as Dave lit the barbecue. The black clouds still hung about like sulky children, but the sun was stubborn. Maybe it wasn't going to rain, after all?

The twins were running along the edge of the water, jumping over the pebbles, splashing each other like crazy things.

Diane carried out the pieces of steak on a tray and set them down beside Dave. 'Okay?' she asked, looking at the curling flames licking the charcoal.

He nodded. 'Sure!' The air was filling with smoke as they both glanced in the direction of the twins.

'Don't let them go right in, will you, honey?' asked Diane. She was staring at the lake as if she didn't care at all and had other things on her mind. He could guess what and it annoyed him.

'Of course I won't!' He spoke too sharply and Diane flashed him a surprised, hurt look that said, *Don't spoil this afternoon, will you?*

'I'll bring Pip out in a minute,' she said. 'He seemed really upset when I went upstairs. I just can't understand what's the matter with him.' Diane went back inside.

Dave looked across to the landing stage. There was no sign of Koppelberg. The fag probably took a couple of hours to change. 'Dolls!' he said under his breath.

At that very moment, Rose let out a high, thin scream. Dave dropped the meat and the fork and ran towards her. She was jumping about, holding her foot.

'What's the matter?' he shouted. She was hopping over to him, crying.

'The stone bit my foot!' He kissed the place where the stone had bruised her. The little girl clung to him and he liked the feel of her warm body. It was then that he saw Teddy was in the lake up to his waist.

'Come out of there!' he shouted. Teddy was glaring, but he retreated. 'What do you think you're doing going in on your own?' he scolded.

'I was looking for my ball!' Teddy replied indignantly.

'Well, it won't be in there.'

'Diep said it was.'

'Then Diep was wrong,' retorted Dave.

Suddenly the afternoon brightened as the clouds got the worst of it after all. The sun had won. Dave put Rose down carefully. 'Okay now?' He straightened as she wriggled out of his arms. He could hear the sounds of Pip's wheelchair crunching its way across to the barbecue area but, then, a blinding flash of light struck his eyes.

He put up a hand to ward it off. It was coming from the landing stage. Dave could see nothing for a moment, and heard only Rose's and Teddy's joyous squeal. A moment later, the light had disappeared and the twins were sprinting round the margin of the shore. Rose had forgotten her bad foot and Teddy his bad temper. Then Dave knew why.

They were running towards a tall, lean figure in bathing shorts, who was holding in his hand something that glittered and twinkled like a wonderful plaything.

'It's beautiful,' Diane half-whispered the words. She was at Dave's elbow. He looked down into Pip's miserable, downcast features.

'His flute,' she added softly. 'I've never seen an instrument like it – and when he plays ...' She breathed in deeply, her eyes fixed on Koppelberg, who now had the twins leaping about him.

Dave saw the music teacher lift the instrument, and the sun spilled its yellow on it, not fiercely like before, but bathing it in magical light.

The three of them listened as the trills shivered and rang through the quiet of the afternoon. Dave shook his head as if he wasn't seeing properly. All he could feel was Pip's pleading hand pulling at the hairs on his forearm. He could hardly take his eyes off the trio but, as he bent down, he saw Pip signing. It brought him back to sharp reality.

'Make him go away, Dad, please!'

Dave patted his son's arm and stood defiantly turning the steak as Koppelberg approached, followed by the twins.

'It was so beautiful,' said Diane, watching them.

Then Dave snapped the spell. 'Who does he think he is? The goddamn Pied Piper? Ow!'

What the hell was he thinking of? He'd only tried to turn the meat with his bare hands! Sucking his burned finger, Dave stooped to retrieve the fork. It was then he saw the agony in Pip's eyes. Trying to make a decision whether or not to spoil the whole afternoon, he masked his anxiety by going to stoop beside the lake and dip his burned hand into the water. He thought the trio would pass him by, but they came to a halt.

'Hi,' said Koppelberg. 'You ought to be more careful. Fire is dangerous!' His voice was high like a woman's and his flute dangled down beside his slender brown legs. He'd been watching Dave stooping to pick up the fork. It was as if he knew Dave's knees felt like they were cracking up. Dave stared at the instrument. Where had the guy found the dollars for that? He'd probably stolen it! Then the flute disappeared. Its owner looked up.

'It's been in my family for generations,' said Koppelberg, twirling it like a sharpshooter in the movies. 'Forever!' he grinned.

Dave didn't return the smile. He just got up.

'Come on, kids,' Diep added, ignoring Dave. 'Let's go over to the barbecue and see if the meat's ready.'

'You didn't say happy birthday, Daddy!' Teddy's voice was unnaturally shrill as he turned his small, fair head in Dave's direction. Rose followed suit.

'No, you didn't,' she said, sounding peeved.

Dave didn't want to spoil their fun. 'Many happy returns, Mr Koppelberg!' he called, then turned on his heel.

Diep looked down at the children and smiled. They lifted small, trusting hands.

'My returns are always happy,' he said, taking their chubby palms in his. 'Come on, I'm *very* hungry!' His light-blue eyes blazed as he made for the meat.

'What *is* Mel doing?' asked Diane indignantly, as they clustered around the barbecue. 'I was hoping she'd help.'

Dave was taking a rest from turning the steak, lying on the grass, supporting himself on his elbows. The wheels of Pip's chair were very close to his face. His instincts told him his son wanted to be near him while Koppelberg was cavorting around, the twins chasing him, going crazy and screaming.

'I'll go and look for her,' he said, about to get up. It was then he noticed the music teacher stop, placing a hand on each of the twins' shoulders. They were all looking towards the house. Dave followed suit.

Mel was coming across the grass, stepping daintily, her black sneakers making no noise. Diane gasped. Her father swallowed. He'd seen her in some things – but that! The lace bikini left nothing to the imagination. It was worse than being naked. It was the kind of thing Dave had seen in the strip club they'd raided a few weeks earlier. Tassels on the nipples would go with it! *How could she come out like that?* In front of *him*. And what if she turned round? Dave imagined what she'd look like from behind with that thong.

He jumped up and met his daughter half way. 'Go and take it off,' he said quietly. Mel's eyes flashed dangerously. He had seen that look on her face before. Insolence.

'No!' she hissed. 'What's the matter with it? I won't! I like it!'

'It's obscene,' he said. The twins were giggling. 'Get in the house!' he ordered, and his eyes glinted dangerously. 'Put your other swimsuit on.' All Dave could see were Koppelberg's mocking eyes.

'You're just horrible,' she said, ignoring her father. Dave was very, very angry. He wasn't going to allow her to parade herself outside like that, whatever she wore in the house.

'Take it off,' he said. Ignoring Dave completely, Melanie walked right past him, towards Koppelberg and the kids. There was nothing he could do, short of grabbing hold of her and dragging her into the house.

Diane's eyes were warning him. He returned to the barbecue to stand beside Pip. Reaching down, he stroked the boy's shoulder. Only the two of them understood. It was like the bond between him and his son was stronger than ever before, joined in hostility towards the stranger in their midst. Dave talked to Pip under his breath as though his son could hear him.

'Don't worry, kid, I'll get rid of the guy. I'll find something on him. Something that will bring your sister and the rest of them to their senses. I will. I promise.'

Mel watched Diep intent on his steak, wringing out every succulent drop, chewing, then swallowing. She quivered as she sat beside him at the wooden trestle table, while her small brother and sister crammed cake down their throats like there was no tomorrow.

The heat exuding from Diep's leg was unbearable. One more tiny movement and her calf would be pressing against his. Her dad couldn't see. Nor could he understand how she loved this guy. This *must* be love. She'd felt nothing stronger in her life. She was drawn to Diep like iron to a magnet. One moment and she'd be there.

As she touched his leg, Diep leaped up with a yell. He'd spilled his coffee all over his trunks.

'Oh, you've been burned!' cried Diane, while the twins stared solemnly, their mouths stuffed full.

Mel was triumphant – not because he'd been hurt, but because she'd *made* him do it. Her touch had startled him so much that he'd tipped up his coffee. He'd felt that same electricity that had given her throbs deep inside.

Diep wasn't red with embarrassment, only from the burn. He was looking straight at Mel as he stood and let Diane soak a cloth in water and hand it to him so he could press it on his leg. His eyes told Mel that he knew how she felt. That it wasn't her fault. She wanted to go to him, comfort him, but he was retreating, holding the cloth to his thigh.

'Well, I guess I'd better go and change again!' he said.

'I can go and get you some ointment,' said Diane, but he was getting further away. Then he threw down the cloth and leaped into the lake, swimming with strong strokes in the direction of the landing stage. They all watched him.

'I guess that hurt,' said Diane. The twins resumed eating.

'As he's off to change, don't you think *you* should?' asked Dave. Mel stared him out steadily.

'Now, stop it, you two. She's been wearing it all afternoon, so what the hell?' said Diane, pulling off her apron. She was thinking of the stretch marks at the top of her thighs. She'd have given anything to look like her daughter. 'Wow, it's hot!' She flopped into the deckchair.

Mel shaded her eyes with her hand, watching Diep climb up the steps to the small landing stage, walk across the boards and disappear into the chalet.

'I wonder how long he's going to be?' she asked her mother.

'Not long,' was her father's dry reply.

Mel looked at Pip. 'Cheer up, it's never going to happen,' she said. She felt mean as hell, even though she knew he couldn't hear. Then, full of remorse, she picked out a cake with a pink heart and handed it to him. But he never smiled.

'Gee, this is a great party,' Mel remarked sarcastically, settling herself in the other deckchair.

Diane sat up, looking at the twins. 'Stop stuffing, you two. You'll be sick!' She was strangely relaxed, feeling she wouldn't care if they threw up everywhere. Suddenly, the sun went in.

At that moment the telephone extension, which Dave had rigged up in the garden, began to ring. 'Oh, no, don't say you're going to be called out. Not today!' cried Diane.

Dave jumped up. He wouldn't be sorry if he was. But, as he walked towards the house, he noticed how white Pip had become. He knew it had been a mistake to let this party go ahead and he was angry with himself for letting Diane cajole him into it. If she hadn't, then Pip wouldn't be suffering. As soon as he picked up the phone, he knew *he* was off the hook at least. Patsy Doran had a story to tell that meant he was going to be out for some time. Now he felt even sorrier for Pip, but what could he do about it?

'Looks like some pervert's on the loose,' said Patsy. It took something to make the big Irishman sound that excited. 'A call came in from the patrolman over at Big Falls. Some kids have been approached by a guy. I'm out there now. You better get over here straight away.' The receiver crackled madly. It was probably the weather. 'I don't like the sound of it. The kids were terrified!' Patsy's tone reflected the urgency of the matter in spite of the poor reception.

'On my way!' Dave replaced the receiver. It would take ten minutes to get to Big Falls. Patsy had despatched another patrol car to the scene of the crime first and then had called Dave. That's all they needed in Sunny Mead now: a sicko.

Mel was watching her father. Yes, he was going out on a call all right. She was glad.

'I'll be back soon!' he hollered. 'Got to go over to Big Falls. Look after the kids, Mel. And find some shade for Pip. Give your mom a rest! She looks as though she's had it!'

Diane made a face from the deckchair and closed her eyes again. 'Trust him to be called out,' she muttered. 'Who'd be married to a cop? At least he's had his meal!' She felt really grumpy.

Mel was angry too. Why should she have to look after the kids? She had better things to do than play nursemaid. Still, she didn't resent Pip.

'Hi!' She leaned over the wheelchair. She felt so sorry for her brother. It must be shit having to sit there all the time. 'More cake?' He shook his head, his lips set in a thin, miserable line. He wasn't enjoying the party either. Pip was on a total downer.

She wheeled him into the shade of the only tree their side of the lake, pulling the peaked cap over his eyes. 'Better?'

He didn't respond. Mel shrugged and left him. Perhaps he'd go to sleep as well. His eyes were screwed up real tight.

Pip was terrified. Sometimes when he closed his eyes and shut out the sky and everything about him, he pretended no-one could see him either. If only it were true.

He opened his lids and, swivelling his head, saw his father about to reverse the car. He was leaving them alone ... and there was going to be a storm! Pip looked up at the sky, which wasn't smiling either. He was really scared.

Then his heart gave a little jump. The car had stopped. Had Dad changed his mind? He was getting out, waving his arms. Mel was running towards him. What was he saying? Pip hated himself that he couldn't hear.

'Hey, Mel! Looks like there's going to be a storm after all. Don't let the kids near the water! Get cleared up and in the house!'

'What about the party?' was Mel's rebellious reply.

'What do you think? Just do it!'

Mel thought how nice it would be if everybody could give orders like that and just be obeyed. Dave turned and jumped back into the Ford.

Pip's heart lurched. Dad was going out after all. The sky was very black as the car headed off to meet the storm on the horizon. Pip began to shake. He couldn't keep his hands still. Suddenly, he was thinking again about the last storm he'd been out in, and what had happened to Dad and him in the accident.

It was almost like night-time in the valley, but by the time Dave was a mile from Big Falls the sky was clearing again. He could see the black and white patrol car in the distance. A small crowd of people were standing around the kids.

The biggest boy was about 14; his brother about nine. They'd been on a hike. The boy's face was white, crowned by a mop of black curls. He spoke very fast as if he wanted to get it over with.

'The guy just walked out in front of us. I thought he was going to ask us the way at first, but when I looked at his face I was really scared.' He looked down at the ground and dug the toe of his trainers into the dirt.

'You don't have to be scared now,' said Dave gently. The boy's obvious distress brought Pip's face into sharp focus.

'Tell the chief what was the matter with him, kid,' said Patsy, with a meaningful look at Dave.

'Well …' the boy looked up and bit his lip, '… well, he had all these spots, you know, like *bites*. And some of them were bleeding.'

Dave grimaced. Maybe the guy had bad acne? He glanced at the little boy, who looked sick. He was staring at Dave as if he wanted to run at him and hide his face like Teddy did when he wasn't being brave.

'Is that right?' he asked.

'Yeah,' the younger burst out. 'They were all over his face! I want my mom!' He began to cry. The big boy sniffed and put a protective arm around the little one's shoulders.

Patsy Doran looked even grimmer. He had heard some of the story from the patrolman who'd taken the call. 'There's a lot more to it than that, Dave,' he said quietly. Then, turning to the big boy, he added, 'You can tell us the rest when we get you back.' They usually got a fully trained child officer on something like this.

As they got the boys in the car, Dave said to the sergeant, 'Well, I wouldn't let my kids out on a hike on their own, not with the world the way it is, but that's parents for you. As for the perv, he'll be on his way by now.' He looked around at the forest.

'No sweat,' said Patsy. 'The guys are going to give us a real good description. Wait until you hear the rest!' Dave lifted his eyebrows.

The patrol car drove off, the boys squeezed into the back. Dave swallowed as he caught the terrified expression on the bigger boy's white face as he looked out of the window: it was so much like Pip's. Then he got into his own car, switched on the ignition and followed them.

It was a miracle! As soon as her dad had gone, so had the storm. And everyone was excited – except Mom, who was fast asleep, and Pip, who had a peculiar look on his face.

Diep was back! He hadn't put on another pair of trunks; instead he was wearing trendy wet-suit leggings, half of yellow and half of red.

Mel couldn't help admiring how he fitted into them. The guy's body was absolutely perfect, glistening and wet from his return swim. His long blond hair fell in damp rings onto his shoulders and his bright blue eyes were the focal point in his tanned face. He was gorgeous.

'Come on, kids, watch me,' he invited.

They were dazzled by him. Walking on water wouldn't have been hard for him. A swift dive here, then another there, in and out of the limpid lake. The twins were squeaking with delight as he crawled out over the pebbles, snapping and snarling, laughing, pretending to be a dog.

Then Teddy was whistling Diep's special tune prettily, hurling his orange ball with its smiling teeth into the bubbling fringe of Branksome.

Diep's antics with the ball left them breathless. It was a dream of an afternoon. Mel felt all her inhibitions slipping away. She was jumping on his back, but he slithered away from her in the water again and again. Mel didn't hear Rose screaming with jealousy, because her world was full of magic and water and Diep.

Later, he stood on a flat stone at the side of the lake and played the golden flute. They sat at his feet, gazing admiringly into his eyes, their receptive faces and ears open to his spell. And in the distance, the thunder rumbled.

The boy in the wheelchair could hear it. Hear it in spite of being deaf. Why did they like his music? To Pip, it was just a frightened shrieking of children and their clattering shoes and, behind, the multitudinous squeaking of a million Snipes. His teeth were chattering with cold fear.

How could they even look at him? The music teacher's legs and hands, scarred by burns, his face, covered in bleeding bites. But they loved him, all of them – except Pip. How could they? The red and yellow of the flames that had burned him hurt Pip's eyes.

He sat, a prisoner in a wheelchair, barred from their golden dreams; a cripple, tears falling down his cheeks. And only a few metres away his mother was sleeping deeply, oblivious to everything, in that sultry afternoon.

Pip watched the music teacher stand legs apart at the water's edge, his arched haunches showing the dark waters behind.

He shivered as Diep Koppelberg lifted his golden flute, then turned and plunged into the lake. Pip blinked. Was Koppelberg walking on the water, the flute to his lips? His eyes, blurred with tears, couldn't focus on the fair heads of his brother and sisters. Instead, their shapes grew in unsteady multiplication until there seemed to be hundreds of children at the water's edge ready to follow Diep Koppelberg.

Pip's mind was screaming out to them, trying to warn them, telling them not to follow, to stay where they were safe, but he could see them ready to enter that world of darkness, ready to follow the Piper into the mouth of the watery tunnel.

They hadn't been able to get in touch with the boys' parents yet, but they'd called in the policewoman who'd been partly trained to interview children. They agreed she'd ask some of the questions. When Dave asked if Patsy would like to be in too, Patsy shook his head: 'No way. If there's anything I hate it's child molesters.'

'You and me both,' replied Dave, as he went into the special room they kept for interviewing kids. It had a few toys and games scattered around, as well as some magazines. The boy called Chas with the black mop of hair then displayed an attitude that didn't surprise Dave, because he was 13.

'I don't want *her* in here,' he said. 'If *she's* here, I'm not going to say anything.' Dave could guess what was coming.

'Neither of us will be at all worried about whatever you tell us, Chas. And it's the officer's job. She's standing in for your mom.'

'I wouldn't tell *her*,' he said.

The little boy was very quiet and looking at one of the toy patrol cars.

'Think of *him*,' said Dave. 'You don't want that man frightening someone else like your brother, do you?'

Chas thought about it for a moment, then nodded. 'Okay, I'll tell *you*. She can write it down.'

'We're going to record this, Chas. Just to help us catch him. Is that okay?' The boy nodded and the policewoman switched on the tape. 'Now, what did this guy look like, besides the bites?' began Dave. The boy's face was already beginning to turn scarlet.

'Dirty blond hair – long, to here,' he touched his shoulders. 'Pale blue eyes. He was wearing ...' Chas looked across at his brother, who nodded, '... kinda – leggings. Yep. Red and yellow leggings and top. A wet suit. And he was laughing.'

'In the forest?' Dave frowned. A red and yellow wet suit? *Laughing. I bet he was.*

'It was wet because …' the small boy hesitated.

'Yes?' said Dave. The little boy looked down at the floor.

'Just wet.'

Dave thought maybe it would have been better to have interviewed Chas on his own, but he knew the boys would be even more upset if they parted them. Whatever that head case had done, he'd frightened the shit out of them.

'He'd been swimming, right?' probed Dave. This pervert had to be caught. 'At Big Falls?' He knew the riverbed had been dry for months. It only flooded in the heavy storms. 'Did you see a car?' The boys were shivering.

'No car. He just came!' said the little one.

'Just came out of nowhere,' added Chas. 'One moment he wasn't there … then …' The boy hesitated.

'… Then he was,' added his brother.

There was silence, although the small boy was getting nearer to Dave.

'You can level with me,' said Dave. 'We're used to this kind of thing. Don't be shy. Did he touch you?' Chas looked Dave in the eyes, then quickly away. 'Did he …' They were both staring at the floor, shuffling their feet on the carpet. 'Did he do anything else?'

'If you mean did he show us his willy …' said the big one. He hesitated. 'Well …'

'Go on?' Dave was waiting, while the policewoman scribbled away. He made a slight, friendly movement with his eyes towards the small boy, who looked as though he was ready to tell him something important.

'Okay, you can say it,' he soothed.

'He had a rat,' whispered the little one in Dave's ear.

'A rat? Tell us about it. Okay?'

The boy nodded, head down.

'Where was it?' The policewoman's contemptuous eyes were telling Dave what *his* mouth wasn't saying – that the bastard deserved a taste of his own medicine.

'He had a rat in his hand; a big black one.'

'He was carrying a rat?' asked Dave, thinking that this was a first.

'Yep,' said the little one, looking at the elder. 'He was …' Next moment, the child's head was down and he suddenly burst into tears. The policewoman went over to him and stroked his shoulder. He didn't stop her.

'Come on, little guy, come on, you're just upset!' she said.

Then the older boy was looking at Dave. His face was white and terrified. Suddenly, he shouted, 'Where's the john? I gotta be sick …'

Next moment, Dave was holding on to him and half-dragging him to the Men's. It was there that Chas sobbed out the story he must have made up to block out what had really happened.

If ever a pervert needed a shrink, it was that one. But Dave just couldn't get the idea of that rat out of his mind. *A rat for a dick?* Kids could imagine anything.

They left it at that for the time being. Once the kids' parents had been contacted and been asked to come over as soon as possible, Dave stood looking out through his office window.

Suddenly Cass's disappearance after Pip had found Bufo slipped into focus. Then he remembered Teddy's foot and his little son's talk of the ball. After that he found himself thinking about Koppelberg: long blond hair; pale blue eyes? But there was no way it could have been the music teacher. He'd seen the guy swim off to the chalet. He couldn't have been at Big Falls.

Dave dismissed the idea, but irrational suspicions kept nagging at him, biting into his consciousness. Through the window, he noticed that the sky was like pewter. He hoped Mel and Diane had managed to get all the things back into the house in time. There was no chance Sunny Mead was going to avoid this storm – and it looked like being a big one. The wind was already bending over the tops of the trees.

The phone made him jump. He picked up the receiver; a woman's voice came crackling on the line. 'Hello. Am I connected to the Sunny Mead police? I'd like to speak to Detective Durrant.' It was a level, unfriendly voice.

'Speaking,' said Dave.

'Good afternoon ...' The woman seemed awkward in her approach as well. She was hesitating. 'I received your message from my office. It isn't open at the moment, but my secretary got in touch.'

Then Dave understood. 'Is that the college?'

'That's right. Voluntree Music College. Miss Lois Reedham speaking.' Her accent jarred – brash New York, still unfriendly. 'This is awfully strange, Detective Durrant. I phoned especially when I saw your exchange.'

'My exchange, Miss Reedham?'

'You are Sunny Mead, New Hampshire?'

'That's right,' said Dave patiently. There was silence.

'And you were inquiring about a Mr Koppelberg?' The voice faltered for a moment, then he heard her clearing her throat. 'I don't quite know how to put this. In 1952 ...'

'1952?' asked Dave. He didn't understand. The voice that returned was elderly, brittle and irritable.

'Yes, 1952. I was then the principal of Camdee College, nothing to do with Voluntree, but – I looked up your query and – you did say Koppelberg?' The woman was quite exasperating. 'A very unusual name. You haven't made a mistake? *Diep* Koppelberg? Flautist?'

'Yes, yes?' Dave prompted. 'What are you trying to tell me, Miss Reedham?'

'I could ask you what you're trying to tell *me*. Especially in vacation. Our records show that, in 1952, we had a teacher called Koppelberg – for a short time.'

'Thirty-six years ago?' What the hell did the woman mean?

'Right. Thirty-six years ago, Detective Durrant.' Her voice was very distant. 'Is this a hoax? Over here in Voluntree, we are not likely to forget 1952.'

'What happened to Koppelberg, Miss Reedham?' Dave's

tone was flat. He noticed he was perspiring freely. It was muggy in the office.

'That is the problem, Detective. After he was offered the vacation post in New Hampshire …'

'What?'

'A teaching post. He unfortunately disappeared.'

'Disappeared?'

'Yes.' Dave could hear anxiety, annoyance, exasperation in her tone. 'Disappeared. Somewhere in your area I believe. That's what you police said. They made enough inquiries. Disappeared, together with …' another long pause '… with his pupils.'

'Disappeared?' Dave felt like a parrot. All he could do was repeat what the woman was saying.

'Two children. Twins. Six years old. It was very painful for all of us. According to the records my predecessors kept, the children drowned. And him. All of them. It was most distressing. I hope you have a very good reason for dragging all this up again!' The tone was peevish and accusing.

'Twins?' That was all Dave could say.

'I don't know why you want to know, Detective. Seeing as it was in your area. It was a very long time ago. I hope this isn't your idea of a joke. Or are you just checking your records?' The sarcasm was instantly discernible, her voice high and piercing.

'Let me tell you,' she continued, 'it took a long time for this college to recover. The scandal, you know. It caused me enough pain in the past. I'm afraid your enquiry has really upset me.'

'I'm sorry you feel like that, Miss Reedham, but believe me, it was a genuine enquiry.'

He could hardly hear her reply. The words kept running through his mind. Diep Koppelberg. Twins. Drowned. 1952? What was happening? He felt he was going mad. Then he controlled himself. There was silence at the end of the line.

'Miss Reedham, it *was* a genuine enquiry,' he repeated. 'However strange that may seem to you, I was not wasting your time. I'm extremely grateful for it. I'll certainly check our records.'

'Okay, Detective Durrant, it seems hard to believe, but that is the only Koppelberg we have ever had at Voluntree. And, hopefully, the last. Thank you.'

'No, thank you for your time. Goodbye.'

She hung up. Dave's mind was reeling. What was he going to do? Check it out? He hadn't time.

Whatever was going on down below in Sunny Mead was happening to his family and, even if he couldn't understand it, he was going to do something about it. *Act first, think afterwards* had never been his maxim, but this was different. He'd think about it later.

The sergeant looked up in surprise as Dave shot by him.

'Sorry, Patsy,' he shouted, 'but I have to get back. It's urgent. I'll call you. And make sure you look after those kids!' As he opened the door and was about to run across the car park a zigzag flash of lightning took him by surprise. The thunder followed with hardly a pause between. The storm was breaking overhead.

As Dave reached his car, great drops of rain were falling from the sky. It had begun.

Pip watched his sister and Koppelberg swimming away, making for the small landing stage. The man's sleek, fair head was like an animal's bobbing through the water, and Mel's hair floated behind her as she rose up and down, her rhythmical breast action matching his crawling movements, stroke for stroke.

Mel was going with him. To the chalet. Large drops of rain pattered onto Pip's forehead. He wheeled himself close to his mother. He shook her. If only he could speak!

But she couldn't or wouldn't take any notice of his frantic shaking. It was like she was under a spell! He gave up trying. The rain was splashing onto the dirty plates, into the beakers and empty cans of coke.

Where were the twins?

He shook his mother again. She smiled as she dozed. The goose-bumps rose on his arms. Why couldn't she feel the rain? Was she dead? But she wouldn't be smiling. It was the only relief Pip could feel.

Where were the twins?

And his mom would be soaking wet through: as wet as if she was swimming across Branksome – like Mel and Koppelberg were doing.

He could feel, right through the whole of himself, that the storm was on its way. He craned his neck to look behind.

It was creeping up on them, its long black fingers probing the whole of their valley, prising it open. Soon it would be tearing at the flimsy buildings, ready to rip them apart with lightning.

Where were the twins?

When he looked turned and looked at the lake, he couldn't believe it. Branksome was calm and peaceful, no heavy raindrops making it seethe and boil. And the twins were there: watching too, staring after those disembodied heads in the water making for the chalet. They stood quietly, hand-in-hand.

What Pip's terrified eyes were telling him couldn't be true. The margin of the shore was dry. Only he and his mother were caught in the rain! And then he saw Teddy and Rose trot off like obedient, small ponies in step.

He knew where they were going, who they were following. He had to stop them! With one last vain shake, Pip left his mother and heaved himself over the grass towards the lake. No way would he let those kids see what was in the chalet. No way! He would follow the path round and head them off. If only he could have shouted to them!

Pip rolled himself out of reality and the grey misery of a wet Sunny Mead afternoon into a world where time was standing still once more; seemingly suspended in golden sunlight, but with no earthly warmth, only the coldness of the tomb.

Dave swore at himself for not exchanging the Ford. He'd known for ages there was a problem with the engine and he'd promised Diane he'd fix it. If the bastard broke down, he'd never make it!

The whole of the world outside the car was one flailing sheet of silver-wet streaks cascading down the windscreen, throwing bits of twig fiercely on the glass. The wipers could hardly cope.

The mountain road that led into the valley was becoming more treacherous every minute; as dangerous as it had been that other time Dave couldn't bear to think of. He fought off any memory of the accident. However bad the storm was, this time he was going to get through. God knew what was going on down below.

Mel's bare foot touched the wooden step underwater. She clung on, while Diep swung himself out and up in front of her. She was disappointed when he didn't offer to help but stood, a gigantic figure above her, legs apart, blocking out the sun dropping low over the roof of the chalet. She felt warm, exhilarated by the swim – and what might be coming next.

He must have been reading her mind. Immediately, he stooped, holding out his hand. She grasped it – and gasped. It was freezing, and his hard nails dug into her palm as he heaved her ashore.

Diep didn't say a word. He just walked across the bare boards in front of her. Perhaps he was shy? She adjusted the black synthetic lace of her bikini. She shouldn't have worn it really; it wasn't meant to swim in. But she'd had to follow him. She'd follow him forever.

She was glad he was in front of her as she pulled the thin, uncomfortable thong of material from between her buttocks. Whatever did she look like from behind?

At the precise moment she went through the door, Mel felt a tiny sliver of fear. What was she doing going inside? Too late. She was in. It was very cold. She shivered again – then jumped.

A slight tickle of wind brushed her legs, a tiny movement. For a split second, she thought it was a cat. She looked; there was nothing.

'This is nice,' she said, looking round the room. The focal point of the living area was where glass display cases were arranged against the wall next to the window. Diep was some collector – and neat too – in every sense.

Strangely the cases had red curtains drawn inside the glass. Mel had seen that done in one of the big stores. It was more personal than having everything on display for every nosy parker who looked through your window. Diep was security-conscious, which was good these days. But she was dying to see inside.

'Diep! Are these your dolls?' she called. She could hear noises in the kitchen like rustling papers. He was probably making coffee. 'I could do with a towel, if you don't mind?'

She was quite cold now, although the sun was blazing through the windows, striking the flute, lying where he'd placed it on the table beside its case. She went over and looked at the instrument. It was fantastic, an antique for sure, hand-carved with the figures of dancing children. She touched it and, to her surprise, it was covered in red dust. Mel made a face. Still, he couldn't be a housewife as well as everything else.

There was an interesting lamp on the table, too, its stem carved like a snake's body – so life-like it seemed real. Mel didn't touch that. She hated snakes.

She was even colder. She turned, thinking she'd go and see where he was, but she hesitated. He might be in the bedroom. He was probably changing. She felt warmer thinking of that. As she was about to cross the room to approach the kitchen she paused in surprise.

She squinted at the cases. She was sure all the curtains had been drawn. But the red velvet of the last case was pushed half-aside. She mustn't have noticed before.

So she went up to it and looked in, her reflection staring at her like a small, white, naked ghost. She gasped. The piercing eyes of two wooden dolls seemed to be staring straight at her … Funny – she would have thought he'd have bought pretty ones with china faces. These had rough-cut features, like they'd been hacked from blocks of wood. They were wearing some sort of odd costume. Mel didn't recognise it but she thought it was a bit like something she'd seen in a history book. The male doll had on a tall hat like a chimney pot and a plain black suit; the female, a white skirt and blouse, both of which were embroidered. Mel squinted at them. It was the same motif as the figures on the music case. She grimaced. They probably came from the same part of the world, wherever that was! Certainly not America. Neither did Mel like the doll's black apron and headscarf. They were creepy.

Suddenly, she found herself thinking about Rose – and Annie. Once Annie had been a lot prettier than the doll in the case, whose hair was braided in a very unusual way. Mel peered – that had to be real hair. Even creepier!

'Where do these dolls come from, Diep?' she repeated. No reply. Just as she was going to walk towards the kitchen, she suddenly felt warmth against her shoulders. He must have come out of the bedroom and crept up on her.

'Ummm,' she quivered languorously, feeling him behind her. Then his arms were hard and tight round her and her body was burning. She couldn't see Diep's face; only feel his quick, warm breath on her neck and shoulders.

Quivering with excitement, she allowed herself, arms pinioned, to be walked backwards towards the couch. Mel was laughing as he picked her right up like a little child and carried her away from the windows.

She was flirting all the way as she nuzzled her mouth into the soft hollow of his shoulder. His hold on her tightened, and she was stabbed suddenly by the sharp pain she'd felt before. 'Oh!' She closed her eyes momentarily. Seconds later, he laid her down on the couch. *I don't want a headache now*, thought Melanie, and opened her eyes seductively – then screamed in utter terror.

The naked old man dropped on his bony knees beside her, his pale eyes burning, his festering thumb pressed cruelly against the nape of her neck, strangling her vocal chords. His narrow, animal-like head with its dry, straggling, grey hair was an inch from her terrified face as he snarled, 'You little fool. Did you think I wanted *you*?'

One minute later, her struggling stopped as Koppelberg dealt Melanie a blow to the side of her face, which sent her into the merciful dark of the unconscious.

Dave struggled on through the merciless rain and mud, feeling the lightness on the steering wheel with increasing frustration as the car periodically slewed across the slippery, narrow mountain road leading to the valley.

The detective clenched his teeth together. All that mattered was that he made it down there. Coming off the road was a possibility he couldn't even consider. He wasn't going to slow down – he couldn't afford to.

Though panic was a stranger to Dave, all he could think about was his family. The bizarre conversation he'd had earlier on echoed in his brain. He was going to check Koppelberg out. A cop should never take anything for granted. There were too many head cases around.

Diane screwed up her eyes and wiped the rain off her face, trying to get her head together. She'd been having a marvellous dream. She and Diep had been swimming across the lake. Branksome had never seemed so golden, nor she so young. She looked exactly like Melanie. She was almost 16 again and quite untouched – by Maby, by anyone. And he had said he wanted her: Diep Koppelberg, the golden flute-player, the man who could make her dreams come true. They had kissed and … She looked round dizzily, down at herself, up at the sky, rain pouring down her face. She remembered where she was.

She was absolutely amazed and very angry. It showed a total lack of care on her children's part to let her sit in a deckchair in the pouring rain. Diane was back in the real world now. She must look like a drowned rat. It was no good getting as tired as this. How could she have fallen asleep outside in the middle of a storm? She didn't understand it. She struggled to her feet and gasped, holding her aching head.

The picnic site was one of devastation. The rain and wind had blown paper cups and plates everywhere. There were even some bobbing up and down in the lake. The tablecloths were ruined. She was soaked right through to the skin and there was no sign of any of her family. It was all too much. Her body felt stiff and her face uncomfortable and sore. She was sure to get a cold out of this. When she got hold of the lot of them, she'd give them hell.

Bending against the driving wind and rain, Diane battled her way towards the house. At least they'd had the sense to go in, if nothing else. She just couldn't understand the mentality of kids. And, as for Diep, what could he have been thinking of?

15

'A wondrous portal opened wide,
As if a cavern was suddenly hollowed;
And the Piper advanced and the children followed.'

The Cosmic Joker had played the best trick in his hand. He had tipped Pip's wheelchair forward, catapulting the boy into a patch of long grass adjacent to Adams's storm drain.

Kiefer Adams and his family, like all good conservationists, had sworn never to cut the grass. They had nurtured that piece of their lawn in the hope it would attract real American wildlife.

The scene was pure black comedy. The grass had been hiding a sizeable boulder, which some kids, playing out there, had moved. It had been lurking beside the path, its razor-sharp edge like the blade protruding from a chariot wheel.

And Pip had hit it. He also had no time to try to heave himself up into the chair again. It would take ages. There was nothing for it but to crawl the whole way to the chalet.

Christ! he swore, not praying now, only sick with fear and apprehension. If he didn't get a move on, he'd lose them all. It was like the fate of the whole of his world was in his hands.

He studied the way he should go. If he cut across the green patch, it would be harder for him to be seen. He might make the back door. He couldn't negotiate the front steps. But what if the door was closed? What would he do when he got there? What could he do?

Pip shrugged off his negative thoughts and began to inch and wriggle his painful way through the long grass. If he'd been a little kid, he could have pretended he was in a rain forest. The grass was high enough – and alive with insects. He had to keep spitting them away from his nose and his mouth. He was sure he'd sniffed up a couple. But he kept going.

The fear of what was waiting for his brother and sisters made him forget the agonising pain. Whatever happened to him, he had to save them. Pip laboured on, feeling his heart thudding inside him with his strenuous effort, tasting the salt drops of sweat running down and dripping off his nose.

He stopped to rest in his jungle-green prison. It was then he saw myriads of ugly insects hanging silently on every blade of grass. They were everywhere, like they'd been in the chalet. They were out to get him.

In a panic, Pip threw himself on, crushing them with his body, flattening the grass. He was shaking all over, remembering what was inside those three terrible glass cases; those unspeakable horrors shown to him by Koppelberg. He found himself hearing the taunting words of the statue man over and over again, in time with his frenzied breathing. *Koppelberg wasn't going to get the twins. Nor Mel.* The thought gave Pip the strength to struggle on, but the next moment was even worse. His hands and his mouth and nose were full of earth. *What the fuck had he got into?*

A gigantic molehill was blocking his way. It was like the nightmare. The smell of freshly-turned earth reminded him of that dreadful dream as he followed the mole, digging his way through innumerable tunnels, following Teddy and the ball. Pip spluttered and sneezed the earth from his mouth, felt it wet between his fingers, vile and disgusting.

He looked up at the sky, as he had done in his dream, and it was dark. Above his head the tall grass waved. It was like being in a grave. And the sky was black. The arch in the sky above was like a dark canvas, framed by the grasses.

Then, suddenly, stringing across it, came the shapes of

reeling bodies, their whirling dull-dark wings folding and flapping. The boy's frightened eyes didn't realise they were herons driven before the storm, saw only the vampire bats seeking out his blood with their needle teeth. He crawled on through the grass and then gasped, feeling a cold companion slithering beside him. A slow-worm? A snake? Not the familiar, warm, dry body of his garter, but the loose, flabby coils of the serpent he'd seen in the dream, fixing him with its dead eyes. It was as if Pip's own skin was crawling with it along the ground, brushing against the earth.

He couldn't turn his head. How could it be Strangler? The garter was safe in its tank. He was going nuts. He felt the creature slither off. He swallowed and, putting his hands carefully in front of him, began to part the tall grasses again so he could move on. It was then he felt sharp stinging on his hands, so sharp it brought tears to his eyes. As Pip grasped the tender, green tips of the common nettle, there seemed to be scorpions dancing through his brain.

Dave stood, cursing, his hair flattened in the wind, his wet trousers wrapped about his legs and the car door juddering, pulling and squeaking against the gale. What the hell was he going to do now?

The tree had been big, but not strong enough to withstand the force of the storm. Half of it had ripped right off and the impact had torn its roots out of the ground like tortured fingernails, blocking the road.

As Dave stood, transfixed, staring, he was thinking of that other tree that had flattened the roof of his car and crippled his son. It brought it all back to him. But this time, he'd been luckier.

He'd just have to leave the Ford and walk. He parked, ran round to the back of the vehicle and pulled out a heavy oilskin he'd had in the trunk for ages. How many times had Diane told him to get rid of it? Now it was just what he needed. Throwing it on, he belted it up. Then, picking up the car phone, he keyed in to the station to warn them of the blocked highway.

After securing all the doors, Dave ran on and up the road to where the trees' leafy fingers were linked, preventing him from reaching Sunny Mead by car. With the scratching branches tearing at his coat, he set off at a run, down the steep narrow road into the valley. He didn't care what the wind did to him, as long as it didn't cause another tree to fall on him. Turning almost sideways, he beat his painful way through the forest, glancing up at the branches above every time he heard an ominous creak.

Ten thousand volts of lightning careered across the sky as he battled his way through to the very edge of the forest and began to run towards the straggling little town below.

When Diane found that the kids were neither in the living room nor in the kitchen, she stood at the foot of the stairs, yelling. She was rewarded by silence. They weren't there!

She couldn't understand it. She went into the dining room and looked through the window towards the lake. Suddenly, her anger dissipated like the rain at the water's edge. It was quite a long way off, but she could see him, waving. Of course, that's where they were! With Diep.

Why had she been so worried and so angry? She turned, her head whirling. What did anything matter? Except being warm. She was shivering. But it had been a wonderful party. What she needed was a rest and a bath.

Diane climbed the stairs like a sleepwalker, unbuttoning her sodden clothes as she went, leaving them in a trail behind her. Entering the bathroom, she turned the taps full on. Then she sat on the edge of the bath while it filled, humming Diep's tune as it mesmerised her brain.

Dave barged in through the kitchen door. One look at the debris-strewn lawn outside had been enough. They must really have been caught in it. The house was silent.

'Di!' he shouted. 'Di? Kids? Where are you?' No reply. He went to the bottom of the stairs and started to ascend. On the third step was a cotton shirt, draped like a damp rag. He recognised it as Diane's. Above that, her bra.

What the hell was happening? Where was she? Cold fear was grabbing at his stomach. What had happened to them all?

The landing was quiet but he could hear the clash of water coming from the bathroom and the thin snatches of a tinny tune, whirling through the house.

He grabbed the door handle, turned it, rattled it. She'd locked the door! She never did that.

'Di? Are you in there? What are you doing?' Something was terribly wrong. Dave put his shoulder to the door. The frail bolt gave way and he almost fell through. He looked at her.

His wife's head was protruding from the water and she was laughing like an idiot. He could see she was hysterical.

Reaching down with wet arms, he dragged her up, her pointed breasts glistening with soapy bubbles. 'Di! Pull yourself together! The kids? What's happened?' He barely recognised her look. It was as if she was high.

The policeman took over. He struck his wife a blow on the cheek with the flat of his hand. Then, holding her wilting body, he pulled the bath sheet around her. Then she came to, was staring at him with frightened eyes, hand to her face, looking round wildly.

'Where are they? Di? Where are they?' He got through at last. She was grabbing at him, gabbling.

'They're with him. Over there. In the chalet!' She cowered, looking up at the ceiling as the thunder cracked above.

Then Dave was gone, sprinting downstairs two at a time and hurling himself out of the door.

It was the nicest place she had ever seen. Rose smiled secretly. She had always known Diep lived in a place like this. She wished she hadn't been cross with him. Nor with Mel.

The sun caressed the twins' heads as they stood at the open

door of the chalet. The wind ruffled their shining fair hair, its fingers playing with the strands. They could hear music. Somewhere inside, Diep was playing his flute.

Rose put one bare, brown, little foot over the lintel, and a downy blue butterfly was flying towards her, then fluttering by.

'Come on,' she said to Teddy, whose eyes were shining. 'Let's look at the pets!'

It was a very bright room with glittering glass cases, like Pip's but prettier. Teddy was blind to the butterfly but he could see his ball, its grinning, boyish face opaque behind the transparent, spherical orange of its body. It was in a very good mood. It wanted him to play.

He didn't need persuading. He stepped into the room behind Rose. The twins' small figures moved towards the cases. They were still hand in hand. Today, it didn't feel sissy to Teddy, just comfortable. They were in this together. If they stayed together, no-one would tell them off for following Diep. Together. Always.

The flute's scissored notes made their legs go faster, like mechanical toys, towards the waiting cases.

Teddy and Rose laughed with delight at the bats, hanging upside down, their winged, umbrella arms hooked onto sticks. Rose put out her fat, soft finger and stroked their cold, grey fur. It was magical, like their sweet, tiny squeaks when she touched them.

The stiff, stalky bodies of the locusts snapped under Teddy's probing. He didn't know that each inquisitive boylike tweak took off a leg.

Like his sister, he was enchanted as they walked through the paradise of their minds, where locusts and gnats were humming birds; and vampire bats just soft night-shadows.

The rat's coat looked like black velvet, its inquisitive eyes flicking over their interested faces. The tip of its tongue was slavering, moist.

'Welcome,' it said from where it sat on the top of the tallest case of all.

'Wow, a talking rat!' Teddy grinned.

'Wow!' echoed Rose. Then she was screaming with delight, her shrill little voice sticking the air like a bodkin. 'Annie, it's Annie! Teddy, look, it's Annie! She's safe!'

He looked – and the ball bounced forward, dazzling his eyes with its light, right into the case. It nestled in the boy doll's arms. Teddy was enraptured. It glinted like a hero's shield. Teddy wanted that boy-doll with all his heart. It crouched, tall and burly, its great padded shoulders ready for the home run. Its crash helmet and visor planted hard on its head. His ideal footballing hero in front of his eyes.

'Gee,' he breathed, 'I never knew they'd made a doll like that!'

Rose didn't hear a word. Her empty arms were aching to be filled with Annie's lovely little body. No-one had eaten up her brains. It had all been a mistake.

Annie was smiling, her raggy lips blowing Rose a kiss; her snub nose, with the dusting of freckles, scenting the summer air; her bonny blue eyes shining out of her red, sawdust cheeks. Rose wanted to cradle her baby-soft head and kiss her over and over again.

The Rat and the Piper grinned as they crouched above the children. They had tasted blood once today – the best was to come.

Now the twins were standing on tiptoe, stretching out their hands. And the glass of the case was melting away. They were willing it to. They were on course for paradise. Behind the dolls, the arch of darkness was filled with light. In the distance, children were running and playing.

Rose and Teddy watched with delighted faces as the automata in front of them beckoned, persuading them to take the dolls in their arms, to step inside.

The children's imagination was transforming the chalet and its dark world into a realm of light. No six-year-old could comprehend the horror within.

The twins' breathing was quick and excited as they reached for the dolls, while a few feet away their naked sister lay unconscious on the couch.

Pip dragged his twisted body erect and wrenched the flimsy back door of the chalet wide open with the hammering wind.

An eerie flash of lightning ripped the sky, revealing to the boy's terrified eyes the horror of the room and the cameo of terror – his little sister and small brother standing, enraptured, before the case, while the whirling, beckoning poopies enticed their victims into the entrance of the tunnel, into the world of Diep the Piper. It was his nightmare come to life.

The deaf boy couldn't hear Diep's piping. Only see the man's fingers as he lured the twins, played on their childishness, promised them ecstasy. And his rat stood fully erect, huge, licking its moist lips, waiting for satisfaction. How it had mocked Pip in the dream, taunted him that Paradise could never be his!

With one wordless scream of fear, Pip hauled his stiff and useless body inside. He crawled slowly towards the arch of darkness, towards Koppelberg's straddling legs, which the two children were approaching, spellbound.

Diep turned, and his smiling mouth betrayed the hatred in his eyes, which he fixed upon Pip. The boy heard the taunting words: *Too late, cripple. They're mine – completely. They'll come with me to the end of the world.*

Diep bent and stretched out his arms, ready to scoop the children up. Then he was transformed into the statue man. His eyes changed from daggered points of salty blue flame to orbs of fire, shooting darts of blinding light at Pip. The boy put up a hand to shield his eyes and was burned by more flames issuing from the tips of the statue's flaming fingers. The twins walked on, entranced, towards the circle of those terrible arms. Pip knew that in a moment they would be lost forever.

All of a sudden, an extraordinary energy, invoked by his anger, surged through his entire body. *He would not let them go. He would fight for them to the death.* Summoning all the strength inside his fast-healing body, he snatched up the carved snake lamp. As he twisted his lips into a scream of warning, his vocal chords awoke:

'*No!*' he screamed. His shadowy, unfamiliar voice hit and

rent the air, electrifying it. Then he hurled the lamp at his adversary. It shattered on contact, drawing the lightning from above, which sizzled through the roof, silhouetting a man's figure, sharp and black, in the doorway.

Then Pip's whole world exploded, sucking him down into an eternity of darkness.

The four walls and doorways were intact but totally blackened. The air was thick with dust, and part of the roof's structure had come crashing down into the middle of the chalet's living area, heaping the smoking timbers high. The hole in the roof was naked under a sky where the storm clouds were now being driven away by a fresher wind.

Out of the smoking debris came a searing noise, the terrifying music of a human scream. The girl's voice was hysterical.

Dave, dazed and lying just inside the doorway, stirred. He had been blown face down onto the floor, a beam missing his head by inches. The shrill scream cut through his brain, and Dave, with horrified realisation, pushed himself back into reality. He groaned with the effort.

Then, over in a corner by the window, came a slight movement. The force of the explosion had been focused in the centre of the room and hadn't penetrated the fringes, which had been sheilded by the debris of the furniture. Suddenly a fair head appeared, blackened with grime; then another.

The twins came crawling out. They sat back on their knees and stared up at the great hole through to the open sky, their faces blank but screwed up in fear like newborn babies recognising familiar objects for the very first time.

The screams were dying. Then Dave was on his knees too, crawling, trying to stand, falling again, shaking. 'Kids, kids, where are you?'

Then Teddy and Rose were scrabbling, searching, looking for him, falling into his protective arms. Blackened, confused, but overjoyed, the trio clung to each other.

Dave disengaged their clinging arms. He had to find Mel and Pip!

Somewhere under there were two more of his children. He began to pull desperately at the wreckage with his bare and bleeding hands.

Later, their neighbours joined the search. Kiefer Adams found Mel tipped under the couch. Diane cried as Dave carried their daughter outside, the dazed twins clinging on to them. She almost vomited when she saw Mel's blackened body.

'Wrap her up in a blanket,' Dave shouted to Diane.

'Have you found Pip yet?' returned Diane.

Dave shook his head.

'The paramedics are on the way. And the fire service!' yelled another neighbour.

'Look after them. I have to go back in again!'

They couldn't stop him. A distraught Diane, who had seen the lightning strike, tried to join him, but was held back by Sam Drury and the storekeeper.

As he searched for Pip, Dave prayed he'd find his son alive, that the emergency services would be quick. They needed firefighters. New fires kept springing up, ignited by the wind, which blew strongly now through what had once been a neat little lakeside chalet.

Diane prayed too as she knelt by Mel with the twins clinging to her. Then Kiefer, risking his life, joined the search again. Outside, everybody knew they didn't have time to wait for the fire chief. It might be too late …

It had been a miracle. Pip must have been close to the table at the time of impact. He had been blown right underneath. The table had lifted suddenly like a shield, protecting his body from falling debris. Two roof beams had fallen, digging into the ground like an X-shaped cross. The cruciform shape and the sideways table had created a niche, where Pip lay semiconscious in the collapsing world of the chalet. His body, though covered in black dust, was quite unmarked.

He had heard them coming. He could hear their frantic pulling then, afterwards, the gentle probing, the precious words, 'Pip, it's Dad! Are you there? Pip? Are you there?'

His dad must have thought it was useless. He knew he couldn't hear him. But he could! He could hear! Biting his stiff, sore lips, the boy realised he had spoken after all those years. Had he saved the twins? He had to know!

'Dad, Dad, I'm here, I'm here!' he croaked, 'I'm here!'

When they brought him out, after uncovering what could have been his grave, Dave and Diane stared at each other, tears running freely down their cheeks.

It *was* miraculous. Pip could speak. He could hear them. He was lifted onto the stretcher, Mom holding one of his hands, Dad the other. He looked up at them, spoke in that unfamiliar cracked voice. 'The twins?' he whispered. 'Mel? Are they safe? Did I save them?'

Diane nodded wordlessly. Her own voice wouldn't come for tears.

When the ambulances had taken the Durrant family to hospital, the fire chief spoke to Kiefer Adams and Patsy Doran. He and his men had made a thorough search of the ruins.

'Dave said there might be someone else in there. A music teacher? There's no-one, thank God! The guy mustn't have been in there. Lucky for him. I hope Dave and Di were insured!' He shook his head.

'I tell you, there's a hell of a lot of damage. Ten thousand volts is one whole lot of lightning. Funny thing, fire. Not everything burnt – this, for instance …' He drew the stiff little doll from his pocket. 'Wood, as well. Here you are, better save it for the kids.' He handed it to Kiefer.

The poopy stared at him woodenly. 'And this.' The fire chief gestured. 'All that damage, but still some clothes intact.' He indicated a pair of red shorts, perfect, untouched by the flames, and a yellow silk scarf wound round an antique lamp with a stem carved into an ugly snake's body. Suddenly the wind from the roof made the scarf dance and pull at its mooring.

'Funny thing, fire,' repeated the chief. 'It seems to choose its victims.' Pushing back his helmet, the man rubbed his black and sweating forehead.

The road through the forest looked like a thin string of white ribbon. As the two ambulances emerged from the tunnel where Sam Junior had met his end, they were like tiny toys dwarfed by the magnificent forest landscape.

The sound of their sirens echoed eerily, reverberating off rock and cliff, tangling itself in the frightened mesh of trees, waiting for fall and death. As the ambulances disappeared, the noise of their whining ceased, carried away by the forest breezes. All was silence.

And then another sound replaced them. It was not the moaning and sighing of an early autumn wind, but a thin piping that filled the air.

It seemed to be coming from a station wagon. Its two-toned colours blended into the landscape, for the ground was muddy and its dark yellow was covered with red dust.

The station wagon sped on, eating the ribbon of the road, rolling it on the tongue of its tyres, digesting the miles like a rapacious beast.

A lone watcher could not have seen the driver through its smoked windows. But through a crack at the top of the glass on the driver's side, a yellow scarf floated triumphantly in the breeze, its silken ears tuned to its master's music.

And the station wagon crawled away, leaving the frightened little town of Sunny Mead to some of its grimmest memories.

16

Burbor Psychiatric Hospital,
Cluj-Napocka, Romania, 1990

Irina had died the week before Marcu's appointment with the bookseller, Nicholas Eisenmann, in Cologne. She had been growing more frail daily and, although her death had been expected, Marcu had not counted on it hitting him so hard. Irina had died with Grandsire's song on her lips; the squeaky-thin piping that played incessantly in Marcu's brain. He had felt depressed ever since she had gone.

As Marcu crossed the rusting Burbor bridge from East to West, he stopped in the middle and leaned against the iron railings, which left a long patch of red on both arms of his white coat. Below him, the rubbish of another hospital week, piled up in and out of a variety of bins, was stirred by the wind and a common crow that pecked miserably at the remains of someone's lunch. As Marcu watched it idly, the bird looked up, squawked and, flapping its wings, floated up on a current that whisked between the buildings and disappeared over the roof. At that moment he wished he could disappear too.

'It would be so easy,' murmured Marcu, leaning over, his eyes on the rubbish, which was probably an ideal breeding ground for rats. He sniffed and felt tears stinging his eyelids, like the onslaught of biting insects in the evening. He put a hand up to rub them away. But no tears came; nor had they when she died, because when he had known the end was imminent, he had been terrified by the thought that she was about to take more important secrets to the grave with her. He had been hardly able to endure it when her lips relaxed from their familiar pursing. He had panicked when he'd recognised the eerie song had turned into a death-rattle and, as a mere mortal, he had no power to prevent her passing. And although he was nearer to the truth about Grandsire, he wasn't near enough.

Ever since her departure, he had despised himself for the anger that had risen in his chest as he looked down at her pitiful, wasted body, feeling she had betrayed him by dying and regretting he hadn't had her force-fed. He could not pretend to himself anymore why he found her death so painful. How many times in her bad moments had she called him, 'Monster!' Perhaps he was worthy of the title? Sighing, he continued across the bridge, wishing that he was anywhere else but Burbor.

Irina's death had brought Marcu's physiological and psychological study of the Arvan female to an end. It wasn't his fault he hadn't been able to tie up his research satisfactorily. Marcu knew he was a good physician but, as an author, he realised he'd been very lucky that his research had been noticed by an American university department and might be published as a full-scale book. He also realised that, from the psychiatric point of view, he had set down a truthful explanation of what he believed had happened in the Arva ritual of 1988. But *why* had it happened?

Marcu was a psychiatrist and he needed to know what was behind it. At that moment, Eisenmann was his only hope. Irina's latest revelations had engendered some new ideas, which he had mentioned in several letters to his German contact. Naturally, he hadn't cited their source, but had passed them off as entirely his own. Something told Marcu that if he'd disclosed they were based on his schizophrenic patient's voices, he might put Eisenmann off. As he'd had no response, maybe the German had been put off already? Anyway, he didn't feel bad about lying to the man. He'd never know, and they were only ideas. Besides, Marcu was searching for facts from which to construct a believable thesis.

He had slight hopes of Eisenmann filling in some of the blanks, which might lead him to his quarry. Marcu was of a different breed from Valentin: the investigating policeman was seeking to identify the Grandsire who was Anka Petrescu's murderer, whereas Marcu was searching for an entity. Shaking his head, he continued on his dreary way to the psychiatric wing to carry on with the daily tasks, which had now become so mundane that he was beginning to question why he had become a doctor in the first place, rather than choosing to concentrate on academic research.

When an exhausted Marcu finally got back to his office after his day's hard work, he found a letter waiting from Eisenmann. The communication was terse and dry; written on paper of the best weight, with an elaborate watermark showing through, which Marcu didn't examine. He scanned the lines, desperate for good news. Then breathed out in pure relief. An invitation to meet the bookseller in Cologne to discuss ritual sources, but also a request to send something of the manuscript first.

As Marcu read the letter through again very carefully, he could feel his heart beating madly in his chest and his depression lifting. This time he noted that Eisenmann did not apologise for the delay in replying to his communications. The man did not excuse himself by citing pressure of work or anything else. Reading between the lines, Marcu realised Eisenmann was promising nothing, but the gist was clear. Initially the man's interest in Marcu's research had been aroused by some minor points, touching on Christianity's introduction in the 7th Century by Arab merchants and its spread by Turko-Afghans; but when in his last communication Marcu had mentioned gypsy folklore, Eisenmann had felt that this offered much more mileage, having brought up analogies with certain rituals practised by Berber-Roumanian *tsigane* or *zingari.*

Eisenmann had signed himself simply 'Nikolai'. The huge signature flowed like a Stygian river across the paper. He had not used such familiarity before; nor the East European derivative. Marcu wondered if it was a sign that the man was warming to his subject at last. If so, what else might he expect from a businessman of Eisenmann's character and wealth? The appointment with him couldn't come quickly enough. Then he began to wonder what 'Nikolai' looked like and how a man in his early thirties had managed to become so influential and successful by dealing in the innocuous business of selling books. He was soon to find out.

17

The restaurant was refined and quiet, overlooking the River Rhine and only a few minutes' walk from the station and the Dom. A long, red Turkish carpet embellished with elaborate scrolls was the only splash of colour against the ice-white walls of the corridor. The shades of the wall lamps threw their shadows up to the ceiling as the waiter hurried along and through the double doors to the small conference room that had been booked by Herr Eisenmann's secretary for his latest business meeting.

Heine, who had been detailed to wait on the clients for the afternoon, straightened his tie. The manager had given strict orders that anything Herr Eisenmann requested was to be seen to at once. 'Sharp!' he'd said. And he meant it.

Herr Eisenmann was one of the hotel's most influential customers. Heine felt a little nervous that things might not be to the man's liking. They said he was hard to please, and this was Heine's first taste of his punctilious requirements. For instance, the secretary had specified that they would be using their own ice cubes in the small refrigerator. 'You may leave their delivery to me. Herr Eisenmann prefers this. The hotel may provide the still water' – which was a very select brand. Their guest had even demanded a specific type of cut glass goblet. Then there were Herr Eisenmann's requirements as to communications, including a whiteboard to be connected up to his laptop. He expected the best, as befitting the reputation he had in business circles. Heine had heard them say in Reception that his influence was global. But today his meeting was, his secretary had said, ' *Tête à tête.*'

Heine hovered outside in the carpeted corridor. Then the wall lights flickered. '*Mein Gott*, I hope it's not a power cut!' But he was saved, as things returned to normal. He swallowed, and with one last flick back of his hair, he knocked.

'*Herein.*'

He entered. Herr Eisenmann was seated with his back to Heine, his black-suited shoulders hunched over his laptop. He didn't look up. The waiter approached nervously, his throat dry.

'Is everything to your satisfaction, sir?' Heine waited. No reply. The young waiter shifted from one foot to the other, not knowing whether he should remain or go.

A moment later, the man swung round and faced him. Heine had never seen eyes like those on a white man. Unfathomably black and unblinking eyes, set under perfectly arched brows into a skin so pale and pure, like fine porcelain. But his hair! It was ripe gold and fell fashionably across his forehead. Heine knew he was staring, but he couldn't help it. A flicker of a smile crossed the man's mouth.

'Well?'

'I'm sorry to have disturbed you, sir. I just came to see if everything was to your satisfaction.'

Heine could feel perspiration under his hair and, to his extreme embarrassment, a drop began to trickle down the side of his nose.

'Yes.' Then Eisenmann added, 'It's hot.'

Heine knew the guest had noticed the drop of sweat. He was probably laughing at him; probably realised it was his first time. Irritability mixed with discomfiture made Heine's face even redder.

'Make sure they ring through when Dr Marcu arrives,' ordered Eisenmann, indicating the telephone. His strange eyes fixed Heine's.

'Yes, sir,' replied Heine, coming to and recovering his composure. What had he been thinking of, staring at the man like that? Suddenly, the red flush suffused his face. Herr Eisenmann's fine brows arched towards the door.

Heine nodded and rushed towards it. He didn't dare look back. Outside, he leaned against the wall and loosened his tie. His mouth was dry and he was burning. He hadn't felt like that since he was a schoolboy and he'd been dismissed for the puerile prank he'd played on ... Who? Heine blinked. Yes, he remembered the whole stupid episode perfectly. It had been really cruel, but he'd been only a kid then. He shook his head. Why was he thinking of that? Was he sickening for something? What was the matter with him?

Wiping his forehead, he hurried off down the corridor, sweat making great dark patches on his white-shirted back.

Nicholas turned back to his laptop to read through again. He didn't really need to, but it gave him pleasure. He did not expect that pleasure to be shared with Marcu, who had tapped into something more dangerous than he could ever have conceived, and for which the unfortunate doctor would ultimately pay the highest price.

He licked his lips, and his dark eyes scored the screen, making the lines shiver and waver as his long, sensitive finger with the well-kept long nails scrolled through the testament of Irina Petrescu's misery.

From: *Dreaming*, the testimony of Irina Petrescu, farmer's wife, formerly of Bedya Farm, Ruare, in-patient, Burbor Psychiatric Hospital, Cluj-Napocka.

Chapter One, *Culled from Her Head, Written in Her Heart's Blood*, as told to Dr Sasha Marcu in *The Feminine Folk Culture of North Transylvania: A Psychological Study*. pp. 1-21.

IRINA: The sixteenth year is a very important year in an Arvan daughter's life. She is prepared for it as much as she is prepared for menstruation. I was not aware then that to have been prepared for neither was as much a mortal sin as not believing in the event. I was naïve then. I felt safe. My own menstruation had begun in my thirteenth year – a good time, according to my grandmother – a safe time. Therefore, 'going up' was not so much of an ordeal.

The remembrance of my initiation is sharp and is a constantly recurring phenomenon. I can only record it in the hope that any other bereaved parent may derive comfort. I have been both witness and victim and I speak with authority.

My clothes had been laid out according to an age-old ritual. Of this I cannot speak except that, in the final stages, my mother and I recited the Six Sorrowful and the Six Glorious mysteries of the Blessed Rosary. This was all done on the evening of 21 July. The clothes consisted of a white skirt and blouse, its sleeves embroidered with black, depicting scenes handed down for generations; a black apron and sleeveless waistcoat and a black cotton headscarf. My mother braided my hair at about eight in the evening, before darkness fell. The hair was not to be touched until coming-down. At no time did I believe I would not return in the same fashion. It is believed Grandsire does not demand a grown woman ...

MARCU: Can you elaborate on this, please?

IRINA: Menstruation had occurred in my case, and only children are involved. Usually those whose health gives cause for concern, those girls sufficiently unformed physically, perhaps lacking a proper diet. I, on the other hand, was extremely well-formed, stubby and short. My only beauty, I think, my hair ...

MARCU: Thank you. Now go on.

IRINA: I slept well and was woken by my mother about one hour before dawn. I was very, very tired. The forbidding of undergarments was difficult for me. I asked Mama where my drawers were. I felt uncomfortable, embarrassed, afraid the wind would lift my skirts. I had large breasts. I wasn't even allowed a band about them. My mother had no answer for me as to my condition. She did not speak, just buttoned up my blouse, dressing me like the girl in the poopy case ... [1]

MARCU: Can you tell me something of this poopy doll, Irina?

IRINA: We all have a poopy case; we all have a poopy case ... [The subject could not be constrained to describe its origin even under hypnosis. The poopy is evidently a deep-rooted fetish.] She was smiling though, doctor. As if she was coming up the ridge with me, clapping her hands ... My feet were set in the path of stones. I was turned three times as the signification of the Trinity. I remember how my feet were hurting. My mother bent and put on my new clogs, black, too – very new. The bells were pretty, piercing the ice in the clouds ...[2]

MARCU: Who was ringing them, Irina?

IRINA: Why, Father Pathan, of course!

MARCU: He was in the church at dawn? [At this interruption, the subject was unhelpful.]

IRINA: It was a very red dawn and cold. The wind

---

1 'Poopy case' – believed to be derived from the French, 'poupée'. See Prof W Meyer's study: 'Derivation of the Latinate roots of the Romanian tongue'. Heidelberg, 1960. The use of 'case' has special significance in 'Arva talk'. Origin unknown, but it may refer to a shroud in which the doll was carried.

2 A local superstition that tolling bells will disperse hail and prevent it from falling and the crops being spoiled.

was freezing me, making between my legs numb. I had no underthings. Even my flower petals were falling.

MARCU: Were they special flowers?

IRINA: Mother planted them in spring – red and gold – in a little patch that Papa could not touch. She told him they were for 'going up'. They pricked my fingers. The others laughed.

MARCU: Others?

IRINA: Sara Divina and Anna Menken. We had fun. Sara said if Basa was cutting hay, he'd look up our skirts. He was a very dirty old man. We knew what he did every summer. We were giggling.

MARCU: You went up together then?

IRINA: Yes, we saw no-one. The grave is railed off with wooden stakes except for an opening for girls to walk through. No-one would ever do that, mind you. The village lads wouldn't go near Grandsire's grave.

MARCU: Your grandfather?

IRINA: Everyone's Grandsire.

MARCU: Tell me about him, Irina.

IRINA: Grandsire's grave stands apart. The cross was cut off in a storm. It is very big, like the mountain. The tombstone is square.[3] The top is shiny like glass, smooth and polished from the weather. There were poopy dolls along it.[4] We knelt and our skirts were blowing up on our backsides when we put the flowers down. Sara looked between her legs and, my god, she saw a black hat bobbing up and

---

3 The subject meant that the tomb is a vault, rectangular in shape. A visit to the site confirmed this. The stone cross is susceptible to lightning. The column has been struck twice in the last hundred years. The last time a strike occurred, the cross was not replaced, owing to expense and the unwillingness of the authorities.

4 The subject is alluding to engravings on the tomb, which are images of children, believed to be the descendants of the Grandsire.

down on the other side of the churchyard!

MARCU: A black hat?

IRINA: Basa the Sowfucker! We saw him!

MARCU: How did you know that?

IRINA: She said he wanted to feel our arses. I didn't like it. Any of it.

MARCU: And that is all you did?

IRINA: All I did, all I did. [Here the subject begins to whistle.]

MARCU: What tune are you whistling, Irina?

IRINA: Grandsire's song.

MARCU: And where did you learn it?

IRINA: Arvan girls all know it. And then we sat on the grave. It was warm for him. None of us had blood.

MARCU: And you were all the same, 'coming down'?

IRINA: All the same, all the same, I was the same ... Anka wasn't ... [Questioning was discontinued owing to the distress of the patient, but continued the following day.]

She spoke before she left us. But only once, mind. I asked her about the blood. Yes, that might seem strange to you, but I had to know if it was true that I was really going to lose her forever. I'll never forget her eyes! When she looked at me she wasn't seeing me - only Him! That was a terrible time for us all. I had believed my daughter was a woman. She had told me she had started to be cursed two months before. Now I knew she had been lying. The voices told me I was guilty, guilty of it all ...

MARCU: Irina, listen, it was not your fault. You didn't know Anka had been lying.

IRINA: There was nothing I could do after that. I had to let my Anka slip away. I was the mother of the Little and Chosen. I had responsibilities as an Arva woman. To make her passing as comfortable as possible. I couldn't let her stay in the hospital. I couldn't even let her out of the village. But they made me. They took her. Out of my sight. They made me! When she came back and they had done nothing for her, only given her blood, Petre was angry; very, very angry. Do you know what he did? He hit me! He said, 'You stupid woman, how could you not know a thing like that about your own daughter? How could you let her 'go up' knowing she was still a child?'

MARCU: Irina, listen, did Petre know about Grandsire? About the secret?

IRINA: No man knows the secret!

MARCU: Stop whistling, Irina. Listen! Why does no man know?

IRINA: Forbidden. The secret is forbidden. Only we girls know the secret of the marriage bed …

MARCU: It's all right, Irina, you can tell me. I won't betray you.

IRINA: No, never, never, no. I shouldn't have let her.

MARCU: You must believe this, Irina. It was not your fault. You had to do it. You were not to blame. How could you have known what was going to happen?

IRINA: Any mother would have. I should have. I let Anka 'go up', 'go up' when she was only a child …

[Interview terminated]

Nicholas leaned back, smiled and pursed his lips into a perfect cipher. Then the telephone rang, drowning his whistle. He picked it up. 'Yes, send the doctor up. I'm ready.'

Eisenmann was tall.

Marcu, who was a big man himself, had to look up into his face while they shook hands. His first impression of the German was his coolness. It wasn't just that he was physically cool, in that his hand was quite cold on that warm day; Marcu's immediate instinct was that the man considered himself superior. Otherwise, he was a handsome fellow who, on account of his eyes, could have been taken to be of Eastern origin, although he sported a wonderful crop of blond hair. Marcu was also surprised to see he wore a diamond stud in each ear, which was the only concession to the prestige of his position, given his almost funereal taste in clothes. Natty dresser, thought Marcu, as he looked at the suit. He was usually oblivious to such things, having a total disregard for style.

'Please sit,' said Eisenmann pleasantly, indicating a chair facing him. Marcu nodded, his eyes straying to the laptop, which was purring continually. 'Yes, I've been looking over what you sent me. It's very interesting,' Eisenmann added.

'Thank you, Mr Eisenmann.'

'Nicholai, please.' He smiled, and the corner of his lips curved quite enchantingly. Marcu blinked. 'So,' he leaned back, 'what are you intending to do with all this?' His hands were flicking over the keyboard, as if itching to begin.

'Well,' Marcu expelled a sigh, 'I would like to get the whole thing published. I've had some interest, but I've ...' He didn't really want to admit it, but that was what the meeting was for. '... I've come to a full stop.'

'Irina is dead.' It wasn't a question. Had Marcu told Eisenmann in his last letter that Irina had died? He couldn't remember.

'Unfortunately.' He still couldn't say it without a slight lump in the throat. She'd meant so much to him.

'And you would like me to help you concerning the Arvan ritual?' The German clipped through the words and, all of a sudden, Marcu thought he could detect the trace of an accent, which he couldn't quite place.

'That's what I was hoping. I need more background. Naturally, anything you tell me will be subject to confidentiality unless, of course, you wish to be acknowledged. I wouldn't want you to be compromised.'

Marcu could have bitten his tongue for his naïveté. It sounded like he was patronising the man.

'That won't happen,' replied Eisenmann suavely. 'So, where would you like me to begin?'

'Anywhere that might be of help. The origins of the ritual, perhaps?' He delved in his briefcase and brought out his notepad. He didn't think he could ask to record the conversation.

'Leading to the secret, I presume.' Eisenmann's voice was almost a purr.

'I'm not that hopeful.'

His joke fell flat. Eisenmann appeared not to be listening. He was now staring up at the ceiling in an attitude of concentration, with his elbows on the table and hands clasped. *His nails are long enough for him to be Chinese*, thought Marcu. He waited breathlessly, his hand poised to begin taking notes. He would have preferred a chat, but had already realised that chatting wasn't something the German did. The psychiatrist knew instinctively this was likely to be a lecture.

'You have no need to take notes, Marcu,' Eisenmann said, without moving. 'I'll fax you the details afterwards. Or I can send you a copy in the mail.'

'Thank you,' replied Marcu, grimacing. As he was wondering why the hell the man hadn't sent the details by post and saved him the trouble of coming all the way from Cluj-Napocka, he was hit by a burning pain that seared through his leg. He prayed it would go, but it only worsened very quickly.

'Christ! … Cramp … sorry!' Feeling incredibly foolish, he jumped up from his chair and tried to relax his leg by turning up his toes. To his embarrassment, Eisenmann offered nothing in reply or sympathy.

'You say you are puzzled by this constant reference to dates,' said Eisenmann. His voice was distant now. 'You are not a mediaevalist.'

'No, I'm a scientist.' Neither was it like Marcu to be on the defensive.

'A religious man?' There was a hint of humour in the German's tone.

'I wouldn't say that.' It was exceedingly hot. 'May I take off my jacket?' No response. So he pleased himself.

'Once, scientists, religious exegetes and mediaevalists were one and the same.' It was a definite reproof. 'Intelligence has decayed.'

'I'm sorry, but is the air conditioning working?' asked Marcu. He hadn't meant to say it out loud. Eisenmann lifted his eyebrows, which made him look particularly disagreeable. Why had Marcu thought he was good-looking?

'You find the room too close?'

'No, sorry. I didn't mean to break your train of thought.'

'Unlikely,' Eisenmann retorted.

Arrogant bastard, thought Marcu. His arm was aching insufferably now. What the hell was the matter with him? Was he trying to sabotage his own meeting?

'I have read through your material,' continued Eisenmann. 'It's very interesting, but I would like a quick run through as to what you can add and what you would like me to help with.'

'I have a very good idea now what happens on 22 July in Arva,' said Marcu. 'Irina has told me most of it, as you can see from the transcript. What I am looking for now is the background to the ritual. For example, why 22 July? I have made a thorough search for information on the date, and it has yielded little. Like many other dates, it has seen certain things happen throughout history, but I can find no particular link to Romania. I am still looking.

'I would like to find out about the song, too. The origin of the music. It was said that Basa was heard singing it on his deathbed. And, yet, according to Irina, it is forbidden to men. All the women I have examined and treated at Burbor know this song, but never divulge it. Personally, I think it has something to do with the dance performed.'

'The dance?'

'Yes, the turning around three times on the stones. Almost a spinning.' Marcu pushed on. 'And then I'm bedevilled –

sorry, a most unscientific term – with the marriage at 19 problem. Each Arvan girl must marry at 19.' He shrugged. 'Why 19? Then, of course, there is the crime.' He looked at Eisenmann, who didn't seem disposed to intervene at any point. 'Not that I am particularly interested in the crime; which I admit sounds callous. Of course, a terrible thing did happen to Anka Petrescu, but it gave me the opportunity to pursue Grandsire further. And I am confident that with your help, I may locate him.'

'You believe Grandsire was the perpetrator?' rasped Eisenmann.

'I don't see how he could have been. I see him rather as an entity. This kind of thing has been going on for ages. I believe the first recorded instance of rape was as far back as 1880. I did note a certain pattern though.' Marcu leaned forward, then wrinkled his nose. He could smell something. Fresh, raw earth. He glanced towards the windows, which were closed.

'Something the matter?'

'I think we should complain to the management. It *must* be the air conditioning after all.'

'I'm not aware of any problem,' replied Eisenmann. He looked completely cool. 'You were saying – a pattern?'

'Yes. Let me see …' Marcu looked through his notes. 'I conferred with the police inspector in charge. Although the records are unreliable, it seems that the same thing that happened to Anka also happened to a girl in 1916, and then to one called Catina Albu in 1952. Catina's mother, Dana Albu, died in Burbor; but of course there are no detailed records. Isn't that amazing? And quite inexplicable.' He didn't intend to let the man know that he was working on the 36-year period avidly and trying to make sense of its numerical background, which was entirely unscientific.

'So you have identified a certain interval at which certain crimes were repeated,' said Eisenmann.

'Yes, I have, and I hope to come up with some answers. With your help, of course. The crimes are a separate issue. Who knows what lurks in the male Arvan psyche? Let's leave that to the policemen. The inspector told me he already has a few leads. I was hoping that you might throw some light on the marriage question in particular. Is there something in the Arvan culture about forced marriage?'

'As I told you in my letters, I have a particular interest in the peasants of this region,' began Eisenmann. 'I have made a study of this particular village. The dialect and the derivation of their surnames. Other villages in the area have little that is special about them. Not like Arva.' Eisenmann rolled the name round his mouth, as if he was gorging on the sound of it.

Marcu's heart bounded. His instincts had been good, then. Eisenmann's input was going to be invaluable.

'Now, take the priest, for instance.' Marcu hadn't been expecting individual identification.

'Father Joseph?'

'No, *Pathan*.' Eisenmann was looking straight at him with black, unblinking eyes.

'Ah, you mean the priest mentioned by Irina?' Marcu consulted his notes, scrabbling through the pages. 'I don't think he's the parish priest any longer.'

'He's not.'

'You know him?'

Eisenmann nodded. 'He lives here in Cologne.'

'But that's wonderful.' Marcu was quite excited. 'Would you be able to introduce me? He must be getting on. I could find out nothing about him. Is he significant to the ritual? There was something about the bell ringing at dawn? Ah, here it is.' He stared at the evidence. 'Yes, the custom of ringing the bell to disperse hail, 'the ice in the clouds', to save the crops,' he added enthusiastically.

Eisenmann smiled, revealing exceptionally pointed incisors. 'As you said, you are not religious.' Marcu flushed. 'The bell is *tolling*.'

'For the *Angelus*?' Marcu was puzzled.

'Perhaps for the centuries when the Vlachs were despised and excluded from the city you call your home.'

'I don't understand. You mean Cluj?'

'Arva's people are an old people. They have long memories.'

'Are you talking about the Continuity Theory?' The debate over whether the origin of the Romanians was Daco-Roman or Magyar had been waged since at least the end of the 10th Century, accompanied by fierce nationalism. 'You are saying the ritual is about politics? We are all Romanians now.'

'It is about freedom,' replied Eisenmann. 'Grandsire led his people to *freedom*. And they must worship how they wish. Not the Pope in Rome or any dictator.'

'You are saying Grandsire is a freedom fighter? Well, he inspires a very strange kind of loyalty that encompasses rape, murder and madness,' Marcu replied drily.

'He cares for his children.'

Marcu looked up from his notes and swallowed. What a strange response. Those eyes were holding his, glowing like a predator's. He shivered involuntarily.

'You were saying about the priest?' He tried to change the subject,

'Does the word *Pathan* mean nothing to you?'

'Only that it's an Indian name. Which I suppose is strange.' He frowned.

'According to your letter to me, your research,' Marcu flinched at the dismissive note, 'has begun to take into account a people whose origins lie …?'

Marcu resented being prompted like a fish played on a line. 'The Roma? Irina told me that gypsies do not take part in the ritual. That they are forbidden. Are you saying the parish priest was a gypsy?'

Eisenmann grinned. 'What else did she tell you, Marcu? Did she speak of wandering musicians from the Middle East? Or a blond-haired boy from Saxony?' Eisenmann stood up, his body blocking out the light.

'I don't follow.'

'Come now. She must have told you more than you are letting on. You are a very lucky man to have learned anything about Arva women. You want to understand why they are married at 19.'

'That is what I'm here for,' snapped Marcu. 'You know, don't you?'

Eisenmann laughed. 'I know what I know. Let's have a drink of water before we continue. You're very near, doctor, to finding out the truth.' He swung round and, seconds later, was crouching in front of the small refrigerator, from which he withdrew a jug and two fine cut-glass goblets. He carried the items over to the table. 'Perhaps you would like to get the ice?' He indicated the open door of the refrigerator.

Marcu bent and withdrew a small barrel heaped with shining cubes, which he transferred to the table. The water was already poured. He felt his tongue lolling like a slavering animal's. For a top-class hotel, the air-conditioning was a joke.

He could hardly wait for the water, and it took several agonising seconds as Eisenmann dropped in one ice cube after another, each of them ringing against the glass. 'Here,' he said, handing it over. 'It will encourage our memories.'

Marcu let the icy liquid rush over his dry lips, quench his dying tongue and silver its mercurial way down his gullet.

'That's better,' he said, sucking on another cube. 'Aren't you having a drink?' The force of Marcu's greedy gulp immediately hit his stomach. 'Oh!' he said, as the cold struck him.

'Later. I am not suffering like you,' replied Eisenmann, leaning back. 'The gypsies then … Did Irina ever mention Eva Kirchma? What did she tell you about Basa?'

'Pardon?' asked Marcu. He felt decidedly peculiar, as he tried to collect his thoughts. 'I heard from Dr Baescu that Eva Kirchma was a prostitute.'

'Ah!' said Eisenmann grimly. 'You look pale. You're sweating. Are you all right?' His words hissed in Marcu's whirling head, mingling with his tinnitus. 'Did the good doctor tell you that Eva was a seer? That, if you had approached her, she might have been able to throw some light upon your secret?'

'I'm a scientist,' replied Marcu weakly. The pain under his

chin was severe and he could focus on nothing except the crushing ache in the chest. His bulging eyes followed Eisenmann as the man came round the table and stood beside him. Suddenly, he felt his shoulder gripped cruelly, but he was unable to do anything about it.

When he tried to move his left arm, he found he couldn't. It hurt too much. His upper body was constricted now by an iron band of pain, while a cold clamminess suffused him.

'Too much ice,' murmured Eisenmann, as Marcu slumped back in his chair. Casually, the bookseller picked up the telephone.

Marcu thought he was back on the train. The girl was there, leaning over him, her sleek, brown hair falling over her shoulder, her bright inquisitive eyes searching his face.

'What's happening?' The pain was cold and vicious.

'You are having a heart attack,' she said.

He was terrified and, in his head, a million chattering voices assailed him as the private ambulance negotiated its way through the traffic beside the great square of the Dom, from where, in the year of Our Lord, 1212, a golden-haired shepherd lad had led 30,000 German children to their deaths.

'Who are *you*?' he gasped weakly, trying to twist the oxygen mask from his mouth.

'Herr Eisenmann's secretary. We are taking you to hospital.' She smiled, revealing sharp, small teeth, but Marcu saw nothing else. He was floating away on a wave of morphine towards the sound of the high, thin siren. Then he lapsed into the black realm of the unconscious.

The Dom was a vast cave of darkness, lit only by the coronas of flickering candle flames. The tourists had returned to their hotel dinners and an eerie void of space and passing time tore out the raucous noises of the city and nailed them to the reverberating emptiness of the mighty cathedral, which concealed in its cavernous maw the priceless bones of the Magi, as precious as any in the Western world, sealed in a casket of gold.

In response to the message, old Father Pathan, frail and stooped, shuffled on his way through the dark afternoon of Marcu's passing, his almost five score years impeding his stick-like legs and laboured breathing. His soul was weighed down with his past transgressions. How many times had he wished his spirit would drag its weary self out and seek the peace and forgiveness it craved for his weak body's sins of the flesh?

Never a day passed when he was not plagued by the remembrance of times past in that scrawny little village on the border, to which he had been sent as a green young priest, unused to the wiles of women and gypsies.

His dark eyes stared out of their hollow brown sockets, squinting up at the Magi shrine, the marvel of tourists from all over the world, who believed in a birth tale in which he himself had long lost faith. He had tasted the myrrh of suffering and its bitterness sickened him. His breath was only a wheeze, expelled rhythmically from his chest.

Every day when Pathan woke and found himself alive, he wondered if that day would be his last; the day when, finally, he would know the secret. Ringing the *Angelus* at dawn had been his Purgatory, announcing the great sin he had committed against his calling and his Maker.

'Let it be soon,' he prayed. 'Deliver me from this monstrous world. Why am I still alive, O Lord? Let me go.'

The old priest dragged himself on past the glittering shrine and into a dark corner, where he opened his breviary and began to mouth his daily prayers. The spit drooled from his slack, lopsided mouth and his palsied hands struggled to hold the holy book.

He thought he could hear the faint sound of a siren blown in from the outside world. A cutting draught assaulted his fragile head as he bent over the book and his eyes swivelled in its direction. A giant shadow fell across the wall, climbing the pillars, moving towards him.

'My son,' he said, turning his head, his voice quavering. What he had spawned, he had spawned. A female child born to a sinful father and mother. A bloodline, begun in sacrilege, that ended in violation, evil and profanity. He crossed himself. '*Absolve me, Domine …*' he began.

'I heard you praying.' The familiar voice was high and cold, the strange hypnotic eyes were beckoning. 'It is time to go.' The frightened priest nodded, moving his lips in silent prayer. His book slipped from his nerveless hands and fell onto the stones.

Mesmerised, he gathered his cassock about him and struggled to his feet, groaning as his knees creaked. Sweat ran down from his hair, making everything a blur. Then he felt the cruel nails digging into his arms, drawing him quickly across the floor and up the steps toward the shrine. Old age, coupled with the fear of his sin, overtook him and, as he twisted his body frantically to escape that iron grasp, he tripped and fell backwards.

His assassin ran lithely down the steps and stood over him. 'Goodbye, Father,' he growled, staring at the fragile head, which had been mashed by the ancient stone as easily as the contents of an eggshell. A brief smile played around his mouth. No human would ever hear Pathan's last confession.

It had been a good day's work. The secret of his origin was safe again. Once more, Grandsire's bloody trail had gone cold. Undetectable, as it had remained for centuries.

EPILOGUE

Simona Murgu had spent a great deal of her time in the churchyard since Grandsire's last appearance two years earlier. She carried many heavy secrets and had no-one to tell them to but the dead. She also knew that she had many years to listen to their voices brought to her on the wind.

But she was strong and had no wish to follow in the footsteps of those of her neighbours who had made their way to Burbor. She had always been strong. She would talk to Claudiu instead of a psychiatrist. Irina Petrescu had done that, and look what had happened to her! And she couldn't even be buried with her daughter.

'It goes on, old man, it goes on,' she whispered. 'Now you know the secret too!' The tears ran down her cheeks as she bent once again over Claudiu's grave, but she wiped them off with the back of her hand. It would do no-one, including herself, any good to weep about what was past and what was to come. Her only comfort was that she shared her black depression with all the others. If she'd had her way, she would have joined her old lover in the grave. But that was not the way of Arva women. They were born to suffer.

Simona straightened as she felt the wind getting up. On that particular day, she had no time to indulge in thoughts of the past, nor to linger, so she hurried off down the stony path to the village, pulling her shawl about her shoulders.

It was meant to be a day of celebration for the Murgu

family. That day, Simona's grand-daughter was celebrating her birthday. There should have been rejoicing in their family but, like Simona, the married women of Arva knew there was nothing to celebrate, because the little girl had been born at four minutes past midnight on the twenty-second day of July, 1988.

THE PIED PIPER OF HAMELIN

Hamelin Town's in Brunswick,
By famous Hanover city;
The River Weser, deep and wide,
Washes its walls on the southern side;
A pleasanter spot you never spied;
But, when begins my ditty,
Almost five hundred years ago,
To see the townsfolk suffer so
From vermin was a pity.

Rats!
They fought the dogs, and killed the cats,
And bit the babies in the cradles,
And ate the cheeses out of the vats,
And licked the soup from the cooks' own ladles,
Split open the kegs of salted sprats,
Made nests inside men's Sunday hats,
And even spoiled the women's chats,
By drowning their speaking
With shrieking and squeaking
In fifty different sharps and flats.

At last the people in a body
To the Town Hall came flocking;
'Tis clear,' cried they, 'our Mayor's a noddy;
And as for our Corporation, shocking
To think we buy gowns lined with ermine
For dolts that can't or won't determine
What's best to rid us of our vermin!
You hope, because you're old and obese,
To find in the furry civic robe ease?
Rouse up, sirs! Give your brains a racking
To find the remedy we're lacking,
Or, sure as fate, we'll send you packing!'
At this the Mayor and Corporation

Quaked with a mighty consternation.

An hour they sat in council;
At length the Mayor broke silence:
'For a guilder I'd my ermine gown sell;
I wish I were a mile hence!
It's easy to bid one rack one's brain–
I'm sure my poor head aches again,
I've scratched it so, and all in vain.
Oh, for a trap, a trap, a trap!'
Just as he said this, what should hap
At the chamber door but a gentle tap?
'Bless us,' cried the Mayor, 'what's that?'
(With the Corporation as he sat,
Looking little though wondrous fat;
Nor brighter was his eye, nor moister
Than a too-long-opened oyster,
Save when at noon his paunch grew mutinous
For a plate of turtle green and glutinous)
'Only a scraping of shoes on the mat?
Anything like the sound of a rat
Makes my heart go pit-a-pat!'

'Come in,' the Mayor cried, looking bigger:
And in did come the strangest figure!
His queer long coat from heel to head
Was half of yellow and half of red;
And he himself was tall and thin,
With sharp blue eyes, each like a pin,
And light loose hair, yet swarthy skin,
No tuft on cheek nor beard on chin,
But lips where smiles went out and in;
There was no guessing his kith and kin;
And nobody could enough admire
The tall man and his quaint attire.
Quoth one: 'It's as my great-grandsire,
Starting up at the Trump of Doom's tone,

Had walked this way from his painted tombstone!'

He advanced to the council table:
And, 'Please your honours,' said he, 'I'm able,
By means of a secret charm to draw,
All creatures living beneath the sun,
That creep or swim or fly or run,
After me so as you never saw!
And I chiefly use my charm
On creatures that do people harm,
The mole and toad and newt and viper;
And people call me the Pied Piper.'
(And here they noticed round his neck
A scarf of red and yellow stripe,
To match with his coat of the self-same check;
And at the scarf's end hung a pipe,
And his fingers, they noticed, were ever straying
As if impatient to be playing
Upon this pipe, as low it dangled
Over his vesture so old-fangled.)
'Yes,' said he, 'poor piper as I am,
In Tartary I freed the Cham,
Last June, from his huge swarm of gnats;
I eased in Asia the Nizam
Of a monstrous brood of vampire-bats;
And, as for what your brain bewilders,
If I can rid your town of rats
Will you give me a thousand guilders?'
'One? Fifty thousand!' was the exclamation
Of the astonished Mayor and Corporation.

Into the street the Piper stept,
Smiling first a little smile,
As if he knew what magic slept
In his quiet pipe the while;
Then, like a musical adept,
To blow the pipe his lips he wrinkled,

And green and blue his sharp eyes twinkled,
Like a candle flame where salt is sprinkled;
And ere three shrill notes the pipe uttered,
You heard as if an army muttered;
And the muttering grew to a grumbling;
And the grumbling grew to a mighty rumbling;
And out of the houses the rats came tumbling,
Great rats, small rats, lean rats, brawny rats,
Brown rats, black rats, grey rats, tawny rats,
Grave old plodders, gay young friskers,
Fathers, mothers, uncles, cousins,
Cocking tails and pricking whiskers,
Families by tens and dozens,
Brothers, sisters, husbands, wives–
Followed the Piper for their lives.
From street to street he piped advancing,
And step by step they followed dancing,
Until they came to the River Weser,
Wherein all plunged and perished,
Save one who, stout as Julius Caesar,
Swam across and lived to carry
(As he the manuscript he cherished)
To Rat-land home his commentary:
Which was, 'At the first shrill notes of the pipe
I heard a sound as of scraping tripe,
And putting apples, wondrous ripe,
Into a cider press's gripe:
And a moving away of pickle-tub boards,
And a leaving ajar of conserve-cupboards,
And a drawing the corks of train-oil flasks,
And a breaking the hoops of butter-casks:
And it seemed as if a voice
(Sweeter far than by harp or psaltery
Is breathed) called out, 'Oh rats, rejoice!
The world is grown to one vast dry-saltery!
So munch on, crunch on, take your nuncheon,
Breakfast, supper, dinner, luncheon!'

And just as a bulky sugar-puncheon,
All ready staved, like a great sun shone
Glorious scarce an inch before me,
Just as methought it said, 'Come, bore me!'
I found the Weser rolling o'er me.'

You should have heard the Hamelin people
Ringing the bells till they rocked the steeple.
'Go,' cried the Mayor, 'and get long poles!
Poke out the nests and block up the holes!
Consult with carpenters and builders,
And leave in our town not even a trace
Of the rats!'– when suddenly, up the face
Of the Piper perked in the market-place,
With a 'First, if you please, my thousand guilders!'
A thousand guilders! The Mayor looked blue;
So did the Corporation too.
For council dinners made rare havoc
With claret, moselle, vin-de-grave, hock;
And half the money would replenish
Their cellar's biggest butt with Rhenish.
To pay this sum to a wandering fellow
With a gipsy coat of red and yellow!
'Beside,' quoth the Mayor with a knowing wink,
'Our business was done at the river's brink;
We saw with our eyes the vermin sink,
And what's dead can't come to life, I think.
So, friends, we're not the folks to shrink
From the duty of giving you something to drink,
And a matter of money to put in your poke;
But as for the guilders, what we spoke
Of them, as you very well know, was in joke,
Beside, our losses have made us thrifty.
A thousand guilders! Come, take fifty!'

The Piper's face fell, and he cried:
'No trifling! I can't wait, beside!

311

THE PIED PIPER OF HAMELIN

I've promised to visit by dinner-time
Bagdat, and accept the prime
Of the head cook's pottage, all he's rich in,
For having left, in the Caliph's kitchen,
Of a nest of scorpions no survivor;
With him I proved no bargain-driver,
With you, don't think I'll bate a stiver!
And folks who put me in a passion
May find me pipe to another fashion.'

'How?' cried the Mayor, 'd'ye think I'll brook
Being worse treated than a cook?
Insulted by a lazy ribald
With idle pipe and vesture piebald?
You threaten us, fellow? Do your worst,
Blow your pipe there till you burst!'

Once more he stept into the street
And to his lips again
Laid his long pipe of smooth, straight cane;
And ere he blew three notes (Such sweet
Soft notes as yet magician's cunning
Never gave the enraptured air)
There was a rustling that seemed like a bustling
Of merry crowds justling at pitching and hustling,
Small feet were pattering, wooden shoes clattering,
Little hands clapping and little tongues chattering,
And, like fowls in a farmyard when barley is scattering,
Out came the children running.
All the little boys and girls,
With rosy cheeks and flaxen curls,
And sparkling eyes and teeth like pearls,
Tripping and skipping, ran merrily after
The wonderful music with shouting and laughter.

The Mayor was dumb, and the Council stood
As if they were changed to blocks of wood,

Unable to move a step, or cry
To the children merrily skipping by,
And could only follow with the eye
That joyous crowd at the Piper's back.
But how the Mayor was on the rack,
And the wretched Council's bosoms beat,
As the Piper turned from the High Street
To where the Weser rolled its waters
Right in the way of their sons and daughters!
However he turned from South to West,
And to Koppelberg Hill his steps addressed.
And after him the children pressed;
Great was the joy in every breast.
'He never can cross that mighty top!
He's forced to let the piping drop,
And we shall see our children stop!'
When, lo, as they reached the mountain-side,
A wondrous portal opened wide,
As if a cavern was suddenly hollowed;
And the Piper advanced and the children followed.
And when all were in to the very last,
The door in the mountain-side shut fast.
Did I say all? No! One was lame,
And could not dance the whole of the way;
And in after years, if you would blame
His sadness, he was used to say;
'It's dull in our town since my playmates left!
I can't forget that I'm bereft
Of all the pleasant sights they see,
Which the Piper also promised me.
For he led us, he said, to a joyous land,
Joining the town and just at hand,
Where waters gushed and fruit trees grew,
And flowers put forth a fairer hue,
And everything was strange and new.
The sparrows were brighter than peacocks here,
And their dogs outran our fallow deer,

And honey-bees had lost their stings,
And horses were born with eagles' wings;
And just as I became assured–
My lame foot would be speedily cured,
The music stopped and I stood still,
And found myself outside the hill,
Left alone against my will,
To go now limping as before,
And never hear of that country more!'

Alas, alas for Hamelin!
There came into many a burgher's pate
A text which says that heaven's gate
Opes to the rich at as easy rate
As the needle's eye takes a camel in!
The Mayor sent East, West, North, and South
To offer the Piper, by word of mouth,
Wherever it was men's lot to find him,
Silver and gold to his heart's content,
If he'd only return the way he went,
And bring the children behind him.
But when they saw 'twas a lost endeavour,
And Piper and dancers were gone forever,
They made a decree that lawyers never
Should think their records dated duly
If, after the day of the month and year,
These words did not as well appear:
'And so long after what happened here
On the twenty-second of July,
Thirteen hundred and seventy-six';
And the better in memory to fix
The place of the children's last retreat,
They called it the Pied Piper's Street,
Where anyone playing on pipe or tabor
Was sure for the future to lose his labour.
Nor suffered they hostelry or tavern
To shock with mirth a street so solemn;

But opposite the place of the cavern
They wrote the story on a column,
And on the great church window painted
The same, to make the world acquainted
How their children were stolen away;
And there it stands to this very day.
And I must not omit to say
That in Transylvania there's a tribe
Of alien people who ascribe
The outlandish ways and dress,
On which their neighbours lay such stress,
To their fathers and mothers having risen
Out of some subterraneous prison,
Into which they were trepanned
Long time ago in a mighty band
Out of Hamelin town in Brunswick land,
But how or why, they don't understand.

So, Willy, let me and you be wipers
Of scores out with all men – especially pipers!
And whether they pipe us free from rats or from mice,
If we've promised them aught, let us keep our promise!

Robert Browning

ABOUT THE AUTHOR

Helen McCabe is a highly regarded author whose love of writing and powerful imagination, coupled with a determination to succeed, have ensured a long and successful career. Her lifelong fascination with literature, history and research and an interest in the paranormal have enhanced Helen's immense gift for creative storytelling.

She graduated with Honours from London University, where she read English, and holds an MA degree in 18th Century English Literature from the University of Keele.

Her long career began with her first novel at the age of seven, with poetry published at 13 and read on the BBC. She started her true career as a novelist after becoming well-known for her short stories and serials in popular magazines. In 1995 her first full-length novel – *Two for a Lie*, about the 19th Century Princess Caraboo – was published, gaining much interest and critical acclaim. Since then, in tandem with work and family, she has written more than 30 novels in various genres, including historical, romance and more recently horror/thriller and crime. She also writes scripts for film, television and the stage.

Alongside her writing, Helen has worked in a variety of jobs, beginning as an assistant librarian and finally as a lecturer and teacher. She is a member of the Romantic Novelists Association, the Crime Writers' Association, the Horror Writers of America and the West Country Writers' Association.

Helen was invited to join Mensa, the high IQ Society, in 1989.

Helen lives in Worcester and has three grown-up children and a grandson.

Her website can be found at www.helenmccabe.com.

ALSO AVAILABLE FROM TELOS PUBLISHING

HORROR/FANTASY

HELEN MCCABE
THE PIERCING
THE CODEX (Coming 2015)

GRAHAM MASTERTON
THE DJINN
RULES OF DUEL (With William S Burroughs)

SIMON CLARK
HUMPTY'S BONES
THE FALL

DAVID J HOWE
TALESPINNING
Horror collection of stories, extracts and screenplays

URBAN GOTHIC: LACUNA AND OTHER TRIPS edited by
DAVID J HOWE
Tales of horror from and inspired by the *Urban Gothic*
television series. Contributors: Graham Masterton,
Christopher Fowler, Simon Clark, Steve Lockley & Paul Lewis,
Paul Finch and Debbie Bennett.

RAVEN DANE
ABSINTHE & ARSENIC
16 tales of Victorian horror, Steampunk adventures and dark,
deadly, obsession
DEATH'S DARK WINGS (Coming in 2015)
Exciting alternative history with a supernatural twist

CAPTAINS STUPENDOUS by RHYS HUGHES
Steampunk humorous adventure about the Fantastical
Faraway Brothers

SAM STONE
KAT LIGHTFOOT MYSTERIES
Steampunk, horror, adventure series
1: ZOMBIES AT TIFFANY'S
2: KAT ON A HOT TIN AIRSHIP
3: WHAT'S DEAD PUSSYKAT (Sept 2014)
4: KAT OF GREEN TENTACLES (Coming in 2015)

JINX CHRONICLES
Hi-tech science fiction fantasy series
1: JINX TOWN (Nov 2014)
2: JINX MAGIC (Sept 2015)
3: JINX BOUND (Sept 2016)

THE DARKNESS WITHIN
Science Fiction Horror Short Novel

ZOMBIES IN NEW YORK AND OTHER BLOODY JOTTINGS
Thirteen stories of horror and passion, and six mythological
and erotic poems from the pen of the new Queen of Vampire
fiction.

KIT COX
DOCTOR TRIPPS SERIES
A Neo-Victorian world where steam is pitted against diesel,
but which side will win?
KAIJU COCKTAIL
MOON MONSTER (coming in 2015)

BREATHE by CHRISTOPHER FOWLER
The Office meets *Night of the Living Dead.*

SPECTRE by STEPHEN LAWS
Something is stalking the Chapter, picking them off one by
one, something connected with their past, and with the girl
they used to know.

TELOS PUBLISHING
Email: orders@telos.co.uk
Web: www.telos.co.uk

**To order copies of any Telos books, please visit our website
where there are full details of all titles and facilities for
worldwide credit card online ordering, as well as occasional
special offers.**

Made in the USA
Charleston, SC
20 December 2014